Also by Gene Hackman
and Daniel Lenihan

Justice for None

Wake of the Perdido Star

Also by Daniel Lenihan

Submerged

ESCAPE FROM ANDERSONVILLE

★

ESCAPE
FROM
ANDERSONVILLE

A NOVEL OF THE CIVIL WAR

★

GENE HACKMAN
— AND —
DANIEL LENIHAN

ST. MARTIN'S PRESS NEW YORK

This is a work of fiction. All of the characters, organizations,
and events portrayed in this novel are either products of
the authors' imagination or are used fictitiously.

www.stmartins.com

Library of Congress Cataloging-in-Publication Data

Hackman, Gene.
  Escape from Andersonville : a novel of the Civil War / Gene Hackman and Daniel
Lenihan.—1st ed.
    p. cm.
  ISBN-13: 978-0-312-36373-4
  ISBN-10: 0-312-36373-7
  1. United States—History—Civil War, 1861–1865—Fiction. 2. Prisoner-of-war
escapes—Fiction. 3. Andersonville Prison—Fiction. 4. Prisoners of war—Fiction.
5. Andersonville (Ga.)—Fiction. I. Lenihan, Daniel. II. Title.
  PS3558.A3114E83 2008
  813'.54–dc22

                                                                    2008005239

First Edition: May 2008

10 9 8 7 6 5 4 3 2 1

To the roughly 600,000 young Americans,
North and South, who left their lives
along with their blood on the battlefields of
our Civil War—and to the hope that our nation
can solve future internal disputes with
a bit less passion and a mite more patience.

★

ACKNOWLEDGMENTS

★

We want to thank our peerless agent, Noah Lukeman, the staff at St. Martin's: editors George Witte and Marc Resnick, assistant editor Sarah Lumnah, production editor Rafal Gibek, designers David Rotstein and Robert Grom, and Joan Higgins in Publicity. Historians Charles Haecker and Art Gomez for their helpful suggestions after reading our first draft. Dan's wife, Barbara, and sister, Patricia, for their advice and encouragement. Gene's wife, Betsy, plays a special role in our collaborative efforts—she is a tireless compiler, advisor, fixer, and when necessary, peacemaker between two strong-willed coauthors. We'd still be working on our first book without her.

ESCAPE FROM ANDERSONVILLE

★

CHAPTER 1

9 July 1864
Monocacy

P | eople say the smell of blood is reminiscent of copper. But copper doesn't really smell most of the time. Now if you run your tongue over a copper penny, well, there it is—you're kind of sniffing through your taster. It was a conundrum that was straining Nathan Parker's befogged logic this evening. He was lying on his back, mortally confused. He could see okay but it was dim; lots of smoke and even the tenacious light of a summer's day was starting to fade. But that coppery blood odor was still overwhelming, it blended with the smell of cornstalks and whiffs of something very unpleasant, perhaps fecal.

He realized he was "coming around" as he'd heard surgeons say of stricken men. He had been half out and was coming back to his senses. Lord, what a mess around him, and the weight on his leg . . . a horse, it was a damn horse. That's where much of the blood was coming from. Actually, it was half of a horse on top of him. God Almighty, it was Phoenix, his own mount, staring past him with fogged-over eyes.

Everything came rushing back; voices, yells. Now that he could hear something besides the ringing in his ears, it was the first he realized he had been temporarily deaf. Someone was calling his name.

"Cap'n Parker, where are ya, Captain?"

"Jesus, Ricketts, them Rebs got 'im that time, I don't see him anywhere."

Nathan tentatively raised his hand and muttered, "Here, here . . . I am."

"There he is!" A scuffle of foot plods and two pairs of strong young hands were under his arms pulling him out from underneath Phoenix.

"Lordy Lord, Cap'n, yer all soaked in blood."

"A course he is; 'at horse is bleedin' on 'im. Bender, give a hand here, wipe Cap'n down."

Nathan knew the voices, it was his men coming to collect him. He could also tell by the voices that they were relieved. Maybe he could dare hope that he was in one piece. It was time to be their captain again—he was almost annoyed that he had no serious injuries. He'd been through this before. First comes the stomach-dropping fear that one's arms or legs are missing, and then the curious contrary notion that a moderate injury would garner him an excuse—something to honorably muster him out—to clear him from the suffocating burden of leadership.

"Lordy, Captain, you okay?" Weed sounded almost panicked.

Nathan gathered himself and finally spoke, "Yeah, I think."

The thin, young soldier was accepting a piece of deeply stained cloth from Joe Bender. Nathan realized Bender must be the one in whose lap his head rested while his face was being wiped. Bender was as strong as an ox but as attentive as Clara Barton when tending his captain. The cloth he'd handed Weed was covered with gore and brown grime.

"Bender, Weed . . . you smell that?"

"What? Smell what?" The two soldiers sounded puzzled.

Nathan took a deep breath. "Never mind."

Rawlins handed Weed a fresh piece of cloth and started pouring water from his canteen over Nathan's face and upper body. Some went in his nose, making him cough heavily; he would have liked a warning. But the rough ministrations were working—he was pulled gently to his feet and, with a little support, he was able to stand.

Nathan looked down at where the artillery round had detonated. Poor Phoenix had taken almost the entire force of the explosion. He was bent around backward with his hind end attached by just a strip of flesh to his front, the part that had been on top of Nathan. A couple of yards away were the horse's innards and enough other detritus that he knew now where those fecal whiffs had come from. The odor was oppressive now that he was on his feet, and Nathan thought for a moment it might overwhelm him.

As his men walked him away from Phoenix he glanced about, taking in the piles of camp ruins, including a ragged Confederate battle pennant. His blue-suited soldiers moved purposefully, ushering prisoners, binding wounds, and going through torn tent fabric, examining papers left in the makeshift Confederate garrison. When the Michigan soldiers realized it was Captain Parker that Weed and the others were tending, they took turns leaving their tasks to walk over to where they could see him and yell encouragement. But as much as anything, they seemed to be reassuring themselves that he was up and about and ready to resume command.

Nathan addressed Weed, "Who have we lost?"

"Nobody, sir. We were all over them afore they had a chance."

"Seems to me there was somebody we weren't all over—look at my horse."

"He's full blowed up, sir," declared Ricketts, a gangly, slow-moving soldier with a knack for the obvious.

Nathan racked his brain, trying to force his memory into some sense of order. He had just led his men of the Fifth Michigan on another mounted attack—only unusual because they were infantry. The idea of doing lightning attacks on fixed positions from horseback had come to him last September at Chickamauga. He'd seen the results of one day's carnage earlier at Antietam and it struck him then that the worst of the nightmare was simple attrition from exposure to hostile fire. The more time one spent standing there, reloading and tearing away at an equally motivated enemy with modern, rifled weapons, the more likely one was to get killed or lose precious parts of one's self.

At Chickamauga, after the bloodbath at Antietam, Nathan had talked General Rosecrans into letting his unit keep some horses they'd taken from the Rebs and use them as mounted infantry. He would ride his whole unit around fixed positions to engage the enemy on the flank, sometimes with two men to a horse. The downside was, such aggressive actions ensured that in short order you'd be in the teeth of the enemy. The upside was, you weren't going to be there long. You either overwhelmed them or they overpowered you. There was only time to reload once or twice at most. Either way it was over quick and the amount of casualties usually smaller than with infantry units. "Parker's Rangers" the Fifth was called. They were often into the thick of it first, but with the help of God, also one of the first out.

Fifth Michigan hadn't fought at Antietam; they arrived right after the savagery was over. It had stunned Nathan—the number of dead—it looked like an entire city full of people had been marched out into the fields and brutally murdered. Blue, gray, men just torn asunder and piled into blood-soaked piles of humanity by the angry hand of Ares. That's when Nathan had decided they must do something to better their chances.

The idea wasn't new. There were some other MIs, or mounted infantry groups, doing the same thing. It wasn't unheard of, but it also wasn't a big part of either side's strategy. There was plenty of regular cavalry, but that was expensive and hard to maintain—the MI was for workingmen. It was one of the few things that worked at all at Chickamauga before the whole damn bunch of them had to run like hell.

So far, they had made three mounted charges with objectives achieved and casualties light. They had quickly won—so the enemy's casualties were also light. If they overrode a position and found they had walked into a meat grinder, Nathan fully intended to withdraw. He was not going to imitate the madness of Antietam. His men trusted him to do the right thing, to get them through this damn war; he could only promise them a fighting chance. Already, he had seen too many men dying for honor; their officers thought it heroic, Nathan thought it tragic.

With all his senses now back, Nathan heard a long, high-pitched wail. It was starting—the groans of young men with broken bodies. There is no quiet after battle, no calm after the storm. One must cope with the screams of the wounded . . . after a while one just wants them to shut up. As he walked by the field hospital, Nathan blocked out the sounds. Whimpers, screams, it was bad, but over time he was becoming inured to it. The buckets of limbs next to the surgeon's tent at the field hospital used to freeze him in his tracks. They seemed a particularly ghastly testimony to unbelievable suffering—arms with fingers on the hands pointing in different directions—the stuff of nightmares. Now he found himself walking by the flesh buckets with hardly a thought, as if it was just the natural consequence of lots of men shooting lots of guns at one another.

The day had been hotter 'n' hell's hinges, but now there was a breeze moving over the banks of the Monocacy. In the distance he could make out the entourage of Major General Lew Wallace. He was riding through to assess their condition and plan his next move.

Theirs was a delaying action as General Wallace saw it; a

damned important one. If Jubal Early and John Gordon's Rebs could rush in before reinforcements arrived, Washington City would be taken—this was something no officer wearing blue was willing to accept.

The corn in the surrounding fields had been mowed down in patches around Nathan by heavy enfilading fire from the Ohio and Pennsylvania boys plus the canister grapeshot of the New Yorkers' artillery. The Fifth Michigan and another contingent of mounted infantry from the 159th detachment of the National Guard from Ohio had been ordered to distract and harass the Secessionists. His men had done their duty. Now they were being called on to withdraw before the full might of Early's forces began to fully engage them. Drop back when the Rebs thought they were into a slugfest and take up positions again—it wasn't a bad strategy—it didn't win battles, but it sure could occupy a stronger enemy force for a considerable time.

General Wallace approached a nearby group of officers and began haranguing them about something, but Nathan felt he'd learn soon enough how the fight was going. Right now he just wanted to get down to the river where he could get the grime and damnable smell washed off. He sent Lieutenant Mackey to give his regrets to Wallace and get his orders while Weed helped him descend to a sheltered cove in the Monocacy River. There he stripped down to his skin, then slowly sat in the waist-deep water, washing dirt and blood off his upper body. He quickly soaked his uniform tunic and wrung it out. Then he sat quietly in the river and gathered himself while his men let him be.

Mackey brought back to Nathan the general's salutations and orders. Wallace said they were getting only a brief break and he hoped Nathan's wounds were minor. Early's men had been stopped cold, but they were a much superior force. They would soon regroup and be back at them. Nathan wasn't surprised. The Rebs were tough—if you ever expected them to back off from hard resistance, you'd be disappointed.

Nathan thanked the lieutenant and waved away the others. It was quiet where he was, and stillness was a blessing he knew would be short-lived. When Nathan was alone he talked to himself. Especially the lines from *Walden*. He started chanting some choice prose from Thoreau under his breath—it was a habit that helped calm him. He had occasionally been caught at it and was embarrassed, but at least it was other officers and not his men who had noticed.

Nathan knew that others thought him a strong leader, an aggressive officer who led his men well. Maybe it was true, but it wasn't for honor and glory . . . not even for the preservation of the Union—it was for survival. He was an old man of thirty-four when he had accepted command of the Fifth Michigan; now he was thirty-six. It was one part of a crazy world that he had some control over—and he was going to get these boys home—in some ways, it was all that mattered anymore.

Nathan believed the nation had slipped into insanity during this war—people who sat at tea tables in polite company only a few years ago were now running bayonets through the necks of their fellow countrymen. Normalcy seemed unattainable ever again. Thoughts of Darien and the people he admired in Boston seemed born of a time when people were still creatures of God, or at least nature. Nathan wasn't religious . . . maybe he was . . . no, he guessed he wasn't. But he didn't think it could hurt praying to God sometimes.

He mulled over how he'd gotten here. Here being the Monocacy River in Maryland, under General Wallace, fighting a holding action against an army three times their size. It wouldn't be long before the time for thinking about things would be gone and they'd be up to their gullets in blood. Blood. It was such an important part of each person yet no one much enjoyed seeing it—especially their own. He had seen a fair amount of it in his adopted home near Harvard Medical School, but that was because people were trying to save lives, not take them.

Nathan had arrived in Boston from the wilds of the rawboned state of Michigan at twenty-four years old to make his fortune. He had only a secondary-school education, but a lust for reading that rivaled anyone's. He had apprenticed for his father in Lansing. He learned to fix watches, clocks, and cameras, but he had also served as a guide and tracker for hunters and surveyors. When he arrived in New England, almost immediately his good fortune landed him a job in the household of a well-known figure in Cambridge who went by the name of Oliver Wendell Holmes.

The gentleman was a doctor who wrote and experimented with all manner of things. He had just advertised for the services of a "fixer," who could help him with some of his mechanical projects—working with cameras and artificial limbs. Although Nathan was of humble means and young at the time, it seemed to make no difference to Dr. Holmes, who liked him and took him under wing immediately. Nathan loved his job and was fascinated with the variety of colorful gentlemen who were Holmes' constant visitors.

The good doctor even, on occasion, let him sit at a side table with some other apprentices where they could hear him hold court with men like Messrs. Emerson and Longfellow. Nathan would listen to the table talk like a young man in a trance. But nothing in the Holmes household mesmerized him as much as the presence of a particular young lady by the name of Darien Crosby.

Darien was as enticing as a rainbow and almost as elusive—she warmed his soul for a few magical years in Boston. She was a delightful pause, an event in Nathan's life, but ultimately a sad one—the angel he could never really have. Of course, he did have her in one sense, but it had been stolen moments, for Darien had become the wife of another man.

"The mass of men lead lives of quiet desperation" was from *Walden*. Nathan had two issues of *The Atlantic Monthly* in his pack when he arrived at Sharpsburg. Thoreau's works were carried as serials in *The Atlantic*. Nathan had been balancing his sanity on the head of a pin ever since Antietam and words such as Thoreau's had become his only real solace in matters of love or war.

Darien was married and out of reach, and then, with child. And the war—what madness, what soul-wrenching madness. Antietam was his moment of truth. Maybe seeing the results of a battle you hadn't taken part in was the most disturbing—sort of like when as a young man he was pulled into fistfights. He was formidable when he fought, but he didn't like them and damned if watching them didn't sometimes make him feel sick.

If fistfights bothered him, Antietam was absolutely incomprehensible to him. He led his men on burial details and kept a stolid appearance through it all. But he holed up inside himself at night. He withdrew and read excerpts from Thoreau's journals by the light of a campfire. This ritual helped him maintain composure and gave him some private ground where he could wrestle with his nightmares and build his strength for his men. His men? Christ, they were boys. But they believed in him and he found strength in their trust—in some ways, in their innocent reliance they had made him brave.

In the Holmes household *The Atlantic* was read by all from beginning to end and every word was subject to discussion and debate. People had variable attraction to Thoreau's writing, many thought him a brilliant but odd duck. But Nathan was an unabashed admirer. Holmes nurtured Nathan as he did others in whom he saw promise. He passed on to Nathan new excerpts from Thoreau's journals that had been posted to the household from Concord by Mr. Emerson, a close friend of ole "Henry David" as Dr. Holmes called him. Some of Thoreau's words went down like smooth honey but he seemed distant to many readers. Nathan couldn't understand certain passages himself until he was swept up in the war. Now, as he finished bathing in the river, he heard the war return.

The sharp sound of musket fire and the heavy thuds of artillery rolled back down the Monocacy River toward them. Nathan motioned his men back from the water's edge and into the cover of a patch of woods near a couple of acres of corn that sided up to the trees. He had fifty-seven men in his company, which was authorized for one hundred. They had reached seventy men and officers at the highest and had suffered thirteen casualties since forming. Eight were dead and five more seriously wounded.

The Fifth Michigan was a regimental designation but, as sometimes happened, there were at least two Fifth Michigans carrying regimental designations at this point in the war. Most of the rest were fighting in Virginia, but Nathan and his men had been sent to help General Wallace. As far as anybody with Wallace knew, his detachment of the Fifth Michigan was all that mattered. They were a funny bunch with strange accents whom the others took to calling Parker's Rangers because of their wide-ranging moves on the battlefield. Many of them had well-developed woodsmen skills, more like Rebs than Yankees.

Nathan rose up when he heard the bugles. His men gathered about him and watched the dust rise in unplanted fields where the Reb cavalry was regrouping and starting another push. So far, the Federals had made them pay dearly for any gains, but the Secessionists now had a full sense of the resistance and were coming across the open ground with no intentions of turning back. As the two armies maneuvered on the field, Nathan judged the tide of battle was set to turn.

He also saw something else, a gap in the ranks of some attacking butternuts. He rallied his men and told them to hang clear after their first volley. "When you reload don't fire, come with me, and leave the horses, all of them." As the Rebs worked their way toward the heights on the Union side of the river, he started moving his dismounted soldiers as reformed infantry. The horses would offer no advantage now. Nathan led his men down a root-pocked ravine and attacked on the flank of the advancing Rebs.

The Virginia boys were surprised all right and temporarily reeled from Nathan's surge, but out from the trees to the south came the soldiers of another Reb detachment that had been biding their time. As soon as Nathan saw them he knew they had finally pushed their luck too far. Ringle and des Fleurs dropped immediately from a fusillade from the large detachment of Rebs that had lucked into a prime position of advantage over them. Des Fleurs was about twenty yards from him, but Ringle was less than twenty feet away. It sounded like he had been hit in the head with a wild swing from a sledgehammer. Nathan could hear the spray of blood and brains in the leaves from a high-caliber impact seconds before the man's body hit the ground.

His men rose to the challenge and fired back intermittently, but they had been blindsided and Nathan ordered them to fall back. On the ridge, the Rebs had cut off any avenue of escape to the high ground. Nathan pulled his boys back to a drainage that snaked down to the river. There was good cover there and soon the Fifth Michigan had stopped the Reb advance and was dealing out some savagery of its own. They might make it out of this mess yet. Then Bender looked past Nathan to the ridge behind them and his jaw went slack. Nathan turned to see that the company of Rebs that had pushed to the high ground had become aware of the exposed position of the Fifth Michigan and their lieutenant was turning them around.

A series of shots rang out and another of Nathan's men fell. Now the men on the ridge were ordered by their lieutenant to hold fire until they could deliver a full field of powder to the Yanks caught below. Nathan looked to Morton, his guidon, and yelled, "Show the white!"

To the men around him Nathan ordered, "Lower your weapons." He didn't tell them to drop them, that would depend on how disciplined the Confederates were who had the drop on them. Nathan could see several of the Rebs raise their rifles, a few fired them but most just held them and glanced over at their lieutenant. The fellow seemed unsure of himself and froze when the chorus of "Sirs?" rang out. Before another soldier could shoot, a sergeant stepped forward and yelled to the men, "Cease firing!"

Nathan breathed a sigh of relief and uttered a brief prayer of thanks for grizzled old veterans. The sergeant yelled to Nathan, "Hear me well, Captain! You and your men are showing a flag of surrender, make sure your boys cool their muskets."

"They aren't going to fire, Sergeant, you make sure you've got your lads in hand and my boys will be laying down their arms."

"Stand tall, men. Fire if one of them moves false." The lieutenant had suddenly found his voice.

The sergeant looked annoyed but snapped toward his men, "Keep tall like the lieutenant says." A lot of the soldiers in this unit seemed young and edgy, as did the lieutenant. Nathan was counting on his seasoned troops to keep calm and avoid a bloodletting.

The sergeant looked over his shoulder back toward his commanding officer, "It's okay, Lieutenant, I'll take care of these 'uns here."

The officer raised his sword and yelled behind him, "I've put Sergeant Boggs in charge here!" then he motioned the rest of his outfit past the ravine where the Fifth Michigan was pinned. Almost immediately a detachment of Confederate cavalry swept past the lieutenant to pursue the remaining Michigan and Ohio troops, who were quickly withdrawing. The Michigan boys were from Nathan's second platoon which was under Mackey. They had been too far away for Nathan to rally during the attack. He prayed that they and the Ohio units they were sharing the ridge with made good their escape. It looked like Jubal Early was in the process of winning the day but Nathan hoped they had held the Rebs back long enough that they were too late to attack Washington.

With the shooting over, Nathan examined his casualties. He didn't know much about des Fleurs, who was comparatively new to the unit, but Ringle was a fine man with a wife and two young sons. It wasn't the sort of thing one needed to be thinking about in the midst of combat, but as an eerie quiet fell over the battlefield, Nathan was free to absorb the full sickening sense of loss that always overcame him in the presence of men who fell under his command. He looked around as the others laid down their weapons and sighed. "Quiet desperation," here it was again. To Nathan, no words could better capture the driving force of most men's lives during this war.

CHAPTER 2

July 1864
Monocacy to Andersonville

Nathan thought the unit that captured Parker's Rangers was composed of a curious mix of Confederate soldiers. Some were mossbacks who, like Nathan and his Michigan lads, had already suffered through a lifetime of warfare during the past three years. But there were also a surprising number of raw green newcomers, most young, some quite old. After three years of attrition, it appeared the South was being forced to convert its home militia to regular CSA troops to fill its ranks.

As their captors approached them, Nathan could tell each of the Reb's level of experience with little effort. Some of the greenhorns were so nervous about suddenly being victors in a real battle that they actually held their muskets out in front of them at eye level, arms fully extended. It looked as if they were trying to keep unruly dogs at bay with broomsticks. Were they to discharge the weapon from that position it would recoil into their faces like a mule's kick.

The seasoned Rebs, on the other hand, held back and watched warily. They knew they were taking custody of veteran soldiers even if some were young—so as they did, they were slow-moving and cautious. Nathan wondered if you could tell the difference between his men and the war-weary Rebs if they switched uniforms. He doubted it. The veteran graybacks had the same deep tiredness worked into the lines of their faces that his boys did. It came from a resignation that life was being traded cheap and their own lives had been on God's auction block a long damn time.

"Lieutenant, I need some attention for my wounded—"

The lieutenant interrupted him midsentence. "They'll be taken care of once our own soldiers have been tended to, we recognize the precedence of men fighting a war of independence for the freedom of their homeland."

Nathan felt the heat rise under his collar. "We've got as many Marylanders fighting for us to preserve the Union as can be found in the Army of Northern Virginia—guess they're the oppressors, eh?" He fought to calm himself. "Well, it shouldn't take much of your medical resources since two of my three casualties had the good sense to die ahead of your tender mercies."

The lieutenant gave a dismissive wave of his hand. "You heard me, when our men are tended to we'll see to your man with the leg wound."

"I appreciate it." Nathan bit his tongue, he couldn't let his reaction to the man's insolence color the way his troops were treated. Although, glancing around, he didn't think the mouthy lieutenant carried a lot of weight with his own soldiers. One wizened-looking grayback had already given Ricketts a chaw of his tobacco and was exchanging thoughts with him on some matter of importance to farmers. How the Reb knew that was Ricketts's background was a mystery only men of the soil could probably answer.

"Hey, Captain." It was Kendall and Corby being marched into the clearing to join the rest of them. They had been the farthest out on the southern flank nearest the second platoon.

"How's Mackey and the boys?" Nathan held his breath for the answer.

Kendall responded quickly, "They're okay, Captain. They weren't caught in the pinch, sir. They skedaddled like you told 'em to if they got cut off."

Nathan breathed a deep sigh of relief. He thought the Fifth's second platoon had made it out of the pincer movement but he couldn't be sure.

"Walleye and me was gonna be worm food if you didn't call it, sir—those damn Rebs stumbled right on us." The Walleye reference was to Corby. Everyone in the Fifth seemed to have a nickname except for Bender, but then, what better name for a wrestler?

"Jeez, they got Ringle," exclaimed Corby. Nathan was always thrown when Corby spoke. Because of his visual impairment one would think he was looking directly at you when he was staring to the side. Nathan assumed he was addressing him when actually Corby was first noticing the bodies of des Fleurs and Ringle, who'd been carefully arranged side by side for burial. Kendall's mouth dropped wide open when he saw des Fleurs was one of the casualties. Nathan remembered that the two of them had been close.

Nathan reached for the right words but couldn't find any. He just said, "Sorry, Kendall, we'll be tending them soon. Gator took one in the leg and we're first trying to get the Reb surgeon to look after him." Kendall kneeled beside his friend; he appeared to be praying.

Borrows and Rawlins came up near Corby, who was still caught up with Ringle and the massive wound to his head. "Yeah, Walleye, Ringle got splatted, sure nuff . . . musta been a buck 'n' ball to do all that," said Borrows.

After a few moments of uneasy silence, Rawlins mumbled, "Rot the luck."

The Fifth had started the "rot the luck" business during Antietam. When they had to somehow absorb death and mutilation on an incomprehensible scale, they found they could soothe themselves with irony. One would point out a Reb's head wedged in the crook of a tree after an artillery barrage and another would comment, "Rot the luck." It even applied to some of the worst of their own casualties. They were carrying Josiah Martin to the hospital tent when his shoe fell off. "Christ, his foot's in it!" Then a horrified pause until one of the others would gather himself and come up with "rot the luck." Somehow it helped.

Nathan turned at the sound of footsteps to find the cocky lieutenant once again approaching him. "If I may ask, Captain, why did you choose to attack with such vigor, yet surrender with such purpose?"

Damn, the son of a bitch—he couldn't let it go. "Not sure what you mean by 'purpose,' but I can't see the wisdom of losing good soldiers when there's no need—our job was done."

"Interesting, Captain. I believe we men of the South have some different notions regarding honor."

Nathan just couldn't help it; some things were beyond his ability to control. "How would you know?"

The lieutenant's face reddened. "Whatever do you mean by that?"

"I mean you can't have more than a few months in those gray britches and no real field time under your belt—I figure I know more about Southern honor in battle than you do."

"I see I made a mistake. I thought you were a gentleman, and denigrating the courage of your captors is hardly the way to—"

"To what? Curry favor with a man of honor?" Nathan had already been worked up before the obstreperous lieutenant had started. He just couldn't get des Fleurs and Ringle out of his mind. Just like that, men he had lived with for two years were no longer of the living . . . and they were fine men . . . and this peacock was giving him lectures on honor. But he also knew that he had gone too far—as was too often the case, he'd let his emotions run away with him. He took several deep breaths.

"Look, Lieutenant, pardon my temper. But I've lost some good young men in the last few minutes. I said I was in a good position to assess the ability and honor of Southern soldiers, and you assumed I meant it was low. In fact, in my estimation, they are fine fighting men. I just don't like hearing about young soldiers on either side in this conflict dying for old men's blustery concepts of righteousness."

The lieutenant's gaze seemed to wander inside for a moment, then he absently nodded an acknowledgment of the apology and moved on. Nathan could tell he was somewhat mollified and the situation reasonably diffused. It seemed that any time Nathan let his heart speak for his head, even for brief seconds, he grew to regret it. The old Reb sergeant with the untamed beard pulled up next to him as they were being marched to a holding area.

"Ya been kicking around in this mess for quite a spell, hain't ya, Captain?"

"I reckon." He glanced at the man, taking his measure. "I get the feeling you have too?"

"Cut my gums at Shiloh."

"Lord, that's a stretch, you have family?"

"Not no more."

Nathan was afraid to ask what had happened to them when the man offered, "Nah, it ain't what yer thinkin'. After a couple years of this crazy war went *by*, she went *bye-bye*."

Nathan nodded his understanding. "Ah, now there's something that don't change much on one side or the other of the Mason-Dixon, Secessionist or Unionist."

"Nah, I expect not." The man was quiet for a moment as they marched along, as if mulling something. Then he said, "That little affair with the lieutenant . . . ya know, he's really okay, just young and confused and trying to be strong. It wasn't that long ago he lost his brother."

So that's where the man's mind had strayed after Nathan's comment. "Jesus, I feel a bit the fool . . . saying what I did."

"Nah, he had it coming."

"Where did the Federals kill him?"

"Wasn't the Federals—it was the Army of Virginia."

Nathan raised his eyebrows questioningly. The sergeant continued, "Yeah, these border states got some of the worst problems—his older brother was a devout Unionist, now he's nothing no more but a memory."

Nathan shook his head. "Christ," he murmured under his breath. Shaking off the gloom, the sergeant remarked in an upbeat voice, "I tell you what, you know my notion about that honor stuff?"

"No. What?"

"I think the most honorable fate for a soldier is to live through this damn war."

Nathan smiled and nodded. "I have to give that notion an amen."

Soon they neared an area where the captives were allowed to stretch out and a loud-voiced corporal was telling them that they'd be given food and water in a few hours.

Sergeant Scraggly Beard told Nathan that this was as far as he went.

"I'm not sure what ole Early's plans are, probably didn't expect prisoners here 'til you boys came sashaying after us. But I 'spect that they'll march you to the nearest train running south and pack y'all off to Camp Sumter; they can separate the officers and such down there. You'll probably be going to Camp Oglethorpe up around Macon way and yer men'll probably stay at Andersonville or Cahaba."

"Thanks for your information and counsel, Sergeant."

"Think nothin' of it, Captain." The man tipped his hat and walked off without another word.

It was things like that that made Nathan wonder. A polite conversation and genuine goodwill in parting; yet if he had the man in his sights a few hours ago, he'd have shot him dead without a second thought.

"Two days earlier, as they marched south and west, they ran into rain and spent two more days slogging to reach a working train track. They weren't given any shelter, but then the Rebs didn't have any to speak of for themselves either. Finally, they came to a ramshackle depot with no name and a waiting string of freight cars. The prisoners were herded inside and were soon chugging toward Georgia.

Nathan found his weariness catching up with him. Gazing through the slats in the walls of the railroad car and mesmerized by the clank and rattle, he saw miles of the old South roll by. There were some run-down towns and Secessionist troops and slaves. The latter, sometimes by the dozen, were still working in the fields.

Nathan disliked the whole notion of slavery, it seemed barbaric. But he also thought killing tens of thousands of men in a day was an awful high a price to pay for ending it. Those piles of butchered humanity at Antietam were some mighty grim currency.

Hell, he'd hardly ever seen a Negro in Michigan. And the Southern boys he'd been alternately killing and running away from? He doubted if even one of those young men in gray uniforms whose bodies he gingerly stepped over had ever owned a slave. And then there was what Dr. Holmes told him about the educated classes in Cambridge. He had been trying to get some Africans enrolled right there at Harvard Medical School and all those right and proper university folks, professors and students alike—they didn't want to have anything to do with it.

It particularly irked him that some of those medical types were abolitionists when it came to judging Southern slave owners, but they couldn't make room for Africans in their own university classes. Ole Doc Holmes was in a snit about it. He wasn't any big fan of Thoreau, Nathan's hero, but he allowed how Henry David was "not only well-spoken but well-acted" on the issue of slavery. Damn, Nathan wished he could meet that man.

And preserving the union? Well, it wasn't that the ideas weren't right—it was just the cost that kept wearing at him. Nathan couldn't help but think that the justifications most men had on both sides didn't start with such high ideals—they were what you fell back on when the war became an endless nightmare. No more parades, songs, and bright uniforms; just blood, screams, and smells one never forgets.

Nathan counted in his head. With the escape of the second platoon under Lieutenant Mackey, he now had twenty-three men with him, counting Gator, who was moderately wounded . . . at least so far. His wound didn't look too bad, but the fear of infection was hard to shake. It seemed that so many of the men he had helped to bury were killed more by the fever and pus weeks later than they were by the nasty wounds that came first. That's another thing they didn't tell the bright-eyed recruits as they got sucked into this war.

Nathan fell inside himself for a spell until he suddenly realized that he was audibly muttering, "Quiet desperation, most men . . . quiet desperation."

★

WHEN NATHAN FIRST glimpsed Andersonville he thought he'd slipped into an Old Testament nightmare. It seemed a huge, rectangular field, barren of trees but surrounded by forest that ended no great distance from its stockade walls. He reckoned its size at about fifteen or twenty acres with no blockhouses along the perimeter. Mainly, the guards seemed to occupy perches on a catwalk along the walls. The treeless field dropped from the far ends of the rectangle toward its center at a shallow angle. Literally thousands of men were crammed inside the walled area with no shelter except what had been rigged by prisoners from blankets and uniform parts suspended from half-rotted wooden posts. There was no escape from the elements at all. A marshy area surrounded a stream that cut through the width of the camp, separating it into two sections—one somewhat larger than the other. On the heights at both ends were artillery pieces set to sweep the campground if there was ever an organized revolt.

From where he was standing, Nathan kept glancing around for a slit trench or privy that a stifling odor told him must be nearby. Suddenly, the grim reality occurred to him—the breeze, rustling leaves beneath his feet, was coming from the direction of the prison. He was as much aware of the presence of the camp from its stench as from his eyes. Then he noticed the low hum . . . sweet Christ, it was the ear's welcome to Camp Sumter—countless flies and mosquitoes. The reaction developing in him to this place paralleled the way he'd been affected by Antietam.

Some, including most of the guards, referred to the prison as Camp Sumter, but most knew it by the name it took from the nearby town of Andersonville. Nathan's men and others who had just arrived had gone stone-silent. Any fantasies of a civilian-style prison facility evaporated; the place looked like it could have been designed by Dante. Nathan had already begun reevaluating his fantasies about him and his men being safe in prison while others carried on the fight. They were soon lined up outside the camp and a Reb officer waved him into a processing area.

"This way, Yank."

Nathan walked to the head of the line and gave his vitals. "Nathan Parker, Fifth Michigan, fighting under the command of General Wallace . . . sergeant."

The registrar, a weary-looking sergeant himself, glanced at Nathan's wide-brimmed hat and the stripe down his leg.

"Sergeant, eh?"

"That's right."

"You know, this here camp is meant for enlisted men. Commissioned officers are supposed to be sent to Macon."

"I'll be sure and mention that to the next commissioned officer I meet."

For a second, the man let a smile pull at the corners of his mouth. Then he shrugged, copied down his name and unit, and bid him "Welcome to sunny Camp Sumter," as he motioned him toward the gate.

The gate guards pointed them to the far right, which suited Nathan as it looked like it might be toward some higher ground. As they made their way toward the general area that had been indicated by the guards, they passed through waves of body odor and filth that almost suffocated them.

They stepped gingerly over and around sick and listless men until they had almost reached their destination, when Nathan became aware that a small group of rough-looking characters, wearing makeshift yellow armbands, was rising and coming their way. There were six or seven toughs, most of them carrying ax or hoe handles.

The other prisoners watched from where they sprawled in the afternoon heat, seeming pretty much resigned to what appeared to be an oft-repeated ritual. Most of the acres of prisoners lying about wore sickly, defeated expressions on their faces. Resignation, Nathan thought, that's what Thoreau saw as "confirmed desperation." He called it "an unconscious despair concealed under the games and amusements of mankind." Even though he believed Henry David's assertion that "it is a characteristic of wisdom not to do desperate things," he also knew that what he felt arising in him now was a warrior's gift—that crazy edge of desperation tempered with cold rage. Nathan wasn't reluctant to fight when the choices were clear. That rarely happened in war—it was impersonal, too often arbitrary. But something in him gloried in battle when doubt was removed—he felt his spirit soar as the thugs approached.

The biggest of the toughs walked up to Nathan, smirking a greeting. It was something Nathan had long pondered, why bullies everywhere seemed to carry that same stupid expression on their faces.

"You the head hen for these Michigan boys?"

Bender and Rawlins both spun around and Weed snapped, "Who you talking to, peckerwood?"

In a low, calm voice Nathan said to Weed, "Enough." He turned back to the big man.

"Are you the one who decides berthing arrangements here?"

"Now, you got that right; Jeremy Gaston at your service. And I must say, you look to be a gentleman. So, for the right consideration we might be able to set you up with a luxury accommodation."

To Nathan, the man's accent seemed to be New York or New Jersey, certainly not the brogue he'd come to associate with Boston.

"But all the space appears to be taken, Gaston."

The man stroked his chin and looked about. "Well now, fancy that. I think you might be right, but don't you worry. I bet me and my boys can talk any of the folks on prime property here to give their spot to you if we ask them nice."

"I guess the high ground is the best. I noticed that you and your associates got up from over near that stump."

"Sure did, and for say, ten greenbacks apiece, I can escort you through camp and have you select quarters just as lovely."

"Thanks anyway, but that won't be necessary."

"And why would that be? You plan to stand up the whole time you're here?"

"It's not that, I've decided where we want to be—I think that patch right there next to the stump would be fine."

The man's face twisted into a snarl. "Why, that's our . . . who do you think you—" Nathan's booted foot slammed full force into the man's groin—the fellow's ax-handle club hit the ground only a couple of seconds before the man himself. Ricketts grabbed up the weapon and applied it to the knee of Gaston's nearest cohort. Bender picked the next nearest thug up around the waist and threw him a full body length. The others, frozen momentarily by shock and surprise, tried to come to their leader's aid.

While Gaston was bent over on his knees, clutching his privates, Nathan stepped back for a running start and kicked the man full in the face. As Gaston went over backward, Nathan followed him, took the ax handle from Ricketts, and placed it across the man's throat—he stood on the left side of it and placed some of his weight on the right side. Gaston's face turned red with a tinge of blue as he began choking. It was clear that he had been so interested in his tough-guy act that he hadn't paid careful enough attention to reading the character of his new visitor.

Nathan thought about that briefly. How he must look to others when his choler was up. He had dark hair, was above average height, medium build, and according to some, had hard eyes. He'd once heard a fellow say that "When Parker's gray eyes fix on ya with his teeth set tight, that's the last warning a man gets." These fellows had also apparently not taken into account that these newcomers were fresh from a military unit that still had cohesion and were in the presence of a trusted leader.

"Tell your big ugly rats over there to give it up." Nathan was referring to the thug reinforcements who were squaring off with the Fifth Michigan.

Gaston motioned his associates back, or at least waved his arm in the direction he thought they were—he was mightily discomfited by the choking ax handle. Then Nathan figured he'd take advantage of the onlookers' perception of his demeanor. A crowd had already begun to gather, so Nathan used the moment as an object lesson for that whole part of the camp. He stared at Gaston and let his inner voice speak. "I can't abide by a man that preys on his own, Gaston. If I ever see you abuse someone in my unit or any of these true soldiers again, I'll kill you—now look right in my eyes and see if you don't think I mean it."

★

SO THE MICHIGAN boys settled in that night as Gaston and his chastened crowd wandered out of sight to browbeat some other men out of a place to sleep. Nathan reflected on the dog-eat-dog prison they had just entered—just one baby step from a dog-eat-dog world. It would be sad another time but for right now it was just the way things were.

His last official act of the evening was to check on Gator. He examined his wound and quietly noted to himself that there was a distinct sharp redness starting to emerge from around the hole in his leg. Assured the lads had made him as comfortable as possible, he withdrew to his own small plot of damp earth. His men had, as usual, made his spot a bit larger and more comfortable than anyone else's except Gator. He had inches to spare when he turned over, unlike the rest of them. It was their habit—the captain always had a special place to retire to, even in the lowest ring of hell.

As Nathan drifted off to sleep he thought of his wounded soldier. He couldn't help but wonder who was the more fortunate—Gator or des Fleurs and Ringle, curled in their comfortable and quiet graves.

CHAPTER 3

3 August 1864
Camp Sumter, Andersonville, Georgia

N athan wished he could control his breathing. He felt the dank earth close in, smothering him as he sought precious air. Red clay muck clogged his ears, caught up under his fingernails, and made for a sharp taste in the back of his throat. Only fear gave him the spark to keep methodically crawling forward in the darkness. Nothing new in that; it seemed fear had been the prime mover in his life for the past three years. He only wished he could calm down; even chanting didn't help. He was ten feet underground and thirty feet from where he had entered the tunnel. His men had dug it by hand, using metal scoops fashioned from their service canteens. They learned from old-timers in the prison camp that holding a canteen over an open flame could melt the solder that held the two platelike halves together. When they weren't using any available flame to boil cornmeal mush or pop lice in the seams of their clothes, they used it to make scoops.

Nathan could feel dirt being kicked back in his face by the man

ahead of him and he detected the odor of unwashed feet wrapped
in rotted leather. It surprised him that he could smell anything after three weeks in Andersonville. After living in indescribable filth,
being able to notice a stench made it seem his senses had come back
alive at the prospect of freedom.

"What, sir?" The question, which came from the owner of the
feet, sounded distant because the man only had room to turn his
head to the side so his voice would carry between his shoulder and
the dirt wall to someone behind him.

"Nothing," Nathan gasped in response. "Keep going, Bender."
He must have been muttering out loud the crazy Thoreau chant . . .
"quiet desperation" . . . "Most men lead" . . . Nathan used *Walden*
the way most men used the Bible. He'd lost most of his taste for
religion—it was probably lying somewhere out there in the
blood-soaked mud between Antietam and Monocacy. He figured
he'd rather share his last few moments with Thoreau than Jesus
anyway.

Sweat trickled in a muddy rivulet down his forehead into his
eyes. He was sweating profusely but not from the oppressive Georgia heat. The air was actually cooler in the tunnel; his effort and
fear made it near stifling. He felt something hit his foot—it was too
tight to even think about turning to see behind, but he knew it
would be Weed. The young man was next in line.

"Most men . . . "He was careful to not say it out loud this time,
it wouldn't do for his men to hear—they'd think he had gone soft
between the ears for sure. Curious, the sorts of things that went
through a man's mind when he crawled through a wormhole in the
Georgia night hoping to escape underneath a stockade fence.

Andersonville wasn't like a regular prison where captives were
locked up in cells and accompanied from place to place by guards.
Once men were penned in the overcrowded stockade they lived
under constant threat of being shot by the guards if they strayed
over a line that came within several yards of the stockade poles.

The "dead-line" they called it. The guards were perched along the wall and artillery pieces were set on a rise at two ends to sweep the mass of human flesh if there was ever an organized escape attempt.

Thirty thousand men were crowded into well under twenty acres with no shelter unless they fashioned some through their own devices. The only relief to the crowding was the daily death count in the camp—a mixed blessing—the irony of which was not lost on the camp's wags. They bet on who might be able to stretch their legs that night because their blanket partner had passed to a happier world.

The decision to chance this escape effort so soon after imprisonment was Nathan's. He knew his men wouldn't be surprised—that's what they expected from the man who led them through battle with so few losses. No, it was Nathan who felt amazed. At first, capture had been almost a relief as the weight of leadership lightened. But scarcely a week had gone by in Andersonville before he had decided to make a break for it. He knew that more than a few weeks in this camp and what remained of their strength and discipline could be drained by the ravages of dysentery, scurvy, and gangrene.

A dirt clod fell from the tunnel roof onto his head. He gasped and inhaled a mixture of air and soil, gagging with the next forced breath—Christ, he had to get out of there. It felt like their progress had slowed to a stop. What the hell, Bender? What's taking so long? They should be about beneath the stockade poles by now. Thirty more feet and they could emerge well beyond the fence on a moonless night behind the guards. After that, getting back to the Federal lines would be damned difficult. The whole countryside was alerted for Union escapees, runaway slaves, and Reb deserters. But even recapture or being shot was preferable to rotting away one's soul in this little nest of Southern hospitality.

Nathan felt Bender's shoe kick suddenly into his face, leaving a sharp pain in his nose and forehead. The man had kicked backward just as Nathan felt a heavy movement of earth and a crushing weight over the front half of his body. Now, Bender's heel poked Nathan's face in staccato. A little more movement of earth and Nathan couldn't breathe. His hand was trapped over his face, so he cupped it, trying to steal enough room to take a breath, but he managed only to inhale dirt. He felt hot blood rushing through his scalp. Then, the approach of oblivion.

He was blacking out . . . dying. Good, it was better to leave this goddamn mess of a world. Good . . . but no, he was coming back out—suffocating pain, hope, and the panic that accompanies hope. Nathan caught one short wheezy breath through clogged nostrils and realized that he was moving again. Weed was pulling him backward through the tunnel. Now he felt a searing in his lungs—drawing enough air in to keep conscious, but not enough to ease the choking. He was moving slowly but steadily, not in fits and starts, smoothly, and he couldn't understand how Weed was doing that unless he too was being pulled by others. Then he was moving more quickly and hands yanked him upright, dragging him unceremoniously from his fresh grave. Damn them all. He felt fingers in his mouth, even invading his nose. Men were desperately trying to save him and he started catching his breath.

"Captain, you hear me? God Amighty, you all right?"

"Okay? What?" For a moment he thought he was back at the Monocacy, but no bleeding horse and no coppery smell here. "I . . ." Then it struck him. "Weed, what happened to Joe? Good Christ . . . Bender's still in there."

Everything went black again and almost as quickly he revived. Somebody, Barsky, was talking. "Wasn't your fault, Captain, wasn't nothing you could have done. It was the damn stockade piles, one fell into the tunnel and squoze him, sir. The men up top saw it happen and the guards, they're in a dither now."

Nathan looked around and noted he was out of the tunnel entrance, but still in the hole from which they had started their burrow. It was six feet in diameter, about twelve feet deep, and lit with a crude birch and rag torch.

"Damn their goddamn eyes, those goober-grabbing sons of bitches," said a scratchy voice Nathan knew well.

"Hush up, Weed, and get the captain up the damn pole." It sounded like Barsky telling the young private to pull him up. Nathan felt himself being lifted from above while hands pushed him from below. Then he was in open air and his eyes began to adjust—bright campfires everywhere. His men pointed him toward the guards' perches on the stockade where they had tried to tunnel under. Two of the poles were sunk deeper than the others by a good two to three feet.

The guards had lanterns placed around their pigeon roosts and one, a tall, sallow-faced sergeant sporting a red sash, made a show of carrying a sledgehammer to the top of the catwalk. Glancing once back toward the compound to ensure he had an attentive audience, he raised the heavy tool over his shoulder and began to pound the lowest pole farther into the ground. This was apparently intended as a brutal assurance to all that whoever had undermined the pole was now being impaled by it.

In a guttural voice with a thick Georgia accent the sergeant made some comment about "Pinning Yanks like doodlebugs on a board," but he was drowned out by shouts from the thousands of men inside the camp. A rain of dirt clods hit the fence and the guards raised their muskets threateningly in response. But it was all part of the ritual. The guards knew the men couldn't cross the dead-line to reach them as artillery pieces were trained on them, and the prisoners knew the guards wouldn't enter the encampment at night. A low plaintive voice spoke from somewhere behind Nathan.

"There just ain't no way to tell how deep yer going once you get that far from the entrance. Hell, he might of been only a couple feet under the post instead of five or ten feet, just ain't no way a tellin'."

Nathan considered the unwashed sea of humanity around him and again became aware of the fierce stench. He didn't know what was more devastating—his near brush with death or that he was still alive. His men apparently had already forgiven his miscalculations in the escape attempt and tried to comfort him, but he couldn't stand it anymore. They loved him and sometimes he hated them for that.

Nathan knew he shouldn't ever show partiality, but Joe Bender was close to his age and had been around more than most of the young men in his command. Sometimes they could even talk a bit, man-to-man. Bender was his friend. Nathan Parker buried his face in his hands and shut out the world. After a few moments in a very even, precise voice he spoke intently into his hands, which were still wrapped tightly around his face, "Most men lead lives . . ." He didn't care if the others heard him, he just didn't care anymore.

CHAPTER 4

17 October 1864
Camp Sumter, Andersonville, Georgia

T he now familiar sight of thousands of soldiers crammed into a compound ass-to-teakettle, clothed in remnants of blue uniforms and surrounded by guards in a hodgepodge of gray and butternut, had set Nathan to mulling the concept of "service." That is, "to serve," as in "service to God and country." Some serve by putting on a blue uniform to preserve the Union and rid the nation of the evils of slavery. Others serve by putting on a gray uniform and pledging to defend against tyranny and to preserve the homeland against rampant Federalism. Then everyone gets in line and shoots one another. It had once seemed logical, even appealing: drums and horns and a rain of flowers tossed by pretty girls. So what in hell was this? Were they "serving" at lovely Camp Sumter?

He rubbed a horsehair toothbrush absently against his gums; if nothing else this gave Nathan some sense of control. Maybe he could keep at least his teeth clean. The soreness in his jaw he suspected was the beginning of scurvy. He sat cross-legged on the ground in front of the lean-to erected by the Fifth Michigan to mark the twenty-five by thirty foot rectangle of prison territory they claimed as their own. It was the territory they had wrested from Gaston and his bullyboys. The wretch had good taste in real estate, Nathan had to give him that. They were on a slight rise in the compound, so Nathan had a full view of the seventeen acres of men interspersed with occasional ragged tents or lean-tos.

Nathan wrapped a worn piece of blanket closer around his shoulders. It was a cool evening for mid-October in Georgia; it usually took longer for the heat of the day to dissipate in the humid air. He pushed another rag underneath his feet. He had boots that weren't rotted through yet, but he kept them off when he was sitting so they could air out. The problem was he couldn't bear to let his feet touch the ground. There was no soil in the ordinary sense of the word at Andersonville, for the ground was alive. Especially during summer, it had squirmed with every imaginable form of vermin. Men were packed so close with such poor sanitation that maggots falling from festering wounds and grubs from rotting cornmeal all thrived together in the slimy land and intermingled with morsels of food and human feces.

The shallow stream that crossed one end of the compound became an open sewer before it even entered the prison grounds. It was the stockade branch of a river called, of all things, Sweet Water. After passing through the guards' camp upstream, it carried human waste and by-products of their cooking and bathing into the prison. As the stream entered the stockade it widened to twenty or thirty feet across and about a foot deep. The consistency of its swamplike border seemed to Nathan similar to thick porridge. Men desperate for water would sink knee-deep in the slime pit bordering the flowing part of the stream. It was hard to believe that men of any civility or honor could have devised an institution as soul-crushing as this place for their fellow countrymen. Even God seemed to object and during a thunderstorm opened a spring in the middle of the camp; Providence, they called it.

Nathan felt a sharp pain shoot up the side of his face when the horsehair on his brush touched an open sore in the back of his mouth. A deep chronic ache throbbed in both sides of his jaw and the back of his throat felt raw—yeah, it was goddamn scurvy. As he mulled his own condition he watched a wasted fellow from another company stagger by, eyes red and streaming, hand over mouth, as was the habit of many of the worst stricken. The fellow turned toward him with an owl-eyed expression common to the prisoners. It came partly from the wasted flesh and partly from the soot of pitch-pine fires highlighting the round eye sockets and whites of the eyes: the "surprised Negro look" as the men called it. And he was sure that his men, many sitting around him and watching, knew that there, but for God and a few more weeks, would go they.

Nathan was startled when the man sneezed. Then the fellow dropped to his knees and matter-of-factly searched the ground for a tooth that had blown out of his mouth. He found it and, casting an embarrassed glance in Nathan's direction, tried to force it back into his jaw before he scurried off. From the total silence around him, Nathan surmised that several of the men around him had also witnessed the bizarre act and subsequent retreat of the unfortunate fellow.

"Rot the luck," muttered Weed.

Some of the others chuckled and shook their heads.

"Least the poor bastard won't be bitin' his tongue," offered Peregoy.

"Hey, Cap'n. Maybe we can have us a competition, you know, see how far we can sneeze a tooth," came the contribution from Red Face Rawlins.

"Yeah," Walleye Corby chimed in. "The winner gets to skinny-dip in the stream whilst the others have to dig his grave."

New ideas for recreational pursuits were coming fast and heavy. But Nathan didn't mind. Men who are laughing aren't gasping their last breath or cutting their wrists.

Ricketts, a sallow, usually withdrawn sawyer from the upper peninsula of Michigan, offered, "Or a blow-it-out-the-arse contest."

"'At's right, Ricketts," said Peregoy. "Yeah, we could put a dung beetle up our butts and aim it at the guards; first to hit one of those cracker bastards in the eye wins."

"There you go, now I'm for that. But men with dysentery can't compete, wouldn't be fair."

Nathan kept silent and returned to rubbing his gums. Yeah, they were hilarious all right. Humor might be a great weapon against despair, but it didn't cure scurvy or stop a hundred men a day in Andersonville from dying of exposure, dysentery, and gangrene. The best Nathan could do to keep those scourges from killing his men was to insist on cleanliness and isolation whenever possible. He shut out the banter and set his mind to considering if there was anything else he could do to increase their chances of getting out of all this alive.

Scurvy was treatable if they could lay hands on the right foods. As hard as he tried to barter for them, there wasn't enough fruits or vegetables to fight off what he thought was the worst curse of starvation. His efforts hadn't been entirely in vain as only one of the twenty-three men under his charge had yet died or become incapacitated from disease or infection. Gator had died three weeks after their arrival. Maybe his loss was predictable given his wound, but the inevitability of it was the worst part. Regardless of how hard they tried, Nathan and all the men of the Fifth Michigan could not prevent Gator's loss from what shouldn't have been a fatal wound.

He was suddenly aware of a sharp pain in his mouth where he had been absently, but vigorously, working his toothbrush. He removed the brush and stared at it—the horsehair was covered with blood and his hand was trembling. Christ, he had to pull himself together.

Nathan continued assessing their situation. Parker's Rangers had isolated themselves as best they could in a camp where they had once been shoulder to maw with thirty thousand other men. Now, in autumn, that number had fallen to fewer than ten thousand, but somehow it didn't seem the crowding had lessened. The mortality rate since August had sharply increased, probably because effects from the earlier conditions were now being felt. Many who had survived the summer were simply too weak to go on. In advanced stages of starvation, they would succumb to infection from even a minor cut.

Nathan watched a death party, a group of men allowed to carry their comrades' bodies through the gates to turn them over to the Negro work crews for burial. Reward for doing this was permission to carry an armload of wood back to the stockade from the surrounding forest, so they were seldom short of volunteers.

Nathan wasn't the only officer who had chosen to stay with his men in prison. But he was probably the most successful at maintaining discipline. They dug their own well, as many had, and Nathan let no one drink from any other source. He didn't know how the damnable diseases worked, but Dr. Holmes had convinced him that being clean was likely half the battle of staying healthy. He made his men overcook their food, pop lice in their clothing seams over an open fire every couple of days, and plan constantly, even when there wasn't much to plan. He had them pool their belongings for trade, when he didn't have them reading, exercising, and foraging. Nathan called this "fighting the darkness of the soul," which he believed was as important as fighting disease and starvation.

The men showed extraordinary confidence in him. They had been incensed over the death of Bender, seeming for some reason to take his demise harder than that of their comrades lost in battle.

For several days, Nathan had been almost useless to them. He was despondent after their failed escape and regaining his composure was nearly impossible.

But when he pulled himself together, Nathan ordered his men to do the same. "Bender was dead before that sot pounded that stake, I'm sure of it," he said. "But if he was still alive they probably did him a favor. Most of all, don't waste time fretting on something you can't fix. That guard is a dead man. Just keep track of where he is stationed on the wall and I promise you, we will settle accounts before we leave." That seemed to calm them down, for Nathan was a man who kept his promises.

He became aware that Weed was tapping him on the shoulder. "Captain, there's somebody here wants to speak with you. He's from Third Pennsylvania and I think he's an officer."

A blond fellow, older than Nathan, maybe midforties, stood over him. How he would have slipped through induction into the camp as an enlisted man was hard to imagine. His insignia was gone and he wore three stripes on an infantryman's tunic, but his bearing, boots, and creased pants should have been a dead giveaway.

Nathan smiled. "Nice to meet you . . . Sergeant?"

The man smiled back. "Lieutenant, Lieutenant Kensington."

"I'm Captain Parker, Nathan Parker. I see you've opted for superior accommodations."

"Heard they were the best Georgia had to offer, to Yankees anyway."

"So you've just arrived."

"I have, and sir"—the man's demeanor became more formal and serious—"I must say that I am absolutely appalled at what I have witnessed in this hellhole. It is positively a blight on the nation's spirit that American soldiers, regardless of their allegiance, should treat prisoners of their own blood in such a contemptible manner."

"Indeed, Lieutenant, I share your distress that it has come to this, but . . ." Nathan had gone through similar conversations at least a half dozen times with newly arrived officers who sought him out after their first few hours at the prison. He didn't know what else to say and was surprised that the full extent of the atrocious conditions at Andersonville remained a surprise to the newly incarcerated. As if hearing his inner thoughts, the lieutenant went on.

"I'd heard that conditions were quite poor here and I expected nothing but spartan circumstances, but this . . . this is unspeakable. Have these Confederates no honor?"

"Actually, I like to think that most who fight under the Secessionist banner have no more idea than you did of what has developed here." Nathan stuck his toothbrush away in his pocket and sat back against a post to settle in for a long discussion. He felt the man needed some soothsaying and direction. The officer's sense of responsibility for his men clearly weighed on him. It reminded Nathan of what he felt like when he first entered Camp Sumter after they were captured at Monocacy early in July.

"Look, Lieutenant, this place is reprehensible, but I don't think it was purposeful. The tyranny of circumstance makes for a place like Andersonville. Families and friends make the worst enemies and brother fighting brother makes for the worst bloodshed."

"Perhaps, Captain, but this atrocity, it's, it's . . ."

"Inexcusable?"

"Exactly so." After a moment the man continued. "But you seem rather accepting of it all, if I may say so, sir."

"No, not accepting, Lieutenant, but philosophical." He offered the man a variation of the same sermon he had been preaching to the others.

"This," Nathan continued with a wave of the arm to indicate the whole of Andersonville, "is a symptom of the whole nation losing its humanity. Callousness, not cruelty, created this place. We Americans have been killing one another with a ferocity that seems to make the whole civilized world uneasy. Hell, during the cleanup at Antietam I saw French and Prussian observers shaking their heads after a battle—'Have you ever thought of giving ground before you've lost thousands?' And 'Have you ever heard of an honorable surrender before there aren't enough survivors to bury the dead?' "

Kensington now also sat cross-legged like Nathan and seemed to be listening carefully.

"This one Frenchman who fancied himself a military historian told me"—and here Nathan spoke in a mock French accent— " 'Accounts of your war of independence showed me the undercurrent of violence that grows on this soil. Only in barbaric lands do men of empire grant countrymen no quarter and take no prisoners. Even knowing that did not prepare me for this—you people will never get over such a bloodbath.' "

"Still, Captain, there's no excuse."

"Yes, there is. Mark my words, I'm no apologist for this place, but merely hating it and the Rebs does not help us understand it enough to protect our men. We don't have the time or luxury to waste energy on outrage. Just consider, the South is starving and Grant won't exchange prisoners. So you put who you can spare in charge of these prison camps and the worst comes out in them and those imprisoned. We curse Wirz, that old Swiss bastard of a prison-master—but remember he gave the prisoners the wherewithal to put down the Raiders. As I hope you've been told, the worst damn predators in here are our own men. In fact," he said, gesturing toward the insignia on the man's arm, "they were called Raiders but most were New Yorkers from New York and Pennsylvania."

The lieutenant shook his head sadly as he listened, but Nathan wasn't through yet. "And we came here after that whole affair and had a new bunch, regulators they called them, already trying to prey on us—these were men, remember, who were part of our own army." Nathan calmed himself down. "So, no, you can't only blame the Rebs, keep an eye on anybody you don't know."

Throwing a twig at the fire someone had started, Nathan said, "And be damn careful of that sorry bunch of Georgia peckerwood reservists we have now for guards. When we had real soldiers on duty here, those Alabama regulars, there was none of the sick goings-on with the dead-line you have now. What do you expect when you have youngsters without the sense God gave a goat and white-bearded shits who were never taken seriously by anyone suddenly given the power of life and death?"

Nathan's voice had risen and he trembled as he finished his tirade. He was aware that his behavior was counteracting his advice. The very anger he was telling the lieutenant not to waste was possessing him. Meanwhile, Lieutenant Kensington grew quiet. He said, "You're right, Captain. One has to become philosophical in this place or he will soon cave in on himself. How long have you been here?"

"July. Some of the boys and I stumbled into an ambush by Jubal Early's men near Frederick."

"The push on Washington City."

"Yeah, the very same. So then we tried our break from here back in early August because we heard General Stoneman had troops nearby and might raid Macon. I figured we could join up with him, that we were better off getting shot or smothering in a tunnel than waiting to die here like dogs."

"And?"

"And, I got my wish. At least one more of my men will never die here like a dog from disease or starvation." After a couple of moments of silence, the lieutenant rose and shook hands with Nathan.

"Thanks for your counsel, Captain. I congratulate you on keeping your men alive as well as you have. I hope to visit you again."

Nathan nodded and bid him good luck, but to himself muttered,

"Make it quick, mister, no way in hell I intend to be here much longer."

★

THE MEN SAT in a circle around him, speaking in low voices. They were in a large shebang, as they called it; a dirt depression partially covered with canvas. It was guarded by Rawlins and Peregoy at the high points to make sure no one overheard them. All had done what they could to appear presentable. To someone from outside, tidying up their rags after three months in Andersonville might have seemed absurd. But these men didn't consider themselves run-of-the-mill soldiers; they were Parker's Rangers. They spent hours beating the grime off their uniform remnants and rubbing the fire soot off their faces with putrid water, all to show their discipline and pride. This was an official meeting and the captain brooked no sloppiness.

"Men, it's time." Nathan removed his hat and placed it on his lap. "First a moment of silence for the men of the Fifth Michigan who have beat us to the grave." They were quiet and motionless for a full minute. The evening murmur of voices from several thousand other men and late-season mosquitoes covered them like a damp blanket.

Nathan placed his hat back on his head and got to the point. "After watching these slack-jawed sots for a couple of months, I'm thinking we can get one person out of here with the right diversion." He saw a glimmer of fighting spirit work its way back into the eyes of even his sickest men. Still they trusted him. He had sworn never to let himself be tied down by emotion, but he couldn't help it; these men believed in him. Damn them. He held their comrades' hands when they lay dying and they smiled at him for making the effort. He pulled himself together and continued.

"It's simple. Boils down to getting someone outside to the other end of the old escape tunnels. You've all seen those crackers take after escapees; they call the locals with their blacks and dogs and head out yonder on one of the trails." Some glanced towards the trailheads beyond the stockade and nodded; the others kept listening.

"We get a man out there and he's going to be caught every time in less than a day. But what if they never head off to begin with?" He paused and looked around for effect.

"I've never seen them come back toward the stockade after a breakout . . . the tunnels out there are yesterday's work, monuments to failure . . . and to Bender. But for us, they're the answer." Nathan let them consider that—he watched eyebrows raise and mouths open questioningly. "If we get a man out there and instead of running, he comes back to the outer end of one of those old tunnel exits and hides—waits 'til the place clears of searchers—by God, then he'd have a fighting chance."

Even the hint of a strategy seemed to bring the men back from despair. "Who's going, Captain?"

"Someone fit enough to run . . . and able to convince our superior officers that we're likely to lose more men in here than on the field of battle if they don't take action." Then Nathan added grimly, "And someone who collects debts for the Fifth Michigan." The reference to Bender didn't need explaining.

"When?"

"Tomorrow."

There followed a brief silence. Weed took in a deep breath and asked, "When you coming back for us, Captain?" The nodding and hopeful expressions of the entire group indicated that this wasn't going to be an argumentative session; there seemed no question who should represent them outside. Nathan knew it was the right choice, but he wanted them to come to that conclusion on their own. He looked around, and seeing no one ready to question the plan, he poked absently at the fire. There were times when more words only shed less light.

"Murphy, Ricketts, Weed, you gentlemen figure out how to get on a burial detail late afternoon tomorrow. Trade whatever you have to for a body, and work out the distraction for when I run. Meeting's over." And that was all. Think long and hard, present your plan, see if anyone had a problem with it . . . if not, act. The men were used to Nathan's way. One by one they worked their way over to Nathan and shook his hand.

"We'll get you out there and keep 'em busy while ya hide . . . but be sure to say hi from me to that red-kerchief-wearing bastard when you're out there, Captain." Rawlins had been especially close to Bender, and there was a simmering look of murder in his eyes . . . along with tears.

"Rest easy, Michael. The sergeant's out there every evening and we don't leave our debts unpaid if we can help it."

"But not at the risk of getting caught, sir. I mean it, we don't expect you to take any chances that could get ya captured again."

Nathan smiled and clapped Rawlins on the shoulder.

"Go with God, sir," said Walleye Corby.

"Best o' luck to ya, suh." Nathan smiled at the Upper Peninsula accent of Vrenka. The ritual parting over, most of the men returned to their individual shelters. Nathan was soon sitting by himself except for Weed and Rawlins.

"Hate for you to go, sir, but you're the best to make it happen." Weed stumbled around for a moment and then handed Nathan a locket. "Don't want some goober-snapper to get that, sir, in case we don't make it."

Nathan placed the locket in what remained of his vest pocket. "You'll make it, son, you'll make it, but I'll carry this for a while if you like." Weed smiled his thanks and went off to find Murphy and Ricketts. Nathan knew they would agonize all night on the best way to get him outside, and he wouldn't interfere; part of them trusting him was him trusting them.

CHAPTER 5

18 October 1864
Andersonville, Georgia/Eastern Alabama

N athan peered cautiously through a mound of rubble. He couldn't believe he was once again in an escape tunnel at Andersonville. There was one significant difference this time: he was outside the stockade perimeter and he had entered from without. He counted on the very unlikelihood of the situation to keep him from capture.

As he caught his breath, he studied the scene outside his burrow, including his pursuers. The search party was composed of several Georgia mounted reservists with carbines. Three Negroes on foot handled a pack of dogs. The hounds began running around in circles getting their bearings and two headed tentatively across the field toward the forest perimeter. A third dog of independent nature hung back, keeping his nose to the ground, glued to a scent he apparently couldn't interpret.

The searchers were in no great rush. It was one thing for a prisoner to get out of Andersonville, quite another to get away from it.

Regular army and militia patrols looking for escaped slaves and deserters doubled well for capturing escapees. Of the tens of thousands of incarcerated men, only a handful of Union soldiers had ever escaped Fort Sumter.

Nathan had seen the abandoned escape tunnel exits while on several corpse-carrying trips to the outside. Some men had actually succeeded in digging under the stockade to come up on the other side. These dated back to numerous attempts by inmates to escape in previous months. Additional obstacles, such as a new moat and in some places a second wall, made such attempts a thing of the past. Most of the exits outside the stockade had collapsed or were kicked in by guards. But others had been ignored; there simply wasn't any possibility of anybody exiting through those holes. They were monuments to failure, which the guards proudly pointed out to visitors and even to inmates on wood-foraging missions.

Clearly the thought that a prisoner would escape, then return to the prison and hide in tunnel exits in the shadow of the stockade was never considered. At least by men—that one damn hound seemed unconvinced and was beginning to make his way toward Nathan when he was yanked back by his Negro handler. The black man cast a sideways glance toward Nathan's hole and held it for a split second before forcefully getting the recalcitrant dog to join the others. Nathan wasn't sure but thought he might have seen the trace of a smile before the man hastened back to the others.

The first part of Nathan's strategy was extraordinary in its simplicity. Fifth Michigan negotiated with the Pennsylvania boys to take some of their dead out of the stockade. The stream of men leaving burdened with corpses was becoming almost continuous. Like most cases of supply and demand the glut of corpses was so great that the privilege of removal was cheap. Two corn cakes, a leather shoe patch, and three pieces of pine for the fire was a bargain for a fresh body.

Nathan and seven of his men had carried the unfortunates to

the hospital and out to the Negroes on the burial detail. Moments later, a diversion caused by one of his men running back into the hospital area distracted the guards long enough for the others to make a break for it—at least until they heard the command "Halt," with which they immediately complied. A couple of hard cuffs were dealt to each of them who had fled, along with head-shaking queries about "how far the dumb Yanks thought they could possibly get." Meanwhile, Nathan had run back toward the fort and dived into the muddy moat. When the Rebs decided he had run, they seemed irritated, but only mildly concerned. Men in the physical shape of the prisoners never got far and the dogs would find them almost immediately.

This last had been the subject of much discussion among Nathan's men—how did the damn dogs distinguish prisoners from anyone else who happened to be traveling in a direction away from Andersonville? The guards never wasted time trying to find an item of clothing specific to an escapee. How were they doing it?

Nathan thought he knew and had bet his life on it. The one thing that distinguished the prisoners from the others was their filthy clothes and bodies. Having been in close quarters with gangrenous flesh and saturated with a buildup of pitch-pine soot from months of campfires contributed to a special Andersonville bouquet. When newcomers to the prison entered, they had to place kerchiefs over their faces as if visiting a morgue in the tropics. Hence, Nathan reasoned, it shouldn't take an overly wise dog to discern inmates from normal travelers.

"Hell, a blind Sunday school teacher could follow their trail if'n he bent over and kept his nose to the ground," was the way Weed had put it. That's why the only object Nathan had in his possession when he hit the outside was a bar of soap purchased from one of the new arrivals. Moments after he was in the trench, he removed his ragged uniform remnants and vigorously took his first bath in months. When twilight descended he emerged from the thick weeds around the trench, moved quickly to one of the tunnel openings, crawled in and blocked the opening with dirt and rocks from inside. He lay there, shivering to beat all, peering through his little slit. It shouldn't be so easy for the dogs to detect him, but he would look mighty peculiar dashing through the countryside stark naked. Nathan had plans for that too—the Georgia reservists had plenty of clothes, namely the ones they were wearing.

As nature called, he watched the guards one by one amble back toward the wood line to relieve themselves. They had a latrine, but like most soldiers preferred open woods to an army shit hole. Finally, he saw what he was waiting for, the sergeant with the red sash making his way ponderously to the woods. Like most of the guards, he left his musket on the stockade pigeon roost and went empty-handed to the forest. He carried a pistol in a leather shoulder holster that also secured a sergeant's billy—an oak club that marked his status and likely contributed to his self-important bearing. The belt hung loose over his hips, covering the latches of his suspenders.

Light was fast fading, which worked in Nathan's favor as he removed the barrier he'd built in the tunnel and headed after the guard. Barefoot and without a stitch of clothing, Nathan padded up to where the guard stooped to do his business. Soon the man rose to his feet in front of Nathan, but facing away. He began pulling his suspenders over his shoulder when he heard Nathan behind him. Annoyed, he protested back over his shoulder, "Sweet Sally, can't a mind tend his innards without some fool comes walking up on him?" Never turning around, he kept grumbling while he fooled with his pants. He had lain the belt on the ground nearby.

Nathan leaped the last few feet and in midair kicked the man in the small of the back. The fellow hit the ground hard, gasping for air. As the sergeant struggled to rise, Nathan threw all his weight on top of him, buried his knees in the guard's shoulders, and yanked loose the colorful sash. When the guard was able with a huge effort to force his head up, Nathan wrapped the sash around the man's throat.

"What in hell . . . ?" The rest he never shared with the living. Nathan grabbed the billy club from the guard's belt and struck him a stunning blow on the back of the head. He wrapped the kerchief ends around the club and twisted the material tight. Somewhere in his half-conscious haze the guard knew what was next and tried mightily to resist. Nathan tightened the cloth until he cut off the man's protesting gasps and felt the panicked fingers tearing ineffectually at his wrists. He garroted the sergeant until his head turned a different shade from the rest of him. Nathan loosened his grip long enough so the soldier could comprehend a few final words.

"This is for Bender, guess it all ain't so damn funny now, is it?" The silent kicking and scratching went on for what seemed a long time and then there was complete stillness. There was a stillness deep in Nathan also, as though he had written the last line of a poem. But there was no satisfaction in it, nor regret, only an overwhelming sense of emptiness that had become such a part of him in this place. He looked down and saw his hands shaking. They were bleeding, too, from the man's fingernail gouges.

As Nathan removed the guard's clothing he considered his situation. He was technically free, but that meant little as long as he was so close to Camp Sumter. There had never been any argument who the escapee would be—a man with the savvy to elude recapture and the stature to influence the outside world that something needed to be done. The only man that made sense was Captain Parker.

It was a questionable honor. The odds against getting away were high and then there was the matter of making it through hundreds of miles of enemy territory to find Federal forces. Brigades attached to General Sherman were not far to the east, but the region between was heavily patrolled by grayback regulars, militia, and locals looking for bounties. If he managed to clear the environs of the prison, Nathan had another surprise for any pursuers. Since it would be predictable that he head north or east, he decided to head west, then south.

Hearing shouts in the distance, he glanced toward the stockade. It was another diversion meant to draw the guards' attention back to the camp—his men had timed it well. None of the guards was looking his way. They all stood tall in their pigeon roosts, gazing warily at the new disruption hatched by the Fifth Michigan. Nathan made his way around the camp to where the stream, the horrid Sweet Water, entered the stockade.

Having deposited the sergeant's body in the same moat where he had stuffed his prison rags, Nathan now wore a faded gray uniform with three stripes. A young militiaman called to him, but he disregarded the hail. He had the privilege of rank and in the dark his self-assured movements seemed to attract no attention—the sergeant must have been a taciturn man who answered people when he damn well felt like it.

Nathan studied the compound from a new perspective. Even in near darkness it appeared a writhing mass of humanity was variably illuminated by sparse campfires. There was a ruckus that sounded like a fight between two groups of prisoners—not highly unusual, but this was probably a fake brawl fomented by his men as a distraction. This perspective from outside was so unusual to him that he was disoriented and couldn't quite tell where Michigan's shebangs were located. The stockade brought to mind a cheese box piled full of night crawlers, like the ones he and his childhood friends used to catch to sell to fishermen.

Beyond the confines of the stockade, no one paid him much attention. He hadn't seen anyone who was clearly of higher rank, and so acknowledged no hails made to him. He located a dark patch of weeds about fifteen or twenty yards past where the stream passed under the fence. This would be perfect. Taking a Fifth Michigan regimental patch from his pocket, he stuck it over the top of a square nail that protruded from a broken board he found in the brush. Then he added the red kerchief that had made the Reb sergeant such a hated figure to the prisoners. He tossed it into the water nonchalantly, like someone getting rid of a piece of junk. He didn't look at it until he was heading back. He knew that inside the camp, any piece of scrapwood was valuable as firewood, so it wouldn't be ignored.

Still acting as if he were vaguely interested in the disruption in the camp, now quieting, he watched the board float under the stockade fence. Almost immediately it caught the attention of a young prisoner. The fellow snatched it out of the water and peered upstream toward the Reb encampment. No activity there. He carried it to show to an older man, maybe his sergeant. Then, Nathan had the satisfaction of seeing the two making their way toward the corner of the camp staked out by Parker's Rangers. His men would be buoyed for many days knowing that Bender had been avenged.

And now Nathan knew something about himself that his men didn't. As sick as he felt, and as empty and unfeeling as he had been over killing the sergeant moments before, he struggled now to suppress a sense of triumph. He fought down the guilt he would feel from the disapproval of his Quaker mother and equally nonviolent, if nonreligious, father. In a funny way he knew his uncompromising intensity came from them. They would never approve of his reluctant propensity for violence, but they were in their own way as resolute as he was.

Nathan made his way back across a poorly lit area with a few off-duty guards huddled around their own little fires and tired worlds, more dozing than talking. He grabbed one of six rifled muskets that were set on their butts leaning against one another in a circle. He had no way of knowing which one belonged to the sergeant, so if the real owner had been watching that would be the end of him. He held his breath until he disappeared in the thickets along the stream, making himself walk slowly, a man in no rush to get anywhere. Now he had a working rifled musket with one shot available and the sarge's pistol, which contained four. He hadn't found any extra ammunition on the sergeant, but wasn't about to push his luck looking for more.

Nathan struck east in the moonlight. He stopped at the ditch to retrieve a couple scraps of his prison garb and after a mile he entered a streambed and tossed the scraps back onshore—something to keep the dogs happy. He then followed the stream back toward the prison and took off again at a brisk pace to the west.

Although Nathan found it served him well in war to do the unexpected, it was difficult to turn away from Atlanta and Sherman's Federal troops and head in the opposite direction. The attraction of being among friendly forces and well fed was almost overpowering. But reason prevailed; he would move quickly at night toward the Mississippi. If his geography was correct, he had some three or four hundred miles to Vicksburg. And if he could get there alive, the river was in Union hands . . . all the way back north. It was the long way to Washington, but he was convinced it would also be the safest. If he couldn't get permission to form an official rescue party for his men through telegraph communication, Washington City was the next place he intended to go.

CHAPTER 6

23–28 October 1864
Alabama

N athan curled up under his lean-to in a small wooded hollow. The smell of smoke from his small fire probably carried as much as a mile downwind, but he had come through that area and it seemed uninhabited. Besides, hot coals were critical to his survival. He had warily approached a small farmhouse four days earlier, the morning after he had escaped. It had proved a horn of plenty to him and the taking was easy. After spending an hour creeping up on a well-constructed and well-kept cabin, watching for any sign of life, he finally decided to walk up to the door and knock. There was nobody home. He filled a meal sack with sweet potatoes and squash and green beans from baskets in the summer kitchen, then lingered to check in the bedroom for another essential item—paper. Before fleeing back to the woods, he snatched a small sack of musket balls and took two sheets of clean paper stock, a quill, ink, and a small vial of sealing wax.

Under his lean-to, Nathan stretched, rolled over, and began

chewing down another helping of beans and tomatoes. He shot several rabbits and spent the better part of a week resting, eating legumes and fresh rabbit meat lightly cooked. Everything he had heard from Doc Holmes about scurvy seemed true, his strength was quickly returning and the early signs of the disease, such as the sores in his mouth, were almost healed. It was incredible how fast the body recovered with the right intake of decent food.

The hollow was ideal; secluded and well wooded, he could even find respite from marauding mosquitoes by distributing the coals in a U-shape about his head where he slept. The smudge of smoke kept them to a low hum with only occasional bites. As fast as he was recovering, he would have the strength to move west in two or three days. Nathan pulled out the quill, ink, and paper, and began practicing on one sheet, keeping the other for the real thing.

The bearer of this document is Sgt. Raymond Forbes of the Fifteenth Georgia Volunteers. All officers, staff, and enlisted personnel of the Confederate States of America and its loyal State Militias are hereby directed to ensure he and the men accompanying him are provided every courtesy and assistance in carrying this dispatch to Col. Nathan Bedford Forrest. He is not to be questioned about the nature of his verbal dispatch or anything else pertaining to this mission.

General Walden
Forwarded as directed and by authority of
General Lee, Army of Northern Virginia

It wouldn't work if he was captured by regulars; they'd know it was a fake and after they hanged him as a spy they'd probably pin it to his body swinging from the nearest tree. Nathan wasn't even sure there was a Fifteenth Georgia, but he definitely had Georgia markings on his stolen uniform. There'd be no problem with the details of the uniform itself as most Reb battle dress at this point in the war was hodgepodged together. He hoped the official-looking seal he was casting on the paper with the wax he'd found would fool most of the area militia, few of whom would be able to read.

Also, he would again do the unexpected. Nathan determined that rather than avoid the bands of reservists scouring the countryside for deserters and runaway slaves, he'd seek them out and demand assistance.

As he was stowing away his newly composed letter and making ready to suck the juice out of another tomato, he heard a rustle in the woods behind him that presaged the approach of either a large animal or a man. Nathan grabbed the musket and laid it across his knees. There was another shuffling of dry autumn leaves and the sound of a small twig snapping. He had selected his perch for its commanding view of a small game trail or rarely used footpath several yards below. A man stepped into view perhaps ten yards distant; he had a round, flat-brimmed hat, a musket cradled in his arms, and two pistols slung in a leather cross-brace under his arms. He wore no uniform, but his clothing seemed in better condition than most men Nathan had seen in the field or prison, including the Alabama regulars who served as guards early on. This was all particularly noteworthy since the man was black.

Nathan clicked back the hammer on the Springfield, a sound that carried import as eloquent as anything he might have offered verbally. When the man froze and glanced up at him, Nathan spoke, remembering at the last second to switch to his faux Southern drawl.

"Mornin', Nightshade. Can I hep ye?"

The man replied, "Hold on there, I'm going about my business, looking for escaped slaves."

"That right, now? Looks like you a funny one to search out runaway niggers, being a blue gum yerself an all. Didn't know massa let ye run around with guns 'thout no one watching over ye."

The black man didn't appear frightened. He even sounded somewhat indignant and clipped in his response. "You're the one who ain't from these parts. I'm no damn slave, but a freeman, and you're on my land, so why don't you lower that rifle?"

"Why don't I pop a hole in yer face and leave here with two rifles and a couple of fine-looking pistols?" Nathan disliked playing this role, but he needed to seem smug, ignorant, and hostile to ensure that no one engaged him in conversation past what he needed for his own purposes. He was afraid of making enough mistakes in his speech inflections to create suspicion. This fellow was not behaving the way Nathan expected a Southern Negro to act in the presence of a gun-bearing white man, and that unnerved him. There was a sneer in the tone of the man's next response.

"Because you'd not get very far. Folks around here know Joe Toby and even they will be out for your fool ass if you shoot me . . . I treat them well. They aren't far off neither, they're helping me look for lost niggas and yaller-belly deserters."

"That so, Joe? Well, I guess I believe ye, but you better leave yore hands away from all that hardware hangin' from yer shoulders while we get acquainted." Nathan lowered his weapon and gestured for the man to walk over and sit by the coals. As he placed the rifle on the ground with his left hand, he nonchalantly slipped his right under his tunic and grasped the hilt of his concealed pistol. But his guest sat down with no false moves and stared at him.

"There's some coffee in that sack, hot water in the kettle. And no, Ah ain't no damn deserter if that's what you were hintin' at, Nightshade." The man's expression didn't change and he didn't reach for the coffee. Nathan continued, "Yer a bit uppity for my taste, but maybe that's the way they do in this part of Georgia."

"You aren't in Georgia anymore, this here is Alabama soil and in particular, it's my land." Glancing down at the coffee sack, he continued, "And that happens to be my coffee and kettle too."

"No kiddin'? So that was your house I commandeered for the cause? Much obliged."

"Now look, mister, I got some escaped niggers moving fast and I need to get after them . . . you, you haven't seen any?"

"Nah, none but what I'm lookin' at right now. But how 'bout tellin' me where I can find some militia afore you go off on your important affairs of business."

"They'll find you once you cross the crick yonder, if that's where yer heading."

"Yeah, it's where I'm headin' right enough. I'm looking for Colonel Forrest's encampment, have a dispatch for him." Nathan almost made the mistake of pulling it from his rucksack, but remembered in time that, judging from what he had taken from his house, this Negro could not only read but would recognize as his own the sealing wax and writing implements.

"Well, I'll let 'em know if I run across them. Now, if you don't mind, I'll be off."

Disconcerted, Nathan was unsure of what he should do. He decided to take his chances and let him go. "Okay, you go on yer way, don't blame ye for wantin' to catch them shiftless niggas' 'fore they get too far. No, sir, we wouldn't let that happen in Georgia. . . . So this is Alabama, that explains it, I guess, with all you freedmen running around."

But he had gotten a tiny rise out of Mr. Joe Toby, as he called himself. The man rose, snatched up his rifle, and was about to stalk off in the direction he had been heading without a by-your-leave, but turned to Nathan and blurted out, "I said I was a 'freeman' not a goddamn freedman . . . never had no slave collar on me, ya understand?"

No, Nathan didn't have the first notion what he was talking about, but the riled fellow continued on in the same tone.

"I been living in 'Bama all my life and leastwise I ain't tradin' with the Yankees."

"Trading with the Yankees?"

"Yeah, you know what I mean." The man shut himself up. "Well, I'm on my way."

As a matter of fact, Nathan didn't know what he meant by any of it. He watched him disappear in the forest and listened to his footsteps recede in the distance. After he was sure he had gone out of range, Nathan gathered his treasures, covered his coals, and headed south, the opposite direction from which he had indicated he would go.

He found himself deeper in the forest with increasingly heavy undergrowth. After only three miles he headed west, trekked three more miles, and set up camp again on the edge of thick woods overlooking a rough trail or carriage road that paralleled the stream where the freeman had told him the guard "would find him." He decided not to build a fire, but burrowed in again for a couple more days of rest and eating. He was tired, but glad to note that he was stronger than when he had escaped. Also, the bone-deep soreness he carried from the several minutes' exertion it had taken to kill the sergeant had started to fade. His anger and determination had carried him through it, but he was aching in every muscle he had employed in that struggle.

Nathan forced himself to remain almost immobile for two more days. He ate even when he wasn't hungry, drank from the clear running creek even when he wasn't thirsty, and rested even when he had enough energy that he felt slightly restless on the fifth day. The more he thought about it, the more he worried why he hadn't fooled the freeman during his chance encounter. Glancing down at his wrists, part of the answer occurred to him. He wrapped one hand around the other and could make his forefinger touch his thumb, something he could not do before the war.

He walked to the stream again, and in a place where the light struck still water with little glare he stared at his reflection. It had been ten days since his escape and though he had been one of the more fortunate at Andersonville in terms of nourishment and was quickly recovering, he still had enough of the gaunt prison look that he contrasted with the rest of humanity. The only thing in his favor was that many regular army troops of the Confederacy were undernourished themselves. Nathan put his ruminations aside when he heard a horse coming from the north on the old road.

He left the stream and regained his high ground seconds before a horse came into view at a slow run. A scout came by, followed by another, then a moment later, two more riding stirrup to stirrup. It was an advance contingent of cavalry moving to cover ground, but not especially wary, as if expecting no trouble. They were Confederates on home ground, but Nathan couldn't see their battle pennants to determine anything more.

An officer appeared, leading a squad of seven or eight, followed a minute later by the commanding officer of the detachment, a captain, in the fore of a long line of mounted troops moving briskly. Nathan hunkered down and counted as best he could. By the time they had passed, he had estimated one hundred and fifty men. Then a pause, more scouts, wagons pulled by dual teams, followed by forty more mounted men. They were followed by wranglers in the lead of a dozen unsaddled mounts and a rear guard of twenty well-armed riders.

Nathan fell back into the role of officer. Instinctively he memorized salient facts in the event that he could pass along the intelligence. He remembered numbers, but he also knew that any Federal officer would be interested in the quality, not just the quantity, of the troops in the detachment. They were fast-moving cavalry not tied to an infantry command, unburdened with wounded, and they seemed very fit. Whatever the rumors he had been hearing at

Andersonville about the South caving in, it wasn't happening here. Within an hour he heard horses again and another mounted force came from the same direction, roughly similar in size and composition to the first. This time he could see their colors better and surmised they were Mississippi light cavalry units.

Nathan reflected again on his own use of horses and Parker's Rangers being dubbed "mounted infantry," which sounded to him somewhat like a "silent drum corps." He knew nothing of the military before being made a lieutenant in the Michigan command. But he had apparently reinvented an old concept of fast-striking infantry that the U.S. Army had experimented with in the past—they were called Voltigeurs. His epiphany after Antietam about never letting his men just trade volleys until one side had more losses had become personal dogma. Long periods of trading blows were acceptable to him in a fistfight but not in armies where each "blow" killed a man.

As far as his superiors were concerned, he was an aggressive officer, even promoted from lieutenant to captain. His group attained some minor notoriety, but to Nathan, the real attraction was speed. His men were hard to hit and there simply wasn't enough time to wreak havoc before the encounter was over. He lost six of the seventy men in his company while killing or wounding twenty-three Confederates in a raid on a hill near Chickamauga. His men dismounted, became infantry again, and held the hill they had won.

Nathan's men caught on to both his tactics and his philosophy. They were game for a fight, but had already seen their share. Now they had a captain who kept them in the heat of the fray, but with fewer casualties.

True, he thought, this tactic had landed them at Andersonville, which was much worse than he figured. But you had to be alive to suffer. Nathan dug deep into his sack of stolen vegetables for the prize he had been saving: a not-too-old head of cabbage. The sack was much lighter now, probably only able to sustain one more of his six-meal days. As he mulled the import of all the troop movement and built a fire, the overwhelming tiredness that he often experienced since prison crept up on him. He dozed off with the soft subtle smell of boiled cabbage in his nostrils and another satisfying meal in his stomach.

CHAPTER 7

29 October 1864
Western Alabama–Mississippi

Nathan slept well and awoke late. Before he could stuff himself with breakfast he again heard horses, this time moving at a more leisurely pace than the cavalry units he had observed the night before. When they hove into his view, it was again clear they were Rebs, but probably not regulars. As they drew nearer he saw they were a mix of young men, boys really, and old men not fit for combat. Unfortunately, he had learned at Andersonville that many of these groups weren't fit to breathe God's air. Many were the town dregs suddenly empowered with some authority. It seemed to him these home guards were one of the war's cleverest jokes on human decency—they ensured that the insanity spread to all parts of the nation, even where there were no battles.

Nathan took a deep breath and stepped out in front of the advancing riders.

"Hey, there."

The startled lead rider pulled back on his reins and the others almost piled on top of him. One of the young riders pulled a pistol from a saddle harness and pointed it. Nathan, musket nestled in his crossed arms, ignored him and directed his remarks to the leader.

"Are you the officer in charge?"

"Who's askin'?"

"Sergeant Forbes, Fifteenth Georgia. I'm here on business critical to the war effort and need assistance," he said with a brusque air of authority.

"That so? Well, mister, 'round hereabouts it takes more than a feller walking up and saying he's somebody to make it so." But the man's tone had lightened and he seemed inclined to be a bit more respectful of someone who might be a regular sergeant in the Confederate States Army.

Nathan handed over the letter briskly and stared unblinking at the leader, who took the document and gazed at the red seal, perplexed. He heard one of the others refer to this jowly heavyset bumpkin in charge as Jonah.

"You read?"

"A courst I read, I just don't have my eyepiece."

Nathan, acting irritated, grabbed the letter back. "It says give all possible help to me by special order of General Lee."

Jonah was still trying to digest it all, his eyes wide at the mention of the revered general. He seemed to be working his jaw side to side under all that flesh as he concentrated. Lee didn't technically have control over soldiers outside of the Army of Virginia, but his name carried weight even where his commission did not.

"Heed me well," Nathan continued, "I've lost two fellow couriers on this run. One succumbed to the fire of a runaway slave which, if you were doing your job, wouldn't have happened. I need to get to Colonel Nathan Bedford Forrest in three days' time."

"Three days? Hell, that's a long ways. And looka here, Sergeant, there ain't no niggers shootin' anybody in my sector." Nathan was relieved to see he had the man on the defensive as the fellow continued. "We just hunted some down with ole Toby. Reckon he knew how to make a example of 'em."

"Yeah, reckon he knows what works, he's one hisself," remarked one of the youngsters. It occurred to Nathan that it was no mystery to him who Toby was.

"Sho' 'nuff," continued the leader. "He nutted one of 'em an' the others got real cooperative all a sudden, didn't they, boys?" He looked around at the others, who shot back grins, but clearly it was Nathan he was trying to impress. The thought of what had happened to the runaways made Nathan sick. The freeman had apparently castrated one as an example and he, Nathan, had made it possible by letting him walk away from his campsite the other night.

"Yeah, ole Toby coming this way in a bit, he's going by Atchafalaya to go home. He borrowed two of our packhosses to ride fo' of his niggas . . . though I reckon that one of 'em is ridin' pretty light in the saddle." Nathan froze. It would be the end of him if the freeman caught up. Joe Toby knew damn well where that seal and paper had come from and he was a lot smarter than anyone in this bunch.

"I need a mount," Nathan announced. He pointed at the youngest rider, a mean-looking kid of no more than fourteen. "Yours will do."

"Wha—?" The boy's jaw dropped.

Jonah, now utterly perplexed, attempted to maintain his authority. "Well, now, Jethro, I guess you can take the pack mule home."

Nathan turned and stalked off, barking behind him a last order, "I'll be ready to break camp in a few minutes and I need at least two to escort me . . . by the way, did y'all see any Mississippi boys headin' south? I tole them to be down Preston way by tomorrow."

"Well, yeah, as a matter of fact they was a couple companies of Mississippi and Tennessee regulars through this way yesterday . . . that was on count of your orders?"

"Not mine. I don't give orders, I carry them, but you better believe they come from men that are used to being listened to." He let that sink in for a second, then, noting the respectful looks, he remarked stiffly, "Be ready to head out in five minutes." Nathan wanted out of there as soon as possible. That a Georgia sergeant of militia should be carrying a communication from General Lee was damned unlikely. That it would be "orders" was preposterous. He was concerned that if Joe Toby caught up to these yokels, he might figure out what was up and Jonah would lead the others after him.

As he headed west with his escort, the sound of the horses' hooves created a rhythm that was putting Nathan to sleep in the saddle. They were moving swiftly, but now that he had others to pace himself by, he realized he still didn't have as much strength back as he had hoped. Luckily, the two men accompanying him were familiar with the country and seemed impressed enough with the importance of the mission that they did their best to lead him by trails known only to locals, as he had demanded. They met few people on the road and when they did, they rushed past them without conversing.

Within an hour they came to a stretch where their trail crossed well-traveled roads, and Nathan's escorts started leading him north. "Whoa, what're we doing?"

"We gotta head north a bit to pick up the Bledsoe Trail. Just a three- or four-mile jog, or so. From there it's a straight shot southwest to Vicksburg."

Nathan nodded and roused himself as best he could. They would most likely be stopped by Rebs even though a few Union patrols did make it this far east from the Mississippi to test the resistance. They hadn't gone a half mile before a small detachment of cavalry passed heading south—his cover must be working well, because they didn't even slow down, let alone ask questions.

About five miles into their "three- or four-mile jog" they ran into two buckboards that resembled supply wagons, but with two armed men on the driver's seat and four escorting each carriage one on each corner. Nathan figured they must be pretty dear supplies as these men looked serious and capable. Three of the four guards moved up to the head of the lead wagon as it stopped. The fourth man deliberately swept both sides, making sure there wasn't anyone lying in wait in the woods. A quick look seemed to convince the rider that this was a poor location for an ambush. He returned to the wagon but stayed behind the others.

Bowman and Rodie, Nathan's escorts, looked at the large wagons closely and Nathan studied the men's uniforms . . . or lack of them. Their clothes were a hodgepodge of gray and brown, as were many others at this point in the war. But that was poverty, not choice, with most men—these fellas all wore shoes, hell, they were actual boots—and not of poor quality. And they were well armed. Now that he was right up on the wagon he could see that the canvas covered bales of cotton. Cotton?

Nathan could be curious later. Right now he wanted distance. He nodded to the group and attempted to pass on as if he and his escorts had pressing business up the road. They were all quiet except for one fellow on the wagon who asked in a clipped Louisiana drawl what they were about. Before Nathan could reply, Bowman answered that they were heading south near Vicksburg, as that's where Forrest was holding up.

Nathan felt the scrutiny intensify.

The man on the wagon glanced at the man who had done the circuit on horseback, seeking bushwhackers. He pulled up front this time.

"You wouldn't be talking about General Forrest?"

Nathan hadn't known that he was now a general, and decided

that playing games wasn't his forte. "Doesn't mean a coot's left nut who we're going to see. We're off to see them under orders from the Army of Northern Virginia and—"

The fellow on the buckboard grabbed for his carbine, but before he could clear the seat he heard the ominous click of a .44 pistol that Nathan was holding in his face. He had produced it from under his tunic with a smooth wave of his hand.

Most of the others were well disciplined. Only two began to draw their own weapons until the fellow on horseback interceded. "Hold it there, fellas, let's not get excited."

Nathan found unnerving the way the others barely paid attention—they returned to scanning the bushes for anyone creeping up on them. The man with the shoulder arm froze in place until the mounted man commented, "Amos, that's okay, put that blunderbuss away. This man's doings are his own business."

"Yeah, Amos, my own business. Now you ease the striker down and kick that thing aside. . . . with one foot, afore you're a distant memory that's bleedin' a lot."

Nathan turned his pistol toward the new speaker's face. "Appreciate your letting me know who's in charge. You're the one going down first, so careful what you say." Nathan only remembered to tag his accent on the last half of his statement.

"Right, right, I imagine so. But you're willing to be shot dead by one of my men as soon as I hit the ground?"

"Why not? None of us lives forever. Been only a matter of dumb luck since Antietam."

The man had both of his hands cupped over the pommel of his saddle and seemed to size Nathan up most intently. "Antietam? Well, you *have* seen the elephant, haven't you."

"Seen enough. You going to let us on our way or not? My hand's getting tired holding this damn thing up, so I'm 'bout ready to pull the trigger and see how many of your men I can kill before the shootin' stops."

The rider never blinked. "Not too many, I reckon. Be a shame, anyway you look at it. Taking the Bledsoe?"

"Right enough," Nathan replied.

"Watch for Billy Yanks, there's patrols getting far east as the Bledsoe."

"Yeah, we know." Bowman likely felt he had to say something, but it was clear that he and Rodie were perplexed by this entire exchange.

Nathan was considering his next step when Bowman and the others looked back up the road to the north. The sound of hoof-beats indicated another contingent of cavalry was coming, about twenty men with Mississippi colors.

The fellow who had taken over as leader for the wagon escorts turned to Nathan and muttered under his breath, "Put that damn thing away and let me handle this."

Feeling as vulnerable as he ever had in his life, Nathan returned his pistol to his holster before the men pulled abreast of them.

The riders slowed to a halt at the wagon and the lieutenant, a hardened-looking fellow, took them all in. After glancing at the wagons and nodding to the fellow who was now in charge of the escorts, he stopped on Nathan. He ignored Bowman even though the young man began talking.

"Now, Lieutenant . . . ," said Bowman.

But the officer kept his gaze on Nathan and Bowman's voice trailed off. "Where you going, mister, got papers?"

He could feel the fear stirring him down to his toes. With an annoyed expression, he pulled the letter from the inside pocket of his jacket and started to hand it to the lieutenant. But his new friend, in whose face he had been pointing a pistol a moment before, took the letter from Nathan's hand.

"Believe I can hep here, Lieutenant. This fella is heading up to the Bledsoe Trace and I've been meaning to see what papers he's got, too."

"Go on, Marcel. Takes me a while to get my spectacles warmed up."

So, the lieutenant knew him, thought Nathan. The man's greeting didn't exactly sound warm, but then he didn't seem a particularly warm fellow. Also, he trusted this Marcel to translate the papers accurately—these days, middle-aged men in the South usually made do with broken or scratched glasses, so reading was a chore. Nathan understood his impatience with the war and life in general. But that meant the lieutenant might kill him without rancor and forget about it five miles down the road. Nathan saw himself in the lieutenant and recognized him too well.

Marcel took the letter and skimmed it. He stared at Nathan, but through eyes that had a curious glint—something between excitement and amusement lurked under the stolid demeanor. "Carrying verbal dispatch to our brethren. He's under direct command of the Army of Northern Virginia with Georgia's blessing. Yep, signed by General Scott."

General Scott? I never said that . . . Walden's head of . . . sweet Jesus, maybe not anymore. Nathan felt himself break into a sweat. He grasped the handle of his pistol under his tunic, considering how far he could get with a company of cavalry on his tail.

But Marcel handed the papers back to Nathan and the lieutenant seemed to lose interest. "Yeah, I suspect he's on his way for the good of the cause, Lieutenant."

With a wave of his hand, the lieutenant simultaneously bade adieu to Marcel and signaled his men forward. Nathan's head spun. It seemed he was done for one minute and all was fine the next. He couldn't help glancing at his strange savior who circled around to the back of the wagon and told his men to get on their way. Bowman and Rodie, confused and a little unnerved, also started to head off.

As Bowman and his other consort forged ahead, both Nathan and the stranger were momentarily left at the rear of their riders.

Marcel stopped and looked at him. Nathan, unsure if his weariness was overcoming him or if he was made dizzy by circumstance, kept watching the fellow. He seemed scarred by battle and something was amiss with his left eye.

"Marcel Lafarge is my name." His hands had returned to his saddle pommel and when he removed them this time he revealed a small but lethal-looking derringer.

Nathan sighed and asked, "You had that there the whole time?"

"Be foolish to talk to a stranger with a gun in his hand while unarmed, would it not?"

Nathan nodded. "Reckon so."

Lafarge removed his hat and fussed with the rim a second before remarking, "Walden's been dead for several months and Forrest, well, it's a good thing you didn't push that too far with any but the oafs you're traveling with. He hasn't been in these parts for a while . . . and Antietam, damn, folks from around here mighta seen that elephant all right but they call it the battle of Sharpsburg." Marcel absently punched inside the crown of his hat, and smoothed out its top. "Yep, gotta respect people's sensibilities."

Nathan could think of nothing to say. He looked at his reins and turned to follow Bowman, who had stopped a ways ahead and looked back expectantly. Lafarge's voice trailed after him, "One other thing."

Nathan stopped.

A bemused expression on his face, the man asked, "Cahaba?"

Nathan briskly turned his mount to catch up with Bowman and Rodie, then stopped and looked back at Lafarge, who had not moved. "Andersonville," he said in a low voice, then rode off slowly. When he glanced back, the man waved his hat at Nathan and rode after his wagon.

★

THEY QUICKLY FOUND the Bledsoe Trail and resumed heading west. Although it seemed similar to the main road for the first few miles, it soon degraded into a secondary trail. Nathan decided he must put the incident aside and concentrate on where they were headed. Eventually he brought the others to a halt and studied the crude map that Jonah had drawn for him on the last sheet of stolen stationery. They were near enough to the outskirts of Vicksburg that his escort was increasingly worried about encountering U.S. Army patrols. The Federals had controlled most of the Mississippi since the fall of New Orleans early in the war and now, since Vicksburg had fallen in a bloody battle of attrition, the whole river corridor was under a Union flag.

To assuage the young men with him he had to remind them of the supposed special nature of their mission and all the sensitive aspects he couldn't share. He prayed that their credulity was as complete as suggested by their blank eyes and mouth-breathing demeanor. He had to admit they were good horsemen, however, and they knew the back trails. Progress had been quick, but he was beginning to share their concern over being discovered. Of course, his reason was different; he was afraid what might happen before he had a chance to explain what he was doing in a Confederate uniform. The North had its own fair share of chisel-heads who would shoot at the first sign of grayback garb.

They rode on for two more days and the next morning, when an opportunity finally came, it was quicker and more simple than he could have hoped for. Rodie, a thin-faced boy who ended most sentences with a breathy laugh, came back toward Nathan and Bowman after a brief scouting sojourn, and he was leading his horse rather than riding. His pistol was drawn and he glanced nervously behind him. He summed up what he had seen with one word: "Bluebellies." At Nathan's behest he led them back where they could observe a meadow with a well-worn horse trail running through it. Within seconds a cavalry patrol appeared, two riding slowly about thirty yards on point, followed by a dozen others. They were alert but didn't seem concerned—it was obvious they were on ground they thought they controlled.

Nathan decided he must act. He pulled an ancient flintlock from his youngest escort's saddle, then drew his own pistol and pointed it at Rodie's startled face. "Rodie, I'm going to ask you once, drop that shooter."

The young man was wide-eyed but Nathan wasn't sure if it was because of the gun in his hand or the fact it was the first time the boy heard him speak without his contrived Southern accent.

"Damn, you's a bluebelly yo'sef."

Nathan pulled back the hammer on his pistol. "Last chance, boy." He was relieved when the young man dropped the weapon. The patrol was far enough away that they likely couldn't overhear the drama playing out in the thicket.

"You's a goddamn Billy Yank."

Nathan reached toward Bowman's saddle and pulled his musket out of its deerskin sheath. He drove his palm hard against the cocks of both boys' old long guns until the striker came off one and bent on the other.

"I'm giving you back your muskets. Get 'em fixed and use them to hunt this winter, but if you're anywhere I can see you in ten seconds, I'll kill both of you. So think fast and decide."

The two young men glanced at each other, back to Nathan, and then down at the Federal patrol that had almost cleared the meadow. Without a word, they galloped away. As soon as Nathan was certain they were truly moving on, he tore his gray shirt off and laid it over his saddle. He tossed away his own rifle and loudly hailed the man bringing up the rear of the patrol. Then he rode out into the clearing bare-chested and empty-handed.

CHAPTER 8

1–2 November 1864
Vicksburg and Environs

T here was a considerable stir amongst the Federals when Nathan rode out in front of them. Four approached cautiously with their weapons drawn. He was impressed again to see they paid more attention to the woods behind him than to Nathan. They were seasoned troops and well led. He was obviously not a great threat, but he could be coaxing them into a potential ambush. Still, there was something disheartening about a young country with so many experienced soldiers. An officer called out to him to advance toward them with one hand on the reins and the other on his head. Nathan could hear several horses moving through the woods on either side of him where the officer had sent scouts to ensure they weren't being suckered into a trap.

"It's clear back here, Lieutenant," came a yell from the trees.

As he approached, the officer with a young face, maybe a Tennessee accent, took him in carefully. Nathan noted he had eyes that seemed older and perhaps sadder than the rest of his countenance.

"I may not look it, Lieutenant, but I'm Captain Nathan Parker, Fifth Michigan, and, good God, man, I need to dismount and sit . . . I feel suddenly very . . ."

Nathan awoke what must have been minutes later. He was on the ground looking up at a dozen curious faces. The lieutenant had the dispatch from Nathan's saddlebag in his hand and the others were going through the rest of his belongings.

"I- I can explain that," Nathan protested.

The young lieutenant looked down at him and smiled. "Sir, I'm inclined to accept your explanation. I can't believe you got the Rebs to buy off on this silly thing. Nathan Bedford Forrest? He ain't within a hundred miles of here if he's alive at all."

Nathan didn't know why he was so weak all of a sudden, maybe the strain of the last few days of riding. He was handed a canteen as he remained sitting on the ground. After drinking deeply he felt better, but surges of emotion confused and embarrassed him. The lieutenant seemed to sense it and told his men to "Take fifteen" and rest the horses. He then sat beside Nathan, accompanied only by a burly sergeant with a New England accent as his men tended their mounts.

Nathan was mortified to feel hot streaks coming down his face. "Pardon me, Lieutenant, not sure what the problem is."

"Take your time, Captain. I don't think you need to say much to me, anyway. Colonel Prescott's people will want to talk to you in Vicksburg—I'm sure you've got a hell of a story."

The sergeant, a middle-aged man, had been absently drawing with a stick in the dirt beside him. He said, "Where you been, Captain?"

"Andersonville." Then Nathan placed his face in his hands and began sobbing uncontrollably. He could hear the horses stir, but there was complete silence from the men of the patrol. After a moment he began to calm down and became aware of a weight across his back. The old sergeant had his arm around him.

Moments later they were on their way. In less than a half hour they came to a plantation house. The environs had clearly been ravaged by war but the house seemed lived in and intact; some of the fields had even been tended. Nathan rode a packhorse and was in the company of the sergeant and two troopers. His strength had returned as it often did for short periods these days, but he had little to say. Appreciative of the care he received at the hands of the patrol, he tried desperately to find something solid in himself to hold on to. He didn't want to embarrass himself anymore, but even muttering from *Walden* under his breath didn't help when the feelings came. At the moment he couldn't imagine breaking down like that again; he also couldn't trust how he'd feel in a couple of hours.

Nathan noticed a woman standing on the porch of the plantation house, not unattractive, although her hair was styled in a severe bun.

"Evenin,' Mrs. Foster." The sergeant removed his hat and spoke to the lady from his saddle.

"What can I do for you?" The woman's voice matched her appearance, polite but standoffish.

"We've a man needs lodging for the night. This here is Captain Nathan Parker." He gestured with his palm toward Nathan. "We're moving east and he'll be picked up in the morning by a detachment from Vicksburg."

The lady seemed to appraise Nathan. He smiled and nodded his head in an informal bow but she gave no acknowledgment. She looked back toward the sergeant and muttered, "He's welcome to the barn and the well. Can't do anything about that, but I don't want him near the house." She glanced at Nathan before continuing to the sergeant, "Reckon he knows better than to come near. I still have two Negroes in my employ who are loyal to me and don't cotton to Yankees any more than I do."

"Yes'm, we understand that. Sorry there's no way to pay you for your trouble but we'll have to insist on the accommodation. . . . Thank you, ma'am."

As he led Nathan to the barn, the sergeant said under his breath, "Coulda been a lot harder on these folks if we wanted to, but they don't have much appreciation for our being here." He helped Nathan lay his saddle in the corner and added, "But then, she's had a hard time of it. Hasn't heard from her husband since Chancellorsville and her son was captured right here at Vicksburg, yeah, she's a cold one all right." He clapped Nathan on the shoulder. "But you can put up with the *warm* hospitality for a night, Captain, and some fellas be by to get ya midmorning or so."

Nathan grasped the sergeant's outstretched hand and shook it. "Thank you," he said, and still holding his hand, he added, "and I mean thank you for everything."

The big man saluted. "You'll be gettin' the rest you bad need soon, sir. You take care now." Nathan felt strangely alone when the man departed.

★

NATHAN AWOKE FROM a nap in near darkness. He felt better and began to arrange the hay and blankets the good lady's Negroes had given him into a comfortable nest for the night. Then he heard some rustling in the fall leaves outside the barn. Somebody or something was approaching and from the sound of it, they were either tentative or trying to be stealthy. Nathan had removed his clothes but restored his boots to his feet, better that way for fight or flight. He removed a wooden bar from its cradle where it served as a lock and hooked the working end of a hoe through the door handle. Raising his pistol with his right hand, he yanked open the big wooden door and pointed the .44 where he thought the intruder would be standing.

Mrs. Foster gave a startled "Oh" and froze in place, the back of her hand over her mouth. He almost didn't recognize her with her hair down. Nathan realized to his horror that he was standing in the last light of evening stark naked except for his footwear. He dropped his hands in front of him in modesty, took a step back, and began a profuse apology.

"Good Lord, pardon me, ma'am, I thought it might be a . . . well . . . somebody . . ."

But rather than stare horrified at him, the lady looked around as though more concerned that someone might be observing them from without. She then stepped through the door and, after a last glance to ensure no one was about, closed the door behind her and put the locking bar back in place. She stood for a moment, letting her eyes adjust to the darkness within. Her breathing seemed labored. Nathan was disconcerted—he continued standing where he was, waiting to see her intention—certain that he had never felt more foolish.

Mrs. Foster remained silent. Now that she could make him out in the dim light she stepped toward him and stopped right in front of him.

Nathan tried again to express his apology and embarrassment. "I'm really sorry, it's just that one can't be too careful. . . ."

"Shhh."

Nathan went silent as commanded and stood still. Both his hands, including the one holding the pistol, were hanging in front of him in a futile attempt to cover himself. He felt her place her hands on his face and begin to slowly caress his cheeks.

"I . . . I don't . . ."

"Hush, Mr. Parker, don't say another word or I will leave."

He felt the blood rise in his face and other places which hadn't seen blood for some time. He slowly reached one arm over to place his gun on a horizontal wooden beam. Her hands started moving over his chest, exploring the ridges of fresh and old scars. Nathan became dizzy and very bothered; his arousal would be more than obvious if she were to brush against him. A second later she did brush against him. He wasn't sure his suddenly weak legs would hold him.

She took his hand and guided it to her breasts. Mrs. Foster wore nothing beneath her night shift. Nathan began trembling. He felt himself grow hard and heavy down below as if a sack of hot lead hung between his legs; his need was suddenly becoming urgent to the point of desperation. She took his hand and pulled him to his hay pallet and lay beside him, her back to him. He wrapped his arms around her as she pushed her bare bottom to him and guided him in. Almost immediately he lost all control and began lunging into her . . . within seconds he gasped and was spent. He lay with his arms still around her.

His conclusion had brought more a sense of pain than pleasure. Rather than move away from him, Mrs. Foster repeated a gentle "Shhh" and kept her bottom glued to him while he regained his breath, his sex now soft but still in her. He couldn't think, confused images kept flitting through his head of home and prison, feelings of fear and joy and sadness as he drifted in and out of an exhausted sleep.

A half hour passed in silence as he recovered; she kept him in place, rubbing her palm up and down the hair on his arms with an occasional drawn-out, "Shhh." Then she slowly began pushing her bottom into his loins again. He quickly regained his hardness and began pushing into her. She showed no response except to hold firm against him. Within moments he had again spent himself. And again it was more like the passing of hot liquid into her, uncomfortable though accompanied by a great sense of release. He dozed off, then lurched awake, unsure how much time had passed, maybe an hour, maybe two. She had gone for a while and when she returned he felt himself surging; this time he knew he would have more control, but when he tried to speak she again placed a finger on his lips and said no in a firm but gentle voice.

She put herself beneath him this time. She had pulled a saddle to the floor and arranged blankets over it. "Now, Mr. Parker, do it like it will be your last chance ever." She lay over the blankets with her buttocks high and guided him into her again. Nathan felt himself totally lose control and all semblance of being a civilized man as he pounded into her furiously. Slowly she began responding and he could feel her back and legs stiffen and faint sounds coming from deep in her throat. When he could hold it not a second longer he exploded deep inside of her, but she kept moving wildly against what was left of him until she too reached a conclusion and turned to jelly beneath him.

After several minutes he withdrew from her and tried to coax her back to lie beside him. She would have none of it. She gathered her shift, knelt beside him, kissed him on the forehead, and squeezed his hand . . . then she was gone. He lay there, watching the light of dawn slipping through cracks in the barn slats, dust motes dancing like fairies in the rays. Had it really happened or was it a crazy dream? Turning his head to the side he could see where the saddle still lay with the blankets piled over the seat.

Among the fantasies that played out in his muddled head there was one of a woman with her back to him on a porch, swinging on a love seat. She was facing away, watching a child play in a grape arbor. He didn't have to see her face to tell she was beautiful and sad and eternally out of reach—he forced it out of his mind.

As the sun crept higher and the damp chill began to dissipate, Nathan crawled from beneath the blanket to gather his kit and meet the escort that would take him to see the colonel in Vicksburg town proper.

Earlier than expected he watched a carriage pull up to the front door of the house. It was his escort all right, and instead of bringing a horse for him they had sent a small open carriage. That gesture bothered him. He wasn't a civilian, he was a captain of a company of Federal soldiers, the leader of Parker's Rangers, after all. He grabbed up his things and headed for the house; the leader of the detail was speaking to Mrs. Foster. He heard a "Thank you, ma'am," and something about disbursement. The lady muttered, "Didn't do anything requiring thanks, please take your soldier and leave my property."

Mrs. Foster's hair was back up in the bun and she looked more lined in the face this morning. Nathan greeted the sergeant, who saluted and jumped into the buggy. Nathan looked up at Mrs. Foster and said in a voice only she could hear, "I certainly appreciate your kind attention. I guess we all have wounds from this war of one sort or another and . . ." His words trailed off.

"Mr. Parker, I have no idea what you're talking about. Good day to you and Godspeed." She had spoken without emotion and with a blank expression. She turned and walked back into her house. Nathan felt tired. He got into the carriage, remarked that such a conveyance wasn't necessary, and fell silent. If the carriage wheels hadn't hit so many pits in the road on the forty-five-minute trip he would have fallen asleep. As he rode he noted the increasing frequency of houses, many burnt or war-ravaged, others oddly intact with life at almost normal transpiring within. The driver announced that he was approaching the headquarters of the occupation forces and he should ready himself to meet Colonel Prescott. Nathan tried to straighten his motley appearance as best he could.

As the driver hitched the horses, Nathan glanced up to a splendid white home sitting on a well-tended grassy hillside. Except for one incongruous shell hole, the rest seemed untouched. A six-pounder had punched through the roof and made a round hole through the house into the pantry. In the distance he could see below the bluffs a shimmering ribbon of green and gray—it could be nothing else but the Mississippi River winding its way out of town. Several officers made their way down a flowered walkway toward him. One approached and held out his hand.

"I'm Lieutenant Nielson, Captain. Welcome to Vicksburg.

Please follow me, as Colonel Prescott is anxious to meet you." As Nathan began to walk up the steep path he felt the damned weakness starting to take him again but then he became lighter on his feet. It occurred to him that soldiers had come up to him on either side and were supporting his arms. He accepted the help but straightened himself as he proceeded. Be damned if he'd go slouching into the presence of a colonel. There they came, those damn womanly sniffles. He fought down the well of emotions and let himself be led to a chair on the veranda, where he was told he would soon be joined by Colonel Prescott. His mind flitted back to Camp Sumter. *By God, boys, it won't be long. Your captain will be coming for you, just hold on.*

CHAPTER 9

Marcel Lafarge
Vicksburg

M r. Lafarge, is it?"

Marcel nodded, noting that the clerk had pronounced his name with a decided emphasis on the "La," making it sound like the beginning of a nursery rhyme.

"It seems, sir, there's been some mistake. I don't find your name listed in our reservations."

Tired after a long trip hauling wagons of cotton and keeping in line a number of cantankerous men, Marcel dug into his inner coat pocket. "Perhaps it's not listed as you say, but because of the tardiness of my inquiry, would be noted on a separate page in your journal."

The clerk made a workmanlike job of leafing through several pages of his reservations book. Marcel thought he would help by sliding a greenback under the ledger.

"Ah, yes, here is your name, sir. Marvelous."

Marcel was used to this sort of trade; it seemed to have gotten worse in these relentless war years. He thought some of the petty enterprising souls from time to time needed a bit of straightening. "What, may I ask, do you go by, sir?"

Stuffing the greenback into his pants pocket, the clerk adopted a more serious demeanor. "The name is Otis, sir. Byrum Otis at your service."

Marcel never took his eyes from the officious man. He folded his arms and leaned against the counter. "A sad thing happened on my way into Vicksburg, Mr. Otis."

The clerk grew nervous as Marcel carried on.

"Yes, we were on the Bledsoe Trace and had just run into a band of thieves and cutthroats. Wouldn't you know, the bastards had just shot a dog, no reason really. Shot this stray female and left it kicking its life away on the side of the road. They didn't attempt to put her out of her thrashing malaise, just stood laughing at the sight." Marcel forced a smile, then pressed forward, invading the clerk's space, forcing the man to join him in his story.

In spite of himself, the clerk couldn't take his eyes from Marcel's scarred face.

"Otis."

He winced as the tall man spoke his name. "Yes, sir." He nodded.

"Righting wrongs should be all our duties these days. Wouldn't you agree? I've always loved animals, what about you, Otis, you like dogs?"

The clerk seemed confused and glanced around, hoping to find something to busy himself with. "Well, sir, I don't really have an opinion one way or another. My wife is taken with swelling around the eyes when in the proximity of cats and such and . . ."

Marcel enjoyed watching the man squirm. Something about the self-consciousness of humans fascinated him. Their "tells," as the poker players called it, were like openings into the very soul of their beings.

"Oh, by the way, Mr. Farge, call me Byrum, please."

Marcel noted the corruption of his name. "Otis, would you see that my bags are placed in my room immediately."

"Yes, sir, I'll have Pernell get on it right away."

"No, Mr. Otis, you do it."

"But sir, I . . ."

Marcel grinned and reached across to toy with the key chain on the clerk's vest. "It's a gloomy day, it appeals to me. I am going to take a walk." Marcel rubbed his drooping eye with a white ker-chief and looked around conspiratorially. "I had to do things on the Bledsoe I am not too proud of, but as my sainted mother used to say, 'Righteousness is like the mighty mountains, judgment like the great deep.'" He stopped to gaze into Otis's eyes. "When I re-turn, I expect my clothes to be hung in the closet, pressed, of course, my spare boots polished, and a spray of flowers to brighten the room . . . *comprenez-vous?*" Marcel dropped his pretense of a good fellow well met. Pointing his index finger at the clerk, he made a pistol-like click with his tongue and walked quickly out of the busy hotel lobby.

★

THE RUST-COLORED YAZOO River that had wound its way from the north, moved slowly in the afternoon rain, dumping reddish earth into the Mississippi at Vicksburg. Marcel recalled standing on the same bluff overlooking the muddy stream one year earlier. After fighting as company commander with Pemberton's Mississippi reg-ulars for nearly six weeks in 1863—bitter and struggling to hold the city—they finally surrendered to Grant's overwhelming forces in July.

He knelt on the colored earth, contemplating his past few days. The trip from Hattiesburg with the cotton and other items of ques-tionable legality had gone well, nothing of note having happened except the chance encounter with a certain Nathan Parker. An interesting sort, Marcel thought. Brave to a fault and maybe a bit foolhardy and desperate. The man's gauntness was certainly a testament to where he had spent the past few months. The notorious Andersonville. It disturbed Marcel that his beloved Confederacy had allowed itself to stoop so low as to degrade and vilify the Federalist prisoners at Camp Sumter. He felt his South should be better than that and that redemption was certainly a possibility.

He gazed out over the horizon, remembering the sharp smell of burnt gunpowder and fresh blood from the past year.

Relentless mortar rounds had whistled overhead close to this spot. The memory still seemed fresh. Marcel ran his fingers over the angry scar on his brow and cheekbone. When he massaged his left eyelid, its decided droop did not respond to his ministrations. His breathing became short when he thought of men who simply rose from these entrenchments and fled in those treacherous days. Not being able to withstand the constant shelling, they just wandered off, many times never speaking a word. He thought of other abandonments. His childhood was rife with disappointment. He attempted to fight off a vision of his older brother, Philippe, who at nineteen had vanished in the night with not so much as a fare-thee-well. His brother's selfish act had infuriated him.

Standing on the weed-bound cliff searching for answers, he knew with certainty there were none. He wondered if his deadly experiences during the war would always haunt him as they had this past year. The shame foisted upon him by Union forces once again seemed palpable and his eyes misted. Marcel's fellow soldiers' retreat from Bruinsburg, south of Vicksburg, became a bloody humiliation. The superior Yankee forces had swept through them at Port Gibson, and Brigadier General Bowen's rapid search for sanctuary around Vicksburg left the depleted Rebel troops vulnerable. Marcel swayed slightly as he recalled the pitiful rout through Hicks's farm. The woods to the north of the verdant fields seemed a likely safe haven, but when Marcel's platoon coutered up to streak across the open field, they were cut down by musketry. Wounded, he lay back, squinting at a red-tailed hawk circling in the clear morning air, thinking it would be nice to lie there, quit the dreaded war and grow corn and feed chickens. Realizing he was not being rational, he rolled to his knees and stumbled his way east, catching up with a headquarters company of Pemberton's army. When questioned about the disappearance of his troops, he was vague and disoriented, and prior to Pemberton's surrender to Grant he was court-martialed in a brief, degrading ceremony. In the confusion of his incarceration and the simultaneous surrender, he found himself not in a Confederate jail, but lying dazed in a warehouse on the outskirts of Vicksburg with several other disabled soldiers in leg irons.

In the days that followed, he fashioned a bandana across one eye and a sodden rag as a compress over his torn face. Taking advantage of the slovenly guards he finally managed to slip away in the night to make his way south. After redressing his seeping head wound and stripping a dead farmer of his clothing, he thought his war over. He headed for New Orleans and the safe haven of his friend, Mother Catherine Spencine.

Hardly a day passed in the previous twelve months when a vision of the war did not disrupt him. His moist hand found his weskit pocket and eased the lethal derringer out of its lined hiding place. He broke the small weapon open and examined the two rounds that lay in the stacked barrel. Ready if needed.

Marcel walked back to the hotel, his vigil at the bluff leaving him exhausted. He realized he was allowing this constant watch-keeping to control his life. He felt a terrible want, to rise up and revolt against—who? The North? It was most likely too late for that. The South was practically on its backside. Removing his hat, he turned his face into the cool downpour. For a moment the water eased his mind.

★

THE RAIN CONTINUED to beat against the glass. Still in his soaked clothing, Marcel sat in a stiff-backed chair, gazing out his hotel window. He could see people scurrying along—some with parasols, others holding coats or kerchiefs high over their heads; all going about the business of their lives. He felt truly alone.

The wet day reminded him of other bittersweet mists. A heavy spring rain falling in New Orleans as he approached the Ursuline Academy on Claiborne to see his friend, Mother Spencine. Two women leaving the illustrious school hurriedly made their way to an awaiting buggy. He remembered having sprung to their carriage door, gallantly sweeping off his hat, and with a slight bow proclaimed, *"Je suis perdu."*

The taller of the two gave him a dazzling smile. "Lost? You have found your way to a girl's school, monsieur. Surely it was what you were looking for."

Marcel heard their laughter as the carriage departed. He remembered standing bareheaded in the downpour, watching the receding vehicle. Later, after several inquiries, he was convinced he was in love, for Mirabelle Chevroux was not only quite beautiful, but educated in Paris and the budding star of New Orleans society. Marcel counted himself lucky to have met her; their courtship left the Crescent City's aristocracy abuzz. His fortune in the import business was nearly assured as he and Mirabelle delighted in each other's company with a fulfilling year of marriage. They soon expected a child, but in his wife's third month of pregnancy, she began to have painful sickness in the morning. She complained of awakening at night, fighting off bouts of melancholy and dizziness. She became distant and refused to eat.

The water on the glass before him drifted down in curved sheets, at once elongating the hurrying figures on the street below and then compacting them into dwarflike figures waddling along the drenched thoroughfare. Marcel fantasized, and as much as he tried to dispense with the vague watery figures, Mirabelle kept appearing below him, passing the shops, greeting others, either stretched in form or painfully squeezed into a rounded pregnant shape.

Coming home from the city to their sprawling estate one wet autumn day, Marcel had stopped his carriage at the boundary gate. As the heavy rain swept a soft mist across the vast cotton fields to the west, he could see a flash of red cloth melting against the white bushes of cotton. Mirabelle had wrapped herself in a heavy burgundy wool blanket, curling into a ball as she clutched her slightly swollen stomach—her life's blood flowing from her wrists.

He had seen his own share of life's blood over the past few years. Confederate soldiers screaming their young existence away in muddy hellholes. Blue-clad enemy soldiers trying to stumble their way back to the comfort of their own lines, innards hanging grotesquely from cupped hands. Yet part of him was pulled to the excitement, the terrible energy of battle, and the closeness of men in arms against a common enemy.

In the time since his war had ended, he had been very successful, having brokered cotton deals, illegal arms transactions, and a number of excursions to the North to purchase contraband to be sold at great profit in the South. The liberation of the Mississippi River had been a wondrous gift to men like Marcel. The South's need for all manner of goods played beautifully into the hands of the enterprising. Marcel made enormous profits, while smuggling bacon, dry goods, cloth, and hardware into the needy Southern consumer's hands. The excitement of meeting a Northern patrol while trafficking in illegal goods proved at times overwhelming. He would often times have several thousand dollars' worth of contraband hidden inside bales of hay or cotton, a simple innocuous businessman, he would insist, merely going about his work. Fulfilling, yes, but strangely he needed more—of what he wasn't sure.

A man of education and culture, he was at once appalled at his lack of tolerance for others and yet angered at his need for justice from the bullies and ne'er-do-wells of society. Calling himself independent from the law, he was much too smart to refer to himself as a vigilante.

The memory of standing in the rain, gazing across the field at the huddled form of his wife still haunted him. Although a brave man in battle and fearing no one, the loss of his wife and child left him wanting for courage. He felt a certain responsibility for Mirabelle's death and in his weaker moments wished to join her.

The illicit arms transfers, his cotton enterprises and such were just not enough to keep his restless soul alive. He needed something else. A challenge, a reason to continue.

CHAPTER 10

November 1864
Occupied Vicksburg—Union Army Headquarters

C olonel Prescott played with a stray lock of blond curly hair that extended over his shirt collar. His pale blue eyes took in Nathan, seeming to harden only when Nathan recounted events bearing on the inhumane treatment of Federal soldiers.

Nathan found it remarkable how the past months all spilled out of him. He was not in command here, and that was a great luxury. Usually he had to weigh every word for its potential effect on the spirits of his men. The officers sitting around him were at least his rank, except for a young lieutenant transcribing his account. There was heavyset Major Hardy; facially scarred Captain Clendennin, who commanded a company of colored troops; and another captain whose name he didn't catch. The latter wore a cavalry insignia on his shoulder. Dr. Donaldson had been silent during the session, having asked all of his questions during the medical examination he had performed earlier that morning.

They were all ensconced in the comfortable parlor of what had been a wealthy mansion high on the Vicksburg bluffs overlooking the Mississippi. The river seemed a flat gray in the midmorning light. Although he had heard steam whistles from what must have been the direction of the waterfront docks, he had yet to see a boat plying its way in either direction since his debriefing had begun.

Stopping for a moment to sip his coffee, Nathan smiled apologetically at Dr. Donaldson's frown. On entering the room after the others, the good doctor had placed a cup of water heavily laced with lemon juice on the table beside his coffee. It was clear which libation he judged a man in Nathan's condition should be drinking. Nathan liked him and deemed himself lucky to be in the hands of such seasoned officers. These were battle-hardened soldiers who weren't fixed on impressing somebody for a promotion. They interrupted rarely and only with questions that had real purpose.

"Those cavalry units heading south, you say were Mississippi regulars?" Major Hardy pulled at a scraggly beard as he posed the question.

"Best as I could tell, and maybe some Tennessee boys. But they weren't green; they were seasoned troops moving fast and weren't carrying any kit. No wounded and no slow wagons or heavy fieldpieces."

The major glanced over to the scribe, and the lieutenant, feeling his gaze, never looked up but nodded to assure his superior that he was getting it all down. Nathan reached for the coffee and switched at the last second for the juice in deference to the doctor. He also offered an explanation for his obstinance.

"Hard pill to swallow, Doctor, hate to have anything spoil the taste of coffee in the morning."

"Coffee for the brain but juice for the body, Captain. You might feel better now than you did in that hellhole but you're a long ways from fit," Donaldson gently scolded. "Scurvy is as deadly as any bullet, just slower."

Nathan nodded but didn't like hearing the comment about his weakness. He was afraid the colonel might get the wrong idea about his fitness to join an assault on the prison. Still, he was delighted with the availability of fresh meats and foods—in all the South, the Mississippi River towns were the few places these days you could still obtain such luxuries. He decided the colonel needed to be reminded of the importance of his being sent back to fight.

"So, Colonel, if you please, sir, I'd like permission to rejoin my men and work with whatever force is sent to Andersonville . . . with my inside knowledge of the place I could be of great assistance to any attack." Nathan looked around at the noncommittal, uncomfortable expressions on the men's faces. It bothered him that even though he was accorded every courtesy, even kindness, his allusions about being reassigned were greeted with little enthusiasm.

"Captain"—Colonel Prescott leaned forward in his chair and looked straight into Nathan's eyes—"I commend your resourcefulness and your courage. No man in this room doubts you have fulfilled your duty as an officer to your men and, I might add, you are among peers who can judge such qualities in another." He sat back in his chair and stared out the window as he continued, as if there were some source of inspiration out there that would help him choose the right words. It was clouding over now as a squall made its way toward them from upriver.

"We've been hearing accounts from others of the horrid conditions in that shameful hellhole. Andersonville is a blight on the nation's pride, Captain; in truth, Grant's intelligence service has probably kept us better informed of it than even our Confederate counterparts. Most Southern officers react as if we're telling tales to besmirch their honor when we confront them on the subject . . . and I'm inclined to think they're telling the truth. They just don't know."

"But—" Nathan started to protest but quieted when it became apparent the colonel wasn't finished.

"Captain, we are trying to end this damn war and committing a force sufficient to not only take the prison but deal with the casualties . . . well, you yourself should know better than anyone the drain it would be on our manpower to cope with thousands of men in your . . . in the condition of many of those prisoners."

"But, sir—" Nathan felt Captain Clendennin place a restraining hand on his shoulder from behind, a reminder to keep his peace until the colonel was finished.

The colonel pulled a piece of paper from his desk. "Captain Parker, I have here a telegram in response to my query about the Fifth Michigan. Your men were reassigned to regular Michigan and Ohio infantry units after your capture. Parker's Rangers no longer exist as a discrete force." The colonel gathered himself to finish his comments but Nathan knew already that any immediate accession to his request was in doubt.

"I am going to post the transcript of this debriefing and its valuable firsthand information back to Washington to the War Department, along with Doctor Donaldson's report. My recommendations for reassignment will go immediately via telegraph." At least he was going to be put back in the field. Nathan felt certain he could talk reason to his superiors to do right by the prisoners in Georgia.

The colonel rose to his feet, signaling the end of the meeting. "I encourage you to rest and eat well. Lieutenant Gore"—he glanced toward the officer transcribing the meeting—"will ensure you have billeting in town and quick access to telegraph transmittals from Washington . . . and, Captain."

"Sir?"

"Godspeed. Remember, you have done your duty already regardless of what happens next. Your men were well led."

Nathan felt confused and listless as he shook the hands of the departing officers, all of whom wished him well. But he noticed that none of them wished him success in what had to be his mission, his expeditious return to Georgia. A young corporal standing at attention met him at the bottom of the walkway. He stood by for him to enter the carriage that would take him to town, not the docks and a steamer departing north. A few drops on his face heralded rain, the squall was on them now.

Nathan studied the well-appointed buggy, which had probably been confiscated from some Vicksburg gentry. Then he returned the soldier's salute, sighed audibly, and climbed aboard. "Thank you, Corporal, but really, I would have preferred a horse."

"Sir?"

"I . . . nothing, Corporal. Carry on. I suppose that's what we must all do now, isn't it? Carry on."

CHAPTER 11

26 November 1864
Occupied Vicksburg

N athan kicked his way along Clay Street. The mud grabbed at his boots like it was trying to pull them off. For the first time in a long time he felt free and reasonably secure. Part of him wanted to run off and spend quiet years purging this ugly war from his gut. But he couldn't. As much as he might want to dream about breathing free, he knew this was a pause; a comma, not a period in his life. He felt the drive to free his men increase in step with his physical stamina. This was turning into an obsession.

The army put him up at Hattie's boardinghouse and left vouchers for payment of his room and meals. He found four dollars and sixty cents in Northern currency a day covered it—meals, bed, and access to the bath. It was also available in Southern currency but at a constantly changing rate in Confederate notes and shinplasters. He wore an officer's uniform that was given to him at the post but as of yet there were no captain's bars to go with it. During the day he slept and ate heavily at all three meals. His strength returning, he was finally finding it difficult to wrap his thumb and forefinger around his wrist.

He mulled over his conversations with the colonel. The other officers told him they sympathized that he wanted to help his men, but most thought he should accept the apparent decision not to exchange prisoners. Grant thought it was harder on the Confederacy than on the Union to feed and house captured soldiers. Confederate prisoners released today would be on the battle lines tomorrow and the Rebs were far more strapped for men. That might be greeted as sound thinking sitting around a crackling fireplace in New York, but Nathan had seen the death rate and misery among the tens of thousands in prison. He couldn't accept that dispassionate reasoning where his men were concerned.

Colonel Prescott had sent a telegram to New York and Washington relating Nathan's observations, asking that he be ordered back east where he could speak to decision makers. A return message congratulated Captain Parker on his escape and confirmed that he should be ordered to recuperate and rejoin the ranks as head of a training academy in Michigan. It did not make reference to his request to speak to the policy people in Washington.

Nathan had no interest in training anybody. He wanted his people out of that godforsaken place and that's all. Camp Sumter was fast becoming decommissioned—its numbers decreasing and the soldiers sent on to Cahaba and other prisons—but he wanted to see that they were gone and ensure they were cared for on the way home. Everybody thought they knew about Andersonville, but one had to be there to appreciate its uncompromising horror. As bad as the war was, the prison camp was worse.

Nathan made his way to the boardinghouse and found one of the few small tables isolated from the community benches. He did this for each meal, arriving early and keeping to himself; good fellowship and cheer were not back in his life yet. He saw that one of the booths in a dark corner behind him was occupied, but aside from that he was alone.

Hattie herself waited on him each night, as if it were a real hotel. She brought him bread and gravy and told him she had okra, corn pone, and pork coming up. He thanked her and went back to contemplating his immediate future. Today Nathan had sent a second telegram back to Washington through the colonel. Once again he beseeched the barons of bureaucracy in the U.S. Army to let him gather forces to make a raid himself if they weren't willing to devote complete units to the task. Prescott complied by sending it, but he was only humoring him. He wasn't sure how much longer he could count on the colonel's support. The tone of Nathan's requests lacked the good-soldier acquiescence that men of consequence had come to expect in communications from the ranks. But fry it all, he wasn't trying to make a good impression, he needed their support now.

"I am simply amazed at what washes onto the shore of our mighty Mississippi." Marcel's voice came from the corner booth behind him.

Startled, Nathan swung around in his dining-room seat.

"Incredible, wouldn't you say? Just a couple weeks ago you were holding me at gunpoint along the Bledsoe Trail. It's Sergeant Who's-is of the something or other Georgia What's-is, if I am not mistaken." Marcel watched as Nathan struggled to catch up.

"Not likely . . . I guess you could say I'm in the U.S. Army."

"Damned if I couldn't. But if I'd said that a few weeks ago you would have been swinging from the nearest oak."

"True enough, Marcel . . . isn't it? Marcel?"

Marcel winked, not really surprised that he had forgotten his last name.

"Lafarge, monsieur. You seem to be a boy in blue with no markings."

"Captain, actually," Nathan answered.

Marcel thought he looked befuddled, perhaps as to why he should suddenly be appearing here in a public boardinghouse in a Southern town under Federal control. Marcel lowered his voice. "A captain from Andersonville, if I remember correctly. Seems you'd have to lie your way into that place as a captain. I expect you'll like Vicksburg a bit better. But anyway, I suppose you're busy, so . . ."

"No, wait. I'm sorry for my rudeness, you did me a great service and I was a bit surprised. I'm Captain Parker. Nathan Parker. Have a seat."

Marcel could tell that this Captain Parker was more than a little curious as to how he had managed to suddenly appear at Hattie's. "Thank you. Don't mind if I do. I've eaten already, but I could do with a glass of whiskey."

The lady herself came by the table and set down two drinking glasses half full of a stout liquid.

Nathan sniffed. "My nose tells me it's unnecessary to explain to you the realities of a wartime boardinghouse in Vicksburg."

There was no bottle to draw attention to, but a sip of the fiery drink made it clear that reality was what you made of it.

"To the devil, may he step on his own red dick," Marcel murmured his toast in a refined, serious voice and both of them took a deep slash of the liquor.

Nathan remarked that it went down well and settled his nerves.

"It's a world full of blackguards and bastards and full-breasted women, my dear Captain." With that, Marcel drained his glass and spun his hand over his head to get Hattie's attention. The community table started to fill up but no one looked at them more than once. Lafarge acting up was nothing unusual—apparently just part of life in Vicksburg.

"Blackguards and . . . surely there's more than that," Nathan said.

"Not really, Captain. If you cite the things that matter in descending order, you might have to reverse the list is all." Marcel noticed that the two slugs of whiskey were already going to Nathan's head.

"Who in hell are you and how in the devil did you just happen to stroll into Hattie Murphy's deluxe accommodations?" Nathan tried to force himself together.

"Ah, a man of few words and little subtlety." Marcel enjoyed the moment, drumming his fingers on the hard oak table. "First of all, I was gazing out my hotel window much in my own world when to my delight I see a certain bender of the truth mucking along Clay as if back on the farm behind a double-shovel plow." Marcel took in the moment and continued. "A fresh uniform, to my eyes, completed the picture, although I suspect there are a few accouterments that are being fashioned as we speak." Marcel motioned with his head to indicate Nathan Parker's absence of grade on his officer's uniform.

Nathan assured him that indeed his rank was being crafted forthwith, as the army would say.

Marcel paused. "You asked who I am? A businessman, a fellow who has found a way to survive . . . a blackguard, a bastard, if you will." He watched Hattie bounce by with a load of mutton for the big table. "A fellow who hates waste, and by the way"—Marcel stopped, amused—"I followed you." He watched as Nathan took in this information.

"Why in the devil's own name would you do that?"

"I am a businessman. An entrepreneur, you might say. I followed you because it pleased me to do so. I was intrigued by your story. I met you pretending to be a ragamuffin sergeant of the Georgia irregulars in the middle of nowhere telling a fisherman's tale of deceit and lies and I next see you mucking your way along Clay Street in a buffed-out uniform of our captors and would-be benefactors. Who in God's name wouldn't be intrigued?"

"I suppose you have a point." Nathan finally had to laugh at his own image. "It does seem like something out of Grimm's. But let me ask you this—who were those men back at the Bledsoe Trail? I mean what in hell were you doing with a full load of high-grade cotton spread over two wagons? And that officer, the Reb, he knew you."

"Did he? Listen, there's a basic truth in life. People need things, some things more than others. You find what they need and you sell it to them."

"Makes you sound like a true servant of the people."

Hattie clipped by with a bowl of sweet potatoes.

"How about women, they need things too?"

Marcel rested his arms on the table. "They need men. And with this war going on their virtue is a loose commodity. If I had a way of supplying that demand . . . at least on a scale that mattered, I would." Marcel took a moment to compose his thoughts. "Now, Captain, let me ask you a question. You held that gun to Amos's face and I asked if you would really kill him if the rest of my men gunned you down. You said, 'Why not?' and you meant it. It struck me that we might even be doing you a favor." Marcel watched as Nathan said nothing, studying the table as if the answer were written there. "What do you want, Captain Nathan Parker?"

"My men. I need to know if they're alive and not living in that scourge of a prison."

"Why?"

"Why? Because they're my men. They trusted me and I led them and . . ."

"Did you do them wrong? Seems as if you led them because the U.S. Army made you lead them."

"What in hell is that supposed to mean?"

"Just a thought." Marcel spun his finger over his head again and Hattie appeared with two more glasses.

Nathan shook his head. "Not for me, thanks."

Marcel shrugged and gulped down half his glass. "You know, there are many ways to get things done, my friend, and they all boil down to money."

"I repeat, what in hell is that supposed to mean?"

"Strikes me as you've got a bug up your ass over those men. Ever occur to you that there's more 'n' one way to skin a cat?"

"Probably a dozen ways, but the most obvious is for me to put together a company of mounted raiders and hit that prison. And damn it if I didn't ask for exactly that, but the people in Washington who allow such adventures will hardly listen to me."

"Well then, let me spell it out for you. You're a serious fellow and you've got a serious problem, but you can't fix everything by wearing a righteous look and begging a bunch of stuffed shirts back east to provide you the wherewithal to do something."

Nathan seemed to be letting Marcel's words sink in. "Are you suggesting doing something about my men on my own?"

"You can't achieve what you want on your own. But you and money, well, that could be something else."

Marcel saw that Nathan appeared dizzy and yet Nathan grabbed the glass of whiskey he had already refused and drank it all down at once. "Mr. Lafarge, I'm a captain in the U.S. Army and I appreciate your suggesh . . . suggestions. But, I am what I am and I must go. Thank you for the whiskey."

As Nathan rose, Marcel shrugged and downed the last half of his own glass. "Think nothing of it, my good man, and good day, or should I say good evening, to you."

★

THEY SHOOK HANDS and parted. Nathan went for a walk before returning to his room. It was almost dark. His head was clearer but he felt tired. Opening the door, he glanced down at his well-made bed, a militarily precise well-made bed. There was a letter, no, a telegram on it, left by the staff while he was out.

He struck a match, lit the oil lamp sitting on the table, and unfolded the dispatch. It wasn't long or complicated; an honorable discharge from the United States Army. He was being thanked for exceptional service to his country and recommended for a Medal of Valor. There was no mention of his request to lead a unit to free the soldiers he left behind.

Nathan was startled by the sound of heavy breathing in the room—before he realized it was his own. How long had he been sitting there with the telegram wrapped in his fist? He wasn't sure, but visions of his men on the verge of death and despair at Andersonville danced through his head. He was suddenly tired, very tired. He would sleep . . . for now. There was much to think about.

★

MARCEL ENJOYED HIS usual breakfast of eggs and bacon. He had sent his toast back twice, for he wanted it to be done to a certain consistency and color, somewhere between a golden brown and butternut, reminiscent of his former uniform.

When returning, the waiter, Albert, seemed perplexed. "I'm sorry, sir, the chef insists this is the best he can do."

The perfectly prepared toast sat uneaten as Marcel drank his third cup of coffee. As he contemplated his day, it surprised him to see Nathan Parker in the lobby of the hotel, inquiring at the reception desk. He called out to the waiter. "Albert, excuse me. Albert?"

"Is it the toast, sir? I can assure you—"

"No, it's not the toast. I wonder if you would be a good fellow and fetch that gentleman waiting there at reception. The one in the uniform."

Albert glanced toward the lobby. "The tall man, sir? In the blue?"

"Yes, in the blue."

Albert quickly walked to the lobby as Marcel thought, yes the one in the blue, the damnable blue. There was certainly something about this Captain Parker, disturbing in a way. Marcel thought it had to do with sheer will. He was his own man, this Yankee, this would-be patriot with the "want" to rescue his forlorn men, yes, the one with the downtrodden look. Marcel stood to greet Nathan.

"Welcome to the Wheeler, Captain Parker. It's not only a surprise to see you but a treat." Marcel glanced at the waiter. "Thank you, Albert, that will be all. . . . Have a seat, Captain."

"Excuse the intrusion, Lafarge." Nathan eased himself into the chair. "I hope, well . . . I feel a bit of a jackass."

"You're not intruding at all, would you like some breakfast?"

"No, thank you. I've . . . well, maybe I will have coffee."

Marcel called Albert once again. "Some coffee for my guest, please. Are you sure you won't eat something, Nathan?"

"No, I don't believe I—"

"Albert, please bring the captain eggs, ham, toast with preserves, and a pot of coffee. Hurry now, my good man, our Northern friend is starved. Oh, by the way, would you like some skillygalee?"

"No, I think I'll forgo that pleasure, thank you." Nathan laughed.

As the waiter left they could hear him mumbling, "Skillygalee."

"We had our own version of that delight." Marcel smiled, remembering. "Except rather than fry the tack at the end after soaking it, we would throw in a piece of salt pork or beef, water it the hell down, and boil it. Called it lobcourse, it was usually awful."

Nathan chimed in, "We were almost always short on sowbelly drippings so we would throw just about anything available into the pot. Put it in the skillet and keep turning it so it wouldn't burn too much."

They fell silent for a few moments.

When the food arrived, Nathan seemed trancelike in the way he devoured the food.

"My God, Captain. I was afraid you would never come up for air. . . . How much weight did you lose in the camp?"

"I would guess thirty pounds." Nathan contentedly wiped his mouth. "Funny thing, sometimes I can't eat a lick, just won't go down. Other times I am a beast. Beats all. Guess it gets to me when I think of my men enduring the filth and deprivation at the camp. Same with sleep. I'll lay my head down and I could swear I'm lying on the cold ground . . . the groans and pitiful calls in the night keep going through my . . ." Nathan fell silent.

"You'll get over it, soldier."

Nathan looked up at him. "I am here because I find myself without a clear solution to my dilemma. Here it is in a nutshell. You call yourself a businessman, Lafarge. Well, as I see it, there's business and then there's monkey business, but regardless, there are things I have to do and as you suggested, it takes money and people. How do I get them and in what order?"

"Let's take a walk, Captain."

As they walked along Clay, Marcel tipped his hat to almost everyone. "Perception is a marvelous thing, Captain. People I greet whom I don't know, nor care to, are usually perplexed. They think, Who is that successful-looking gentleman, should I know him? Do I know him? And best of all, do I want to know him? It's an amazing process, my friend. Truly amazing how many souls one can flirt with in the course of a day. . . . Speaking of perception, I perceive you're of a mind to skin some cat? Correct? Have your circumstances changed?"

Nathan allowed the morning sun to beat down on his face for a moment. "I have been unceremoniously kicked out, booted, discharged from the army. When we spoke last night I had not been informed. Fair or not, in truth it's probably for the best, my wrath seems to be exceeding my good sense, what little there is left of it—"

"Let me come to a quick point." Marcel could tell this was confusing and painful for Nathan and yet he felt it necessary to be pointedly strong with him. "I am, if nothing else, an aggressive, combative servant of my own needs and wants, hence my proposition is as follows." He stopped as if an inspiration had swept over him. "I say 'proposition,' as if one is making a proposal to a banker to finance a business opportunity." Marcel once again paused. "I don't mean that, forgive the equivocation. What I should say is simply that I would like to help you." Marcel sensed immediate doubt from Nathan.

"It's been my experience, Lafarge, that 'I would like to help you' really means 'I see something in this for myself and I'm going to color this in a way that makes it appear rosy,' am I wrong?"

Marcel needed to present himself differently. "Roses, my friend, have thorns. My prop—excuse me. Once again that word, sounding as if I'm soliciting a lady of the night for favors of the flesh." Marcel tipped his cattleman's hat to a corpulent man in a too-tight business suit. "My idea is as follows. I will provide you with a band of jolly bastards, rogues, and ne'er-do-wells to complete your mission. Will they be soldiers, used to discipline and regime? No. But I promise you this—they will be gunners and jailbirds spoiling for a scrap. . . . In a word, ideal for what you have in mind."

Nathan stopped their stroll and put his hand on Marcel's arm as if to end not only their walk but the conversation. "Look, Lafarge, I appreciate your taking the time to state your case, and under different circumstances I would be delighted at your proposal but—"

Marcel started to interrupt.

"Wait, Lafarge, hear me out. These men are dying, can you understand that? Goddamn it, they're starving to death, eating worms and grass. The place is alive with pestilence. The water tainted with death, many of them asleep in the open with nothing but God's dark sky over their heads." Nathan stopped to catch his breath. "I can't make this so-called raid with your band of jolly bastards and rogues, for Christ's sake. What in the hell are you thinking, fellow?"

Marcel's features turned dark. "First of all, take your hand off of my arm."

Nathan did so with an attitude that projected misunderstanding and loss of hope.

"Now you hear me out, *fellow*"—Marcel pointed his finger at Nathan's chest—"I am nothing if not a man of my word. When I use the expression *rogue* and *jailbird,* I do so to describe a certain kind of man. Will there be rotten apples? Yes, there'll be thorns and bastards, but at the center there will be a core of hard, determined men who are looking for a payday . . . do you hear me? A payday. Why am I doing this? You may well ask. To be honest, I love a good fight. It's my life's blood. I am dying, not literally, but each day I slip further into a morass of commonplace bullshit. I need out, whatever it takes, my friend. I am attracted to you and your ideals."

Nathan frowned as Marcel continued.

"Listen to me, Captain. I will provide you with fifteen to twenty fighting men, call them what you will, but they will raid your so-called Camp Sumter and free your men . . . that I will promise." Marcel stopped and shoved his open hand toward Captain Nathan Parker. "You have my word on this, monsieur, we will return to Vicksburg in triumph. Let's part now and agree only to the following. If after twenty-four hours you have changed your mind about my brigands, we will meet at the Wheeler to discuss details." Marcel pulled out his pocket watch. "Shall we say 10:00 A.M. *demain? Bonsoir, mon capitaine.*" After a brief handshake Marcel marched off, still nodding to the occasional passerby as if he had not a care on God's green earth.

★

NATHAN WALKED AWAY from the docks with his heart and soul in an uproar. He weighed the options as he approached the Union army headquarters. In exchange for his silence he could probably have his commission restored. Apparently, they were brooking no interference with anything that would slow the war coming to an end. Made sense . . . from a distance.

What he was forced to do to obtain the resources to free his men was not illegal, but it was against all his soldierly instincts. Ulysses S. Grant, the very one who refused to engage in exchange or parole of prisoners, was also the officer most opposed to the copperhead trade of permitted items to the South. Odd, because he was the one high-ranking officer whom Nathan truly admired.

With his discharge intact Nathan wouldn't be breaking any laws by engaging in private enterprise. But he cared little about that—whether or not laws were broken meant less to him as time went on. It was the principle of the thing. He accepted Marcel for who he was. There was no pretense of virtue on his part. He was a survivor and an opportunist. Marcel had made him an offer: he could be righteous and morose about the fate of his men or he could be ruthless, unscrupulous, and successful.

Nathan had no son, to say nothing of a wife. But then, he had twenty-two sons of a kind at Andersonville. Raid the camp if they were there or influence their disposition if they weren't. Marcel had put it well: money was the great mover. But could he do it? He was proud of being a soldier even though he wanted his service to be behind him, something he looked back on while he muddled his way through life. He hated the war and was consumed with one thing, freeing those he felt responsible for.

He rounded Mississippi Street and saw some soldiers escorting a group of what appeared to be ten or a dozen barely clothed skeletons to a medical facility. The ex-prisoners looked like a series of bones erected into human form, clothed in old Federal tunics and left in the mud and smoke for a year. An escort remarked to Nathan, "I can't believe this . . . can you accept that these men were captured by fellow Americans?"

"Are they from Andersonville?"

"No, Cahaba."

"Cahaba? I thought that place was better . . . that it had indoor lodging and steady food."

"Has indoor incarceration and even oil lamplighting, but as you can tell from the way these fellows look, it ain't the Wheeler."

One of the men lost his footing and tripped in front of Nathan. As he helped the man to his feet he could smell the familiar fetid breath and body odor that went with the look of despair in the man's eyes. Nathan and a young private from the local command helped the man up the stairs. He was probably a hundred-and-eighty-pound man who had shrunk to no more than a hundred and twenty.

The fellow turned and with a swollen tongue spoke to Nathan. "Thanks for the lift, brothers, I've been dreaming of getting home for so long I can't even figger where I am . . . are we going to be all right?"

Nathan looked closer at the man's eyes; they were clouded over. He extended his hand in front of the soldier's face but the man didn't blink. "Can you see?"

"Oh, yeah, I think so."

"You think so?" said the astonished private.

Nathan helped the man into the infirmary, where another prisoner turned and took over. "I got him. He's having a hard time of it."

The private was standing outside as Nathan emerged. The young man had tears in his eyes. "That fella, he can't see?"

Nathan patted the boy on the arm. "No, he'll be fine. I need to go, but keep on assisting them, will you?"

The war and well-reasoned, strategic decisions be damned. His men were not going to be left to the whimsy of fate in Andersonville.

CHAPTER 12

November 1864
The Mississippi Steamboat Belle Marie

O nly the *Belle Marie* remained, her companion boats having left for more lucrative regions. Fully loaded with as many as six hundred bales of cotton, her guards on the main deck swelled with product stacked five bales high and ten deep. A small path had been left on her starboard side to allow passengers to reach the staircase leading up to the boiler deck, where accommodations were located. Marcel acquired a spacious, comfortable stateroom and had arranged a respectable cabin for Nathan, if in fact he arrived.

Their meeting at the Wheeler that morning proved difficult. Marcel found Captain Parker to be a man of considerable integrity and purpose and not without a quick intelligence. He had to admit disappointment that the good captain had not agreed to his proposal of financing his so-called raid on Andersonville prison. But Parker insisted on giving Washington and the correct channels one last try. It amused Marcel that it had become difficult to give away not only his services, but his money as well.

Marcel had a light meal and spent the evening exploring the boat. He remained on the stern of the boat listening to music drifting back from the dining room, which had been converted into a lounge for the evening. Lafarge marveled at the endless need of people to travel. One would never suspect that a war raged only a few hundred miles away.

A familiar voice along the outside guard caught his attention—Clete Wilson, a character he knew from the river. A man who plied his trade of cardsharping and confidence games along the Mississippi. He seemed to have struck up an acquaintance with one of the powdered ladies from the ballroom. Marcel eavesdropped on their innocuous, dreamy-eyed conversation. He owed Wilson money; it might be a problem in the coming days. He would have to see. Running into each other on the boat was probable.

Pleased to be traveling again, the comfortable bed seemed to swallow Marcel. He had a certain wanderlust, and the idea of selling his cotton in Memphis excited him. He went over, once again, the various possibilities. It could be lucrative if all went well. He envisioned his bales sitting on the main deck, their brethren crowded next to them, each waiting patiently for their chance to become yards and yards of finished goods.

★

A GROGGY MARCEL stood next to the portside guard as the vessel came alive. He had given up on sleep and dressed for the day.

Steam built up in the boat with the crew waiting to let go the fore and aft shorelines. The gangplank had been pulled into a vertical position, although the steamer was still close enough to the dock so that the shore party could leap aboard. Marcel stood overlooking the bow, hearing the captain shouting to the crew above him on the Texas deck. The 6:00 A.M. departure time approached, and he made his way to the starboard side rail as he saw a figure in the distance hurrying along through the mist. Nathan Parker carried himself well for so early in the morning. His two valises swung easily at his sides, conveying a relaxed demeanor that surprised Marcel. Nathan could see the shorelines close to being let go and he heard the shouted calls from the crew, yet he proceeded along the quay seemingly unperturbed. Marcel paused before speaking, anxious to see how it played out. Six bells rang out in the crisp morning air. The sound resonated from the wheelhouse with the captain bellowing simultaneously, "Stand by to cast off your bowline, Mr. Peters."

"Aye, aye, Captain," answered Peters in an equally strong voice.

Nathan was still fifty yards from the boat but hadn't increased his pace. Marcel admired his poise if not his judgment. The line handlers were waiting patiently at the dockside stanchions. The captain ordered for Peters to cast off the bowlines; Peters shouted to the two men at the bow stanchion; the lines came off and the men leapt aboard. The bow of the boat started to inch easily from the dock. After the order came for the stern lines to be let go, Marcel could feel the thirty-foot starboard wheel start to move. The stern of the ship was still pinned to the dock as the bow slowly came away. The portside wheel had been put in reverse to bring her bow clear as the boat crept forward. Marcel noticed that Nathan, at the last moment, stepped easily onto the boat's sternpost as she cleared the dock. He watched as First Mate Peters went aft to help Nathan with his bags. The mate had a clipboard and Marcel could see him going about the business of checking Nathan in. Walking aft, he stood directly over Nathan on the lower deck.

"That was quite a display, monsieur, *comportement décontracté*. Bravo. Cutting it a bit thin, though, weren't you?"

Nathan looked up and smiled. "Good morning . . . breakfast?"

Marcel nodded and disappeared behind the guard railing. He

envied Parker, as it had taken him many seasons to gain such self-assuredness. The years before the mast were difficult. Cabin boy to first mate had been a struggle, his development coming slowly and with much loss of blood.

★

LATER IN THE morning, passengers crowded the dining room, their breakfast dishes clinking a high-pitched symphony. Marcel and Nathan sat in the aft portion of the room away from the buffet table, attempting to have a conversation amid the din.

Marcel drank down the last of his third cup of coffee. "I honestly didn't think you would make it. Were you reluctant to be off on your voyage of destiny?"

"Reluctant to go to Washington? No." Nathan shifted in his chair. "Hell, no. Hattie, my landlady, promised a buckboard at five thirty that didn't materialize so I had to hoof it. Sorry if you were concerned, it was not my intent."

The *Belle Marie* steamed along, grunting mightily. She made good time, occasionally dodging flatboats and river snags as Marcel and Nathan strolled the wide hurricane deck.

"There's a game being stirred up in the lounge after supper tonight, are you ripe for it?"—Clete Wilson, the gambler Marcel had eavesdropped on the previous evening, came from behind them—"And I hate to bring up old wounds, Lafarge, but—"

"I owe you one hundred and forty dollars, Clete," Marcel interrupted the riverman, "and you'd like to have it, correct?"

Wilson tipped his hat and proceeded along the walkway as Marcel watched his back.

"A friend?" Nathan looked at Marcel, smiling.

"Hardly, I am always reluctant to trust these river rats. They're interesting to a degree, but they'd slice you up and have you for breakfast and think nothing of it." Marcel stepped to the rail. "I've owed that rascal money for quite some time, it amuses me."

"I would be more than happy to sit behind you at the game, Lafarge."

"Would you do that? It would give me some assurance. Thank you."

They parted, agreeing to meet at suppertime. Nathan's naïve invitation to protect his hindquarters amused Marcel. If anyone needed protection, it would be Wilson.

CHAPTER 13

November 1864

M arcel spent the day lounging on the promenade deck while the *Belle Marie* made her way past quaint villages and mile upon mile of harvested cornfields. Dotting the banks of the river, the depleted stalks looked like exhausted warriors. Scraggly weeds, searching for moisture, grew down to the river's edge.

They slowed once while a long skiff piled five feet high with cordwood tied up to the starboard side of the *Belle Marie*. The paddle wheeler progressed slowly upriver while third-class passengers, who had signed to work off part of their passage, along with the crew, unloaded the skiff. They then set it adrift, the owner allowing the current to carry him back to his original roost. Watching this, Marcel thought there were easier ways to make a living.

Late in the afternoon, Marcel once again ran into Wilson. "I think I am going to have to forego the pleasure of attending your game this evening, Mr. Wilson. I have work I must attend to before we arrive in Memphis."

"Why, Lafarge, you're not getting a case of cold feet, are you?" Wilson said.

Marcel didn't like the gibe but chose to ignore it. "No, Mr. Wilson, business. Some of us have to work for a living, you know."

"I am sure we'll meet again. I am up and down on these boats several times a month." He paused. "Not much gets by me on the river."

"Meaning?"

Wilson's eyes narrowed as he lowered his voice. "You owe me money. Pay up or watch your back, Lafarge." Wilson bolted along the promenade.

Marcel and Nathan spent time pacing the boiler deck after supper. Music drifted away from the ballroom like the last of the late diners, the ornate room being readied for an evening of entertainment, from the out-of-tune piano accompanied by an equally off-key violin. Marcel thought this to be part of the charm of riverboat travel. He stood outside his small cabin, leaning against the starboard side rail, waiting for Nathan to return from his room. He wasn't entirely sure if he should engage Wilson in the proposed card game or not. It might be amusing to best the man—the "cold feet" and "pay up or watch your back" remarks had not sat well with him. He caught himself laughing; of course he would play cards with Wilson, he knew himself too well. It would be too tempting not to.

★

MARCEL GLANCED AROUND. A group of four men sat in the corner of the ballroom engaged in their poker game. A rotund fellow wearing a red flowing cravat matching his florid complexion laughed as he raked in a pot of chips. He recognized the man as William "Big Bill" Duff who fancied himself a ladies' man and gambler par excellence. Marcel remembered him as a bully. But to each his own, he thought.

Marcel willed a half smile to vanish from his face as he and Parker approached the table.

After introductions, Marcel observed several hands before producing his paper money. "It's table stakes, is it, gents?"

Duff shuffled cards and glanced at Marcel as he dealt. "It's whatever you're big enough to handle, Forge."

Marcel cleared his throat. "It's Lafarge, and I'll bet fifty on my queen." He won the first pot and players responded with pretentious "Ohs" and "Ahs" accompanied by good-natured laughter.

"If it's not beginner's luck, it's downright mystifying. Damn it all." Duff smiled but seemed to be put off by Marcel's first-hand luck. They played on for another half hour.

"Lafarge, that's at least three times you've folded your cards when I would have sworn you had the table beat." Clete Wilson's brows arched. "What's the trouble?"

It pleased Marcel that Wilson verbalized his anxiety at not being able to engage Marcel directly. Once again his instinct told him that the man's desperate need to beat him had nothing to do with money. "Just don't have the cards, Mr. Wilson. It's that simple."

"My name is Clete. Don't be calling me mister, it riles me. Makes me think you might be funning with me, having sport." He took the cards roughly from the man on his right. "I recognize it ain't rightly my turn to deal but with these other gents' permission, why don't you and I play a couple hands atween us, just us two. What you say, Slick?"

Marcel could barely hold in his excitement as he turned to Nathan Parker sitting behind him. "Captain Parker, what do you think? Should I engage Mr. 'Clete' here in a mano a mano with the pasteboards or continue play as before?" Marcel winked at Nathan as he delivered his facetious line. He could tell the captain was well aware of what was going on.

"I'm not much of a gambler, Marcel. My experience doesn't go much beyond the occasional flipping of coins for drinks. But from what I can see, I don't believe you'd be in a great deal of difficulty." He then added quietly, "Slick?"

"What did you have in mind, Clete?" Marcel saw Wilson bristling but he had taken the bait and seemed determined to try and best Marcel.

"Let's play a man's game, Lafarge. Five-card stud, hundred-dollar ante. Think you can handle that?"

"Why not get right to it, Clete?" Marcel adopted a grave expression. "Let's just cut for high card, five hundred a round, so I can get back to the real poker players."

Whispers arose from the other seated players and the small crowd who gathered behind them.

Wilson quickly glanced around, his bravado beginning to fade. "All right, do your damnedest, big man," he called out to Marcel in a somewhat shaky voice.

Perspiration formed on Wilson's forehead as he shuffled the cards and set them in the center of the table. Marcel lifted a third of the deck and turned them over, exposing the nine of clubs. Wilson quickly picked up half the remaining pile but before he could turn them over, Marcel grabbed his hand.

"Before you turn your hand, would you like to double the bet?" Marcel gave Wilson a hard stare. "Let's say a thousand on the turn. . . ." Marcel waited while Wilson's stiff smile began to fade. "Can you handle it, Mr. Wilson?"

The beat of distant paddle wheels thrashing the muddy waters was the only sound heard as Wilson glanced around the table. "I don't carry that kind of money on me."

"Then it's payday stakes . . . agreed?" Marcel smiled.

"Agreed." Wilson dropped his eyes, already feeling beaten.

Marcel released his grip on Wilson's hand and watched not the turn of the card, but Wilson's face. As the man's eyes came back up from the cards, the anguish in his expression gave Marcel pure delight.

Wilson threw the cards on the table and kicked his chair backwards, his fists tight to his sides. "I'll be a son of a bitch. . . ."

"You certainly will, my friend." Marcel smiled. "You certainly will. Shall we meet in the morning prior to disembarking to discuss payment?"

Wilson nodded reluctantly and pushed his chair away from the table. Marcel played well for the next few rounds. He pulled in his chips and glanced at Duff's beefy hands. "Trust me, sir, it's strictly the luck of the uninitiated." He smiled, elevating the mood.

They played on, Marcel holding firm, never overbetting, biding his time, waiting for Big Bill to "overplay." It finally came, though Marcel was somewhat surprised when Duff said, "I see your bet, Mr. Forge, and raise you five hundred."

"I thought this was table stakes, Mr. Duff." Marcel could not sort the fellow out. He was certain he had him beat as Duff drew three cards and had checked on the opening. Marcel held a spade flush. "I'll call your bet, Mr. Duff." He went into his wallet, producing the required money.

Duff smirked as he spread his hand—a full house, beating Marcel's five spades. Nervous laughter circled the table as the players seemed to sense something amiss.

Marcel played several more hands, watching Duff closely. It seemed the man almost always won when he dealt. He observed Big Bill expertly shuffle the cards. Marcel couldn't actually see him deal "seconds," but knew that he was. After careful consideration, Marcel decided there wasn't much he could do at the moment. "Gentlemen, you've cleaned me out. I'll call it an evening. Thank you for allowing me to sit in."

The men answered with polite acknowledgment as Marcel excused himself while starting across the stately ballroom.

From the table, Duff called, "There's a penny-ante game usually stirred up in the negra section on Polk in Memphis. I'm sure they'd be happy to oblige you, Forge." He slapped his hand on the table. "Deal 'em."

Marcel made his way down the stairs avoiding other passengers, not wanting them to see his rage. He hurried along the promenade, needing to get back to his room. Nathan trailed behind him, offering solace and little else. At his cabin door he gathered himself and made a good show of assuring the captain that the lost money was simply the fare for doing business on the mighty Mississippi. They parted, agreeing to meet on the dock midmorning in Memphis.

He was not angry about the loss of the money but about the way it had been done. He knew without a doubt that Big Bill Duff cheated him and he would have difficulty living with that. Marcel stood in the center of his room, several times running his hands along his weskit front, feeling the reassuring bulge of his two-shot derringer. The more he reasoned that he would just have to let it go for now, the more he was convinced that he couldn't, that he would at least have to confront the man and express his views. Whether it would lead to other more advanced repercussions would be left to Mr. Duff.

Marcel watched from outside the lounge as the men gathered at the table continued to play. He felt like a petty thief pacing the lonely deck. Far ahead to the west of the snakelike river, dim lights could be seen. Was it Memphis, he thought, no, that sparkling city would be on his right on the eastern shore. Most probably, it would be Helena. The Arkansas town's pale glow was still ten miles away. A chorus of loud laughter came from an open doorway of the lounge. Marcel eased into an alcove as the card players spilled out onto the wide deck, the game over. He watched as the men said their good nights. After several minutes just two of the players remained, Clete Wilson and Big Bill Duff. They gazed at the dark passing water, chatting amicably. Listening to their conversation, Marcel began to have second thoughts about a confrontation with the corpulent Mr. Duff. After all, it had been a game of chance and as the name might imply, nothing was guaranteed. Just as he was ready to ease his way out of the alcove and slink off to his room he heard Bill Duff's deep-seated belly laugh followed by an exchange between him and Clete Wilson.

"You took him to school good and proper, that's for damn sure." Duff responded once again with a loud guffaw and spouted something about penny ante and the game in the Negro section of Memphis that their pompous Mr. Lafarge might be right for. Marcel's resolution about letting bygones be just that quickly evaporated. He pressed his back hard into the bulkhead, breathed deeply, and waited. After several minutes Wilson left for bed, calling out for Duff to cuddle up warmly with his newfound stash of money. Marcel bit his lip and tried to control his intake of air. When it was apparent that Duff was comfortable for the time being, Marcel waited for the man to move to darker environs. Finally the bell-shaped cardsharp looked both ways as if needing privacy. Then, as Marcel watched, the man walked quickly to the companionway stairs and made his way down to the cargo deck to the dark spaces between the stacked cotton bales.

Marcel stepped quickly and arrived behind Duff while he fumbled with his fly. "What you feel pressed against your fat neck, sir, is a small-caliber pistol. Its power is of sufficient means to send a pea-sized chunk of lead swiftly circling the inside of your brainpan, almost certainly disrupting your thought patterns to a fare-thee-well. Your money or your life, Duffy."

"How do I know you have a weapon?" Duff said weakly, his hands still at his fly. "I don't see it."

"Do you need to?" Marcel worried the derringer's twin barrels into Duff's neck.

Duff's head dropped and with a deep breath he started to turn, but then thought better of it. "All right. What do you want? Your money? You know, Forge, you're a sore loser."

"Nothing sore about me, Mr. Duff. I don't abide cheating. I don't mind losing to a fair game, but I watched you. You're a card cheat, you dealt yourself several hands from the bottom. And as I said before, my good man, your money or your life."

Marcel sensed Duff's doubts about whether a firearm existed. "Big Bill, is that what they call you? Well, Mr. Big, I'll tell you what, let's walk aft to the paddle wheel 'til we get to the port side axle." Marcel prodded the heavy man in front of him. "I'm counting to three, Duff, and then—" Marcel looked down as Duff wet himself. "Well, well, the Big Boy has pissed himself, 'fraid he's gone too far with the wrong poker player." Marcel reached around and pulled a thick folded wallet from the man's vest.

"Some of that I earned from the other fellows," Duff whined. "Take what you think is yours and leave me my fair share."

Marcel stepped back, never taking his eyes from Duff's neck as he slipped the small derringer into his vest's padded hidey-hole. Surprisingly, some of his anger and frustration diminished with Big Bill's complete degradation. It was laughable. Marcel thought about how strange life could be. This lout, this despicable bully, soiling himself in front of Marcel, seemed now to be but a harmless schoolboy. He obviously had been at his trade as a card cheat for a number of years but had more than likely always managed to bluff his way through any tough situation. Maybe this time, Marcel thought, a good scare would be enough. The wallet stuffed full of banknotes pleased Marcel as he replenished his losses, taking only what belonged to him. A full moon darted behind the starboard paddle wheel as Marcel turned back to his frightened quarry. "Your billfold is going to be—"

Without warning, Duff kicked his right leg backward, striking Marcel just below the knee. With both hands instinctively going to his leg he was suddenly vulnerable as Duff spun and charged. "You bastard, I'll kill you, you motherless—"

Marcel had time only to raise a hand to the other man's throat as the two of them struggled on the slippery deck. Duff was strong, but Marcel was quicker, managing to get both arms around the heavyset man's neck, pulling his head roughly to his body.

Once again, the gambler lashed out with his feet, momentarily loosening Marcel's grip. His arms were occupied with the bully's head, leaving Big Bill's wild hands free to search for a weapon, his fingers groping as they came upon the pistol. He ripped it free and raised his arm. As the Frenchman's knee drove mercilessly into the man's groin, Duff howled in pain as the two large men wrestled at the railing protecting the thirty-foot revolving wheel. Finally, Marcel was able to bend Duff's hand gripping the derringer slowly back toward his ample belly.

"Loosen your grip, Duff, or I'll put both of these rounds into your fat gut."

"Do your damnedest, Forge, I've got the weapon, you frog-eating bastard." They slid closer to the pulsing giant wheel, struggling and falling heavily, Marcel's weight squarely on top.

"Have you had enough, Duff?" Marcel could feel the fight had gone out of the man. "Duff?" The pale moon cast a reflective glint, shining brightly off the nickel-plated derringer. He rolled off the body, gasping for air. During the struggle to the ground, Marcel's hand had squeezed Duff's, inadvertently firing the weapon into the gambler's chest. He could hear him wheezing, and then, nothing. Marcel's rage gradually subsided, remorse quickly replacing the pent-up frustration from being beaten at his recent game of cards. He wondered if it was all worth it and if anyone, in the end, would believe it was fate. He got to his knees, retrieved the bloody weapon, and rinsed it in the spray of the wheel. The body rested on the deck between stands of guardrail; Marcel eased it into the churning river. He washed his hands in the brackish liquid of the Mississippi.

CHAPTER 14

Late November 1864
The Mississippi Steamer Belle Marie *and Memphis*

I understand the *Belle Marie* is going to be laid up with repairs for several days. It will give me time to settle a few of my affairs in Memphis."

Nathan Parker didn't answer. He quietly adjusted his tunic as Marcel scanned the expansive dock area.

Marcel continued, "You haven't changed your mind about going to Washington, Captain?"

"I feel it's important I try to get this raid, if that's what it's going to be, done as an official act. If there's misadventure, there won't be any civilian repercussions later. . . ." he trailed off, trying to meet Marcel's eye. "Understand, I appreciate your offer. But I would feel more comfortable if this were done in military fashion."

"Totally understandable, monsieur." Marcel nodded. "The offer still stands. What say we leave it at this—if your Washington soirée doesn't pan out, I'll give you an address here in Memphis where I can be reached." Marcel quickly scribbled the name and particulars of his Memphis hotel, paused, then continued to write. "I'm also including the name and address of one Israel Pennington, bar owner and provocateur par excellence, who could very well be the lynchpin to our putting together an agreeable band of . . . shall we say, handy-type souls?"

Marcel handed Nathan the notation, who, after a quick glance, folded the paper and put it carefully into his breast pocket.

"This Israel, is he a patriot of the South, a freebooter, or just what?"

Marcel smiled. "Mr. Pennington is a devout believer in just one thing: himself. He will be our man if the occasion demands . . . shall we say, you'll let me know your intention?"

The two men parted on the busy cotton-laden wharf, Nathan vowing that if the need arose he would take advantage of Marcel's offer.

The dock area came alive with teams of horses and laborers hoisting bales of cotton onto heavily loaded wagons. Marcel watched Captain Nathan Parker striding purposefully up the busy Memphis street. He admired the man's perseverance but he knew that if the roles were reversed he would at that very moment be re-cruiting a merry band of cutthroats to ride with him to the Georgia prison.

Marcel waited for more than an hour for the erstwhile card-playing Mr. Wilson. When he arrived he was not alone. Marcel watched as Clete Wilson and two other men appeared on the top deck of the *Belle Marie* along with the captain. Amid much arm-waving and shoulder-shrugging the group made their way down the companion-way stairs. At the gangplank, the riverboat captain gave the trio a desultory salute and turned back to his ancient boat.

Marcel boosted himself onto a vertical cotton bale and waited. The three men dodged through a group of workers and he called out, "Mr. Wilson, are you looking for me?"

Clete Wilson led the way as if anxious to confront Marcel. "You know anything about Bill's whereabouts, Frenchy?"

Marcel eyed the two other men; one seemed vaguely familiar, the other was a sizable man with a badge pinned to his vest pocket. "Bill? I know lots of Bills, which one would you be speaking of, Clete?" Marcel could tell Wilson was indeed upset.

Clete turned to the lawman. "This here is Constable Josh Perkins, and we're looking for Duff. Supposed to meet me for breakfast, never showed." Wilson paced along the dock. "His room's cleared out, he was booked to go onto St. Louie . . . you seen him?" He looked hard at Marcel perched on his cotton bale.

"I saw him last night"—as if he were concerned, Marcel eased himself off his perch—"at the game, Clete. I retired early. If you remember, you probably saw him after me."

"What's your name, fella?" This from the heavyset constable.

"Marcel Lafarge, sir." He looked directly into the officer's eyes. "How can I be of service?"

"Wilson here says you took a beating at the table last night, we're talking to all the players." The man stopped and took a deep breath as if he was bored and turned to Wilson. "I don't see any foul play here, I swear, the fella's room was cleared out, his bed hadn't been slept in, for the life of me I don't see it. The captain explained to you, Mr. Wilson, that some passengers got off in Helena, Arkansas, last night late. I think your Mr. Duff just made an early departure."

Marcel thought "early departure" to be a polite way of putting it. He was also pleased with himself that he had the foresight to take Big Bill's room key off the body and arrange his quarters to appear used—the expensive valise and linen suits having floated in the Mississippi for only a few moments as he watched from the dark starboard railing. The constable surveyed the three men briefly. Glancing about the *Belle Marie,* he tipped his hat and left.

Marcel looked at Wilson's companion. "You're Rene Sangnoir, *oui?*"

Sangnoir nodded.

"My, my, Clete your knife-fighting friend is quite well known in the Baton Rouge area," said Marcel.

"Don't try and get off the subject, Lafarge." Wilson remained angry. "What do you know about Big Bill's whereabouts?"

"Clete, I can honestly say I have no idea where our Mr. Duff is." Marcel reasoned that it was not strictly true—that he knew he was facedown in the Mississippi, but just exactly where he would be hard-pressed to say.

Wilson seemed to cool down finally and signaled to his friend Sangnoir to leave him and Marcel alone.

"Lafarge, the way I see it, we should be about even. Hell's fire, you owed me money for quite a spell . . . what with interest and all, I'd say we're square." Wilson took a stance as if he wasn't going to budge from either that spot or his position about the gambling debt.

Marcel, with his thumb, had eased the handle of his derringer out of its vest pocket, the bone handle hooked casually over the brocaded weskit. "Clete, let's not get in a fuss about this. I owed you money, now you owe me money. You looking like a schoolboy ready to scrap is not going to change that."

Wilson dropped his head. "What you got in mind, Slick?"

Marcel thought about what he was going to propose to this lout. "You're usually ready for a scrap, Clete, how would you and your friend Sangnoir like to get paid for doing just that?"

Clete looked suspiciously at Marcel. "What we gotta do?"

With little detail, Marcel explained to Wilson about the proposed raid and meeting him in Tuscaloosa at Israel's tavern. To Marcel's surprise, Clete knew Israel; he liked him, had worked with him on the river. They talked about money and how Clete would work off his debt plus obtain another thousand for himself and five hundred for his unsavory associate.

Wilson also assured Marcel that Sangnoir would be agreeable to whatever he proposed. They didn't shake hands but nodded at each other and parted. Marcel felt relief in being able to distract Wilson from needing to find the whereabouts of his friend Duff and instead, diverting him to being part of Captain Nathan Parker's raid. Marcel knew there would be very little chance the two ruffians would arrive, but heaven help the enterprise if Wilson and Sangnoir actually showed up at Israel Pennington's tavern in Tuscaloosa.

As the two men swaggered on their way, Marcel wondered if, on the outside chance these river rats did arrive in Tusca, he was doing Captain Parker a disservice. He thought if Nathan wanted a military operation he certainly wouldn't get it at Israel's. Military bearing, disciplined hours, and the pursuit of a righteous cause would be the last thing on the mind of any man willing to fight for money. Wilson and Sangnoir being no exceptions.

CHAPTER 15

December 1864
Memphis

A fter two weeks in Memphis, Nathan had only one more day before catching another steamer north and east. He stopped by the Federal garrison in Memphis to see if Major Canby was there. Nathan knew the man from Chickamauga, where he'd been responsible for his promotion to captain. While Nathan had been commanding officer of the Fifth almost since the beginning, it had been as lieutenant through a field designation. He got his captain's bars for real through Canby's doing.

Fifth Michigan's initial captain was killed the first week in the war. Lieutenant Mackey and he were both assigned platoons with Nathan as commanding officer. Typically the Federals had a captain over the whole company and directly over one of the platoons. Mackey was a good man and Nathan heard that since their capture at Monocacy the lieutenant and second platoon had escaped without casualty. Colonel Prescott had told him in Vicksburg that Mackey had recently himself been promoted to captain.

Nathan's hope was that Canby, well connected in the U.S. Army's political world, could help him on his mission to Washington. His endorsement would mean more than even Colonel Prescott's support. This trip simply had to work. It was inconceivable that decent, rational men would allow the horrors at Andersonville to continue. Nathan refused to accept the necessity of a renegade action from a gang of the sort Marcel would assemble. It was, in fact, surprising to Nathan that he was even seriously considering such an extreme solution. Did rational men really take something like that beyond the talking stage? Maybe not, but could Nathan accept a solution that didn't result in his men being out of that camp . . . rational or not?

Nathan was feeling dizzy with the implications of it all. Would he have to accept mourning Weed, Peregoy, and Rawlins like he had to accept mourning Bender? It was the rational, reasonable thing to do. All the right-thinking veteran officers at Vicksburg said the same thing: stay out of it, try to help them after they were released if he was really that set on helping them. It would be so easy to accede to those recommendations, who could blame him? Even his men themselves wouldn't blame him . . . but there was one person who would—Nathan Parker would blame him.

It then occurred to him that maybe Marcel was all windy talk himself. Maybe he wouldn't even follow through on his boastful offer. Maybe he would find a score of excuses if Nathan took him up on it. But he knew he was kidding himself. This fellow he met on the Bledsoe Trace escorting a wagon full of cotton; he was the real thing. He really would take this thing on for the hell of it. No rational reason would be sufficient; this man would never do it for profit—that would be too risky, plain bad business. The reason he would do it was because he was goddamn Marcel Lafarge. Nathan didn't know what drove the man but he had little doubt he'd be there come hell or high water.

When Nathan arrived at the garrison he found how quickly the army forgot their own. He was mere days from leaving his commission and they weren't even going to allow him in the HQ. But as it turned out, he didn't need to be there long anyway; a thin-lipped, self-important lieutenant deigned to extend the courtesy of informing him that Major Canby was dead.

"How, I mean where . . . I just heard in Vicksburg the man was here and there's been no action to speak of over the past few weeks. . . ."

"No, Mr. Parker. He wasn't in action. He tried to jump aboard a troop transport at the dock and fell in and drowned. It was an accident."

Accident? Nathan had forgotten that people still died who weren't in battle or prison. He absently patted the folded paper in his breast pocket. Possibly, just possibly it might come to using Marcel's offer—Nathan made sure the contact information for Marcel and the fellow in Tuscaloosa, Ishmael or some such, was safe.

As Nathan quietly made to leave the HQ he saw a list posted in a corner. The pane of glass it was under had been streaked from people anxiously running their fingers down the long list of names with the heading, CASUALTY NOTICES, OCTOBER/NOVEMBER 1864. Nathan ran his own finger down the list. He was about to turn away, then stopped and gazed at one name intently—he involuntarily took a deep breath. The import of the death in battle of this Federal soldier would take some time to sink in.

He wandered down a side street past a place called Cooper's Hideway. He stepped in and took a seat. Soon he was sipping down an ale as his mind absorbed the implications of what he had seen on the casualty list. Harmon Cantrell dead . . . unbelievable. Although it seemed logical that his own name should appear on one of those lists read by anxious hands throughout a war-torn nation, it seemed impossible that Harmon's should.

A parade of emotions marched through him. Darien, the woman

he had loved, was no longer married, she was . . . she was a widow. Nathan felt shame that a part of him undeniably sparked at the death of a good man. How could his time with Darien, so joyful, if illicit, end so sadly? When Darien Crosby married a friend of Dr. Holmes and became Mrs. Cantrell, it was no great surprise. She had been betrothed to Harmon Cantrell since childhood in an arranged marriage, the sort of which the rich were particularly fond. Harmon, almost forty, was a decent man but staid, with none of the soul fire of the young fixer who'd been taken in by Dr. Holmes. Nathan didn't sweep Darien off her feet; they both were unwitting prey to their own natures. Having innocently spent time together at Dr. Holmes's estate, they soon discovered a love that neither was prepared to cope with.

That other factors could prove so overwhelming had never occurred to her until it was too late. Nathan was bright, hardheaded, and difficult in many ways—but she found him also a passionate and attentive lover. Harmon traveled often, giving Darien plenty of time to let the immediate attraction she had to Nathan overwhelm her. Both lovers were in their early twenties with an intensity to their longing for each other that neither seemed capable of resisting. Then Darien was with child; when Sean was born the unspoken question for them both was who the father was. For almost four years, Nathan and Darien continued their trysts in starts and stops—sometimes both feeling too guilty to proceed. Except for her infidelity, Darien was a caring spouse to Harmon. Nathan's difficult choice to leave Boston, thereby removing the source of temptation, was the reason he was back in Michigan when the war broke out.

He agonized over his mug of ale. Would he pen a letter, no, he hadn't the time; he would send a telegram . . . one offering his condolences. On a small piece of cotton cloth that he found he could obtain cheaper than paper, he penned a short message. He expressed his condolences over Harmon's death. But the crisp formal wording also carried an unwritten statement—that he was alive and still cared for her. He dropped it at the telegraph office before heading off to conduct his business in Memphis. There would probably never be a response. But he had to do something or he would never have been able to think of anything else. Memphis absolutely bustled. There were Confederate deserters and anxious merchants, sensing the close of the war, who scrambled for positions of advantage in the new South. Others were Rebels to the bone and acted as if another quick turnaround by Lee would mean the capitulation of that drunken sot Grant and a negotiated peace. Everybody was an expert and everyone had an opinion. He climbed a rise near the outside of town.

From the rise he could see below him smudge pots being lit to run off the mosquitoes and gas lamps being lit to make sure they were attracted in the first place—nothing made sense anymore. He followed a road running south parallel to the river. When the light fell away from the sky and shadows lengthened, he decided to turn back. A small homely dog took after him and marched about six feet behind, as if trained.

"Hey, pal, how are you doing." The dog perked his ears but hardly looked up, just kept following.

To shorten his trek by a good half mile, Nathan took a shortcut through a field and came upon a couple of figures seated around a low fire. The last rays of light were tickling the rim of the horizon when he approached the two Negroes, a boy of ten or eleven and an older man. Whiffs of fish frying in an open pan made Nathan realize he was famished. He cleared his throat.

Startled, the youngster looked up at Nathan. "What's at?"

"Evening, didn't mean to scare you," Nathan said.

"What you want, mister? We ain't hurtin' nothin. Man what owns this place says it's awright to come here." The boy's nervous voice carried a tinge of hostility.

"Relax. I'm only passing by."

"Thass right, Jeeter, be polite." This from the old man, who had been leaning forward, poking the fire with a long stick. He sat back and studied Nathan for a moment, then jutted his chin toward a rock near the fire.

"Come set a spell, mister. Jeeter 'n me jus havin' some crappie 'n' cawn."

"Been fishing, eh?"

"Yessuh, that's the trufe, been fishin'. Jeeter, 'member yore manners and offer the man sumtin' eat."

Looking up at Nathan, Jeeter added, "You hongry, mistuh?"

But Nathan didn't think Jeeter was partial to giving up any of his hard-won crappie and cornmeal. "Thanks anyway, I've eaten, but maybe I'll sit a spell." Then Jeeter saw the dog.

"Hey, mister, you got a dog."

The hostility had vanished from the boy's voice.

"Yeah, this fella is a knight of the road, Sir Galahad is his name."

"He hongry? Can I holt 'im?"

"Yes, but be careful, he's used to nothing but the best." The boy began tending to him as if he were a thoroughbred. Sir Galahad was soon muzzle-deep in a black fist full of fried fish and cornmeal.

A steam whistle sounded and all three turned to follow the progress of a boat negotiating the river below the bluff. The riverboat seemed similar to the *Belle Marie* from this distance, maybe even bigger. There was an odd trail of little lights in front of the boat strung out toward the channel.

"That's funny, what are those lights in the water?" Nathan asked.

"Oh, them, they's lanterns" said the old man, "yessuh, that skiff up front, see it there? They strings out little candle-lamps floating on cork floats afront of the riverboat." Nathan watched the big steamer slowly bring its bow around to where someone in another skiff handed up one of the lanterns and got quickly out of the way. The huge riverboat began edging over the trail of minilanterns toward the safe waters of midchannel.

"Yessuh, 'eatin' up the lights' is what they call it, yep, they calls it eatin' up the lights."

Eating up the lights? What a curious scene it was. The monstrous craft did seem to be consuming one light after the other as it picked up enough steam to fight the stiffening current and head confidently into the channel. Nathan was stirred from his reverie by a question from the old man.

"You a soldier, ain't cha?"

"Was. How'd you know?"

"I'm old 'n black, mistuh, I ain' stupid. It's the way you walk an' wear yore clothes. I speck you were in the bad stuff, too."

Nathan was curious now. "And what makes you say that?"

"Ain't many men get that close and me not hear 'em, mistuh. You walks with yore feet kinda pushin on the groun, an' you was movin' the leaves aside wif the edge of yore boot afore you lit with yore heel. Only ones does that is injuns and woodsmen. You a hunter?"

"Yeah, I was for a while, but what's that got to do with 'bad stuff' and the army?"

"That's in yore eyes, mistuh, no disrespec' intended, now, none at all."

"But you couldn't see my eyes when I walked up."

"Didn't say I could see 'em. Jus' said it was in yore eyes, don' matter none ifs I can see 'em."

Nathan accepted a piece of fish from the old man and studied him closely as he returned to poking the stick in the fire.

"I suppose I did see some bad things . . . did 'em, too."

"Everybody been doin' bad things fo a while, mistuh. Ain' never seen nothin' like it. Whole world's gone crazy's what I think."

"But it must be better for you now since the emancipation and all."

"Heck, Ah been free a while, din' need no 'mancipatin,' but these times comin' now, I figger these here gonna be the wust."

"Why's that?"

"These Southern folk, the white 'uns are bad put. I mean they's hardly richer'n niggers anymore an' they got their pride hurt. Thass bad for everbody."

Nathan stared at the fire and nodded. He glanced at his host, encouraging him to continue.

"Yessuh, no offense to you, but already them Yankee fast-talkers comin' down here wit' dey own niggers and startin' to cause trouble. Dem and 'em copperheads. This river been Federal fo' a while an' they comin' now mo' an' mo'. War end an' it gonna be crazy."

Nathan was impressed by how well informed he was. He finished with his makeshift meal and rose to leave. "Thank you much, I'm beholden."

"You more than welcome, mistuh, an' take care of yourself now," said the old man. Then the man abruptly stopped poking the fire and fixed Nathan in a steady gaze. "'Nother thing, mistuh: you do know ain't none of us is to fault for all this? God is just settin' us all straight who's in charge."

Nathan contemplated that. And he thought about Marcel and his men in that damnable prison. He rose and said, "You two, take care."

"Hey, mister, yore dog!" yelled Jeeter.

"Dog? Oh, yeah. You know, he was telling me on the way here that he's about had it with wandering and was looking for a young man to care for him."

The boy's eyes widened in the glow of the fire. "You mean Galleyhat talks?"

"Not much. You have to spend time with him and listen careful."

The old man shook his head and laughed to himself. Jeeter petted Galleyhat with great fervor, to make sure he was treated well enough that he might talk. He smiled and half waved as Nathan departed.

Nathan trudged back toward the Fairmont. Beale Street seemed indifferent to the turmoil at the docks. In no mood for gaiety, he took a back alley to avoid the brunt of the sounds of music and laughter. Backstreet Memphis was bigger and more alive than Vicksburg. Passions were playing out in the rear of its establishments.

He passed silently in the shadows and noted, as he had seen in Boston and Atlanta in better days, that the action took a different form in the half-fenced yards behind the taverns. In one, some friends tried to talk two fellows out of a fight—their reluctance to disengage seemed feigned. In others, there were silent trysts between customers and ladies of the night. He stopped short when he realized he wasn't twenty feet from a couple he hadn't yet noticed. The sounds of casual sex were somehow comforting, as though it were a statement that life went on in spite of it all. Still, he was afraid he might be discovered and thought to be a Peeping Tom.

He was starting to slink off when he heard a woman's deep Southern accent admonish a customer to quit grabbing her head. Two steps away he looked back again. It was difficult to ignore such a spectacle. The man, an older Federal officer, was breathing hard, almost raspy. In the dim glow of a lantern, Nathan saw a surprisingly well-dressed woman on her knees in front of him, her head bobbing frantically. Each time she stopped it seemed the man would expire, but she was making it clear she was going to do things her way if it was going to happen at all.

"These have to come down all the way." She fumbled for a second with the man's trousers and soon had them down around his ankles.

"Lean back, mister. Leave your darn fingers off my bonnet and study the sky while I finish doing what's needing done."

The man complied. With his arms splayed against the wooden wall and agonized expression to the sky, Nathan thought he had a sort of bizarre, Christlike appearance. The woman renewed her efforts with her right hand and furious head-bobbing over the man's groin. Meanwhile, he noticed that her left hand was deftly feeling through the pockets of the trousers that were now draped at her knees. Nathan was intrigued—professionalism in any form always impressed him. The man moaned to the heavens and the cords stood out on his legs as he started to reach his conclusion, but that only gave the woman more leeway to be thorough. She removed a roll of bills and, to Nathan's astonishment, only peeled off three or four before sticking the roll back from whence it had come.

Then it was over. The spent fellow slumped down the wall to a sitting position as the prostitute straightened herself. She glanced around and looked right at Nathan. He started to recoil but held her stare until, apparently judging him as no source of threat, she went to surveying the alley behind him. She returned her attention to the man on the floor, who was struggling to his feet and, sure enough, patting his pocket to ensure he still had his fortune intact.

"How about a tip for a working girl, mister?" The officer reached in his pocket, pulled out a bill, and handed it to her before turning away to head back inside the tavern. The woman brushed past Nathan without a word. She had handsome features, a dress that had been expensive in better days, and a conservative bodice. On her head was what looked for all the world like a churchgoing bonnet. From what he could see in the dim light, her face was lined and a bit hard or maybe sad, but not without dignity. A quick whiff of stale perfume and fresh sex and she was gone in the shadows. Survival, Nathan thought—it was the ultimate art form among any species.

CHAPTER 16

23 December 1864–January 1865
Memphis and Annapolis

N athan sat back against an elm and watched the activity on the Memphis docks. He reflected over the past few weeks. Marcel would serve Nathan's purpose well by providing finances for the sword if the pen and pleading didn't work. It dispelled some of Nathan's desperation to know that his attempt to convince the Federal leaders wasn't his last chance. In a way he kind of missed Marcel when he wasn't around. Most of the people in Nathan's life for several hard years were people he had to take care of or who he took orders from. Marcel was neither. He seemed at times obsessed and at others a totally free spirit—he was a living paradox whose effect on Nathan was to breathe freshness into all life's routine affairs—nothing was routine in Marcel's world.

At times Nathan wondered about his own motives. The drive to get his men was overpowering. Dying in the process would be no help, yet he was sanguine about that prospect. Maybe it was because death was also a ticket to a certain kind of salvation. It had one great advantage over life—a release from responsibility. Death meant he would no longer have to carry on his shoulders the burden of knowing he was eating well and getting healthy while the young men who trusted him were gagging down maggot-ridden mush.

Just then a chill wind found him on the rise and pierced through his woolen overcoat—he knew how difficult it would be to avoid that icy-damp breeze at Camp Sumter. His soldiers would try to find warmth by clustering close in their cloth and wood shebangs and keeping coals burning when wood was available. Merry Christmas, lads. Various reports said the population of the prison was shrinking, but its death rate was climbing even higher than when he had escaped.

Nathan absentmindedly tossed a rock down the hill and rose, pulling his tunic in close about him. He swore the sunny South could feel even colder than Michigan sometimes—it was the damn wet that was laced all through the wind. Christmas Eve was tomorrow but he had no inclination to recognize it; there'd still be Christmases when his job was done. As he ambled toward the waterfront he counted the money Marcel had left with him—enough for passage both ways and then some. He said he would present Nathan with a sum equal to the task of raising a gang of renegades if, when he returned to Memphis, he had decided to take Marcel up on his offer.

Nathan figured he'd catch a riverboat to St. Louis and change for one plying to Pittsburgh. From there he'd probably go by rail to the Washington area. Grant was there and Nathan would seek an audience with him. Nathan had come to the conclusion that the only person who could actually make a release possible was the general himself. The Federal army wasn't like the Secessionists, who had a confederation of tribes called states; the Union forces had one leader, and his name was Ulysses.

From what he knew of the man through reputation, he was

gruff and tenacious but also a battle-hardened officer. He had little time for bureaucrats and kiss-asses but the one person who might have an effect on him was another battle-hardened officer who had been there and seen as many elephants as he had. There were very few officers imprisoned at Camp Sumter and certainly none that had escaped. If he could only get the man to fully appreciate the realities of the place and the horrors that could be mitigated through an exchange, even a specific one just for Camp Sumter . . . hell, Nathan didn't know what his chances were, but he had to try.

As he reached the docks he became more aware of the nature of the crowds. The number of entrepreneurs was already climbing. Christ, those sons of bitches really had carpetbags just like everybody said. He went to the office of the Pennsylvania and Tennessee Steamboat Company as busy men of means, often with a black freedman in tow, arrived in numbers that raised the prices of the rooms. The ticket-seller said there were problems on some portions of the run back east with flood damage and even some Rebel raids on the ships. Even though the next couple of voyages were booked, for a small consideration he'd slip him in. It made Nathan wonder how many others had been offered the same deal and how much past their weight limit these boats were running. Nathan declined and said to book him by next week. That would put him in Annapolis about January 7 or 8, when Grant was supposed to be there.

The week in Memphis went slowly but provided a temporary respite from the driving obsession that had been dominating his life. He had made his battle plan and would live by it. He smoked a cigar he had just purchased from a fellow at the livery. He didn't know why he'd done that, as he rarely smoked pipes or cigars. He was not really enjoying the taste, but the smell of tobacco and the ritual of blowing warm smoke out of his mouth was somehow soothing.

He sat in the hotel lobby where it was warm and he was lulled by the constant hum of busy, important men buzzing about their affairs. It provided a comfortable backdrop for his internal voyages. With his course set and decisions made, thoughts of Darien started breaking back into his consciousness. Harmon was dead . . . still hard to believe. Suddenly he was startled by a burning feeling in his finger—he didn't know how long he had been sitting there in a trance but the stogie had burned down an inch since he had drawn inside himself.

Embarrassed, he glanced around to see if anybody noticed but all were oblivious to anything but their own affairs. His thoughts had been of Darien, why, for God's sakes, he didn't know. She had been the source of stolen romance and she'd probably be only vaguely interested in his telegram if she had ever even received it. That ready smile, deep blue eyes, throaty laugh, and her ability to pull him up from the depths of self-absorption with a promising glance . . . all of it had been warm and wonderful . . . but wrong. And the three years that had passed since then left little room for anything but survival. Why was her memory forcing itself into his head, so strong, so clear? He took a deep breath and pushed it away.

Tonight was New Year's Eve. He would depart on January 3. They were on the cusp of 1865 and most people in Memphis, blue or gray, undoubtedly hoped the damn war would soon be over. Nathan stopped back at the hotel for drink. He sat by himself for a moment but his week of inactivity had made him restless. He rose from the parlor chair and looked about, trying to decide whether he should visit a party down at the docks when a fellow looking around the hotel crowd fixed on him, then came his way. What could this be about? He held an envelope in his hands. Marcel? Had Marcel already sent him a letter? He tipped the runner and stared at the small package. It had come from Washington—who did he know there?

On opening it he gasped. The handwriting—he knew it immediately; the high flourishes on the *t*s and *f*s and the smaller rolling script; it was a letter from Darien. And the paper, it smelled of woman. He returned it to its envelope, sat down heavily, and let it lay on his leg. There was no way he could open it here . . . he wasn't sure he could open it anyplace. He made his way to his room; any thoughts of the party at the docks were a distant memory.

He sat on the bed and stared at the envelope. Finally he worked up the courage to open it.

My Dearest Nathan,
May God help this missive find you.

I am so relieved to learn that you are well. The news of the capture of some of your company at Monocacy left me only with the hope that you had survived amongst the captives. But there has been no casualty list available from the battle and little word of any prisoners at Andersonville or Cahaba.

The death of Harmon at Darbytown has been most grievous to me and has weighed heavily on Sean. It weighed even heavier thinking you might have preceded him in death and learning, as we just did, that Dr. Holmes's son, Oliver Junior, returned wounded, made my worries for you all the more real. This war, this damnable war! I believe I would leave the South to its slavish ways before I would sacrifice so much life.

Beyond the joy of seeing a telegram from you rather than, God forbid, about you, comes the further surprise that you will be journeying east soon to see General Grant. As I write this I am on my way to Washington to reclaim Harmon's personals and to visit Auntie Ruth. If you find the general in Annapolis, is it possible I will be blessed to see you in the quick?

Oh, Nathan, this war is a horror, I only hope it will soon end. I find myself lifted from the world of grieving and launched to some dizzying conclusion by hearing from you. We have both strived to keep our honor in the wake of a passion that persisted despite all. Your parting for Michigan was a great blow for me, but I thought then a sign of your strength and righteousness.

There are two things I must tell you, Nathan, one that you

surely know and one that you surely don't. The first is that I love you and always have since the day we first met at the home of dear Dr. Holmes.

I wear black in mourning for my husband and I truly cared for him. But I have longed for you for almost three years now and I can hold back my words no longer. There, I have said it. But shameful as that may be I know it is probably of no great surprise.

The second thing is this. Nathan, you should know that Sean is yours.

I hope God may grant us some more moments together again, but if not, I am most joyous that He has spared you.

With Love,
Darien

Nathan read the letter several times. On the *Eastern Flower* from St. Louis to Pittsburgh, he kept reading it over and over again. He followed the news from papers he purchased at the steamer stops and returned at night to his letter. He had never found any communication so stirring, yet so unsettling. Harmon died in October at Darbytown, according to the casualty list he had seen in December in Memphis. Now she was collecting his things in Washington. The speed of Darien's reply was unnerving, no more than ten days. He still hadn't gotten used to the speed of communications these days—the war did result in some strange benefits.

As he boarded a train for Annapolis, he had to some degree taken back control of his senses. He was preparing for his meeting with Grant. He arrived at Annapolis Junction on January 10 and started the process for gaining access to the general. It was here that he learned the true meaning of patience. He expected it would take time, perhaps a day or two, but he found himself in hell for a week. He saw captains, even a colonel, and was treated with courtesy but still had no moments with the general, who was in constant meetings or gone on short trips. The only thing that gave him a prayer of an audience was that he was Captain Parker, U.S. Army, retired. Some of the general's underlings were brusque and others seemed truly sympathetic and he believed they meant it when they wished him luck.

On January 19 his patience was at an end. He heard from the office scuttlebutt that Fort Fischer had fallen in North Carolina and there was a stream of couriers bringing updated news of those events. Nathan had never been good at waiting. When he saw the general and his retinue leave an office at the far end of the hall and come his way, Nathan Parker did what he was known for doing—he took a measured risk.

"General," he said in a respectful but insistent tone, and not softly. Immediately a sergeant-at-arms in the outer vestibule said, "See here, sir. You've no cause to—"

Nathan turned to him sharply, feeling the flush rise in his face. "I'll be goddamned to hell if I have no cause. Three months at Andersonville is cause enough for any officer to have the courtesy of a hearing with his superiors."

A colonel in the company of the general walked up to Nathan and said, "As an officer and a gentleman you ought to know better than to cause a stir—"

"Shit and damnation to you . . . sir." There was no going back now and it was clear that he would either get his audience or be ejected from the building. It looked like it would be the latter as several guards came in at the sergeant's signal. But Grant stepped forward from the others and barked, "Enough, Sergeant. Let the man speak."

The scribes and accountants returned to their work, at least outwardly, as the leader of the Union forces walked over to Nathan and continued in a conversational tone. "Andersonville? You're Captain Parker who's been keeping vigil in the hall here for some days."

"Captain Parker, retired, sir." Nathan was surprised that Grant knew who he was and that he had been there for all this time.

"You headed Parker's Rangers, a feisty bunch from the Upper Peninsula of Michigan who even gave the Reb cavalry some worries."

Nathan was stunned at his level of knowledge.

"Your boys were 'mounted infantry,' whatever in the hell that is . . . but ballsy bastards all right, I'll give you that." The general rapped his hat against his fist a couple of times as if reflecting on something, then added, "All right, say your piece, Parker . . . and make it quick."

"I want my men freed from that hellhole."

Even the general blinked in surprise. "Well, I'll give it to you, that's quick."

"Seems you already know my purpose, sir, so no reason to draw this out."

A look of what Nathan could swear was sincere sadness passed over Grant's face for a second. He looked at the floor and responded, "Yes, I know what you're here for."

In the awkward silence that followed, Nathan looked past him at the covey of annoyed-looking officers, then back to the general. He said in a low, calm voice, "Sir, I know you've a great weight on your shoulders already, but I feel if you could know the impossible circumstances of these fine young soldiers, their suffering . . ."

Grant seemed to come to some internal conclusion and he had a harder look when he went back eye to eye with Nathan.

"Parker, I respect your looking out for your company, but I've got roughly a million men to worry about. I can't afford to be human, I've got to do what's needed."

"That's no excuse for turning your back on soldiers who could be helped without jeopardizing the others. It would not take a large force to free those men, particularly with me involved, who knows the system inside out. I could have my commission restored and—"

"A diversion for the sake of pity would leave me undermanned somewhere else. I'd be saddled with the care of thousands of men needing medical treatment along with repatriation. . . ."

Grant held back whatever else he was going to say and placed his hat on his head. He began pulling on his gloves in an agitated, I'm-through-with-this-nonsense demeanor. He looked Nathan straight in the eye and added, "Is that understood?"

Nathan held his stare. A realization was dawning on him. "That's it, General, isn't it? You aren't concerned about sparing enough men for a raid or having to exchange Rebs that you'd have to fight again . . . not anymore, you're not. This war is almost over."

Grant snorted and in a rare display of uncertainty he shrugged his shoulders, not in assent, but not in retort either.

Nathan continued, his own voice showing resigned understanding. "You don't want to be encumbered by thousands of soldiers needing medical assistance—you already know the extent of the misery at Camp Sumter then?"

"You can come to any conclusions you like, Captain . . . you've had your audience, now please, leave me to attend to this goddamn war." Grant said the last in parting and Nathan dropped his head as the general and his coterie began to leave. Nathan said nothing. He felt surges of anger and frustration but was speechless.

Grant turned back to him for one last comment. He was less harsh this time. "Parker, I'm no fool when it comes to judging men. I know you were a good soldier and not one to give up easily on a mission. You've done your job and you've been released from your duty, now give me a chance to finish mine. But mark my words—don't do anything to hurt the war effort to save a few men. I won't forgive that, Parker. I mean it."

"Yes, sir, we've both jobs to do and I haven't the intention or means to interfere with yours." Disregarding his lack of a uniform or commission, he saluted, and Grant returned it. The general silently regarded him for a moment, then walked out.

A colonel in the retinue who seemed particularly annoyed at Nathan's intrusion let the others pass him on their way outside. He advised Nathan that he had better act wisely and leave the general to his weighty affairs. "Believe me, your impertinence won't be tolerated a second time."

He was full of himself, this officer. And it seemed the Union army was becoming full of the likes of him. Young, brimming with importance, sails fully set to follow astern of the flagship that had just filled canvas on its way out the door. This type seemed common to the higher ranks of power near Washington—they were different from the veteran officers he had met in Vicksburg. The jaunty tilt of this fellow's hat, freshly returned to his well-groomed head, the smug expression. Nathan heard himself respond in a low voice to the officer; a response that came from somewhere deep inside him.

"Mister, don't you make the mistake of threatening me when I'm no longer under your authority. I've made my peace with the general and I respect him. But believe this, if you don't wipe that sneer off your face, I'm going to slap it off."

The colonel's visage deeply reddened. He turned and made full-ahead in the wake of the general's entourage.

Nathan breathed deeply and urged himself into a cooler state of mind. General Grant's words had saddened him, but the colonel's had enraged him. He knew it was partly his feeling of impotence to change things and the colonel had simply opened his mouth at the wrong time, and he shouldn't take out his anger on the wrong person. The office he had been occupying as a guest for a week was dead silent as he made his way out.

Nathan wandered to the hotel's dining room and ordered a coffee and overpriced breakfast. His heart ached but so did his belly; he needed to eat. Nathan asked the waiter to get him a piece of paper and a quill. The price of the paper astonished him—why so

much? It seemed the one thing the war ensured was high prices for
the basics of life.

In some strange way his ire was settling. No longer was he torn
over what he must do. All had come abundantly clear. He started
to compose a letter to Marcel Lafarge.

> Marcel,
>
> If you are reading this then my faith and trust in the U.S. Mails
> has been restored. As you have probably guessed

Nathan felt rather than saw her walk up to his table. The scent
of jasmine and hollyhock preceded her and it was like the last three
years were a dream. She was there like a feminine vision from a
different life, he felt it literally to his toes. When he rose he found
his tongue tied to the back of his throat. "Dary, I, my God, I . . ."

She placed her hand on his shoulder. "Sit, Nathan." She bent
over and pecked him on the cheek before sitting. For a public place,
that was as far as she could go for a lone woman wearing a mourning dress. But he felt her hand squeeze his knee as she sat. It was a
reassuring, strong touch.

"Your silence, you do remember me?" The teasing smile drew
him from his paralysis long enough to respond awkwardly.

"Of course, I, uh . . . good God, Darien."

"You weren't that hard to find, you know."

"I wasn't?"

The waiter came by and Nathan asked him to bring a bottle of
wine.

"No. I walked into the command vestibule two days ago looking for you. I saw you there grinding your teeth and . . . and well, I
knew that wasn't the time to talk to you."

Nathan drew a deep breath and composed himself. "Darien, I
don't know what to say. I, I mean your letter, there was so much in
it that . . ." He felt her take his hand again and squeeze.

"Nathan, calm yourself. I know you've been through much and I don't wish to increase your burden."

"No, I didn't mean that."

"I haven't but a moment. What I said in my letter is true, all of it."

"Yes, but there was so much."

Just then a young fellow walked up to them, looking to Nathan older than his eight years. Darien turned to him. "Sean, my sweet, how are you?"

"I was just looking for you, Mother. The carriage is ready and we should be leaving soon."

"Oh, yes, don't worry. But before we go I'd like you to meet Mr. Parker, do you remember him?"

"Hello, Sean."

The boy seemed to light up. "Oh, yes, from Boston. You helped Dr. Holmes, it's great to see you again, sir."

"That's a fine uniform, but you look a little young for the Army."

"The academy, sir. I'm hoping to be a cadet. It will be . . . some years before I can serve."

"Where would you like to take your education?"

Sean smiled, the origin of which was no mystery. He was definitely his mother's son.

"Well, perhaps VMI."

"VMI? But that's . . ."

"Yes, mother says our country will soon be one again and we will put away our differences. I think the Virginia Military Institute would be a fine place."

Nathan reflected a moment, then responded. "So it would, so it would."

Darien placed her hand on Sean's wrist. "And now you must get to the carriage and tell them I am coming."

The lad turned to Nathan, who offered him his hand. Sean

shook it firmly and said, "It was excellent seeing you, sir." And then he rushed off excitedly, his youth for a moment overcoming any military bearing.

"My God, Darien. You've a wonderful son, but why would I expect differently?"

Darien fixed him quietly with her gaze. Then she rose and kissed him, probably less than properly this time, given the glances in their direction from fellow diners.

Nathan rose also, in reaction to her apparent need for a sudden departure. "But wait, Dary, there are things I want you to explain. . . ."

She stepped up and leaned into him so that none but he could possibly hear her voice.

"Dear Nathan, listen well. There are signs women know when they are with child—neither you nor Harmon are aware of when I truly learned of my pregnancy. Suffice it to say that the tyranny of basic math is absolute—Sean was not a month premature, he was full term and, Nathan, Harmon was not in Cambridge when Sean was conceived. Only my mother and Nanny Rose and I knew."

She turned and was out the door in the blink of an eye.

The trip back to Memphis was as if time had stopped. Nathan's mind tumbled over a kaleidoscope of images—General Grant, Darien . . . Sean.

He would be back by February 3 or 4 and hoped to be gone for Tuscaloosa in less than a week. He rubbed a gloved finger along the windowsill in the stateroom and studied the dusty stain intently. Nathan was a father . . . of a son of a woman who loved him and who, for the first time in his life, might be attainable.

CHAPTER 17

February 1865
Memphis

N athan made his way to the hotel from the waterfront. He had been gone a little more than a month from Memphis, but so much had happened it seemed it had been a year. Although the recent revelations in his personal life could overwhelm a man in ordinary times, he wouldn't let them now. These weren't ordinary times and somehow what he'd learned made him feel even more compelled to wrest his men from the jaws of disease, starvation, and despair.

After all, his soldiers were the sons of other men and they were under his care. What would he think of an officer that didn't do all he could for Sean if he was in Andersonville? What would Sean think of him if he knew? This was absurd. He had met the boy and talked to him for a couple of minutes and now he was concerned whether he could live up to the lad's expectations? Harmon was the boy's father in all ways but the physical, and he must take care to remember that.

He forced his attention back on his divided nation and the little piece of the vast puzzle that was his to solve. His instincts told him that even worse than the purgatory of a war of secession would be the honeymoon in hell that would derive from the forced reconciliation. He only had to look at the greed-driven carpetbaggers around him to be convinced.

The riverboat he arrived on carried news of Sherman turning his demonic attention to the Carolinas. It was a move designed to hasten the crumbling of the Confederate war machine and seemed perfectly in line with Grant's cigar-chewing commitment to what needed to be done.

Lee was still holding out at Petersburg and Richmond and there were desperate last stands being taken around the South, but starvation and a breakdown of order were the rule below the Mason-Dixon.

This was the worst news possible for Nathan's men. CSA soldiers would have seen it as a matter of honor to maintain some semblance of propriety in the treatment of his men. It was the looming chaos that he feared more than anything else. The Southern states in disarray; most families missing loved ones, unaccounted for or worse; daily reports of atrocities against their brethren by Sherman, none of which was likely to ensure the well-being of enemy prisoners. Nathan was having increasing trouble reconciling the needs of a nation with the needs of its citizens; maybe that's why he was a captain and Grant was a general. There was no time to lose, he must head back to Andersonville.

Nathan pulled the crumpled piece of paper from his breast pocket. The name of Marcel's Hotel in Memphis was Monserrat. When he arrived at the desk of a very upscale hotel with blacks serving the same roles, as they always had, holding doors and carrying bags, he asked for Marcel Lafarge.

"Monsieur, you are Captain Nathan Parker."

"Well, retir—yes, I'm Nathan Parker."

"Mr. Lafarge has departed but he left a note should you show up." The man read it aloud. "Please pass this information to Captain Parker—I have received his cable from Annapolis; if he will be so kind as to proceed to Tuscaloosa, I will meet him there. Other players will be present as discussed who are eager to be dealt into our game. The package I have left is to be given only to Captain Parker, no surrogates. Then he signed it—'Santé, Marcel Lafarge.'"

As the concierge handed the package to Nathan, he further stated, "Monsieur Parker, as Marcel was leaving I spoke with him a bit about some of the latest rumors that have been passing through here and he asked for me to relay one of them to you as he thought it pertinent to your affairs."

"Rumors?" Nathan knew that anything that happened from New Orleans to St. Louis was passed with the speed of wagging tongues up and down the Mississippi. The Western Rivers channeled not only cargo and people but information. But of particular interest was what the concierge told him of the developments at a camp near Vicksburg. It was a parole camp set up through an informal deal between certain Rebel and Yankee officers.

Two officers, one Union and one Secessionist, seemed to be arranging what Nathan had often dreamed of—an accommodation of desperate prisoners at a time in the war when the weight of the greater good seemed to be crushing the souls of individuals. These men were forging a plan to get sick and starved men from hell to purgatory—a definite step up. Both were having trouble with their higher-ups—a plight to which Nathan could relate.

Nathan thanked the man for his help, handed him ten dollars in greenbacks, and carried his newly acquired package back to his hotel room. The package contained $3,500. As he expected, Marcel Lafarge was a man of his word.

Nathan's room became the preparation area for his foray to Camp Sumter. On the floor he had a new rifle with sixty rounds of ammunition. A Colt Whitney with the new rotating barrel and self-crimped cartridges lay next to it, along with a Navy .36 with a holster he could conceal under his pants leg.

The arms were in good shape but the money was a mess. The confusion with currency was getting exceedingly complicated as the war moved toward a close. In fact, the money was probably the earliest and surest indicator that the Secessionists' days were numbered. Bankers seemed to have a sixth sense for that sort of thing and hedged their bets ahead of the rest of the population. The new paper money being printed the last couple years by the Federal government, greenbacks they were called, was by far the most stable. Nathan sorted them out along with the rest of the currency he had picked up in his travels.

Nathan had seventy-two dollars in U.S. gold and silver coins in one pile. Then the $3,500, most of which he still had in greenbacks, but some of which he'd converted into state notes from the Bank of Chattanooga and treasury warrants from Arkansas. He also had some Confederate States of America currency printed by the Rebels from their capital in Richmond. He'd bought it cheap four or five weeks ago but it had already lost another two-thirds or so of its face value.

Nathan held an Alabama note up to the light in the window. There was something poignant about Secessionist money—the careful early attention to detail in the art and printing of the Confederate bills seemed to herald the ascendancy of an idea. Then the lessening of paper quality in the more recent print runs, and now bills printed only on one side. His plan was to conceal most of the greenbacks under his saddle in a canvas pouch and leave the state money, CSA dollars, and a few shinplasters as the currency he would deal with for most things while heading toward Georgia. Having too many greenbacks could be a giveaway that he wasn't Southern and he wasn't on his way home.

With the demands of the immediate addressed, Nathan's thoughts once more drifted back to his son. The prose in Darien's first letter proved even more portentous than he'd guessed. He recalled Sean's birth which he and everyone else had thought to be a month early. How withdrawn Darien had gotten at the time; how she and her midwife and mother had journeyed to Maryland for the first few months. The upshot of that turned out to be that he had a son.

But was Harmon oblivious to this condition? Did he know that his wife had slept with Nathan? Were there others? Did Harmon know Sean was the son of his wife's paramour? There were sufficient compelling questions to spark his imagination, but no time to seek answers.

As Nathan headed to the livery, he clutched his various monies and belongings. It occurred to him that he was actually a rich man for the first time in his life. Curious how unimportant that could be when there were matters of life and death to tend to. The fellow running the stable was a freedman. He squinted at the Confederate bills Nathan shuffled in front of him. But being this close to the river it looked like he wasn't going to settle for less than Federal green for the color of his money. That and silver and gold coins would do fine, he allowed.

Nathan selected a healthy, spirited-looking mare and an expensive used saddle. The latter wouldn't need breaking in and it had room to secure a hidden cloth bag without rubbing on the mare's flanks. He'd left his uniform top and anything that wasn't critically important in a bag for the concierge at Monserrat to keep for him. Although he still had new officer's pants that had been given to him in Vicksburg, he planned to dispose of them the first opportunity he had.

He mounted up, pointed the horse's muzzle southeast, and started out of Memphis. He figured he would be there mid-February and Marcel would meet him as planned. Why he was confident in that he didn't know. Marcel was unpredictable in many ways, but in some Nathan completely trusted him. If he wasn't there when he arrived, well, he'd deal with it. But for now Nathan was bent on making the acquaintance of one Israel Pennington and buying his services and that of as many others as he could convince to make a little trip to Andersonville. Everything he'd been hearing led him to believe that it was mainly inertia that kept his soldiers in Rebel hands. His conviction was that most militiamen would not be ready to die in the service of inertia or in order to keep control of a bunch of a few starving men. He'd soon find out.

CHAPTER 18

February 1865
On the way to Tuscaloosa

N athan, deep in thought, made his way on horseback toward Tuscaloosa. His pace was slow and deliberate, which suited both his mood and his new persona as a man of the cloth. Wearing the remnants of a Federal officer's uniform was out of the question with the chaos of war parting the social fabric of the South. The best he could come up with for neutrality was a minister's garb. He had been raised by reluctant Quakers and since most of the area he was passing through was wide-eyed Baptist of one flavor or another, he was more than a little uneasy.

It was becoming clear to most that the South was going to have to yell uncle sooner or later. Some of the grayback soldiers he saw weren't much better fed than the prisoners at Andersonville. Although some disciplined Southern units controlled wherever they were at the moment, as soon as they passed on, poorly led militias, deserters, and renegade gangs emerged from the woodwork. These outlaws fed voraciously on the uncertainty and community collapse around them. But one benefit of this growing chaos for Nathan was a decided lessening of travelers on the public roads.

Nathan's journey had taken some interesting turns. As the mare he'd bought in Memphis plodded on, he pondered his future. He ran his finger over the back of his head where a fresh scalp wound was still giving him a fair amount of discomfort. The horse had come easy, it was a straightforward transaction, but the black frock was something else.

He had seen some women washing the garment in a river eddy along with a bunch of other clothes just east of town. It struck him that it was the right thing for his travels. But his offer to buy it was refused and not very graciously at that. A middle-aged woman told him where he could stick his Yankee money no matter how much he offered.

Finally, frustration and a lack of time drove him to act. He jumped down from his horse and grabbed up the tunic. The damn horse, not yet used to him, had paced off several yards away, leaving him to be chased by the gaggle of women who commenced cursing like drunken sailors. He finally caught the nag and ducked as a cobble that could have killed him whizzed by his ear. Even drawing his weapon and shooting it in the air did little to slow the harpies. As he galloped unceremoniously off, a walnut-sized rock hit him in back of the head. Hours later it was still throbbing.

He mulled the course his life was taking. Here he was on a mission to free his men from a prison he felt was more dangerous than a battlefield. While he picked his way over a well-worn trail east toward the men in his unit, his unlikely partner Marcel was probably already headed downriver to join him. The weight of the pistol concealed in his waistband and another in the pocket of his frock were his only sources of comfort. More and more it seemed guns were the keys to his being. During the seemingly endless years of warfare they were tools of necessity, now they were . . . more.

Who was he becoming? Everything had changed. But one thing

was clear—wherever he went afterward, even if there was no afterward, he must see to his men. His parents, his friends, they seemed so distant—like poorly written characters in a play. The thought of Darien, who could smile through her eyes and make his heart soar at the sound of her voice, intruded briefly . . . of recent, maybe more than briefly.

He had taken to pushing away her ghost as quickly as he could. Memories of happier times had no place in the real world of today. But thoughts of Darien were suddenly much harder to ignore. After all, what was real? The brisk breeze was real, the burning feeling in his scalp was real, and his mission was real. Yes, his mission. Above all, that was real—he shook away the half-formed fantasies and concentrated on his quest.

Nathan's first stop was to be Israel's saloon in Tuscaloosa. Apparently Israel Pennington could be counted on to do what needed doing. If anyone could make that judgment about a man, it was Marcel. Where did his sympathies lie? He'd asked that about Pennington, and Marcel had answered, "With himself." The more he thought of that, the more it made sense. It never would have before. Nathan had felt honor to be as real as night and day; and men who sold themselves for gold were worse than whores.

But who was he turning to now? The army he had served so well? Prayer? The law? No, the only way to bring the young men of his command through the remaining days of this blood-soaked horror was with the help of hired guns, mercenaries, the very snakes he used to despise.

The horse rode well at a canter, but it was a struggle keeping her there. Ahead, he spied a group of riders, but because of his distracted flights of imagination he had no time to take cover before they passed him by. He would have to exchange greetings, which could be dangerous.

"Morning."

"Morning, Reverend."

He was passing by three men and their families. As he struggled to sound believable it started to dawn on him that these men were more nervous than he was. He politely dispensed hope for the cause and confidence in the Lord before asking where they were headed. But the men seemed defensive about where they were going.

He noticed wounds poorly bandaged on one man's hands; two fingers were gone and a series of boils traced up his arm under his sleeve. Nathan knew it wouldn't be long before the fellow was missing more than a few fingers. The quietest of the three riders kept back, one hand holding something beneath a blanket on the horse. The families were all in one wagon with two women and a passel of youngsters visible on the buckboard.

The irony of the situation almost brought him to tears. He realized the men were deserters. They were Rebs who . . . who what? Cared more about saving their families from a sinking ship than they cared about honor? Christ, he sensed they were just shy of shooting him, not for being a Yankee spy, but for being a real Southern minister who might have a big mouth.

Nathan ended the conversation. "Bless your children and the future of our land." He tipped his hat. "Fare thee well, pilgrims." As he rode off he kept expecting a bullet to plow its way through his back. He rounded a copse of trees and glanced back as nonchalantly as possible. The others were gone but the silent fellow was still watching him.

Please go on, mister. You saved your young 'uns from a bad memory, now save yourself. Nathan had his pistol in his hand now and knew he'd have the advantage if the fellow decided he'd rather be safe than sorry about potential informers. A few moments later he glanced back again and the man was gone.

He was just letting out a long sigh of relief when he heard more horses. It was a company of Alabama regulars with a few Mississippi butternuts rolled in. They hardly noticed him as he pulled off the road to let them by.

And so it went. Almost a full week's ride to Tuscaloosa but most of it uneventful.

There were occasions he had plenty of warning from hoofbeats and voices that people were coming and he would make a toilet stop, with his back purposefully to the riders. On others, he seemed to be no stranger or more anxious for privacy than were his fellow travelers.

No one seemed to react to his faux Southern drawl. Whether he used it or not seemed to make little difference. Southerners were preoccupied with the course of the rest of their lives right now; not the nature of strangers' accents. Since he first fled from Andersonville he had noticed a growing change in the South. A sense of waiting for the next shoe combined with a certain restlessness. Everything that was a given four years earlier was now open to question.

It seemed the women were less protective of their virtue and more open to invitation from the victors. He'd heard a Southern man complain of it and Nathan believed he was right. The losers were simply less attractive and their women's legs more open to the conquering males—this, for some reason, Nathan found very unsettling. It was hard to accept such pragmatism driving fidelity no matter who was winning.

As Nathan rounded a bend in the outskirts of Tuscaloosa, he became aware of a commotion in the thick brush off to the side of the road. He reined in his mount and quietly looked and listened. To his right he could make out the shape of a Conestoga-style covered wagon that had pulled off into the trees.

He could hear clearly a distressed female voice telling someone to "Keep back."

Nathan loosened the .44 in its holster under his frock and edged closer to the wagon. He heard a man's voice, thick with a Louisiana drawl, telling the frightened woman to "Shet yerself up." Casting a glance over his shoulder to check for others, Nathan saw no

one. Barring the yelling that had caught his attention, it was unlikely anyone on the road would be attracted to the spot. He considered for a moment that whatever was going on back there was
none of his damn business and he'd almost turned away when he
heard another frightened voice. It too was female but more
low-pitched and came from inside the wagon. It was followed by
the wail of a child, a loud slap, then silence.

Nathan could hold himself back no longer. He rode directly to
the clearing behind the trees and pealed out loudly, "Mornin' folks,
y'all need any help back here?" A hard-looking fellow pushed himself away from the wagon wheel against which he had been pressing
a woman—one who seemed less than interested in his attentions.
His mouth dropped open and his eyes scoured the ground looking
for something. Nathan saw several feet behind the man a heavy
belt, which held a holstered pistol as well as a large blade. It looked
like it had been hastily tossed aside when other things absorbed the
fellow's attention. As he took a tentative step toward the gun, Nathan drew his own weapon and suggested, "Hold it right there."

The fellow was tall, with short hair and mustache but no beard.
He was one of a multitude of cold-looking bastards roaming the
countryside these days—although something about him was somehow familiar.

A fellow causing the commotion inside the wagon suddenly
pushed aside a canvas curtain and stared out at Nathan. He cast a
ridiculous figure naked from the waist down with his pendulous
sex quickly losing its perch. Ridiculous to Nathan perhaps, but
menacing enough to the black woman he had been raping. She
quickly pulled her skirts over her nakedness and cast a look behind
her where a very frightened white girl maybe eight or nine was
huddled in a corner.

Romeo wore a black weskit made of what appeared to be some
sort of velvet. He was dark-skinned and lanky with shifty eyes that
flicked from side to side as he leaned out of the wagon to measure

the situation. Before Nathan could act, the Negress lashed out viciously from her supine position with her foot. She kicked the man headfirst out of the wagon where he almost hit Nathan's horse as he tumbled to the ground. She then turned her attention back to the little girl, crawling to her over boxes. Nathan tried to collect his wits—both men were staring at him, both caught unawares, one literally with his pants down.

"Mister!" screamed the white woman. "Please, these 'uns saw us resting here and acted like they was gentlemen 'til they seen we have no menfolk with us."

Nathan was stumped. Now what? He was in the middle of something he didn't want to be just outside a town where he wanted to draw no attention. The fellow who had been kicked to the ground raised himself up and pointed at Nathan.

"Reverend, you better think on what you're getting into. We was just riding by and these two offered us something they just decided to take back."

"Yeah," the first fellow added. "Rene's right, they was hot for it and the lady here said we could have some of the nigger girl afore you came up."

"Damn yore eyes, Ah did not! You're just like the rest of the yaller scum around here who didn't have the sacks to fight for our ways against the Yankees."

Nathan couldn't deal with this. He had to get them on their way before they attracted passersby from the road. He turned to the black woman and asked if the men had hurt her. She had grabbed up the little white girl and was comforting her, the girl's face buried in her ample bosom.

"Ah cut 'im if Ah get the chance."

"That's not what I asked. Were you forced? Did anyone say you had to do that? Did the missus?" To Nathan's surprise, the woman closed up tight and looked away. Nathan glanced at the white woman in disbelief.

She gave an annoyed eye roll and explained, as if to a child, "Yeah, I told Jenny to give 'em some. We're in bad need of money and they said they'd pay for a taste a chocolate . . . but it didn't give 'em no right to mess with a white woman."

"You mean . . ."

"And then, that crazy bastard jumped in there and started taking her in front of Maya."

"See, Preacher?" The fellow called Rene grabbed up his trousers, which took him closer to his gun.

"Sweet Jesus, don't you move a goddamn inch." Nathan was half a mind to shoot all of them. He pulled back the hammer of the .44 and quickly gave them an ultimatum.

"Now look, all of you, listen hard 'cause my patience is about spent. First, you ladies get the hell out of here and—" He realized he needed to know more before he gave his marching orders. "But first, tell me where are you going?"

"We going west," said the white woman.

"Okay, do it. Quick. Meanwhile, you two, get yourselves together and stay right there til they're gone. And you're going into Tuscaloosa whether you like it or not."

"That's fair enough, we're heading there anyway."

Nathan motioned to the women to hurry and then turned his attention to the men. As the man called Rene pulled on his trousers Nathan asked him, "Where you from?"

"Vicksburg, Reverend. We was just getting a little taste from the black and the missus here started looking like she wanted some and—"

"Vicksburg? That's a funny place to be coming from since it's in Yankee hands."

The first man took over for Rene. "Look, we're working for the CSA, we been sent here to help with—"

"Sent by who?"

"Sent by Mr., eh, by Colonel Marcel Lafarge."

Nathan let out a long sigh as the women hurriedly made their way off and the men looked up at him expectantly. He dropped his attempt at a drawl and when the women were finally gone he said to the two of them in unvarnished Yankee, "Colonel Lafarge, eh? You're some of the fine gentlemen he sent here to help a certain Yankee, aren't you?"

"Well, uh, how'd you know?"

Nathan looked down at the ground, took a breath, and holstered his weapon. "You can pick up your toys, fellas, but before you get any ideas, you shoot me and you're shooting your paymaster."

The man who had been struggling with his pants looked up with a surprised expression and blurted, "You're Captain Parker?"

"That I am. And I expect you're the very Clete Wilson I met one evening on a Mississippi steamer in the company of the redoubtable Mr. Lafarge."

"Well, now, that's somethin', ain't it? Looks like we're on the same side."

Nathan glowered down on the two of them. "We're not on the same side, I'm hiring you for a job. After that you can both hold hands in hell for all I care."

Nathan turned from the two and urged his horse toward town. He spat over his shoulder and muttered, "You men come into town when you're ready. But don't come around the boys at Israel Pennington's place 'til tomorrow night."

As he entered a large mudflat on the approach to town he forged through the worst of it until he could become lost in the crowds. In a half hour's time he was at the doors of a place called Israel's Saloon. His nose told him that this whole end of town could have used the help of the Union's newly created Sanitary Commission. But the saloon was cleaner than most of the area's establishments. It felt lively and strangely inviting as he entered.

"How can I help you, Reverend? Most folks hereabouts aren't

lookin' to have their souls saved; seems it would be a sorry waste of holiness."

"I'd like a drink of whiskey and the pleasure of Mr. Israel Pennington's company."

Surprise and curiosity pushed up the barkeep's eyebrows. "Well, you make yourself comfortable and I'll see about rousing Mr. Pennington."

Within moments Nathan felt, rather than heard, the presence of men surrounding him.

Then "Good day" from the shrill voice of an odd-looking fellow. He had a patch of hair in the middle of his bald spot and a surprisingly thick spread of hair down the sides of his head. Nathan noticed two men had sidled up next to him at the bar. Apparently Mr. Pennington didn't even have trust in men of the Lord.

"I understand you're looking for me, Preacher. How can I be of help?"

"I was referred to you by a friend of yours, Mr. Marcel Lafarge."

"Marcel? I know he's given to quoting the good book at some of the oddest moments but I never figured him for a religious man."

"Mr. Pennington, as I think you've surmised, I'm no more a minister than is General Grant and my trade runs not to the saving of souls but more to releasing them from their mortal husk . . . the times, you know."

Israel let a grin play across his face. "The Lord's got some hard eggs going around selling his word."

"If we might sit down and discuss the matter I'd be most grateful," Nathan added. "And the gentleman who keeps nudging my back looking for weapons will also get to sit down without having to remove my foot from his arse."

At that, Pennington and his entourage broke into laughter.

Israel glanced at the barkeep and motioned for him to bring a bottle to a nearby table. The man who had been nudging Nathan slipped over and said something to a group of men at the table. They got up and obediently moved away.

"After you, Reverend."

"Thank you, sir."

"By the way, *do* you have a gun?"

"Of course." Nathan thought it a minor sin of omission that he didn't mention the second one.

Although four men sat at the table, only Nathan and Israel did the talking.

"Mr. Pennington, times are changing, as we all know. The Confederacy has fought a noble fight but the fortunes of war and the weight of Northern industry are bringing the whole mad mess to a close." As he spoke, Nathan removed the folded piece of paper from Marcel and placed it on the table.

Israel let the paper sit in front of him and remarked with a half smile, "There's people around here as might disagree with you."

Nathan shrugged. "Might be, but I don't think you're one of them. The carpetbaggers and scalawags are already heading this way. They're looking for a new dance step . . . and it probably isn't going to be the Virginia reel."

Israel unfolded the note of introduction and read it, then looked up at Nathan. "What is it you want of me and my humble associates?"

"Marcel assured me that you gentlemen would be willing to assist me in making my way to Camp Sumter and doing what has to be done to free my men. As I'm sure you've gathered, I'm a former Union officer."

"Free your men?" Israel looked genuinely surprised. "I thought they were releasing most of those Yankee prisoners 'cause they couldn't take care of 'em."

"I've heard those things too, but there's really no telling. Information coming out of places like Andersonville isn't known for its accuracy."

Israel stared at him for a long minute. "What's all that got to do with me? Why do you think I can help?"

"Because you're unscrupulous. No offense, it's an understandable way to be these days."

Israel kept his gaze but remained quiet.

"Marcel has great faith in your contacts, your abilities, and your ruthlessness. It sounds like an excellent combination of virtues to deal with my problem."

"And what's in it for us?"

"Money, lots of it."

Israel looked around at his associates, who reflected his interested but cautious expression. He ran two fingers absently over the bald patches on his head. "You say Marcel is coming here, too?"

Nathan nodded. "I'm not asking you to take any risks before you have a significant down payment. He should be here later today."

"We'll wait to talk to him. If you can back what you say, we might be interested."

Nathan rose, bowed to Israel Pennington, and excused himself. He wandered about and found himself a place to eat. The town was a scary place; formerly home to magnolia blossoms, sweet music from citizen bands, and the scent of faux shy Southern belles, it was now as businesslike as New York with a mean undertone.

A woman approached him and asked if he needed some comforting. He wasn't sure about comfort, but he damn well needed a woman. After a few moments' hesitation and stalling, Nathan for the first time in his life paid for female favors. By that night he returned to Israel's saloon. He was calmer and his hands had stopped shaking but the encounter with the woman had only made him sad. It wasn't that their coupling was bad, she was attractive under it all and serviced him well, but somehow it brought him low.

Those few moments with Darien in Annapolis had changed his world in many respects.

When he walked in, again he asked for Israel. One of his former tablemates approached him and said that they had yet to see Marcel.

"That's no bother," remarked Nathan. "When Marcel decides to appear he'll make waiting worth your while." The fellow looked skeptical but Nathan didn't give a damn about his opinions. He retired early to a room he rented on the second floor of the establishment and fell quickly asleep.

The next day went much like the first in Tuscaloosa. Nathan drank and waited, but didn't take part in the doings of the brothel. That sort of comforting wasn't what he needed. As evening fell, Israel Pennington approached him.

"Seems as if our mutual friend is mighty late. It'd be a shame if he didn't show as I've gathered a group of gents that would probably suit your purpose . . . although they're not the patient type."

Nathan glanced over toward the bar. The group was getting restless and well into their cups.

"My apologies for any delay, Mr. Pennington. I'm sure Marcel will be here directly." Israel shrugged, patted Nathan on the shoulder and walked off.

Nathan was becoming concerned. He had no doubt that Marcel would be there in due course, but he didn't want to lose track of the group that was starting to gather at Israel's call. He went down the street and found his Union dollars gladly accepted for a nice steak. Close to midnight he returned to the saloon. Still no Marcel.

As Nathan sat down and began nursing a drink, a couple of fellows pretty far gone in their spirits approached him. A tall individual with mean eyes sat next to him with a bright-bladed Arkansas toothpick, a bowie knife, extending from his waistband. His associate was heavyset and hard-looking but with a slightly brighter expression. The heavy fellow asked Nathan if he mighta been deserted by his good friend and was going to be stuck with the holding fee if he didn't show.

Nathan waved to the barkeep and motioned for him to leave the bottle. "Holding fee?" He felt that cold darkness creeping over him. Thugs, bullies; they always insinuated themselves in situations where order was breaking down. He thought of Gaston and the New Yaarkers at Andersonville.

"Now, didn't Israel tell you about that?" The man went on. "Holding fees can cost quite a bit when professionals have to wait at their own expense."

"No, I guess he didn't." Nathan poured himself another drink and gestured toward the men, asking if they wanted their glasses filled.

"Don't mind if we do," said Mean Eyes. Nathan filled the man's glass and motioned to his heavyset friend that he'd like to also fill his. As the man leaned forward with the glass, Nathan slid his grip thumb-down over the neck of the bottle, lifted it, and smashed it across his face. Heavyset spun backward into a heap. The bottle remained unbroken in Nathan's hand. But Mean Eyes never looked at it; he sat still as death and seemed more concerned about the cocked .44 pressed into his cheek from Nathan's left hand. The man was hardly visible to Nathan through the angry red haze that blurred his vision.

The saloon went silent. All fixed their attention on Nathan and the thin man whose color had drained from his face and whose eyes seemed somewhat less mean. Their attention was only slightly diverted by the heavy man groaning over his broken teeth and bloodied nose in the corner.

Then Nathan noticed something curious. Mean Eyes had a second gun pressed into his temple from behind him . . . a derringer. It was Marcel.

"Lord Amighty, Cap'n Parker, you've a terrible temper for an officer and a gentleman." Marcel Lafarge sat next to the thin, and now very nervous, collector of holding fees. He smiled broadly at him and slapped him on the back before returning the derringer to his tunic. In the corner, the heavier man was being helped to his feet by some of Israel's sidekicks. Marcel gestured to Nathan to be generous with his bottle and fill his own and Mean Eyes's glasses. Nathan obliged after also returning his own pistol to his frock but their skinny guest seemed to have lost his thirst for whiskey and good fellowship. He rose slowly, keeping his hands far from his bowie knife, and quietly left. Israel Pennington took the empty chair and showed he was far from squeamish when it came to drinking from another man's glass.

"Good to see you, Marcel, we've been trying to keep your friend here entertained as we waited. He was worried you wouldn't show even though we tried to reassure him. I think he took a bit of umbrage to some of the fellas wanting to charge him a fee for wait-ing." Israel winked at Nathan, who sighed and poured himself yet another drink.

CHAPTER 19

February 1865
Tuscaloosa, Alabama

A fter a night of heavy drinking, Marcel's head throbbed as he tried to align his thoughts. He knew he must be in a hotel room, but to save his life he couldn't remember where. Peeling wallpaper hung in random strips. As he moved his head carefully toward the light he could see through the grime of the glass window and a suspended sign—ISRAEL'S. Thoughts of the previous night returned. The usual morning-after regrets of too much drink were accompanied by a pressing need for hot coffee.

When he tried to raise his head it felt as if a crown of thorns strapped to his forehead had been tied to the bedsprings. So much for Pennington's cheap corn liquor. As his senses began to displace his lethargy, Marcel's thoughts rearranged into some semblance of rational order. He took a moment to reappraise his preparations before heading to join Nathan.

Marcel had purchased a mare and a young gelding at the Morris stable in Bovina just east of Vicksburg. He bought a used

Confederate States' saddle, military holster, pistol, and two duffle bags, which he strapped to the back of the mare. He traded his black wool trousers and white shirt for the delighted stable master's gray-striped army pants and suspenders along with a tattered cavalry hat and belt with CSA buckle. A faded red color-less shirt completed the package. All in all, he looked much like a mustered-out Confederate soldier on his way home.

Marcel went to the sink and spent several minutes throwing water in his face and changing his shirt and underclothes before deciding to venture out into the world beyond the privacy of his hotel room.

★

THE SUN WAS high in the late morning as Nathan joined Marcel and Israel at a table by the window of the saloon.

"Morning, Lafarge, Pennington. Any chance of coffee here-abouts?"

Pennington gestured toward the bar. "Coffee on the stove, be-hind the counter."

Marcel could tell that Nathan was also under the weather. "Would you like a drink, Parker? Nothing like starting early."

"I'll never touch another drop of liquor as long as—" Nathan paused. "Well, maybe never is too long a spell. Let's just say not in the near future . . . by the way, any luck in recruitment?"

Marcel gestured for Nathan to sit. "We have two fellows com-mitted to our endeavor so far. Israel assures me that a couple of brothers he knows and maybe their father will accompany us. I think the plan should be a small group that can move quickly as one, rather than a big mob who might pose a discipline problem. There's a small town about twenty-five miles east on the Cahaba River—Centreville— where we can maybe pick up a couple other boys Pennington knows." Marcel noticed Nathan hadn't raised his head from his coffee. "We can pack out of here within the hour. That is, if your infirm body will allow it."

Nathan's red eyes met Marcel's. "I know that you're always half joking, and I appreciate that, but as far as my infirmity is concerned, hangover or not I'll outride your Rebel ass 'til hell wouldn't have it—I'll get packed."

Marcel and Pennington glanced at each other as Nathan stopped his painful climb up the stairs.

"Israel, I think we should follow suit, don't you?"

He nodded and went up the stairs to his room.

Marcel rose and then counted out loud. "We've got Israel and his two, plus Clete and Sangnoir; that's five aside from us."

"Yes, I recently had the pleasure of renewing acquaintance with those two gentlemen," replied Nathan.

Marcel gave Nathan a puzzled look but rather than distract from his count to ask about their meeting, he continued on. "Then, Sangnoir sent a group of rather scruffy individuals east from Vicksburg to meet us north of Camp Sumter . . . and, I must say, Captain, I think that bunch will be mostly deserters and renegades. I mean, you do understand that we aren't talking soldiers or even militia here? These are generally murderous rogues; not much better then the sort as runs with Quantrill."

Nathan noticed Marcel cut his eyes at him a couple of times as he spoke. He had to be weighing whether or not Nathan was accepting of the quality of the force he was assembling. In truth, Nathan wasn't sure; Marcel was right to ask. He'd been comfortable leading his Union soldiers and knew he was pretty damn good at it. But those men were farmers, chandlers, apprentice printers, and carpenters; the sort of people he respected as fellow citizens. The scoundrels he'd dealt with in the bar the night before, the likes of Wilson and Sangnoir; that was different. These men were mercenaries. Their fidelity was bought and owed nothing to patriotism or honor.

Well, he reflected, at least losing them in combat might not be as devastating.

Over the past few months Nathan had heard more and more of Southern soldiers breaking away from the CSA and the state militias to run with malcontents and ordinary criminals. These were men not inclined to accept the discomforts or shame of living in the homeland of a defeated cause. Such were the likes of Quantrill and his men, as Marcel had said. They were a seedy crowd, but he had no other option—he had to either accept the notion of "men" his friend had in mind or stop it all now. He addressed Marcel.

"I suspect that choirboys aren't the type of men we're looking for, my friend. I know that righteous folk wouldn't approve but I'll be damned if there's a lot of them lining up to volunteer to help me."

Marcel kept his peace, he knew Nathan was still weighing it all. Then Nathan added with finality, "I appreciate your efforts on my behalf, Marcel. But understand this, if these recruits get out of hand, or if they forget that accomplishing the mission is the only way they get paid, they're going to wish their Southern brothers had hung them for desertion."

"Fair enough," said Marcel. Then he returned to his count. "So, that gives us seven, counting all of us here, and Israel knows about four or five more recruits along the way to Camp Sumter. So, figuring Sangnoir probably sent six to twelve on their way to meet us in Georgia, we'll number somewhere around eighteen to twenty-four when we're set to raid the fort."

"That'll be enough," Nathan said. "We'll win this by being wily and motivated—our bunch has greed on their side and that's more than those militia boys can count on now. If the garrison ever got themselves together to really fight us off in a disciplined way, we'd never succeed, but given the situation . . . I think we'll have enough."

"One other thing I've been considering." Marcel kicked absently at the ground. "None of these boys really know that area over in Georgia. We're going to need a scout or somebody who knows the lay of the place."

"True, anyone in mind?"

"Actually, I do. I was talking with Israel here and he says we should try Freemarket Street, Gosset's corner or some such. There's some local boys there that really know the countryside—scouts, traveling hagglers, and slave-wranglers and the like."

Israel nodded his agreement.

A few minutes later the three of them ambled their horses into the center of Tuscaloosa and stopped at a place with a big sign above it that read GOSSET'S. But the sign never explained what Gosset's was. It seemed a cross between a livery and an outfitter. It was also one of the few places in town that seemed to show little wear from the war.

Among the crowd examining horses and talking were a couple of black men. Nathan watched them chatting and sharing a bottle when suddenly he felt his heart jump into his throat. He knew one of these men. The fellow was still distracted by another's talk but was slowly walking his way. Nathan leaned down from his horse and muttered toward the back of the fellow's head when he passed.

"Damn if it isn't Nightshade."

The colored man wheeled around and stared at Nathan for a long moment.

"Well, bless me for a fool; damn if it ain't the Georgia sarge. An' you can drop that nightshade talk, I got a name."

"What is it? Oh, wait, I remember, Tobias . . . Jodie Tobias."

"I go by Joe, Sergeant, but you can call me Mr. Toby."

Marcel was nonplussed at first, but then he fired, "You got a helluva mouth on ya, talking that way to a white man . . . what are ya? A freedman?"

"I already tole ya, guvner, I'm Mr. Toby. You gentlemen want something from me or don't ya?"

Israel muttered under his breath, "Uppity, but he knows the direction you're going as well as anybody within a hundred miles."

"I'm not interested in that fellow, no matter what he knows." Nathan didn't know why he disliked the black man so much; he knew he shouldn't let it stand in the way of his mission but he couldn't help it.

"Suit yerself."

Marcel seemed unsettled with Nathan's quick dismissal of the Negro. Israel looked as if he might feel the same way. But all Nathan could think of was the cruelty the man had dealt out to one of his own kind.

"He's from right back that way, Nathan," Marcel observed. "He'll really know the country, being a slave-wrangler. How in the hell do you know him, anyway?"

"Had the pleasure of meeting him on my stroll west from Andersonville. He's a cold, bloodthirsty son of a black bitch."

Marcel blinked at Nathan's language; it was the first he'd ever heard him talk that way. "Look, my holier-than-thou friend, he's got as least as much reason to be cold-blooded as you do. You said yourself we ain't looking for altar boys."

Nathan watched Joe Toby move down the street negotiating some sort of deal with a white man. He recalled how self-confident the man seemed in Georgia and how the white militia boys even seemed to have respect for him. It sickened him but he must play the hand he was given. He turned to Marcel and Israel and nodded in resignation. Marcel looked at Israel and signaled him to catch up to Toby and see what could be worked out.

The sun was very high by the time the men and their horses moved away from Israel's saloon. They forded the Black Warrior River south of town, taking a country lane since the main road with the bridge seemed to have an unusual number of riders. They were aware of a large fire burning somewhere near the center of town.

Nathan looked back several times toward town, where dense smoke had spread out over the western sky. Marcel sensed he was troubled. "Something going on back there. Thought I heard reports from a Spencer."

The rest of the afternoon, Marcel remained quiet, thinking that Nathan was best left alone. He dropped back to the end of the procession of their horses on the rutted road. Behind them, he could hear a group of riders approaching hard. Marcel noticed the cavalry comprised young boys aged fifteen to sixteen years. They numbered about twenty in crisp uniforms but several of the boys were spattered in blood. Carrying outdated muskets, they were led by an older man who seemed unsure of himself. Marcel and his group pulled up to let them pass. Only minutes later, several more horsemen came past but at a much slower pace—white-faced and frightened, their horses exhausted.

"Sergeant, are you all right?" called out Marcel. "What happened?"

A young boy with three stripes on his sleeve turned to Marcel as they passed. Marcel saw a face reddened by tears, his eyes seeming to dart in fear.

"Commandant Murfee ordered us to retreat." The boy's feet were out of the stirrups; his dangling legs gave him a rag doll posture. "Bastard Yankees burned it down. The university, they just flat burned it, we couldn't do nothing. . . ." He looked at the musket frozen in his hand and shook it free, dropping it in the ditch. Gathering himself and his two companions, he trotted off.

Marcel could see Nathan was troubled by the entourage of youngsters who had passed. They rested by the side of the road, Nathan never taking his eyes from the musket lying in the ditch. Finally, he looped his right leg over the saddle horn and eased off the mare. Marcel saw him crouch down, examining the musket—turning it over, loosening the ramrod, sighting down the barrel.

"I don't know what I think of this."

"It's only a musket, an outdated one at that." Marcel slid off his horse and joined Nathan.

"Devastating to see this kind of courage." Nathan shook the dirt from the tarnished weapon. "The frustration that must be—"

"Coming from a former Federalist and devout Yankee, I'm surprised you care, Captain." Marcel walked back to his horse, which had started eating the grass along the side of the road.

Nathan didn't answer, but mounted up after strapping the weapon onto his packhorse.

It was but ten minutes when once again the sound of troops could be heard coming up the pike. The three men stepped their horses off the road and waited. This time the young soldiers marched on foot in quickstep, two and three abreast. Exhausted, many of them labored to keep up. Carrying packs of various shapes, their attire seemed to be a replica of a Confederate officer's dress uniform. They were a disheveled lot.

"Honor thy name, oh, men of the South, honor thy country's name," Israel called out in song to them. "Carry our flag, oh, men of the South. . . ."

Soon, the young soldiers picked up Israel's theme and began in unison. "Courage thy name, lead us to fame, carry our flag on high." The young troops seemed buoyed by their battalion song and picked up their step, disappearing down the road in the dust cloud of their own making.

The men watched the sad departure.

"They're from the university cadet corps. Poor little bastards." Israel looked back at the burning city with concern. Marcel, Israel, and Nathan watched the smoke billowing above Tuscaloosa. The dark clouds shut out the sun and in the dim light the three riders continued east toward Centreville.

CHAPTER 20

February 1865

Marcel, Nathan, and the two riverboat gamblers enjoyed an uneasy peace while waiting at an orchard for Israel, who had ridden into the hills overlooking the Cahaba River. "Back in less than an hour!" he had shouted, his bald pate shining in the sun.

"We are a feeble little band of raiders, eh, Cap'n?" Marcel found Nathan's gaze hard to read.

"I guess I'll have to take credit for our lack of troops, Lafarge. My hammering that lout yesterday in the saloon was the liquor talking. I let it get the best of me and we lost two men."

"But look on the bright side, Captain. We've gained two stalwart lads from the mighty Mississippi and a black who would just as soon slit your throat as look at you. My man, you can't tell when their particulars might come in handy."

Nathan glanced at Mr. Toby, asleep on his horse, then to Wilson and Sangnoir, who had drifted several hundred feet down the dusty road. "I think describing those two as 'stalwart' would be a stretch of the King's English."

Marcel quickly added, "As for the two in the saloon, I'm not too sure that wasn't providential in the end, Nathan. *Baudets* like that would sooner or later be trouble, best you took care of them sooner. Speaking of Providence, we may have been extremely lucky getting out of Tusca when we did. Sounds like your Yankee friends raided the town."

Head down, Nathan whispered, "Sounds like, indeed."

Israel returned with four men, three of them on horseback and the fourth, a black man on a mule without a saddle. "Lafarge, Captain, say hello to Floyd and Bill Walter and their daddy, Floyd, Sr."

The two young sons of Walter looked to be eighteen or nineteen, each more unkempt than one would have thought possible. The younger fellow wore a Confederate cap, the other the hat of a cavalryman. Both had jammed pistols into their belts. They were unlikely candidates for Parker's Rangers.

"Who is the gent sitting astride that fine mule?" Nathan smiled at the black man, who dropped his eyes to the ground.

"Lemuel is kinda shy, he works for me as a hand at the farm. Truth be told, I was scared to leave him alone at the farm, with the girls and all." Floyd grunted a dirty laugh and was joined by his boys. Marcel didn't think he was going to like the elder Walter much.

"Is he going to be able to keep up, Mr. Walter?"

"Well, he damn tootin' better or I'll have his black hide."

Walter's boys chuckled at this. Marcel sensed Nathan getting agitated as he spurred his mount out of the group and rode over to the black man.

"Name's Parker, Lemuel, glad to meet you. Have you fired a gun, Lem? Can you shoot at all?"

Lemuel worried his toe along the inside of the mule's front leg. "Reckon I can, massa . . . I shoot me some—"

"He's a good shot, Captain," interrupted the elder Walter. "He can hit about anything he aims at, squirrels and the like—"

Nathan wheeled his horse back around, facing the group. "We'll not be shooting any squirrels, troops, let's get something clear. Every manjack of you is now under my leadership. You have agreed to come along on this raid for a monetary sum. All of you with the exception of Lafarge at equal pay, correct? By the way, what's Lemuel's pay? What's the agreement with him, Israel?"

"Don't rightly know, Parker, nor do I give a damn. That's up to Floyd. It's his nigger what's sitting on the mule."

Marcel thought Nathan was treading on shaky ground with Israel and the Walter clan.

Marcel quietly eased his horse back as the air began to get heavy.

"I'll ask it again, what's his pay, what's the arrangement?" Nathan looked each of the Walters in the eye and settled on Israel.

The older son of the clan spoke up. "You're biting off a hefty piece, mister."

"Hold it right there, gentlemen. Let me see if I can mediate this." Marcel moved out and away from the group. "Seems to me, Israel and the Walters are fine with their one-hundred-fifty-dollar fee, am I correct, gents?"

They answered in agreement.

"Why don't I take care of Lemuel's share so we can be on our way. This little misunderstanding can be forgotten and—"

"That won't be necessary, Marcel. I instigated this gathering and I'll be responsible for any expenses incurred by the group. I was hasty, gentlemen—"

Marcel decided it might be easier if he stepped in and took care of the situation. It was obvious the Walter clan did not want interference from outsiders about what they were going to pay their man Lemuel, but nevertheless, Marcel was relieved when Nathan interrupted.

"My passion for this endeavor tends to cloud my good judgment. Lemuel, at first opportunity, we will get you a saddle. Mr. Walter, your business with your help is, of course, your own business. I would like us to be a tight group and proceed without difficulty. It's going to be tough enough once we get to where we're heading."

"Hold your hosses here." Mr. Toby had been sitting back, listening to the proceedings. He moved his horse up between the elder Walter and Israel. "If'n I'm 'spected to die like the rest of you I 'spect to be spoken to without the word nigger coming up every time you feel the need, and I reckon that dumb bastard Lemuel over there probably feels the same." Mr. Toby adjusted his twin bandoliers of pistols. "My name be Joe or Ivory Joe or Mr. Toby but not nigger, nigra, or blacky." With that Mr. Toby reined back his horse and lined up alongside of Lemuel; he had stated his position clearly and with a wide quizzical grin on his face sat relaxed and nonthreatening on his mount. Marcel caught Nathan's slight shake of his head as if to say what next. He spurred his horse into a trot and called back, "Anytime, gentlemen, anytime."

The group began making its way down the country road when, shortly, Israel rode up between Marcel and Nathan. "The Walters want to know where we're heading, can I tell them?"

Nathan indicated for Marcel to do the talking.

"Why don't we see in the morning if the Walters and monsieur Lemuel are still with us. If so, we'll discuss it then." Marcel looked across at Nathan, who nodded his consent.

They rode on into the heart of the small community of Centreville. Floyd Walter disappeared for a half hour and returned with two more recruits—a giant of a fellow with flaxen hair and a woman, both fairly well dressed. They brought along a packhorse with two oversized saddlebags.

"This be J. T. and his wife, Wilma. J. T., Wilma—this is Captain Parker. That's Clete and Rene back there."

Marcel noticed he purposely neglected to introduce Mr. Toby.

"This here is Marcel . . . I always forget your last name, Frenchy." Walter grinned.

"Lafarge."

"Right, 'course. Israel, you know . . . and my boys Floyd and Billy. I know you didn't contract to have no woman as part of the troops, but Wilma says she'll do the cooking and whatever else what's needed doing. So, what do you think?"

"Excuse me, Nathan." Marcel interrupted as Nathan started to speak. "Floyd, you seemed to take on a lot bringing along your friend's wife. It looks to me as if you have already told them they're coming."

"Pardon me for being alive, Frenchy." Walter tried to smile. "I thought you needed help, you gonna be particular. Hell, we could all just pack up and head for home."

"Being particular, Floyd, is not it at all. We want to keep things friendly." Marcel glanced at Nathan. "How about it, Captain?"

"Lord Amighty," Nathan said quietly. "I never knew recruitment could be so devilish." He then addressed his merry band. "If Mr. J. T. and his wife want to come along, I think that will be fine, with the understanding everybody has to pull their own load. That suitable with you, ma'am?"

"I look forward to the trip. You and the other dandy with the tight drawers, what's doing all the talking, need to get something straight atween ya, never you mind 'bout Wilma taking care of her end."

Wilma was not a timid soul. She slapped her ample behind with her open hand. "I can pull my load and youse too, big fella." Wilma laughed self-consciously with Israel and the Walter bunch joining in. "Didn't 'xactly mean it in a boy-girl way, Captain, but I think you get my drift."

Nathan mounted his horse. "Let's ride out of town a spell and camp for the night, get an early start tomorrow." The group now numbered twelve. As they cleared the last small building of Centreville, Marcel kept staring at Nathan until he finally turned. "What is it . . . *Frenchy?*"

"Fine little army you got here, General."

"Marcel, I swear sometimes I—ah, hell. I thought about a small group of eight to ten real soldiers willing to do battle to right a terrible wrong. And what do I get? A bartender, farmer with two loutish sons. A black man on a mule and a blond-haired mammoth with a fat foul-mouthed wife—ah, piss and corruption."

They camped early, and true to her word, Wilma stirred up a fine soup of lentils and scraps of pork rind; delicious after what had turned out to be a very difficult day. Four small Sibley tents full of rents and patches were rigged close to the fire. Soon, everyone was wrapped in their bedrolls except for Nathan, who stoked the flames. Marcel pulled up his woolen blanket.

"Get some rest, Captain. Lots of miles to cover tomorrow."

"I was thinking about those young men today—those cadets—sad, truly sad." Nathan warmed his hands against the pine fire.

Marcel adjusted a leather flap on his saddle on which his head rested. "Well, they had their baptism of fire. Something they'll never forget, certainly."

"The musket, the one I took from the ditch?"

"What of it?"

"There were three rounds stuffed in the barrel. It hadn't been fired. In his haste, the boy probably did what he had been practicing for months. They would have been short of ammunition at the academy, and more than likely only dry-fired their weapons. It happens sometimes in the excitement of battle—a soldier forgets to fire. In this case, three times. He will later recall something incomplete about the process, but he more than likely won't remember what it was."

Marcel noticed Nathan's eyes misting.

"The dropped weapon, I think, meant defeat to him. It's strange how unfinished a war can be. Whether you're winning or not, there's never a sense you've done something truly good and worthwhile. My son was . . ." Nathan trailed off.

"Son? What of your son?"

"Another time maybe, another time."

Marcel kept trying to listen to Nathan, acknowledging him with grunts and "uh-huhs," but his eyes were closing. His last thoughts were ones of soft bosoms and flowing red hair, and the Walter clan arguing about blankets late into the night.

★

WHEN CAMP BROKE the next morning, Marcel was pleasantly surprised to find their little band of soldiers still intact. Just outside of Montgomery in the small town of Prattville, they bought Lemuel an inexpensive saddle and picked up a second horse for Nathan as well. Marcel and Wilma were in charge of buying provisions while Nathan and Israel stocked up on ammunition. They spent little time in Montgomery, carefully fording the Coosa River just north of town.

Farmer Walter complained constantly. "Damnation, I didn't sign up to be no river rat, hell, me and the boys are soaking wet. We coulda took the bridge in town. What the hell's the difference. I'd like to know."

Marcel rode up beside Floyd and his boys. "We forded the river so as not to be asked too many questions, Floyd. You know you fellows are welcome to leave anytime you want. Just pull up and turn your mounts and hike on out of here. Take all the bridges you want back to Tusca."

"Yeah, well, maybe we'll do that, Frenchy. Pay us off and we'll be on our way."

Irritated, Marcel turned in his saddle and called back to Nathan. "Walter and his boys want to hightail it for home, Captain.

Shall I pay them in full?" He watched as Nathan slowly loosened his pistol from inside his belt.

"Pay them what you think they have coming, Lafarge."

Marcel looked to Nathan, who responded with a slight nod. The blow, when it came, knocked Floyd clear from his saddle. He hit hard on his left shoulder and ended up on his back in the middle of the road with Marcel standing over him, pistol in hand. He placed his right boot strategically between the man's legs. "Don't call me Frenchy, do you understand? Call me, hey there, or whatya name, or pissant, but don't call me Frenchy. It's derogatory." Marcel felt relieved when Nathan rode up in front of Floyd's sons.

Floyd tried to squirm out from under Marcel. "You a big man when ya got the drop on a soul aren't you, Fren—"

"Don't say it, sodbuster, I'm telling you." Marcel eased away and dusted his trousers. "Now here is what you're going to do, Floyd. Rustle your lanky ass up, get astride your mount, and head back into the sun with your bastard children, but first turn over your ammunition to me, and I mean all of it. I'll give you money for grub and enough to buy rounds and powder on your way back through Montgomery. Now, Floyd, let me explain something. I don't want any trouble from you or your idiot boys. If there's trouble, I'll kill you sure as your country ass is lying in this road. *Comprenez-vous?*"

"Do what the man says, boys, dump your rounds on the road." The farmer grew mean-eyed. "You too, Lemuel."

"Let Lem make his own decision." Nathan never took his eyes from the boys. He then turned to the black man with half a grin. "What say you, Lem, do you want to tag along with us?"

Lemuel nodded, but wouldn't look at Walter or the brothers.

"Marcel, while I collect this ammunition and look after the boys, why don't you get old Floyd there to sell me his rights to Lemuel?"

Marcel looked at Floyd quizzically.

"How you gonna force me to sell my nigger?" His chin dropped. "What with witnesses and all knowing it was did under harassing."

Marcel called out that unless they wanted to join Floyd, the rest of the raiders should move on up the road a hundred yards or so. They moved out of earshot.

Turning back to Floyd, Marcel continued, "Now, dig out some paper and write the following: 'I, Floyd Walter . . . ' "

Walter found paper used previously for wrapping meat and a writing stick in his pack. He scribbled as Marcel dictated a long document with a legalese touch about Lemuel being his faithful servant and how he regretted that he had to let him go—but for his own good and a hundred dollars, he'd do so . . . and how Walter would do this with a certain joy but a heavy heart knowing Lemuel was with a fine new master.

"Now sign it and have your mouth-breathers to witness it."

"You can't call my boys that . . . besides, they can't write much."

"Well, put down their names and have them plant their *x*. They can do that, can't they?" Marcel gave Floyd twenty greenbacks and stood in the middle of the lane as the hapless trio rode off. Just before they were out of sight, Marcel thought he saw the elder Walter shake his fist back toward him.

Nathan rode up to Marcel. "I wonder if we have seen the last of Mr. Floyd Walter."

"You are now the proud owner of one black man, Mr. Lemuel, last name unknown." Marcel handed the bill of sale to Nathan. "And as far as the last we've seen of Floyd, it'll take him a half day to get back to Montgomery and a half day to get back here. Plus, he doesn't know where we're bound unless our friend Israel has told him."

Nathan booted his mare along the road toward the merry band. "Lord save the innocent and the little children, for it's damn sure I can't."

★

"TAKING THESE BACK roads *is* extending our trip, Captain."

"Part of the plan, Marcel." The riders had fed and watered their horses at a farmhouse set back in the trees near Crawford, Alabama. The lady of the house treated them to cherry pie and coffee. "Glad I could entertain y'all, my menfolk been gone quite a spell." She paused to wipe her eyes. "I pray they're heading toward home, and the good Lord saw fit to keep them a piece." She busied herself on the porch, refilling their coffee from a large tin pot. Marcel didn't know if she would be insulted if he offered her money, but he slipped a five-dollar greenback between the saucers.

When they remounted, Marcel began wondering, once again, if his decision to join Nathan on his quest to Andersonville had been a wise one. Impulse always played an important role in Marcel's life and he prided himself on his knack for making the right decisions. He hoped this was one of those times.

The riders made their way carefully along a fence line bordering a small stream. The woman at the farmhouse had given them directions to Columbus, Georgia. "Follow your nose east t'word the sun, always keeping it to your best hand. When you've gone farther than nearer to two hours, you'll see a community church to your weak hand and the Chattahoochee be trickling afront you. 'Course, your animals would of told you there was water long aforehand. Thank y'all for the visit. If you see a couple ragtag soldiers name a Sparks traipsing west, tell them to skedaddle on home. The fields need tendin'."

Nathan and Marcel remained silent for the better part of an hour. Behind them, J. T. and Wilma quietly sang a song about the flowers that bloom at night, how the jasmine's sweet smell rekindled their love.

Nathan finally broke their silence. "I been trying to think what's the proper thing to do about Lemuel."

"He's certainly yours, Captain. There's no doubt of that."

"That's it, exactly. He's not mine nor should he be. It's ungodly to own someone. I'm not sure what I feel about equal rights or what in the hell constitutes what a Negro man's place should be, but it sure in hell ain't being owned by another human being."

Marcel stayed quiet as Nathan went on.

"My experience with coloreds is limited, but I swear it's not proper. Tell me you don't think it's a crime against mankind to own a slave?"

"You got me there, monsieur. But to my way of thinking that's only part of the problem." Marcel could sense Nathan getting angry.

"All right, let me ask you this before we address what is the other part of the problem."

"*Oui.*"

"You don't like being called Frenchy, right?"

Marcel nodded.

"In some strange way it's the same—being called that sounds as if you're being thought of as different. You're not, of course, but it's annoying to be thought of as such, correct?"

"Yes, it annoys me. But on the other hand I like being different. I actually work at being different but on my own terms."

Nathan appeared to be chewing on this for a while. "What was the other 'part of the problem'?"

Marcel stopped his horse and dismounted. With a small stick, he drew a crude map in the dirt. "Here's the United States." With a quick swipe he divided the drawing into two parts. "Here, the Mason and Dixon line. Tell me, sir, why should these people at the top of the map"—he indicated the northern states—"tell these people at the bottom how to run their state governments, farms, business, schools."

"You can run your institutions any damn way you like, you just can't run them with slaves."

"You really think that's the end of it? That the Union government won't interfere with states' rights?"

The other riders moved close into the group. "I am not sure of anything, Marcel, except it's un-American and ungodly to own a slave and I believe this war will bear me out."

Israel spurred his horse through the dirt map and galloped down the road. "Piss on you, Captain." J. T. and Wilma followed him at a slower pace. Wilson and Sangnoir whispered to each other while walking their mounts down the road.

Lemuel looked to Marcel and Nathan. "Thank you, suh. But you pay me no mind 'bout all this, I'm tickled to be shut a them Walter folks. Lord, they was a feisty lot, I tell you."

Marcel remounted his mare and addressed Nathan. "Maps in the dirt, my friend, they're so easily wiped out. State lines and people are another story." Marcel moved down the dirt road to join the group. He looked back to Nathan handing Lemuel a piece of paper while Mr. Toby, a little farther back, sat on his horse, one leg looped over the saddle horn. Marcel could hear him laughing at Lemuel.

"You think that piece of paper gonna set you free, nigger? Lord Amighty, you sitting there all misty-eyed and looking like you just got offen your mama's tit. Lord, I'm ashamed of you. Why I'd take your butt into Tusca or Montgomery and sell you, paper and all, in a jig's time."

Lemuel heeled his mule past Mr. Toby. "Maybe, maybe not, Mr. Devil."

CHAPTER 21

February 1865
On the Road to Georgia

I t was midday, but still Nathan was mulling over the morning's events. The more he thought about it, the less it made sense. The people in the South weren't that different from country folks he had grown up with in Michigan, but they were a world apart from his adopted home in Boston. This was the first time he knew any Southerners in a personal way; that is, when he wasn't shooting at them, chasing them, or running away from them.

Those boys from the academy—that had been hard to see. They reminded him too much of his own men in Andersonville. True, his men were now hard-bitten soldiers and a bit older than the academy lads, but Christ, Weed couldn't be more than twenty-one now. He was eighteen when he first joined Nathan's company. The young Federals in the patrol Nathan had turned himself over to near Vicksburg might have been wet behind the ears, but their powder was dry and they needed little direction from their officers. A wave of the hand, a nod, a pointed finger—they were battle-hardened teenagers who knew their business. There really was something troubling about a country full of so many hardened warriors of such tender age.

And that slip with Marcel, about Sean . . . he was usually much more guarded. He wondered if in any way the loss of Darien . . . and now, for God's sake, Sean . . . if that could in part be the reason he was considered so daring in combat. Like most soldiers, Nathan lived in constant fear of getting maimed or rotting in prison. But he couldn't say he had feared dying since parting years ago from Darien. And his "boys"? Maybe there was something about them that . . .

"How 'bout here, Nathan?"

"Looks good." Marcel had found an excellent place to take their midday repast and gather themselves. They could see the road both ways for a hundred yards and put their backs against the tree line. It was unlikely passing troops would bother them and they outgunned most anyone else.

Nathan found a spot apart from the others and pulled his boots off to air out his feet. Damn, they looked ragged, an unpleasant combination of calluses and raw meat. Nathan pondered again what he had learned back east. He thought he had done the right thing with Darien—God knows, leaving was painful enough to be a right choice—it made them miserable but at least assuaged their guilt. Nathan thought their parting would be the end of it, but the first couple of seconds in her presence and his feelings came rushing back as if they had parted yesterday. He also wondered how all the rest had come about: Andersonville, Marcel, the motley crowd of raiders he was leading. In one way the story was completely unfathomable, yet in another, it seemed as natural as could be. Everything had changed with the war. Men died like flies from bullets, bugs, infections, and plain old neglect. It was inconceivable at the dawn of 1861 that the world would become the way it was in the first knell of 1865. How could the same people he had listened to in polite parlor conversations, people who would commiserate with one another over a nasty blister, how could those same damn people run a bayonet through the throat of a man now that they were the "enemy"?

And Marcel? Marcel had to be the craziest son of a bitch he'd ever met. He was a devil, clever as a snake charmer, but the Falstaff in him had a touch of Cyrano. Underneath the bravado and uncaring exterior there was a core—something rock-solid about him. And then, of course, for further inspiration, he was graced with the company of that great wordsmith, Israel Pennington: "Piss and damnation on you, Captain, on you, yes you, Captain, I say piss and damnation." But even with him, Nathan sensed something strong and dependable.

Nathan breathed deep as he reclined against a handy stump, still well inside himself, his boots temporarily cast aside. His eyes half open, he saw Marcel glance over at him a couple of times. He knew that he would soon walk over to check him out. It was time to shake the darkness, he had much to do and must calm himself. *Most men lead, most men lead lives . . .*

"Marcel." The call came from behind him.

Nathan cocked an eyelid to watch Marcel, who had already been heading his way with a studied nonchalance, turn back toward Israel. The saloon keeper was pointing to a lone rider coming toward them from the west, the ground over which they had just passed. The group kept a wary eye on him as he approached; they still thought there might be a chance of the Walters finding some ammunition or their friends and following them. But as this fellow drew near he gave a wide-sweeping hat-off salute to the group and a jovial, "Howdy damn to y'all."

Israel returned the greeting and J. T. and Wilma wandered over to exchange pleasantries. Marcel didn't join in the banter but casually mounted his horse and ambled around behind them. Nathan noted the newcomer didn't seem to be armed, but was an exceptionally seedy-looking character. There was a strange red-brown discoloration encircling his leg above his knee; Nathan had seen that kind of marking before, but couldn't quite get his tired mind to remember what it signified. Anyway the man was a welcome distraction, allowing Nathan to keep his lonely vigil sitting back against his tree while the others chewed the fat.

The traveler was more grist for Nathan's mulling. Why couldn't he take people for what they were anymore? This fellow obviously wasn't going to jump the whole lot of them. Wilma walked up to J. T. and placed her hand under his arm as her big husband, hands in his pockets, joked loudly about the damn Yankees, the darkening sky, there being no cotton around 'cept rottin' in the fields or headed to Federal mills, "Courtesy o' the damn copperheads."

Nathan was slipping his slouch hat over his face for a short nap when he heard something behind him scuttling through the brush; perhaps a deer. Almost simultaneously he remembered why the discoloration around that fellow's leg bothered him . . . guns. That marking came from the practice of gunfighters to strap down the bottom of their holsters, particularly the new six-shooters, to keep the leather from sticking to the iron when they grabbed them.

A loud hoot came from behind him, a Rebel yell, accompanied by the sound of a group of men charging out of the brush toward Marcel and the others in the road. Gunfire rang out from the attackers, accompanied only by a shot from Marcel, not at the bunch who had come through the trees but at the rider who had first greeted them. Less than a second from the sound of the yell, the rider looked like he had been poleaxed out of the saddle. He fell to the ground with his foot twisted in his stirrup. As the man lay on his back, fumbling under his jacket for a weapon, Marcel reached down and blew his brains out with a second shot.

Nathan leveled his Springfield and pulled back the hammer. It was difficult to find a target without endangering his own people. Despite all the smoke and noise, no one except Marcel's victim had fallen. He heard Bill Walter yell, "You Frenchified son of a whore!" as he rushed by him from the woods, raising his rifle toward Marcel. The attackers obviously weren't aware of Nathan's presence. He trained his sights on Bill's back and felt the recoil rock his shoulder. The younger brother was picked up by the force of the blast and deposited on his face, probably dead before he hit the ground.

Nathan put down his rifle and drew his pistol. The scene in front of him looked like a stage melodrama he had seen in a Boston theater where all the actors seemed impossibly close to one another but somehow still missed easy shots. Israel drew down on one of the newcomers and hit him the same time Marcel did. The fellow did a strange kicking backward somersault before lying still.

Nathan saw J. T. on the ground, holding his arm, when someone—it was that goddamn Floyd Walter—shot him again before starting to back off from the melee. Wilma, who had been crouched with a heavy cooking pot in her hand, howled and unleashed the pot at Floyd. He ducked, or it would have hit him in the head and probably killed him.

Lemuel had come back to the scene from the bushes where he had been making his toilet. He had a tree branch with which he tripped old man Walter and then slammed him with it on the side of his face. Floyd's handgun skittered away from him as he went down, but he jumped up and headed for the woods like a stunned jackrabbit.

Nathan hadn't been able to fire again for fear of hitting his own people, but now he saw Floyd, Jr., heading toward the road at a full run. Before he could even aim, the older boy went down—he must have been hit by either Marcel or Israel. Floyd, Jr., yelped and rolled on his stomach, then sat upright as if he had been pushed, but he seemed incapable of getting to his feet. Nathan crouched and started to make his way toward Marcel and the others as bullets ripped past him with alarming frequency. He looked back at Floyd, Jr., where a red spot was deepening on the back of his shirt and pants. The other attackers faded into the bushes and the place grew silent.

But it was just a lull in the noise. Wilma resumed a wailing shriek as she cradled J. T. in her arms.

"Jesus, look at J. T.," said Israel.

He was shot at least three times. Nathan had seen this sort of thing before; a big man taking the brunt of all the fire in a fight. None of the rest of them were hit, although Marcel's horse seemed to have hurt its leg jumping about. Marcel was beside himself, in his rage seeming like the angel of death.

"Floyd, you sorry bag a shit." He looked toward the woods. "I'm going to hurt you bad when I find you."

Wilma was gathering herself to shriek again when Marcel told her to latch her mouth. Looking past her, he said, "What's that I'm hearing in the trees?"

"That's Walter's son, Floyd, Jr.," Nathan said. "He's pulling himself along by the cypress roots over there . . . I think he took one in his spine."

The gaze of the rest followed Nathan's outstretched finger to where they could see Floyd's son pulling himself slowly away. Even Wilma quieted herself for a second as Junior let out a plaintive wail.

"Daddy, Dad, I'm hit. Come get me."

Marcel advanced toward the stricken boy and yelled over his shoulder back toward the woods. "Come on back and get your boy. One of your spawn is still alive and calling for you."

A couple of shots came from the woods, but landed nowhere

near them. The raiders weren't coming back. Marcel was muttering about "Murdering philistines" and "The Lord's judgment," when Lemuel, with J. T.'s rifle in his hands, pushed past him toward Floyd, Jr.

Marcel tried to point his pistol down at the boy but Lem walked into the line of fire, saying, "No, sir, I take care o' this." To Floyd, he said, "Hello, massa."

"Lem, godsake, get my daddy will ya, ya lazy ole nigger."

Nathan and Marcel watched Lemuel kneel down closer to Floyd, Jr., and stretch him gently back on his side. The front of his pants were stained with urine, the back with blood.

"I don't feel nothin down there, how come's that, Lem?"

"'Cause yer back-shot and it got yer pain glands."

Lemuel put Floyd, Jr.'s head in his lap. "Well, boy, I'm sorry, but you finally got what you deserved." Lemuel sounded strangely regretful. "And see yer brother yonder? He's daid too." Floyd dutifully looked over toward his brother's body.

"Yeah, no fuss now, boy, you'll be okay. Ole Lem raised ye and knows what's best." With Floyd, Jr., still staring at his brother's corpse, Lemuel reached behind him and picked up a heavy limestone rock. Without another word he raised it and brought it down hard on Floyd, Jr.'s skull.

Just then, Mr. Toby came limping out of the woods, shouting about how he thought he busted his leg from a fall in the woods and couldn't get engaged in the fight.

"I'll hep ya bury that cracker tho, sonny, will I ever."

Lemeul shrugged. "Suit yerself, Toby"—he trailed off—"you usually do."

Nathan and Marcel left the men to tend to the boy's body and walked back to where Israel was standing over Wilma. She was delirious with grief over the obviously dying J. T. The big man looked confused by all the blood seeping from his bullet holes. He looked up at Israel. "Damn, I think I musta been hit."

Suddenly, he let all his air out and expired. For a second, even Wilma was totally quiet.

"Lordy," said Israel. "They sure kilt the hell out of J. T."

They all stepped back when Israel's observation was followed by a banshee wail from Wilma. Marcel, still beside himself with fury, glanced toward the woods. "Guess that son of a bitch found some ammo and those yahoos on the way home . . . talked 'em into getting rich by killing us off."

Israel spit. "Yeah, those ole boys'r sure looking rich, ain't they?"

They started cleaning up. The fellow traveler that Marcel had shot first still had his foot in the stirrup and was being slowly dragged around by his horse as it looked for grass to graze on. Marcel pulled the man loose and relieved him of his best belongings. He rigged the horse's reins for following as a pack animal. The four men dragged the bodies of their attackers to a gully as Wilma kept rocking back and forth and crying forlornly with J. T. clutched in her arms.

Nathan approached her before the others returned from disposing of the attackers' bodies. "Sorry about your husband, Wilma, it was a rotten piece of luck. But we can't spend any more time here; we have to get going before we attract attention."

Wilma just wailed louder and grabbed up a handful of dirt to toss in Nathan's face.

He said nothing, but started gathering up his things and making ready to depart. He took stock of himself, noting he wasn't touched by bullets or hurt in any way except that his head still burned where that woman had hit him with a rock.

Inside? Inside Nathan felt great. His low feelings had dissipated. He sat upright in his saddle, no gut-sickness, no darkness. It was bizarre; all the morose reflections and agonizing over right and wrong choices in life—they were for a while laid to rest. This is what he knew how to do; he felt good. He looked down at the others and gave clipped orders for them to make ready to leave. Finally he turned to the black man.

"Lemuel, gather up some trenching tools and we'll bury J. T. on the other side of the road from the gully. If Wilma keeps acting up, leave her or shoot her."

"Right, suh."

Lemuel was sounding pretty good himself.

CHAPTER 22

2 March 1865
On the Way to Andersonville

arcel's mare limped badly and he stopped several times
since the shoot-out to stretch her tendons and joints.

He asked Nathan to hold up as he had kept a wicked
pace over the last hour, taking the lead following the emotional
burial of J. T. Marcel called out again that he had to do something
about his mare. He eased off the animal, uncinching and sliding
the saddle off her back. He reached up inside her rear haunches, his
hand coming back wet with blood. She had been hit, taking a
round right in the thick part of the muscle. It looked as though it
had lodged in the joint.

Wilma, still whimpering over the death of her husband,
screamed out. "It's a sign, oh, good Lord we're all gonna be dead.
My John Thomas is gone, God Amighty—"

"Shut that woman up," Nathan called back to Marcel. "She'll
have everyone in the county wondering what in the hell's
afoot."

Marcel ordered the distraught woman to get ahold of herself. She annoyed him but he felt sorry for Wilma.

"Don't you tell me nothing, you horse's ass." The heavy woman wheeled her horse around toward Marcel. "Damn your eyes anyway, you bastard. You got my John Thomas kilt, starting that fuss with old Floyd back there . . . you got my J. T shot dead. . . ." She drove her fists viciously into her eye sockets and screamed about the Lord taking vengeance on her. "Hep me, God. Hep me."

Marcel reached over and grabbed the reins of Wilma's horse. "Get down off your mount."

"Don't you tell me—"

Marcel grabbed her arm, pulling her off the horse and slapping her hard twice across the face. "Stop your wailing, woman. Cry all you want. But don't raise your voice. If I have to tell you again, I'll shoot you." Marcel had his pistol out, standing in front of the woman until she settled down. He turned from Wilma, slipping the bridle off his mare. He dropped it on the ground and walked the horse off the trail into the heavy trees.

Marcel led her to a small stream. She smelled the air and snorted but didn't drink from the creek. Her eyes were glazed and unfocused. Marcel ran his free hand gently over her brow. "Rest now girl, lie in peace." The shot rang out over the valley, echoing through the hills and seeming to come back around and settling in the copse of trees where Marcel stood. "And the Lord said, 'Blessed are the animals, praise them for they are innocent.' "

After distributing his gear to the other riders' packhorses, he saddled the gelding and joined Nathan as they started off along the narrow trail.

In time, Nathan reached across and placed his hand on Marcel's shoulder. "That must have been difficult."

"What? Slapping Wilma? Not at all." Marcel spurred his gelding ahead along the dirt path.

After several more miles through the dense wood, the band

came upon a road skirting the forest and heading east, bounded by a wooden fence to the north opening up to rolling hills and vast open farmland.

"Keep a sharp eye, Lafarge," called out Nathan. "We're pretty well exposed to your left hand."

Marcel waved a quick acknowledgment and proceeded to lead. After no more than a quarter hour he held his arm up for the horsemen to stop. He stretched himself in his stirrups to look across a series of plowed fields toward what appeared to be a group of small buildings in a valley that he thought might be the better part of a couple of miles.

As he rode back to Nathan, he could see him rummaging through his pack, probably looking for binoculars.

"Those structures down in that cut up ahead could be the church that Sangnoir told us about. Captain, can you see anything with the glass?"

Nathan panned his field glasses back and forth. "Can't rightly tell . . . seems to be some animals grazing. At this distance, could be cows, maybe horses . . ." He called out to Sangnoir up ahead. "Rene, come back here and have a word, will you?"

Marcel thought Sangnoir to be annoyed as he slowly mounted his horse and rode back. "*Qui est ce baudet?*" mumbled Marcel.

"My French is confined to *oui* and *femme*," Nathan nudged Marcel. "What did you mean?"

As Sangnoir approached, Marcel replied, "It means, who is this jackass?"

Nathan turned to Marcel.

"You hired him, monsieur, you tell me." Nathan called out, "Rene, follow Marcel and see if that structure yonder is the church you told us about."

Rene looked back over his shoulder. "I wouldn't rightly know, Cap'n, never seen it afore, but if its got a dozen or so nasty-looking, hell-for-leather heathens hanging 'round pestering the devil out of the locals, that'd be it, I reckon."

★

MARCEL AND RENE stayed on the road approaching the buildings from the south. They were on a rise looking down on a small community of a dozen or so structures surrounded by a heavy forest.

Rene's gleeful expression belied his weathered face. "You're gonna meet some real ones down there, Lafarge. Yes, sir, some of the toughest bastards you ever set eyes on, you can believe it."

Marcel thought that was just what they needed—more renegades, louts, and *pistoleros*. He began wondering why he hadn't just shot Wilson on the boat rather than involve him along with this jackass, Sangnoir, and now these thieves, waiting in the building down below. He already heard shouting from what appeared to be the church. Real doubts about involving Wilson and Sangnoir in this venture started to trouble him.

They trotted down the rise and reached the end of the field, where they came upon a post with two arrow signs: TWIN CROSSING, pointing to the south, and FRIENDSHIP, to the north toward the church.

"I understood you told Captain Parker that the men would be at Twin Crossing's church?"

Sangnoir batted away a horsefly and looked across at Marcel. "What's the difference, Lafarge, we found them, didn't we? Friendship, Twin Crossing? Makes no never mind. Fellow just told me state o' Georgia, 'tween the Twin Crossing and Friendship." They rode on for several minutes, Rene looking in mean spirits. "Leave it alone. You hear? Let it be."

Marcel decided now would not be a good time to start up with Rene so he would "let it be." But he thought there would come a time . . . yes, indeed, there would come a time for his Cajun friend.

Streaked spring clouds blotted the sun for a few moments, causing a chill to pass. A light breeze rustled dried leaves on the hard-packed pike. Marcel's horse whinnied at scenting other animals in the air. "Whoa, now, whoa." The horse settled as Marcel patted the animal gently on her neck. Someone up ahead was singing about a "fair-skinned gal in a calico dress, waiting by the old millstream." He wondered if he had done right by Nathan. After all, the captain's intentions were certainly honorable. His need to free his men could not be argued. But try as he would, Marcel found it difficult to foster real feelings for the "quest" or the imprisoned men.

Nathan hated having his effort associated with adventure, the word that he, Marcel, so cavalierly used to describe their trek. Marcel actually didn't see the problem with the word *adventure*, after all, what else would one call it? He decided that on the way back to Nathan, he would stop at the arrowed sign and tack on an addition so the captain could see it as he passed. "Adventure." This way. Pointing east. Marcel knew he really wouldn't, but the thought still amused him.

He paused to gaze at the church before him.

"Whatsa matter, soldier?" Rene chuckled. "You think those fellows gonna bite your white ass?"

Marcel ignored the comments and proceeded cautiously until they were leaving from a copse of trees near the church. "Ride up ahead of me, Sangnoir, and call out to your brethren yonder."

Rene spurred his horse, taking the lead, then looked back at Marcel with a wide grin before calling out to his brothers in arms. "Oh, there, Tommy boy, hear me now. St. James, you terrible giant, it's Sangnoir the savior, what say ye?" Rene galloped hard toward the church. "Call out or be damned, you ne'er-do-wells."

Marcel noticed the church's front door had been broken, suspended by just one hinge. One of the tallest men he had ever seen emerged from the interior with a roast chicken dangling from one hand and a bottle of what looked to be whiskey in the other.

"*Qui est ton ami, Rene—l'homme dandy?*"

"His dandy friend goes by Marcel Lafarge, *Pasteur*." Marcel moved his horse forward. "And you would be?"

"Name of St. James . . . Lamont to my friends."

"Well, Lamont, gather your band of merry men, fix that door back to the way you found it, and mount up. We need to cover some ground before nightfall." Marcel rode back up the trail thirty or forty yards, dismounted, and busied himself with the cinch on his saddle, all the while watching the mercenaries file out of the church. St. James and Rene appeared to be in a heated argument, glaring occasionally toward Marcel. A robust woman in leather trousers and a filthy flannel shirt pounded nails into the hinge on the suspended door. She was dutifully using the butt end of her Beaumont-Adams steel-handled pistol to drive in the three-inch spikes, the holster for her weapon slapping her ample thighs with each blow. Marcel waited while sixteen or so drunken riders mounted their horses to form up behind him. He was sure it was the vilest band of brigands he had ever seen. It was going to be interesting to see Nathan's expression as he presented him with his newest "recruits."

As they caught up with Nathan, he signaled for St. James and his roughnecks to fall in behind. Marcel eased his mount alongside Nathan's and peered straight ahead, trying to resist the temptation to look at the captain. "Maybe with some work they won't be too bad. . . ."

Nathan stretched in his saddle and turned to look back at the troops. "Work, you say? First of all, that band of cutthroats wouldn't know the meaning of the word. Secondly, we'll all be lucky if we wake on the morrow with our scalps intact. Christ on a crutch, help me." He spurred his horse forward.

"Many hands make light work," said Marcel. "Proverbs six . . . oh, the hell with it."

They rode for several hours, the only sound being their animals' hooves on the soft, rich dirt. As the sun cast long shadows along their trail, Marcel thought he saw movement inside the tree line, which he called to Nathan's attention. Nathan wheeled his horse around and tethered both his pack animal and his mount to a fallen tree branch, telling Marcel to ride back and alert the others.

Marcel made his way back past Wilma and Lem to Israel. "We've got something going on in the trees up forward. Keep your eyes open."

"Any chance it's that yahoo, Floyd?"

Marcel shook his head. "If he's alive, I don't think he's had time to collect his wits about him, get help, and get back at us again. It's not him, but walk your horse into the woods there and sniff around some." Marcel rode back, telling Wilma and Lemuel to stay tight. He moved Clete and Rene off to the north to keep watch.

Still upset and red-faced from crying, the woman called out as he passed, "What's going on, why am I stuck back here with Lemuel?"

When Marcel didn't answer, she raised her voice. "Damn it to hell, who you think—"

She stopped when Marcel pulled his horse up and looked back. He was getting close to the end of the line with her. He rode back toward where he left Nathan and dismounted. Not seeing him, Marcel walked cautiously into the woods thick with brambles and overgrown thicket. Unable to walk quietly, Marcel paused to listen. Voices could be heard coming from his right. He called out, "Captain Parker, I've got the second mounted platoon deployed along the south perimeter awaiting your orders, sir."

Nathan answered back, "No danger, over here, Lafarge."

Marcel made his way toward the sound of Nathan's voice, which seemed to come from a small opening in the trees where two Confederate soldiers sat propped against stumps. Another man sprawled out on a tattered blanket.

The older fellow, in obvious pain, wore a blood-encrusted kerchief tied around his eyes. With hardened blood also on his face and neck, his thinning hair stood up in matted clots. The uniform, such as it was, hung limply from his emaciated frame. "Who's there?" His voice trembled. "We can't do you harm so let us be, you hear?"

"We don't intend you any harm, soldier." Nathan knelt down next to the man. "What do you need?"

"Hell in tarnation, I need 'bout everything. Could stand a Thanksgiving turkey for my son and I, and the corporal there. I'm just funning with you, fellow. You sound to be a Yankee. My eyes are . . ." The man's breath came in short gasps. "We were in a hellacious fight, I tell you, got separated from our troops . . . been on the move now. . . ." The man paused, being careful what he said. "Donny, how long you figure we been lost from the Twenty-fifth Guards?"

Donny looked at Nathan and Marcel. "You fellows regulars or what?"

"We've been mustered out, Donny. Is that your daddy there, son?" Marcel sensed these soldiers were probably deserters and knew Nathan would pick that up also.

"Yes, sir. He got hit by a minié ball 'cross the forehead at Selma and somethin' peculiar going on 'bout his belly. We was with old Bedford Forrest over there . . . but got separated somehow."

"Where you heading, Donny?" Marcel felt the men were close to being finished.

"We live over Alabama way, sir."

Nathan called Marcel to follow him, and once they were out of earshot he stopped. "These boys are probably lying about their outfit and all, but they're in bad shape. What do you think, Lafarge?"

"What do I think? About what? Hell, leave them, we can't take on every orphan we find along the road, for Christ's sake."

"I'm going to give them my pack animal and some food." Nathan paced around between the broken branches and shrubs. "Stay with Israel, the women, and Lem while I handle this."

"Ah, hell, Captain. . . ."

" 'Hell' is right, my friend, it surely is that."

Marcel walked back to his horse and dug out a pack of hardtack and a canteen of water as Nathan stripped his packhorse.

Marcel stuffed the items into a pack on the gift horse and then mounted his own animal. "You shamed me, Captain. You surely did."

"That old lady back in Crawford who treated us to pie and coffee, the one who was waiting for her menfolk. You remember her, what if that was her kin?"

"That would be highly unlikely, don't you think?"

"Yeah, but what if?"

They continued to pick their way carefully along the rough path, dodging the dark threatening shapes of night. The moon hadn't come up yet and they were deep in a blackened wood.

★

IT GREW COLDER and darker as the night pressed on. The riders were beyond being tired and hungry.

Israel called out to Nathan, "Captain, what say we bed down, have some hardtack and coffee. Ain't nobody following us. If old Floyd wasn't hit, he was scared shitless, and probably halfway home by now. He's not gonna come after us nohow."

"We'll press on for a spell." Nathan never looked back. They rode for another hour, when Nathan suddenly raised his hand for them to stop.

"What do you hear, Captain?" Marcel listened intently for other horses or men traveling in the woods.

"Can't tell, we're close, real close." Nathan dismounted his horse quietly and signaled for the others to do the same. He pointed at Marcel and motioned for him to follow as he drew his pistol and proceeded along the path. After several hundred yards, Nathan signaled for Marcel to join him. He whispered in his ear, "We're within fifty yards of the west fence line. I don't like what I hear."

"What's that?"

"I can't tell. Just seems something . . . can't put my finger on it just . . ." With one knee down they waited.

Night birds whistled and somewhere Marcel thought he could hear an owl hooting in the distance. A brisk cool breeze rustled the dead leaves scattered under the tall oaks. Something in the air Marcel couldn't identify seemed reminiscent of times past. A combination of smoke and something more pungent. Something unpleasant, just hanging there.

Nathan lowered his head as if to concentrate and hear better. "Let's go back to the horses."

They made their way carefully back to their band of riders. "We're going to move several hundred yards back west and bed down for the night. No fires, no tents, keep your horses saddled and ready to go. One of us has to stay on watch at all times. I'll stand the first session." They led their horses back into a group of tall cedars. "Get some sleep."

It seemed Nathan stopped to gather himself a moment. "But before you bed down, let me speak of this. You men who joined us at Friendship had your propositions explained to you earlier by Mr. Lafarge. We want you to understand the following: no one wins a battle by laying down their life. We don't expect that from you. We don't anticipate that you will be heroes of any kind. What we ask is simple loyalty. If you are asked to supply a diversion of some kind, that's what we expect. No questions asked." Nathan walked about the men, their attention rapt. "If it's concentrated fire on a certain target, that's what we want. Marcel and I will do the planning and we ask only that you ride hard when asked. Fire your weapons only when ordered to do so, and maintain a sense of pride among yourselves. This is extremely important, men. And oh, yes, a nod, of course, to the ladies." Warm laughter rolling among the men seemed to encourage Nathan to continue. "As we are a small band and expect to be greeted by superior forces, we must be disciplined in our firepower. We will expect only the best from you." Nathan paced in front of the group, who had fallen silent again.

Nathan's air of command intrigued Marcel. He watched as Nathan reached down to retrieve a long branch from the ground. Extracting a short-bladed knife, he carefully cleaned the leaves and small twigs from the stick. The group remained mesmerized as he swept the branch through the air several times; a high-pitched whistle echoed through the trees, each time just a little louder, then with a flourish he raised it high over his head.

"With this poor knotted saber, I swear on God's name to right the injustice done to men bound to me as my responsibility—my command."

Marcel watched in awe as Nathan held the ill-gotten gang of cutthroats as if rooted in tar.

Nathan dropped his head, still holding the wooden saber on high. "Lord, save us in these troubled times. Bless our beasts of burden who support our wares and bodies, we give thanks for your comfort. The blessed clear water, the bountiful harvest of vittles you have provided. We thank you in Thy Father's name."

The chorus of "Hallelujahs" and "Amens" at the end of Nathan's speech impressed Marcel. The men broke up in small groups as Nathan walked quietly away from camp. Marcel caught up to him as he stood rooted, overlooking a rocky precipice bordered by a small stream, the wooden saber still in his hand.

Nathan glanced Marcel's way as he approached. "I know. I know. Don't say it. I went too far."

Marcel paused. "On the contrary, monsieur, you went only as far as was needed." Quietly, he added, "It was, in a word, *parfait*. I think the men and ah, yes, the ladies, if they can be called that, were impressed. *Supérieur, exceptionnel, sans pareil, bravo.*" Marcel applauded softly as Nathan looked into the misted waters below.

★

MARCEL AND NATHAN exchanged watch duty through the long, cold night, having decided between them that the others either weren't to be trusted or, good intentions aside, would probably have fallen asleep on duty.

In the soberest part of the night, after Marcel had just completed a quarter-mile swing around their campsite, he could hear Wilma weeping. She had been at it on and off for the better part of the night. She lay alone in her Sibley.

Marcel stood at the canvas flap of her shelter for a long moment before he called softly to her. "Mrs. J. T., I have another blanket for you." He could hear her rustling on the leaf-strewn ground.

"Don't need it. You slapped me, damn you."

Marcel crawled through the tent opening. "Take this and wrap it around you. Maybe it'll help your blubbering."

"What you doin' in my quarters, dandy?" She started crying again, deep painful sobs of pain and regret. "He weren't no bad man, was John Thomas . . . kind to a fault, put up with a hell of a lot from this pitiful old fat woman. . . ." She sniffed, trying to catch her breath. "He woulda been twenty-six in a few days. I . . ."

Marcel sat beside her, putting his arm around her heavy shoulders. She shuddered but didn't move away. He eased his stiff body down and wrapped the thin blanket around her. She breathed a large sigh between her weeping. "Why does the Lord take the good ones, can you tell me . . . never lifted a finger, or raised his voice. The poor sweet dumb bastard wanted to show me he was a man . . . wanted to come on this, this, raid or whatever you call it . . . his momma's gonna be fit for nothing when she hears . . . I ain't gonna tell her, no . . . somebody got to chop the kindlin' and do the chores . . . who'll feed the chickens and mind the mules? His face was all red with blood . . . I knew soon as I heard that shot that I . . ." Her breathing became heavy; a slight whistle through her nose accompanied her mouth dropping open and then the sound of snoring. Marcel slipped out of the Sibley and closed the flap.

"Marcel?" Nathan stood just outside the circle of tents. "What the hell you doing in there?"

Marcel motioned for Nathan to follow him a few yards farther down a wooded trail. "I might have been a little rough on the widow before. She'd been wailing and carrying on most of the night—"

"I know, I heard her."

"I gave her my blanket, seemed to help. I think she finally drifted off."

"It'll be light in an hour or so." Nathan stooped down to pick up a stick, fiddling it in the dirt. "Want to take a walk?"

Marcel motioned for Nathan to lead the way. They started out east again toward the prison camp, staying on the high side of a filthy ravine, keeping away from the sludge-laden water. They moved slowly, Nathan with his pistol out, picking his way carefully through the dense trees. Staying away from a trail below them, they approached the crest of a small hill when Nathan signaled for Marcel to stop. Nathan listened closely as Marcel thought he was trying to separate sounds of the forest. Broken by a rabbit, the tension eased.

"Damn, thought that was a Confederate dwarf for a minute." Marcel could tell Nathan was trying as hard as he could to control his breathing. Nathan again whispered, "Another fifty feet or so, we can get a view of the camp when the sun comes up. Won't be but a half hour or so."

They moved on and stretched out under a fallen tree. Behind it they lay head to head, staring up at the misty, gray sky.

"It's hard for me to believe I'm back here."

Marcel couldn't quite understand what Nathan was feeling. For him, it was just a damp cold night in the middle of Georgia. "What's your plan? Are we going to take the camp by storm? You know, attack them from all four sides?"

"You're an amusing fellow, Lafarge. But as I said to you once before, I'm deadly serious. I thought some of our troops would start a diversion probably on the east side—a fire or rapid gunfire. Haven't really thought it out yet." He raised his head. "Listen."

"What?"

Nathan came up to his knees. The sky in the east turned a dirty yellow, streaked with dark blue clouds. "I don't know, damn. It's something . . . last night, before we went back to the horses. There . . . can't quite place it." They both listened.

Marcel once again smelled that odor. "What's that in the air? That . . ."

"That's human waste and pain and blood and piss," Nathan said and raised himself. "That's death and twenty thousand men struggling for dignity." He stood briefly next to an oak, quietly reached up to a branch, and began pulling himself high into the tree. The sun stretched across the open field below and in front of him. "Lord amercy, now I know."

Marcel got up, standing next to the tree.

Nathan whispered to Marcel below. "There were as many as twenty to thirty thousand men down there. Nearly a third of them died, some of them in my arms. And now they're gone."

"What?"

"They're gone." Nathan made his way down through the branches. "What I heard was nothing. The sound of the trees and birds and such, but not of swarming flies and men struggling through the night to live and breathe. It was hell on earth both day and night and now it's not there. I don't hear it, they're gone." The two men looked to the trampled field below. No movement. As it got lighter, they saw what looked like a young boy with a rifle walking lazily through the camp. A few men could be seen on the south side beside some buildings. Nearby, one or two fellows stirred in the center of the camp, rolling painfully out of makeshift shelters. Nathan had tears in his eyes. "Why hell's fire, we could just walk right in there." And so they did.

CHAPTER 23

March 1865
Camp Sumter, Andersonville Georgia

N athan was dumbfounded. That the number in the camp would be reduced was expected; the population of the camp had significantly lessened even while he had been there. The misery and death rate had, however, increased after his escape, probably the results of so many men being so sick. The fatalities in the camp were catching up to the abuse. But this . . . what had happened?

As their small group made their way around to the west gate, Nathan became increasingly perplexed. There were more people in the camp than he had originally observed from his vantage in the treetop, but they still numbered no more than the low hundreds. Many of them were Rebel militia, but they were doing very little guarding. He rode up to the west entrance gate leading his . . . his what? Raiders? The whole idea of raiding the camp seemed absurd now.

Two boys, no more than fifteen years of age, stood at arms. Their faces suggested they were happy to be able to do something official now that they were being approached by someone they didn't know.

Nathan dismounted and strode straight up to the lads, with Marcel and Israel right behind. "Where in hell are your prisoners?"

The boys' eyebrows raised at the sound of his accent. Nathan felt the blood pounding in his temples and knew he was pushing his luck, but he needed to know what was going on. He felt Marcel come up behind him and take over the discussion with the guards.

"This fella's a Yankee and he's been told he could come and take home his brother."

"No shee-it? A Yankee? I thought he was Jeff 'son damn Davis." The taller of the two boys had taken charge of the situation and was showing he had authority, no matter how the camp had changed.

Marcel glanced out of the corner of his eye at a Georgia regular about thirty years of age, a sergeant with his arm in a sling who had checked them twice and looked like he might have more to ask if he came their way. Rather than let his temper take over, Marcel lowered his voice and in a casual manner asked if they might be allowed to look over the prisoners to see if his associate Michael's brother, Sam Finnerty, was there.

The older boy seemed mollified that he was being asked rather than told something by the strangers and remarked that it made no never mind to him. "Most these Yanks been sent on to Jacksonville, 'bout five thousand of 'em, just a few days ago . . . we got left some real sick 'uns. Them boys in a bad way and we're guardin' 'em more to keep the locals out than these 'uns in. Shoot, they so sick they look like you could knock 'em in the groun' side by side and make a picket fence."

"How did they go to Jacksonville? Forced march?"

"More like a forced stumble. They went to Albany by the train yonder and I don't know what all from there, ain't my business."

"Can my associates and I go on in?"

"Help yourself, just don't take no arms in there." Pointing to a shaded area nearby, he added, "Just leave yer hardware there on the hosses and let yer nigger watch over it." The young man seemed to tire of the encounter and turned aside to his duties, such as they were.

Nathan felt Marcel glance at him but he never rose to comments like that anymore; it was just the way things were. He gathered himself to enter the prison. Marcel and Israel entered also, but Wilma held back with Lemuel. She allowed as how she hadn't lost nothing in Andersonville she needed to go looking for.

For Nathan, the sights and smells took him back to what had been his world for what seemed an endless amount of time. While some things were familiar in a dreamlike way, others seemed very different. The most dramatic change was the lack of crowding—it was a different place now that you could see the ground. Much of the maggot-ridden cloth and soil had been raked into piles and burnt. Most of the work was being done by Negroes, and along the wall on the east and north sides, it looked like large shebangs were set up. Some men had been moved there, who before must have been in the hospital on the south side.

He tried to say as little as possible, grateful for Marcel's and Israel's presence. As he walked toward the area covered with Sibley cloth he noted quite a few Rebs of one sort or the other, which had been rare when the prison was a mass of humanity. Now, only a few blue uniform fragments were visible on standing men; the rest were lying on their backs. There was a Southern doctor talking to a couple of militia and prisoners when Nathan strolled toward them. Marcel pushed ahead of him and asked about the Fifth Michigan, were they gone or were any still here? He explained Nathan was here with a pass and—he was cut off midsentence by the doctor, who didn't seem to give a damn for passes or bureaucracy of any sort.

"I think there was a contingent of those Michigan boys here that went on to Jacksonville," he offered. "I remember them because they were well known by the others—their captain was in here with them and made it out."

Marcel glanced back at Nathan and said, "Sounds like the right bunch, Michael, guess that's where your brother went."

"I guess so, but how about these fellows?" He gestured toward the long line of tents.

The doctor said he didn't think any Michigan fellas were there, but a militiaman who'd been listening interrupted. "Hey, there's a Michigan boy in the other end, he might be from Five."

Nathan made his way in the direction of the pointing finger.

Marcel again forged ahead before slowing and stooping down over a fellow at the far end of the structure. Then he knelt over him on his hands and knees. Nathan knew he was warning the man not to reveal to anyone standing around the true identity of his next visitor. Then Marcel and Israel, who had also ventured forth, turned and gestured for him to approach. Oddly, neither Marcel nor Israel would look him in the eye, they just ambled off some yards away and stood looking over the camp.

Nathan hastened to where the soldier lay, but was immediately disappointed; this wasn't one of his men after all. The poor fellow was in that final state of dissipation where his lower jaw fell back and he appeared to have the endemic underbite of the starved.

"Cap'n?" came a very low voice. Something about his voice inflection was familiar, still it couldn't possibly be anyone from—"It's me, Rawlins."

Nathan couldn't believe it; it was Red Face Rawlins. Only now he was white of face and more corpse than man. "What the hell, Rawlins? What in hell happened to you?"

"I knew it, it's you, Captain." Rawlins had forgotten the warnings but there was no one in earshot anyway. "We was waiting for ye and it just got worse for some of us. I got the dysentery real bad, been diarrhea 'n' brown water all over the place."

"Jesus, you look starved."

"Yeah, and that ain't the worst of it, look here."

Nathan actually thought he might faint for a second. Burns and gangrene both had the same effect on him. When Rawlins raised a rotten blanket the odor that Nathan thought was from outside hit him hard. The man's left leg, deformed anyway from starvation, seemed to end in a brown stocking . . . but his leg was bare. The foot had been removed to slow the infection's progress but it hadn't worked. Rawlin's upper leg was turning the same color above the knee as below. It was fast-moving gangrene.

"Rot the damn luck, eh, Cap'n?"

Nathan sat back and put his face in his hands. He simply didn't know what to say. Weakened by the few moments of excitement, Rawlins lay back and caught up with his breathing.

"Where are the other guys, Red?"

Rawlins jutted his finger toward the west side of the camp. "The train."

"They went on the train? Where?"

"To Albany and on to Jacksonville is what we heard."

"Jacksonville?"

"Jacksonville, Florida. Prison and maybe exchange, dunno."

Nathan felt Marcel place his hand on his shoulder. Israel was standing back some, but staring at Rawlins and some of the others strung along the back of the shelter. He couldn't blame him. Nathan had seen gore and emaciation before, but nothing like this.

Rawlins was tired from the exertion of speaking. Nathan held his bony hand and told him to rest his head back and sleep.

Rawlins shook his head. "Can't, Cap, the pain keeps me up most the time."

Nathan had to get out of there. He rose and said, "Rest easy, soldier. I'm not leaving 'til things are taken care of for good this time."

The three men silently left the area of open shebangs and headed toward the gate. Nathan saw the Reb doctor again and called him aside. They talked for several minutes and then Nathan and his friends walked out of Camp Sumter. Nathan walked to his horse, which was resting with Lemuel in the shade.

"Lem, let me get under that saddle a minute." Nathan removed several hundred dollars in greenbacks and headed back to the medical dispensary. He gave the money to the good doctor. The man would be needing it for sure in the near future when he could count on his scant supplies becoming even more scant. In exchange, the doctor gave him a small cloth packet, which he took with him when he returned a last time to see Rawlins.

"Red."

Rawlins looked up at him and smiled. Nathan kneeled down and poured a dose of laudanum into the side of the man's mouth from the pouch . . . a lethal dose. Then he handed him a tin cup of water he'd scooped from a dingy bowl. "That'll make you feel better, Red."

Rawlins, again out of breath from his exertion, looked up at his captain's face and smiled. "Thanks, sir. Say cheers to the boys from me, hear?"

"I'll do it, Red."

Back outside the camp, Nathan made ready to ride south to Albany. He turned to his group, who sat astride their horses silently. "We're finished here. We need to head south. No trains today or tomorrow, so let's go by horse to the station in Albany."

Nathan hadn't any idea how long the ride to Albany took. It seemed they'd started yesterday, rested somewhere, and now they were riding into town. He was lost somewhere deep inside of himself where there was an empty camp, a wind blowing, and one less man in pain. He crawled out of himself to see the town. As they headed for the train station, they started to hear noise. It was troops . . . prisoners. They were being loaded up on three flatbeds and a couple of old coach cars.

"What's going on?" Nathan asked of a guard at the station. "Where these boys going to?"

"Hell, they ain't going nowhere, they're coming back."

"Coming back?"

"Yeah, ain't easy for me to shed tears over Yankees, but this here is crazy. These boys been on their way to Jacksonville and now they back here. Craziest damn thing I ever seen."

Nathan wasn't sure if he was dreaming this or not. "Please, tell me that you're not sending these boys back to Andersonville?"

"Yeah, we are. Sorry, but they ain't gonna be able to release them in Jacksonville, don't know why. We want to be shed of 'em. Can't figure what's going on."

One of the guards added, "But it ain't all of them. We forwarded on half of 'em to Vicksburg. They settin' up some kind of parole camp there—Camp Fisk they call it."

"What's that?"

"I don't rightly know except they're waitin' for our boys to be released from up north and we're going to trade 'em out. But I tell ye, these boys here are in bad shape. Been real hard here, I mean on everybody. Don't take much to guard 'em now, that's for sure, it's keeping them alive is the problem."

Nathan's head spun. They'd taken his men at Monocacy, kept them at Andersonville until they were near dead. Led them out twice since Christmas and now they were taking them right back to hell on a train. He listened in to the conversations and realized that most of the prisoners still thought they were going to Macon and repatriation. He didn't share with them what the guards had said, but asked if any of them knew the whereabouts of the guys in the Fifth Michigan. A lanky private from New Jersey remarked, "Yeah, that Fifth Michigan bunch, heard tell part of them were sent to Camp Fisk, Mississippi. . . . But most of 'em are a day's ride back east, toward Jacksonville, probably round Clyattville. Got train trouble, so I heard tell."

Vicksburg, Camp Fisk. After all this time, his final objective was now going to be the place he first escaped to and where he was decommissioned from the army. His concerns about the health of his men had been confirmed the night before at Camp Sumter. He only hoped they could sort this all out by the time he caught up to them. It seems some officers in the Vicksburg area dreamed up an exchange of prisoners that only the most hardened could deny. He'd find out about that in due course, but for now he'd fall back himself and discuss the situation with Marcel.

But one thing was for sure. If this craziness was eventually taking them back to Vicksburg, it was taking them to where he, with the help of Marcel, wielded clout. He could either personally ensure his men were included in the early exchanges or, if he had to, bust them loose and get them on a ship north himself.

CHAPTER 24

April 1865
Georgia

M arcel watched Nathan closely, sensing his frustration and anger. The news that Nathan's troops were shuttled back and forth between Jacksonville, Florida, and Andersonville Prison was difficult for a sane man to imagine.

Nathan paced along the weathered tracks. "Damn it to hell. What's to become of us?"

Marcel exchanged glances with the group.

"I don't mean 'us.'" He waved toward his small band of would-be raiders. "I mean 'us' as a civilized people. Are we doomed to behave as animals? To treat our fellow man so mean of spirit? Do we . . . oh, the hell with it." Nathan swatted the side of his leg with a small switch, tossing it to the side while he stalked down the track.

"You're heading east, Captain, and Vicksburg is a long way in that direction."

Nathan appeared as if he were about to bite the ass off a wild cat. "Some things in this cursed life you just have to set straight. Vicksburg will have to wait; we are heading east, the majority of the Fifth is somewhere near a godforsaken burg called Clyattville, Georgia. . . ." He turned to Marcel. "See to it, will you? Get us on a train headed toward Valdosta and that town . . ."

"Clyattville?" Marcel smiled to himself.

Nathan left the tracks, not looking back. Confederate soldiers in complete disarray were stretched out on the station platform, several of them laughing at Nathan's outburst. Marcel made his way into the depot, glancing at a red-faced lout leaning against the station doorway.

The slovenly corporal took a long drag on a nasty cigar. "Whatsa matter, y'all having a baby? Mister, your wife looks to be long overdue." He pointed toward Wilma and several other soldiers joined him in the joke.

Marcel made arrangements for all of Nathan's recruits to board the 4:00 P.M. train to Valdosta. The horses were to be loaded onto a flatbed open car with slatted sides. It was not ideal, Marcel thought, but lacking a closed cattle car it was the best that he could do. They camped nearby the Flint River.

With four hours to departure, Marcel walked the streets of Albany, aware of what could best be described as a pall on the town. A decided lack of energy and listlessness shrouded the locals; they weren't walking with purpose. A group of men in front of a barber shop spoke of a surrender. Farther down the muddy street, Marcel overheard two women saying, "Maybe it was better, maybe it was near to the end."

His curiosity aroused, Marcel crossed the street. Having seen a sign for the local news office, he entered the small shop to read the paper posted on a bulletin board. The headline was LEE SURRENDERS AT APPOMATTOX. Marcel looked around, wanting to share this news, wishing to ask someone if it was real. He didn't know how he felt. A part of him wanted to rejoice, but having lost so many friends at the siege of Vicksburg, any sense of elation troubled him. The waste of life seemed incomprehensible. While the fighting continued, there was never a moment to consider the right or wrong of the conflict. It was simply "them against us." But now . . .

A man in a dark blue apron walked up to Marcel slumped in a chair, asking if he needed help. Marcel fixated on the printer, asking, "The headline? It's true?"

The young man wiped ink from his hands, answering only with a nod as he turned away, his right leg dragging behind him.

In the stark daylight of Albany Street, Marcel understood what he had felt earlier about the atmosphere of this country town. He himself now seemed to lack energy in his step. A sense of loss settled on him. He was surprised to realize how deeply he felt about the South's capitulation.

★

THE FLINT RIVER moved lazily under the old stone bridge. Marcel felt like a kid, tossing pebbles, wondering what Lee's surrender might really mean. Was the war truly over? If he had given up his army, then the end was certainly in sight. Marcel gazed at the passing water while his thoughts drifted back to his wife, Mirabelle, and the kind of life they would have shared had she lived.

"Are you going to jump?"

The voice startled Marcel. It was Nathan, who seemed to have walked off his bad mood. Marcel tried to shake off his own bloody thoughts. "It's neither high nor deep enough to do the job. Have you heard the news?"

"Of your having purchased tickets to Valdosta? Yes, Israel told me. Four o'clock, right?"

Marcel scratched the rock surface of the old bridge with the sharp stone in his hand. "No, damn it, the war news."

"Yes, of course, it's all over the streets. Wilma and Israel are in disbelief and Lem doesn't know what to make of it and as for your Friendship conscripts they are restless to say the least."

"I thought you would be celebrating, Captain. Your men are obviously safe now."

"Not by a long shot, my friend. They aren't any better off now than they were a week ago. I am going to continue to pursue a fair resolution and make damn sure they get repatriated and back home in one piece. You still with me?"

"I'm along for the ride, Yank-o." Marcel looked into the eyes of the captain. He didn't feel up to it but smiled weakly. "We should replenish our store of vittles, monsieur."

★

ON THE TRAIN for almost two hours heading east, they stopped to take on wood for the boilers and water to make steam. Marcel eyed a redheaded brakeman tapping the wheels with an iron hammer and inquired if they would be making Valdosta that evening. The man never stopped his patrol looking for hot bearings, but replied they would pull off at a siding by the Little Banks River, spend the night, and head out at first light. Marcel shifted his weight on the hard bench, thinking they had their Sibleys and would make the best of it.

CHAPTER 25

April 1865
Trouble on the Train

A stocky man in a heavy wool suit and a bright-colored tie approached Marcel. "They don't like to push on much after dark. The tracks are so bad they can't make any time. Their lanterns only shine out there a couple hundred feet or so; the engineer can't see the condition of the tracks." He rustled around in his heavy floral rug-covered bag and pulled out a piece of wrapped cheese. "Care for some?"

"Thank you, no." Marcel wondered how many hands had caressed that particular chunk of dairy product. "We've come pretty well prepared."

"Many feel we would've won this damn war if old Jeff Davis had expanded the rail lines and kept them in better shape. But I guess the money was going for other things. Well, I suppose looking back, one can always see pretty clearly, wouldn't you say?"

Marcel agreed and feigned a need to speak with his friend. He settled in on the bench next to Nathan. "Lots of opinions about the war, Captain. You share yon scalawag's thoughts?"

Nathan looked out the window. "It was hell while it lasted." His gaze seemed lost in the distant hills. "One wonders if anything has truly been settled. If indeed the war is over, it'll take years for the country to recover. Years."

★

FIFTY PEOPLE, MOST of them asleep, all breathed the same fetid air in the rattling passenger car. Marcel remained wide awake in the enclosed space. The landscape trudging past his window seemed tediously repetitive. The plowed fields, the occasional farm. If not for the steady sun darting through the cloud-peppered sky, Marcel would have sworn they were traveling in circles. Watching multiple heads swaying in unison in front of him became hypnotic as the train followed the curving tracks. He wished it would put him to sleep; but each time his eyelids grew heavy, he would be jolted awake by the occasional uneven track joint. He was certain that the South's inability to transfer their troops in a timely fashion had more than a little to do with their losses in the war.

Marcel got up and walked to the outside area between the cars, joining a Confederate soldier whose left arm was presented as an empty sleeve. The soldier braced himself against the swaying train as Marcel passed him a cigar, asking the corporal where he made his home. He smiled, saying he hadn't seen hide nor hair of his kinfolks back in Tallahassee for nearly three years. He said his daddy was going to wail when he saw his arm—or where his arm used to be. Falling silent, the soldier started to weep, saying he wasn't crying for himself, and hoped Marcel understood.

Marcel cupped his hands as he lit the young man's cigar, allowing as how they should all weep for a solid year after the events of the recent past. "Better days ahead, better days."

Lemuel, who had found a place in the forward car with a group of Negroes heading east with a white slave owner, joined Marcel in the open vestibule.

Marcel greeted Lem with an offer of a cigar.

"No thanks, sir. Never did try one. Except rolled a few ciggies with corn silk and such, but didn't take to it." Lem breathed deeply of the morning air. "Friend of mine said he caught his seven-year-old with a smoke and swatted him upside the head. Said to him, 'I tolt you about playing with fire, didn't I?' " Lem laughed and although Marcel didn't think it was that funny, he joined in.

"You like a good story, don't you, Lemuel?"

"Yessir, I surely do that."

The train pulled into the siding for the night. It was a weary group that built fires and set up Sibley tents. All pitched in to gather wood for a thin supper of porridge and hardtack, with quick good-nights called out amid banked fires and warm blankets. Somewhere close by the sound of a mandolin strummed softly and several deep voices sang what sounded to Marcel like "Annie Laurie."

★

AS FIRST LIGHT spread across the wooded grounds, the train's whistle awakened the bundled campers. Sometime in the middle of the night, Wilma had made her way back into the train. Marcel found her massive form stretched indelicately across a hard wooden bench. He shook her foot gently. "Wilma, we're fixing to leave. There's porridge by the tent, best be quick."

Bleary-eyed, she rolled over. "Can't abide it, give Israel my portion."

Marcel stood at the open back of the passenger car watching Israel, Lem, and Mr. Toby on the bank of the stream, their shirts off, bathing in the cold water of the Little Bank River. He had felt its refreshing sting an hour earlier when he walked back from an extended hike along the tracks. He could readily see why it was dangerous to travel at night. In some places the ties had simply sunk from not having been properly bedded in gravel and tamped.

Marcel shook Wilma once again as the train's sharp whistle sent the balance of the passengers scurrying back to two cars becoming full to overflowing. "Better sit up, Wilma, we're going to need the space."

He watched as Wilson, St. James, and Sangnoir bullied their way through the passenger car, having little respect for civilians on the train. St. James gave Wilma a hard look, a wink, and a "You sleep alone, *ma chérie?*" before flopping down in a seat next to Marcel. "What's the plan, general? Are we backing down now?" The passengers seated nearby became quiet, recognizing the ruffian's attitude.

Marcel decided not to kindle any fires at this point. "All in due time, Lamont, just be patient, we'll let you know as the day progresses." Later, Marcel, deep in thought, was startled by a salesman across the aisle.

"Have a nice breakfast, sir?"

"Passable, just passable." Marcel didn't know if the man was being facetious.

"I would give an eyetooth for a decent cup of coffee, or for that matter a hot cup of tea, haven't had tea in some two years, I deal in herbs and gingerroot. If you're feeling a might under the weather, sir, I sell an extremely fine elixir recommended by the surgeon general himself. A potent mixture of dried dogwood, willow, poplar bark, and fine spirits, all blended and cooked into a secret recipe."

"If you tell the ingredients, how can you call it 'secret'?" Israel took a seat next to Wilma.

"It's all in the blending and cooking process." The salesmen paused. "And, of course, the amount of each ingredient in the stew."

Israel nudged Wilma. "I'll bet they stir that bark and willow and such through a barrel of whiskey, enough to scare it a bit and call it . . . what you name it, bud?"

"Uncle Taylor's Spring Tonic for the Smile of Your Life. One dollar."

The train bumped forward as Israel dug his hand into his wool pockets. "Here's my dollar, friend. Cash on the barrelhead."

The salesman dug a glass bottle from his bag, the brown liquid alive with small bits and chunks of what looked like wood chips. He passed the bottle to Israel and dug another from his bag. "Anyone else?"

They all refused, being more interested in Israel's ability to extract the cork from the bottle and downing half of its contents in a single swallow.

"Damn, that's 110-proof pure Kentuck." He belched. "Nothing like an eye-opener at seven A.M., Lord Amighty. What's your name, fellow?"

"I'm Uncle Taylor of Atlanta and points south." He stood. "Pleased to meet y'all, and bless you." The salesman proceeded up the aisle showing off his goods, quickly selling out his stock of Uncle Taylor's Spring Tonic to the rowdy bunch.

Nathan once again seemed lost in the distant horizon. Marcel watched him off and on for the better part of an hour, with the hypnotic clicking of the wheels meeting the rail ends almost lulling the two travelers back to sleep. He found Nathan's introspection unlike him, for most of the time he was energetic and positive. Marcel wondered if the salesfellow ever had a thought not tinged in blue skies. Must be nice, being content to sell some harmless brew to anxious buyers, drift along from day to day just . . . a heavy bumping sound caused most of the passengers to spring for handholds. The train's brake squealed as the rattle under the passenger car increased. A whistle screamed several long blasts as people ran for the doorway, and the train lurched to a stop. Caught in the middle of the car in the crush of passengers, Marcel already heard people outside shouting. Marcel saw Nathan's shoulders droop. "Ah, damn it all to hell."

Working their way out the door, they dropped to the ground alongside the train and walked forward toward the locomotive. The wood tender behind the engine had a strange faded painting on its side—ornately clad women dancing in a large antebellum mansion, smiling coquettishly at uniformed officers of the Confederacy while black slaves served drinks. Bent over the top of the painting in elaborate script was the epithet THE SOUTH FOREVER.

Up ahead, Marcel glimpsed the engineer and the fireman speaking with a man gesturing down the tracks and holding a red flag in his hands. Marcel and Nathan waited for word. "Well, monsieur, as our good friend Captain Rogers of the *Belle Marie* says, 'If it 'taint one thing, it's 'tother.' The two men were still there when the conductor passed by, saying that a troop train up ahead had either been derailed or disabled.

Nathan started toward the horses in the rear cars.

"Let's saddle up. Get the others started. This hunk of iron will be here for hours."

After retrieving their horses from the flatbed, they packed their belongings and started heading east in less than ten minutes. A long line of travelers struggled with bags and personal possessions on both sides of the tracks. The ragged troop of horsemen made their way along the iron rails, Captain Nathan Parker in the lead. Marcel noticed a group of men ahead of them at a curve in the tracks. They appeared to be Confederate soldiers. He alerted Nathan, but the captain, having already seen the men, nodded and turned in his saddle.

"Men, keep your weapons holstered. We don't want trouble at this stage. They seem to be just a patrol. Steady."

The soldiers looked unkempt, some sitting on the rails, others with tunics removed, their weapons lying carelessly against the train track. As Nathan's group got closer, they saw more soldiers scattered along the tracks. A seven-car passenger train around the curve rested idly on a siding farther ahead. The locomotive didn't appear to have steam up.

"Howdy, son, what gives?" Nathan asked one of the soldiers. "You having difficulties?"

The man continued chewing on a stem of dandelion. "Who wants to know?"

Marcel saw Nathan adopting what looked to be his best smile.

"Don't mean to be nosy, soldier. We're just a bunch of out-of-work farmers passing through." Nathan gave a little signal with his hand and the group proceeded, paralleling the sided train.

Confederate soldiers stood guard at each doorway, gaunt faces appearing at the windows. As they drew abreast of the fourth car, Marcel heard a shout from the coach.

"Captain Parker, it's Corporal Watson, Fifth Michigan. Christ Almighty, Captain. What ya doing here?"

Nathan spurred his horse to the train window. "Watson, what the hell . . . where are the others?"

Marcel watched Nathan speak excitedly through the open window when a shout came from the front of the train. Two Confederate officers and a squad of foot soldiers hurriedly approached Nathan's mounted group. A slight man whom Marcel deemed to be the senior officer called out.

"You there on the bay mare, pull back away from the train. Do it now."

Nathan reined back his horse as he glanced Marcel's way. Reading Nathan's distress, Marcel eased his mount gently toward the gray-clad officer.

"*Allô, Lieutenant, bonjour.* Sorry, sir, didn't mean any disrespect. We're just some out-of-job souls looking for a day's pay and a warm *repas.*"

"You look to be pretty well armed to be laborers." The lieutenant cast a look of disdain over the band. "Horses look well fed and you all don't appear to have missed many a meal. What's your story? You deserters?"

Marcel eased off his horse, thinking this little Napoléon would be more comfortable eye to eye. "No, sirree. We've all put in our time, done our duty and our damnedest.

"We're just trying to work our way home. Vicksburg, that is. What with the war just about over and all—"

"What's that you say? The war over? Don't you be flip with me, son."

"All respect, sir, the war's over. For all intents, Lee's finished. They're talking surrender at Appomattox. It's over."

Turning to his other officers, the man seemed stunned.

Marcel couldn't hear what was being said but they appeared to be arguing. He glanced over toward Nathan, who gave him a nod to try and get closer to the group.

"Keep them engaged, they're going to take a while for that news to sink in." Nathan glanced quickly back at the stalled coaches. "We've gotten ourselves into a bind here. I was hoping to take over the train in a surprise move, now this . . . maybe our martinet will listen to reason." He looked at Marcel hopefully.

"You there—" The lieutenant came striding forward with hands clasped behind his back. "One of my men said he heard one of our prisoners in the passenger car call you by name." The officer took several steps toward Nathan. "What's your name, fellow?"

"Darien."

It impressed Marcel that Nathan came up with a moniker so quickly.

"Well, Mr. Darien, why would that man, that prisoner, yell out 'Larker' or some such, at which point you immediately rode over and began a conversation?"

"Don't rightly know." Nathan grinned. "Just thought to be neighborly, suh."

"Browning"—the lieutenant wheeled around to one of the other officers—"put these riders under arrest until this blasted engine gets fixed and we can look into this." The officer turned sharply and started back toward the locomotive.

Moving away from the group, Lamont St. James crowded his horse in front of the man, looking down at him from his high perch. "The war's over, didn't y'all hear that explained to you? Why you want to be difficult, fellow?"

The officer gave St. James a hard look. "Move that horse, fellow, or you'll find yourself in a passel of trouble."

St. James eased a Colt from his belt and laid it casually against his thigh. "You're one dead sum of a bitch, little man. Afore you arrest me y'all better give it some thought—tell your soldier boys to put down their weapons, or say good-bye to your head."

Marcel felt the officer getting nervous.

"Second Lieutenant Browning, do nothing rash." The lieutenant's voice broke slightly. "Tell the men to put down their firearms and be calm."

Marcel watched the squad of soldiers lay their rifles down next to the steel rails. The horses began milling about, acting fractious, sensing the tension. He moved his mount close to St. James. "Well, Lamont, you have certainly gotten us into a fare-thee-well. What do you propose?"

St. James remained silent, never taking his eyes from the startled officer.

Nathan crowded in next to him. "If just one of my men suffers as a result of this action—"

It seemed to Marcel that Nathan could barely control himself.

"—just trust that you've pushed us into something that was better left to cooler heads."

Nathan yelled toward the train. "Corporal Jimmy Watson, Fifth Michigan, keep your heads down, remain peacelike, wait for further orders."

Loud voices still came from the train; and both Marcel and Nathan kept an eye on St. James.

"I count thirty-five or so Confederate troops." Nathan seemed worried. "If it comes to it, we're outnumbered, but mounted, we're more mobile." Nathan stood in his stirrups, looking back at the flatcars behind the coaches, then, disappointed, he settled in his saddle. "At least for the time being, I see two flatbeds with probably fifty mounts, saddled . . ." Nathan addressed the gray-clad lieutenant, "sir, we may have acted hasti—"

A rifle shot whistled past Nathan's head, appearing to come from the east where the slovenly group of soldiers had been stationed, followed by a volley of rounds overhead. Men scattered as shots rang out from both sides. Marcel sprang from his horse as St. James fired his pistol into the lieutenant's face. The man slumped to the earth, dead. Marcel sensed a recognition of disaster from both sides, as Nathan's raised but calm voice called to his troops to ride behind the far side of the train and regroup. The soldiers who had been ordered to drop their weapons quickly tried to retrieve them as Nathan's band rode through them, firing indiscriminately, dispersing men and officers. The Confederate troops fled in panic across the tracks and into the pines south of the train. Several Confederate soldiers had been killed and were laid close to the tracks. One man, dragging his wounded leg toward the distant tree line, cursed loudly that he had been hit. At least a half dozen of Nathan's men had dismounted to stretch their legs before the shooting began. Their horses bolted during the melee and followed the rest of the Friendship gang's mounts behind the train. The horseless men crouched out in the open and attempted to take refuge between the main track and the depression of the siding. Marcel and the others assembled behind the passenger cars on the north side of the train. It was going to be a long siege.

CHAPTER 26

April 1865

Blood on the Tracks

N athan drove his horse hard, trying to restore order. "You tarnished son of an idiot!" he shouted to St. James as he passed. Marcel's horse reared in anguish amid the rapidly increasing gunfire. In the chaos, orders from both sides commanded men to take cover or set up defensive positions. Marcel saw Nathan dismount to help one of the Friendship group back on his horse, the man looking gut-shot and pale.

"What a hellish fix this is," uttered Nathan angrily. "Keep those Rebs away from those mounts on the flatbeds!" he shouted. Then to Marcel, "Maintain a sharp eye, we're going to need some of those horses."

There began a steady stream of rifle and musket fire from Confederate soldiers on the other side of the train; several rounds broke windows, others ricocheted off the steel tracks. Nathan pulled a Henry Repeater from the scabbard under his left leg. "We've got men stranded, exposed to concentrated fire out there hunkered down behind the tracks. I am going to take a half a dozen troops and show a false flanking maneuver to the east. If the Confeds fall for it and redirect their fire, see if you can't get those yahoos who are pinned down back here behind the train. I underestimated the number of troops across there, seems to be closer to fifty."

Marcel tied his mount to the handrail of the third coach as Nathan rode off, gathering his troops for the ruse. Heavy caliber rounds bounced off the metal tracks, their high-pitched twang full of menace. Marcel crawled carefully past the scarred wheels, gravel from between the tamped ties sent flying by the insistent rounds. Shards spat up and stung his face and hand; he moved his head quickly behind a set of huge brakes. A hundred feet ahead of him to the south he could see the haunches of the six men trapped behind the far set of rails. He shouted to them several times, but in the heat and noise of the continued firing they appeared deaf to his calls. It was a brave thing Nathan was doing, Marcel thought. Risking his life to create a diversion to try and rescue a group of idiots who by their own stupidity had gotten themselves in a box by getting off their horses. They knew it was a dangerous situation. He wondered if it wouldn't be best to just leave the bastards out there. Probably not, but it was a thought. Marcel kept watching. He called again. No response. He rolled over the final rail and started crawling toward the men. Head down and moving slowly, desperate to find the smallest of depressions, volley after volley flew over his head like angry bees sailing past at astonishing speed. He dug with his elbows and knees, the dirt, gravel, and thistle grinding relentlessly through his clothing.

"Hey, damn it, can't you hear, for Christ's sake?" He remained jaw down, pressed hard against the rugged earth. Feeling a dampness on his cheek, he fought the urge to wipe the blood from his face. He felt wet spots on the back of his neck and hands and it was with some relief that he realized it was sprinkling. Softly at first, dust formed above the ground as the rain pelted the dry earth. The sound of thunder rolled like distant artillery. When he started to move again it became easier, the wet grasses sliding him along toward the prone immovable men ahead. He was worried, as it had been most of ten minutes since he had spoken to Nathan. He suddenly remembered the name of one of the men lying in front of him. Better yet, his nickname, likely because of his outlandish hat—a bowlerlike disreputable specimen that had seen better days—was lying cocked against the foremost track.

"Hey, Banker, look here. It's Lafarge."

Marcel paused.

"Banker, we need to retreat back to the train, you hear, damn it?"

He remembered the man's laugh. Like a jackass's. Hee-hawing and snorting out of his nose to much delight of his fellow oafs. Lying next to Banker some ten feet to his side, a man turned to look back at Marcel. He shook his head, closed his eyes, and pointed at the sprawled figure. Marcel crawled the last few feet and rattled Banker's booted foot to no response. As he got closer he saw a fixed expression on the man's face, a spoon-sized puncture to his throat. Marcel rolled him to his side to see rain-washed blood puddling from a gaping hole in the back of Banker's neck. White vertebrae shone clear as the downpour continued. Marcel inched closer to the man who had shaken his head. "Hey, bud, what's your name?"

The man shifted slightly before answering. "Name be Fred, but if I get my ass out of this mess you can call me gone."

Marcel pushed a laugh the man's way. "Fred, if we survive this day I think it will be a crowded exit for all of us. Now listen to me. Captain Parker is about to kick up a fuss out to the east of us, as if he was trying to run a flanking maneuver on these fellows yonder in the woods. When we hear it, we think the Confeds will direct their fire that way, then we're going to make a run back to the train. Pass it along to the fellow to your right. Tell him to make sure everyone to his right is aware that with my pistol shot, we're hightailing, got it?"

The man acknowledged Marcel and started inching west. Marcel did the same, going east, passing the word, reassuring the stranded men that all would be well.

One man with a leg wound, curled in a ball, encircled his hands and arms about his wounded calf. He rocked back and forth muttering a prayer, "Oh, Mother of God, come to my needs. Address thy Lord's servant . . ."

The shower slackened, the gray sky still puffed full of corpulent clouds. A howling wind from the south peppered light rain into the faces of the abandoned group. They squatted down, Marcel straining to see the eastern tree line where Nathan said he would be. It had gotten cold; Marcel's clothes were soaked with spring rain. He wanted to rise to his full height and shake himself, wrap his arms tightly across his chest, and beat some heat into his body. But he dared not. There seemed to be a lull in the fighting, fewer gunshots coming from the south. Marcel wondered if Nathan was holding off for this. How in the hell would half a dozen mounted men convince the Confeds that they were being attacked in force? He marveled at Nathan's approach. He waited another five minutes when finally from the distant eastern tree line he could see Nathan emerge with the group of six other troops, firing rapidly with rifle and handgun, racing toward the flank position of the entrenched Southern troops. It seemed as if the good captain had just begun his charge when he suddenly darted back into the trees. But Marcel could hear continued fire coming from the forest. After several moments, Nathan, with his familiar black hat and blue-and-yellow kerchief tied at the brim, came bursting from the woods once again, continuing along the tree line, firing rapidly with his rifle, only to be answered by a withering volley erupting from the Southern troops.

Marcel thought this was the moment. He fired his pistol into the driving rain and urged the troops back to the coaches. He drove the men on as the fire from the Southern soldiers erupted toward the fleeting images of Nathan and his phantom group. The horsemen wound their way through the woods so one could never see the beginning nor end. Marcel pressed his orphaned band to scamper back toward the safety of the train. The rain-soaked men crouched low to the ground as they doggedly sprinted toward the coaches. It was working, Marcel decided. But no sooner had he thought that than one of the men went down, clutching his hip and screaming bloody hell. Marcel grabbed him by the arm and forced the wounded man to continue running. As they clambered under the train, the Southern forces once again directed their fire toward the coaches. They gasped for breath, writhing with pain. It had worked, Marcel thought, but just barely.

The men were sprawled behind the raised track siding as Nathan finally rode up.

"Did you get them all?" It surprised Marcel that Nathan seemed so cool.

"One dead, had to leave him. Shot through the throat. What a mess. Two wounded, painful, but able to ride, I reckon."

Marcel watched as Nathan alighted his horse, soaking wet, and took shelter behind the sturdy iron wheels.

"I've got troops onboard this blasted train and I think it's high time we get them out. I wouldn't have planned it this way, but certain loutish cretins have forced our hand. What say you?"

Marcel nodded. The man was a demon, no doubt. He had just run a gauntlet through the woods for the past half an hour and now without even a kiss-my-behind, he spouts a "What say you." *Damn.* "All right, lead the way, Captain." He would put up a gallant front for the man but he didn't have to like it.

Nathan swung easily up to the stairs of the coach and ducked into the vestibule. Marcel stiffly followed. The fire from the Southern front continued, shredding the windows and the sides of the blackened coaches. The rain, though light, continued, washing through the shattered windows. It looked to be fifty men scattered along the aisle and nestled down between the seats. Some had been hit but most were just huddled in fear. Nathan crawled among the men, reassuring them and asking for the whereabouts of the Fifth Michigan.

"Up here, Captain," said Corporal Watson, whom Nathan had spoken to earlier as they rode up to the train. "There's nine of us here and another three forward in the second coach."

Nathan edged his way toward the corporal. "Are you hit? Everyone okay?" Watson and Nathan shook hands, the thin young man assuring the captain that he was fine along with the others huddled protectively behind the double walls of the toilet.

"Mr. Lafarge and I are going forward—" He was interrupted by a hail of bullets piercing the sides of the stalled train. Keeping their heads down, Nathan explained to Corporal Watson how they would get the other survivors of Fifth Michigan and meet Watson at the tree line north of where the train was parked. "Go to the back of this coach and when you see Marcel and me cross the coupling into the other car, slide out and down the far side steps. You understand?"

Watson nodded and gathered the other men and crawled to the back of the train.

When Nathan saw they were in place he signaled to Marcel and opened the vestibule door, bolting across the coupling to the forward car. Marcel was right behind him. Nathan turned the knob of the door only to find it locked.

"Damnation and hell." Nathan pounded on the door as bullets began ripping pieces of wood from the overhead.

The two men kicked at the door several times before breaking the latch and as they finally tumbled into the coach, Marcel yelled that he had been hit in the back of the head.

"You've got a wood splinter the size of a butcher knife caught in your locks," Nathan examined Marcel's long hair. "Must have not been your time, Lafarge."

"Ah, hell, if I can't get this out I'm going to look like some damn wild Indian." Marcel lay flat in the aisle trying to rip the wood from his knotted hair. He wondered about the marksman who had fired the shot. Just a few inches down and to the right . . .

Nathan started crawling toward a group of men in the forward portions of the car. "If you don't move, you may not have to worry about how you look. Come on." Several bodies were scattered under the metal stanchions of the seats. One man's arm had been blown off; the other arm extended toward the severed member, the fingers pointing as if to tell the whereabouts of the separated limb. The two men continued to crawl through the slime, with Nathan calling out for the Fifth Michigan while Marcel followed.

A man more dead than alive raised his hand feebly. "Here, Captain . . . James Fitz, Fifth Michigan." He attempted a smile, his slack jaw and cheekbones gaunt reminders of the horrors of Andersonville.

"Good to see you, Jimmy," said Nathan gently. Giving him a quick hug he asked him, "You by yourself?"

James gestured weakly, pointing toward four men crouched against the far wall. Even in the midst of the action Marcel could tell that Nathan was shocked by Fitz's and Watson's emaciated appearance.

"Did the guards leave any weapons when they got out of here?"

"Gun locker, but you can't get in 'cause it's padlocked." James pointed toward a metal chest bolted to the back wall.

Nathan signaled for Marcel. "Break open that chest, see what we've got."

Before Marcel could act, a volley of rifle fire ripped several windowsills and ricocheted along the length of the car, making a deafening horsewhip sound.

"We need more firepower." Nathan stole a quick look out of the train window, then bent down. "Damn, we've got men in the field heading this way. How you coming, Lafarge?"

"During the next volley I'll dispense with this piece of rusted junk." Marcel had worked his way to the back wall and examined a large steel lock on the gun cabinet.

It wasn't long until the Confederate sharpshooters once again raked the train with their lethal rounds. Marcel fired his pistol twice, spinning the lock crazily on its hasp. Three rifles and a half dozen pistols sat in the locker along with an adequate amount of ammunition.

Nathan passed the weapons out along the length of the coach to the willing recipients and told the men to hold their fire until the Confederates got up to move again.

Marcel watched Nathan scan the field, observing the gray-clad troops some one hundred yards away.

"Hold . . . hold easy now, easy."

A distant metallic whistle across the wet field signaled some thirty men who rose as one and began running toward the train, led by their chilling high-pitched Rebel yell.

"Hold people, hold, take careful aim." Nathan nodded to Marcel. "Now fire, boys, fire."

Marcel quickly rested his pistol against a windowsill and began firing. Several men in the field had gone down from the rifle fire but they were still too far away for the pistols to be effective. Nathan fired and reloaded rapidly when he noticed they were turning. He told the men they were heading back but to keep at it, keep firing. The men on the train emptied their weapons at the retreating Confederate troops.

"Jimmy Fitz, get outside now!" shouted Nathan. "Outside on the tree side, double-time, get out."

A number of sickly men stumbled off the train, moving toward the woods where the horses were waiting. Marcel and Nathan followed alongside, giving a hand to the weakened men. Nathan was speaking, almost to himself, "I count eighteen. There's only supposed to be five from our coach—fourteen altogether, counting the nine that Watson took off the train earlier—what the hell?" Nathan trotted alongside a gray-haired man in tattered blues. "What's your name, Dad?"

Breathless, the man tried to speak but couldn't. He raised his hand and stopped moving. "Name of Willoughby, son, and no, I'm . . . not part of the Michigan whatever the hell it is, but if 'n you think for a minute I'm not going with you, you got another think acomin'."

Nathan put an arm around the man's waist and half carried him toward the tree line. "Well, ole-timer, you got the best of me, this was supposed to be the Fifth Michigan's party but I guess as you say I got another 'think acomin'." Nathan and Marcel remounted their horses at the tree line. Marcel spurred into a gallop toward the front of the train, where a group of men were beating a Confederate soldier who had fallen to the ground. He shouted for them to break it up, the men falling back as the bloodied soldier dashed around the front of the locomotive, hightailing it across the tracks only to be shot inadvertently by one of his own men in the distant woods. As he lay sprawled on the rail right-of-way, Marcel heard an order shouted from across the way to "Cease fire!" Two Confederate soldiers came running out of the pines, ducking low and heading toward their fallen companion. A rifle report from his left startled Marcel and almost immediately one of the two soldiers went to his knees, crying out he'd been hit and lordy, how it hurt.

Nathan rode toward Marcel, bellowing. "Gather our men from the front of the train and fall back into the woods."

A high-pitched woman's scream came unexpectedly from behind the coal tender. A Friendship camp follower, a large woman the men called Ruth, wearing leather trousers, had been hit. As Marcel rode up, one of the Friendship group had taken her off her horse, trying to apply a compress on a bloody wound to the woman's stomach. Lathered in blood from chest to knees, she tried to catch her breath, her face rigid with pain. "I'll be good. In a moment . . . I'll be, I just need a breath of air, all I need is . . . a . . . whiff. Can't catch my, oh, Mama." Marcel watched her eyes fix on Nathan.

Her friend stood, his hands and arms covered in a red syrupy gore. His reddened face was bathed in tears. "She were a trooper, I'll tell you. A regular hell-raiser. Rest, big one, rest now."

Marcel read the tension on Nathan's face as the captain wheeled his horse about and charged back toward the caboose.

The woods to the north were full of brambles, crowded by disease-ridden pines with spindly branches drooping to the forest floor. Pleas for help came from the train. It seemed that most of the Union prisoners of war had simply sought shelter on the floor of the passenger cars when the shooting began.

"Form up on me, let's make haste, troops," directed Nathan once again, as he circled his arm above his head.

When everyone gathered, Marcel noticed the captain seemed overpowered with concern.

"We don't have a lot of time so I'll explain just once what we are going to do." Nathan slipped easily off his horse. "You men off the train other than the Fifth Michigan, make your way back to the railcars and reboard. Do it now."

"On whose authority do we reboard?" One of the healthier Union soldiers walked toward Nathan.

"On mine. I'm Captain Nathan Parker of the Fifth Michigan. Now do as you're told, soldier. I apologize for this debacle, son, but at this point it can't be helped. I thought I could take you but I can't. Follow orders and reboard." Nathan stepped back and shouted to the men straggling back toward the train. "You, men, are only a couple days from Vicksburg where you'll be sent north. In case you hadn't heard, a surrender of the Confederate army at Appomattox took place." Nathan paused. "It's good news, people. We can all rejoice in that at least, and again, I apologize for this—"

The men from the train looked back at Nathan. A pitiful group. Marcel carefully eased his horse toward them as if to gentle them along.

"Hold up, Lafarge." Nathan stood with hands on hips, feet apart. He seemed, for the moment, resolute. "You men go on now, do as you are told, like I said before—"

Marcel watched as Nathan stopped midspeech, appearing as though he couldn't comprehend the events of the last five minutes.

"Ah, damn it." The good captain once again looked away toward the rear of the train; the two flatcars still held perhaps as many as fifty very nervous horses. "Marcel, take half a dozen men and see if you can't liberate fifteen or twenty of those Southern mounts. The rest of you spread out along the tracks under the train and give covering fire. Israel, Wilma, you people of Friendship redistribute our supplies. Every manjack is to carry his own share of rations and water. I want those extra horses and mules fitted for all of these men, not just the Fifth Michigan."

The extra men from the train gave a weak shout of joy as Nathan hurried his horse across a clearing and tied the mare to a tree branch. Marcel watched briefly as he greeted his men, embracing their skeletal forms standing with his arms extended, clasping their shoulders, looking into the sunken eyes of desperate souls. To Marcel they didn't seem much better off than Rawlins at Camp Sumter, though it looked like they might be able to ride a bit. They seemed confused, like it was hard for them to make sense of what was happening, they even acted somewhat unsure of Nathan. As Nathan directed the covering fire, Marcel, along with Israel and four others, sped back toward the flatbed cars. The horses on the train were skittish from the gunfire and straining at their tethers. Marcel swung up to the slat-sided car and searched for the gate. He called back to Israel.

"These mounts are going to come off this platform hell-for-leather. I'll try and slow them down, catch as many as you can, let the rest run free." When Marcel let the gate down several of the horses that had broken free from their tethers leapt from the train, one mare going heavily to her knees and rolling over being quickly caught. The others were rounded up into groups of four or five and hustled back toward Nathan's position. As they approached, Marcel called out.

"Captain, I am going back to try and release that batch of ponies in the second car so that rambunctious lot across there in the trees can't use them."

"Help get these men mounted first, we've got to find better cover!" Nathan shouted back.

One of the Fifth Michigan boys looked to Nathan. "Cap'n, who're these fellas riding with you? Where's our soldiers? Damn, it seems forever since we seen ya."

"Men, I'll catch up with each of you later, individually, but for now I need you to mount these horses and follow Mr. Lafarge. He'll lead you back into the woods to an area he thinks might be safe from Confederate troops. This bloodfest was not my intent but now we've no choice. I'll explain later what the plan is. But just let me say this—it gladdens my heart to see you and I'll do my damnedest for you."

A light chorus of "Hurrahs" came from the men, and with help from Israel and Lem, they began to mount the packhorses.

Nathan signaled to Marcel and the two men led their horses away from the others. "Have you ever witnessed such a hellish nightmare? That oaf St. James has put us into a dangerous situation. I'd like to horsewhip the bastard."

"You told your men you had a plan." Marcel tightened the girth of his saddle. "What is it?"

"Plan? My plan is to get the hell out of here. That's my plan."
Nathan kicked at a rock with his muddy boot. He gave St. James a
look that chilled Marcel. Lamont remained surly and impatient as
usual.

Marcel almost wanted to tell St. James to back off, that he was
balancing his life on the head of a pin . . . almost. Instead he said
nothing and looked to Nathan for orders.

"First of all, Marcel, get all of these people pulled back a half
mile or so where they're safe. If those Confederate troops are smart
they'll let this thing go and be on their way. If not, we'll deal with
them as needed. I'll stay here with the rest of our band and the
Friendship group. I think I can depend on Israel and Lemuel for
support." Nathan remounted his horse. "We'll remain here for an
hour or so to cover you. Head due north, we'll find you."

CHAPTER 27

April 1865

Marcel rode past his mounted ghosts, most of them looking very uncomfortable on horseback. Single file, they made their way carefully through thick woods. After what Marcel thought to be a half hour's ride, they came to a wooden fence bordering a vast open field and he instructed the troops to dismount. There, they would tether their horses, stretch out, get rested, and wait for Captain Parker. Marcel would circle around to the rear on watch. He studied the men as they slid weakly off their mounts onto the brush-laden ground. Marcel left them and began backtracking. Riding for several minutes, he tied his horse to a tree and began a foot patrol from east to west, stopping occasionally, listening.

After a number of such passages he sat on a fallen tree where he could observe to the south. It had been, in the words of Nathan Parker, a "hellish nightmare." What, he thought, was in the mind of jackass St. James? For him to draw down on the Confederate lieutenant was beyond belief. It had certainly compounded a difficult situation into an impossible one. Of course, the rifle fire from the ragtag group of sharpshooters hadn't helped circumstances either. The vagaries of war remained a mystery to Marcel. He wondered if the men who were killed today would be remembered as having died after the war was over. How ironic, he thought, to go through years of battles, starvation, bitter cold, and the heat of summer only to be killed a day after Lee surrenders. He thought Nathan had made a tough decision taking the remains of his troops from the train. Plus the hangers-on. Marcel mused it was better that Nathan made those decisions rather than himself.

After an hour, Marcel heard horses coming from the south, breaking through the brambles. He watched as Israel stopped at the edge of the clearing to check if it was safe to cross. Marcel called out for Pennington, signaling for the rest of the band to come forward, meeting them in the center of the clearing. Nathan led the way.

"How are the men, Marcel?"

"They have bedded down to rest farther on. A fence was either going to have to be skirted or broken so I decided to wait." He took a breath. "Nathan, I'm not even sure they can stay mounted for much longer."

Marcel led the way back to the Fifth Michigan's rendevous area where Nathan checked on his men again and then motioned for everyone to gather.

"As some of you in the rear have reported, we're being followed. Whether it's the whole damn bunch of those Rebs or just a patrol, we don't know yet. But in any case, followed—"

"Who are you to spout off about Rebs, Yankee bastard?" St. James interrupted.

Nathan rode toward the man, easing out his pistol as he approached.

Marcel felt a calm come over him. Anyone this stupid deserved what he got. Lamont had underestimated Nathan and there was no longer any doubt in Marcel's mind of the outcome.

"You know damn well I meant no disrespect with that remark," Nathan said softly but clearly. "Damn it, man, can't you put your mouth to rest for a while? You drew down on that officer, precipitating this mess, do you want to stop in the middle of this flight to settle petty differences?"

"I'm on your right flank, Captain." This came from Marcel. He said it as much for the consumption of the rest of the Friendship crowd. They needed to know where he stood in this.

"Let's hear your answer, Lamont." Nathan's eyes grew dark.

All Marcel could think was for Lamont, the damn fool, to shut up.

St. James grinned and looked to his gang, attempting to laugh his way out of having been called out. He turned in his saddle, reaching for his sidearm hidden from Nathan's view. As he spun back and raised the weapon, Nathan shot him in the chest. The man slumped forward with a loud grunt, his horse dancing in circles.

"Israel, catch that horse and kick that big oaf out of the saddle," said Nathan. "No, wait, I'll help." Nathan shuffled his horse to Lamont's side and shot the man again in the shoulder, the impact knocking him cleanly out of the saddle. "Israel, now please bring that good mount back here, we're going to need him."

A shout came from the back of the group. "You got some nerve at these wages, killing one of our own, calling him an oaf, why hell's fire . . ." The voice died out as Nathan rode up and down in front of the Friendship group, saying nothing, looking each man in the eye. One after another they averted their glances. He rode back to Lamont and methodically emptied the last four shots in his pistol into Lamont's face and body—after each shot he looked back at the horsemen until they turned away.

★

NATHAN TRIED TO make sense of it all. He moved away from the others to a copse of small trees. He dismounted and sat on the ground, extending his arms to the side, resting them on the sticky surface of some dwarf pines. He lowered his chin to his chest and breathed deep. It helped to keep his head from spinning.

This wasn't the way it was supposed to happen—his men weren't supposed to be here. This was not the place for his moment of triumph . . . was it triumph? It didn't seem right to finally accost his men in the midst of chaos. But isn't that the way it always was? Anticipation, hope, dread, then *pop*—ugly reality. Christ, they looked bad, even though alive.

All men lead lives . . . then you kill them. Something about killing St. James reminded him of killing that goddamn sergeant at Andersonville. How did it make him feel? If anything, kind of good. But he had just pasted four rounds of a .44 into Lamont's face. How do sane, reasonable men do that? To Nathan's mind they were merely intended as exclamation marks at the end of his sentence—that damn renegade band of his and Marcel's—they didn't take subtle hints—he meant what he said and had to be clear about it.

Something about Watson and Fitz, yes, that was it, the odor. The smell of Jimmy's fetid breath and disease-ridden body had taken Nathan back to Andersonville like no other memory could. It was the smell. "Hello, Jimmy," then a hug, and Andersonville wafted through the clearing.

Nathan began shaking; he had to gather himself and get going. He raised back to his feet and looked around. He saw Marcel staring right at him. Nathan returned the gaze until his friend looked away. Marcel was changing; he knew he would. He had followed Nathan's lead in battle and was finding it drew him. Marcel was a rough character, but beneath the brashness and cynicism, he was steeped in a sense of honor as much as any man he had ever met.

Though older and wiser than Nathan's Michigan troops, Marcel too was succumbing to the drug of combat—a sort of opium that seduced men even while it repelled them. Marcel had been hurt in Vicksburg in many ways—particularly that direct wound to the soul—one that left him trusting no one—especially anyone in uniform.

Marcel feigned cynicism, but Nathan believed that more than anything, the man wanted to fight with comrades he could believe in—and Marcel had never fought under Nathan Parker. Nathan didn't know why men were so drawn to him in combat—it often made him uneasy—but sometimes, truth be told, it also thrilled him. He knew that growing gleam of battle-lust in his friend's eye. Marcel was sipping blood from the crystal goblet—the grapes of wrath—and Marcel knew that Nathan knew where they were stored.

When Israel returned with the horse, he nodded for Marcel to lead the way. As they moved off, Nathan called out over his shoulder, "Any man not satisfied with either the wages or the company, ride on out. But do it now, not in the middle of the night. You hear?"

At the fence line, Marcel stood next to Nathan gazing out at the open fields.

"You've let the genie out of the bottle, Captain. That band of fire-breathers will be looking for redemption."

Nathan kept peering at the vast plowed field.

"Captain?"

He finally turned to Marcel. "The way I'm feeling just now, I'll welcome all and sundry attempts at redemption." He paused for a few moments. "You see that stand of heavy trees yonder, maybe three hundred yards? It appears that, because it's slightly raised ground, the farmer had to plow around it all these years. In any case, it looks almost a quarter mile long and I think a perfect little island for us. Let's mount up, get some of the men to break down this fence, have them spread out across this field, make no attempt to cover our tracks. If, in fact, those Rebs are following us, we want to appear to be wandering."

It had taken the better part of an hour for the Fifth Michigan boys, the Friendship and Tusca groups, and the hangers-on from the train to get settled on the wooded plot in the middle of the plowed fields. Marcel thought it was one hell of a little army. There were eleven from the Fifth Michigan and four hangers-on. These men would ordinarily be excellent fighters but due to their condition they were more burden than asset.

Considerable discontent came from the likes of Sangnoir and Wilson. Marcel wondered what he had been thinking of when he invited Wilson to work his debt off by coming along on this debacle. He knew his judgment at times seemed less than clear, so why should he be surprised that this river rat and his friends would be anything but trouble? With the demise of St. James, Rene Sangnoir seemed to be in charge of the Friendship group and Marcel heard him grousing, "Why in hell's name are we exposed out here, Christ Amighty. They could surround us and pick us off any damn time they wanted." Marcel, in the midst of unsaddling his horse, turned to Sangnoir.

"Hightail it on across that open ground, Rene. Explain to those troops filling up those trees how you had nothing to do with that pissant lieutenant's death. I'm sure they'd lend a sympathetic ear."

Sangnoir and Wilson looked to Marcel, each waiting for the other to say or do something. Marcel just showed his teeth to them and kept at his business.

"We might just do that, Lafarge—" as Sangnoir spoke, a volley of musket balls shredded the branches above the men's heads.

"Everyone get down, weapons at the ready!" shouted Nathan. "No firing, I repeat, no firing."

The men sought shelter behind fallen trees and depressions as the barrage continued.

"Lafarge, have you got something white, a cloth, a shirt, anything?"

Marcel tore open his kit bag and found a crumpled light blue shirt. He scrambled to where Nathan was tucked behind a tree stump. "Best I can do, Cap'n, what are you planning on?"

"Well, with a white shirt, I was planning on tying it to the end of this musket to get those yahoos 'cross the way to meet me to see if we can't talk some sense. But I don't know what the hell kind of message this thing is going to send." Nathan attached the colored shirt to the musket's bayonet and started creeping toward the tree line. He looked back. "You are welcome to come along if you want to keep an eye on your blouse, monsieur."

Marcel followed the captain as musket fire decimated the branches and trees around them; a shriek from off to their left seemed to be evidence of someone being hit. Livid, Nathan continued to crawl, his weapon extended before him. When they reached the edge of the clearing he paused behind a fallen tree and began waving the musket high over his head. It took several minutes for the rifle fire to diminish. "It's the blue shirt. They don't know if we want to talk or make love."

Finally, the firing seemed to let up. More anguish came from their troops behind them; someone else had been hit.

"Christ in a basket. This is a nightmare." Nathan stood abruptly, vigorously waving the musket while walking into the open ground. Several rounds came whistling overhead.

"Cease fire, South! We want to talk, cease—" Marcel followed, shouting.

A musket ball ripped the cloth under Nathan's left arm, causing him to drop the overhead weapon. Marcel rushed to him.

"Are you hit, Cap'n?"

Nathan had gone to his knees in pain. "Smashed my rifle stock and rammed it against the underside of my arm. Wave that damn shirt, Marcel. Get them to stop."

"Stop the damn firing, for Christ's sake. Cease fire!" Marcel grabbed the musket and moved it forcefully over his head.

Finally, the deluge stopped. A strong voice came from the tree line across the way, "What you want, Yankee?"

"We just want to talk to y'all."

"The two of you drop your side arms and proceed to the center of the field."

"I'll get Israel to go with me." Marcel helped Nathan to his feet.

"No, I'm all right." Nathan clenched his left armpit. "Just steady me for a moment." He leaned against Marcel as they finally proceeded unsteadily across the plowed field. When they got to what they thought was the center, Nathan went to one knee while Marcel continued to hold the musket over his head, moving it gently.

"I don't see any movement on their part, Captain."

"They're trying to play it tough with us, we'll just wait." Nathan leaned against his bent knee and examined his trembling arm. "Christ, this son of a bitch hurts but it didn't penetrate, just spanked my arm with the stock hard enough to draw blood."

After several minutes, Marcel lowered the weapon and blue shirt down to his waist. Almost immediately, a musket ball plowed into the earth to Marcel's left.

"I think they're telling us you need to continue waving that flag."

Marcel hoisted the musket into the air once again. "These bastards are beginning to annoy me."

From the tree line, a high chorus of laughter.

"Did you hear what I just heard, Nathan?"

Nathan nodded. "That frivolity could come back to haunt these sons a bitches if I have anything to say about it." He struggled to get to his feet. "Let's go back to the tree line. Obviously, they're trying to unnerve us. We'll attempt to talk again, later." As they turned to walk back to their own line, several shots once again kicked up the earth to either side of them, accompanied by gales of laughter from the distant trees. The duo once again stopped and turned, Marcel glaring in the direction of the hidden troops.

"I guess it was a mistake on our part to get ourselves in this position. We can't go back, I can't drop this damn peace flag and they won't come out and talk. What do you propose, General Grant?"

"If this wound didn't sting so damn much"—Nathan took a couple of deep breaths—"maybe I could think straight. I—" He stopped.

From the far tree line, three soldiers started making their way toward the center of the field. It had stopped raining. As they neared Marcel and Nathan, the man in the center, obviously the officer, spoke out. "I am Lieutenant Anthony Browning at your service, gentlemen."

Nathan cleared his throat. "Captain Nathan Parker formerly of the Fifth Michigan, and may I ask, Lieutenant, wasn't it made abundantly clear back at the train debacle that Lee had surrendered and that the war was practically over? Didn't we explain that? Didn't we tell you that an armistice was imminent?"

"Don't speak to me of surrender, we have no word of an armistice and don't adopt that condescending tone with me, you jackass. You killed one of our officers, shot him in the face like the cowardly bastards that you are."

"The man responsible for that act has been summarily dealt with." Nathan gathered himself. "I extend that information along with my personal and sincere apology for the death of your officer. Now listen, damn it. Can we stop this nonsense before both sides sustain more casualties?"

" 'Nonsense,' you dare speak of nonsense, Captain? I have half a dozen dead soldiers, goddamn it. You took prisoners off that train that had been left in our charge. Return them immediately or we'll drive you out of those trees and walk through you like a dose of salts, so-called armistice or not. Incidently, First Lieutenant Moore had sent for reinforcements long before you fellows arrived on the scene. I expect them forthwith."

"I would need to speak to my superior officer back at the tree line," Nathan lied. He staggered, trying to gain a better footing in the soft field. "If you will allow me and my adjutant to retreat temporarily, I'll be back posthaste with an answer for you."

The Confederate officer nodded his approval as Nathan and Marcel made their way back toward their troops. Halfway there, Nathan looked over his shoulder. The Confederate trio hadn't waited and were hastily making their way back to their own lines. Before Marcel and Nathan could make it to their own tree line, musket fire began whistling over the two men's heads. "So much for our treaty agreement," Nathan lamented. The gunfire increased as the two men stumbled, exhausted, into the comfort of their home ground.

One of the Friendship men yelled sarcastically. "Can we shoot our guns now, *General* Parker?"

Nathan winced, shouting back, "No, absolutely not! I'll tell you when."

Marcel helped him deeper into the woods where they would be relatively safe before attempting to dress his wound. After cleaning the jagged tear, Marcel hefted a small metal flask to Nathan's lips and then took a long pull for himself. They both stopped abruptly, listening to the sounds of a bugle blowing notes of assembly. Marcel and Nathan looked at each other and said in chorus, "Cavalry."

"I asked you earlier, monsieur, of your plan, if any? Has it changed now that it appears the enemy has mounted horsemen?"

Nathan stretched his arm up high, carefully bending his elbow and flexing his fist several times. "It's not as bad as I first thought, thanks for asking. I would have bet my boots that the officer's remark about reinforcements coming forthwith was bull dung." Nathan got up from the fallen tree and paced for several minutes. "I want you to take half a dozen men and their horses and go to the far western end of our treed little island, about fifty yards in from the edge and as deep into the forest as possible. Start a campfire, you're going to have to search around for dry wood. But I think that's possible; tell them to strip the bark if necessary. Leave one man and his horse there to tend it, then start back this way another seventy-five yards or so and do the same. Work your way to the far eastern end with as many fires as it takes every seventy-five paces, leaving a man at each fire. Then, come back here to the center . . . build a very large fire. Then we'll talk."

CHAPTER 28

April 1865

Marcel headed back to the clearing. The musket fire decreased to an occasional round, scattering through overhead branches. After collecting Israel, Wilma, Lem, and Mr. Toby, Marcel recruited three more men from the Friendship group and proceeded west toward the end of the copse of trees. They gathered wood, lit a fire, and left Israel and his mount to tend the flames before starting back. Wilma remained stationed in her separate little camp. Marcel hurried to the far end with the Friendship men and finished his trip with Mr. Toby, who insisted he wasn't interested in being left at the far reaches of the wooded area. After starting the final fire in the center of the enclave, Marcel looked to Nathan, who had been conversing with the men of the Fifth Michigan.

Nathan waved his hand over his head for the troops to gather; when they did there were twenty-two including Marcel and Nathan plus the men from the train. "People, we're hopelessly outnumbered. I have a plan to get us out of here with the least amount of casualties." Nathan paused. "Here's what we're going to do. As it gets darker, I want you to break up in parties of three. Marcel and I will stay here at this central fire while those with horses will make your way in separate groups to the individual fires. When you get there, cook your supper, sing, carry on in a carefree manner. At ten thirty, I'll fire two quick pistol rounds, begin to make your way back here. Stop the singing; it will be as if you have turned in for the night. Kindle the fires well so they'll burn for several hours. Once we're all assembled back here, I'll explain what's next."

"I'll get you some coffee, Cap'n." Marcel noticed Nathan was pale and a little weak.

"Never mind. I'm going to see if, in fact, those foot soldiers yonder have been reinforced—see what's their strength." Nathan took his binoculars and started toward the tree line.

"I'll help you there, Mr. Parker, suh." Lemuel had been given the job of stoking the central fire. "Yes, suh, I can surely do that."

Marcel and Nathan exchanged glances.

"You think you could skirt around to the east and take a gander at those troops, Lem? See how many horses there are?" Nathan approached the black man and put a hand to his shoulder.

"I'll do you better than that, Captain, suh." Lem started toward the edge of the trees, stripping off his clothes as he walked. Marcel followed. By the time they reached the view to the darkened open field, Lem was down to his long gray underwear.

"You don't have to do this, Lem. You know that, don't you?"

"I owe Captain a lot, Mr. Farge. I'll be back, directly."

Marcel watched as Lem took a few steps into the field and then eased down on the soft wet earth and began to crawl; he was indistinguishable almost at once.

Marcel picked his way back to the fire where Nathan was huddled, clasping his wound. "He's one brave son of a bitch. I'll give that to him." The two men watched the bright flames, listening to the various attempts at music and laughter coming from the other fires scattered on either side of them.

"I don't think Confederate officer Browning ever really knew how many men we had," Nathan spoke softly. "There was such hellish confusion and I am hoping they'll think twice about attacking us. I'm trusting our fires and faked frivolity will keep them at bay at least until morning when I plan to be long gone. In any case, we'll know more when Lem gets back. . . . That is, *if* he gets back."

"What a sight, seeing him all buffed down when he eased out into that open ground." Marcel stirred the fire with a long stick.

"You know, Lafarge, you have to take some responsibility for all this."

"How do you figure?" Marcel glanced at the captain.

"Your careless choice of associates has proved disastrous to say the least." Nathan stood with considerable effort. "The fact that you would involve this illiterate band of cutthroats, rapists, thieves, and the like, on what you knew was considered by me a serious endeavor, rankles me. I don't leave my own anxiousness out of the mix, but you, my good friend, must at some point decide who the hell you are. Do you gallop through life caring only for your own pleasure? I consider you a friend, Marcel . . . you need to make some kind of choice—whether your sense of adventure supersedes your obligation to those who have committed to you. You made unfortunate choices because you thought the results might be amusing. I hope for all our sakes my men of the Fifth Michigan don't fall prey to that amusement." Nathan looked deep into the fire. "Go back to the tree line and wait for Mr. Lemuel."

Marcel started to speak but thought better of it, choosing instead to make his way silently back to the edge of the woods. He stared out into the moonless night. His dressing-down by Nathan stung him, more than he was ready to admit. The captain had laid him bare, no doubt. It hurt because he hadn't thought it possible.

He couldn't remember when he'd been spoken to in such a direct and intimate fashion, certainly not since his marriage.

A strange sense of dampened joy coursed through Marcel. He thought he should be upset and angry but his heart told him that someone had been brave enough and cared sufficiently to tell him who in the hell he truly was. It was humbling, and he didn't quite know what to think about it. One thing was obvious though, Nathan was deeply upset. The man was a soldier, not a marauder, and his mission was turning into a cutthroat's ball. Nathan seemed reasonable except when it came to the welfare of his Michigan soldiers—then he was the most single-minded and cold-blooded son of a bitch he'd ever met. That business with St. James showed a dark side of Nathan beyond what Marcel could have imagined.

Marcel sat with his back to a tree for nearly an hour before he heard what was rather a poor imitation of a whippoorwill coming from the darkened field. He answered with an equally poor night bird sound, and waited. After several minutes the whippoorwill repeated but this time was considerably weaker.

Marcel once again answered and waited, after several minutes he was startled when Nathan suddenly appeared from behind him.

The captain knelt down next to Marcel's spot against the tree. "That sounds like it might be Lem out there. Wonder why he doesn't come on in?"

A slight cough followed another attempt at birdsong.

Marcel took off his pistol belt and dropped it to the ground, pulling the heavy weapon into his right hand. He looked to Nathan and began his journey into the black field. Whoever had made the bird sounds now moaned softly some sixty or seventy feet off to Marcel's left. As he scurried over the broken ground, he strained his eyes trying to see into the darkness. At one point he thought he heard sounds coming from farther back in the field. Crawling forward he was startled to hear once again the labored attempt of the whippoorwill. Marcel whispered, "Lem, you there?"

"Yes, suh, but I'm poorly, suh," Lem answered. "I got myself pig-stuck for sure."

Marcel moved to the man stretched out on the damp ground. "You been stabbed, Lem?"

The black man took in deep, labored breaths, not answering. Marcel rolled him onto his back, then lifted him to his shoulders. He could feel the warm blood on Lem's body.

On the way back to the tree line, Lem whispered to Marcel. "I think they followed me, suh. I think there's maybe two of those devils out there in the field. . . ." Lem's voice trailed off.

"Cap'n," Marcel stage-whispered to Nathan as he got closer to the edge of the field. "Lem's been stabbed or something. He's gonna need some fixing." Marcel laid Lem's blood-covered body down next to the tree where Nathan had propped himself. As the two men tried to make the Negro comfortable, Lem opened his eyes.

"In my hand, Captain, suh, in my right hand. I can't let it go, prize it out, Captain." Lemuel's right hand clenched tightly around a piece of cloth.

Nathan gently opened Lem's hand and a banner of bright yellow fell from his fingers. Nathan held it close to his face, trying to catch light from the distant bonfire. "Looks like a cavalry guidon with the number five. Lots of wear. They're a company, probably at least thirty plus the bunch from the train makes close to sixty or so. Well, he got our answer for us, damn it, but at what price?"

Marcel examined Lem's stomach to see a deep puncture under his floating rib on the right side. "Can you staunch that blood flow, Cap'n?" Marcel asked. "I have some night crawling to do."

The two men stared at each other as Nathan carefully folded the cavalry banner and pressed it against Lem's wound. Without looking at Marcel, he addressed him. "I admire what you're going to do but remember, your death cannot help us."

Exuberance filled Marcel. He tucked his pistol into his belt at the small of his back and started toward the tree line.

"Take this," Nathan said as his bowie knife and sheath lit at Marcel's feet.

Marcel retrieved it and sprinted away. Reaching the soft earth, he bent over deeply so as not to show a silhouette against the flickering campfire. After slowly elbowing his way quietly across some twenty yards of mud, he stopped to listen. He could only hear the singing, which seemed to be dying out, and an occasional owl, but the longer he remained still, the more convinced he became that someone was out there. A clicking sound that could be mistaken for a cricket or cicada came to him softly from in front, probably thirty feet. Another similar sound emanated from his left. After a while he understood a pattern—one cricket would call and then ten seconds later call again, just that little bit closer. Then the other cricket would sing out his song softly, move, and call again.

He reasoned that the crickets were moving toward him. He would just wait, as this one in front had about two more calls to make before Marcel would say hello. They were good, he thought. Well trained, steady, and patient. But, Marcel thought, there would soon be a third cricket. He steadied his breathing, deep and quiet, concentrating on allowing his toes to lose their tension. His ankles and on up . . . his legs releasing the bound muscles, he sucked in air, concentrating on his neck, trying to relax his arms and shoulders. The bowie knife handle he had placed under his chin he now held with both hands, ready to lunge quickly forward.

In front of him within ten feet came the call of the amateur cricket accompanied by the heavy expulsion of air from its creator. After the first utterance, Marcel knew the caller would start to move. As the night sounder's silhouette came into view, Marcel rose onto his elbows to hear a startled, "Jimmie?" Marcel then drove the eight-inch blade hard into the cricket's exposed throat. He struggled for a moment as Marcel clamped his hands roughly over the man's mouth until he stopped moving. Multiple insect sounds came repeatedly from the east . . . and then nothing. Marcel waited once again, trying to calm his rapidly beating heart.

A rustling, then a quiet, "Rupert?"

Marcel clicked his best cricket imitation.

Shortly, someone whispered, "What was that noise, Rupe?"

Marcel muffled his voice with his hand. "Snake," then quietly called, "Jimmie, come 'ere." He was aware of Jimmie crawling toward him. When he got to within twenty feet, the soldier started speaking in a quiet voice, about how he hoped the news was true of the war being over, how they would have a heck of a good time back in Atlanta. All the while Marcel clicked away, leading Jimmie to the inert body of his friend, Rupert. Marcel had moved to the man's right side; as he got nearer he drove the knife viciously toward the back of the young fellow's exposed neck. But the soldier's heightened instincts caused him to roll at the last second, the knife catching him high on his right shoulder. He screamed in pain and slashed his cradled musket across Marcel's face, breaking the skin above his left eye. They wrestled, Marcel continuing to strike out with his knife. The soldier dropped his weapon and grabbed both of Marcel's wrists, twisting with alarming strength. Marcel, sensing the battle starting to turn, crashed his knee repeatedly into the groin of the combative man, who arched over in pain. As the soldier's grip loosened, Marcel plunged the blade deftly into his chest.

Marcel buried his wet hands into the damp earth, trying to rid himself of the young man's blood. Rolling onto his back, he gasped for air. Finally able to open his eyes, he watched a black-shrouded image of the moon. Dark clouds rolled past a sad, reddened face. He wondered what these dead men in the field lying next to him had dreamt of. Had they looked, just minutes before, at this same moon? It seemed to matter not. They were gone now, that was for certain.

CHAPTER 29

April 1865

Marcel sat by the fire with Lem, who was stretched out with a blanket under his head.

"I am feeling a might better, Mr. Farge. Captain Nathan made me swallow some of that corn liquor. It sure does rattle a soul. Lordy."

Marcel murmured his awareness to Lem that he had heard him and went back to his visions. For whatever reason, he couldn't seem to shake a pervading sorrow that had come over him. After the wicked fight in the field culminating in the death of the two soldiers, he was near exhaustion. Whether it was grief or merely the aftermath of the incredible shock, he wasn't certain. So stimulated one moment, only to suffer this depressing letdown the next, Marcel didn't know what he was sure of. A terrible lethargy overcame him. He prayed he wouldn't be called upon this night to engage in any other supreme efforts. He cradled his head in his hands. It would pass, he was sure, but when?

"Mr. Farge, suh, someone's hustling t'word us."

Marcel roused himself and slipped his pistol from his belt. He was relieved to discover it was Nathan.

"How did your reconnoitering go?"

"It was fine, I took care of our problems in the field."

Marcel paused to reflect on the past half hour. "I think we bought ourselves some time. Speaking of which, shouldn't our troops be drifting back in soon?"

Nathan glanced at Marcel but didn't answer. He looked at his watch and walked to where the horses were tied and began to saddle Lem's mare. "Lemuel, you gonna be able to ride? 'Cause we're fixing to skedaddle out of here directly."

Lem propped himself up on one elbow. "I am resting my bones now, suh, just give me a might of time."

Marcel checked his pistol for rounds, wondering why Nathan hadn't answered him. He walked to his horse, noticing that riders were slowly coming into the campground. As Marcel saddled up, the troops drifted in, Nathan meeting each one with a swift whispered conversation. He helped Lem onto his mount, then cut a short hank of rope, tying the black man into his seat and leading the line to his own saddle horn. Nathan finally mounted and led Lem to where Marcel waited on his horse.

"I'll tell you what I told the others," said Nathan quietly. "As soon as Israel and a couple of the Friendship gang are here, you will ease on out in single file. Can I trust you to bring up the rear?"

Marcel nodded.

"You are going to slip out of here and move north through that clapboard fence. After several miles and only if you are not being followed, turn west. I am betting our bonfires and camaraderie will have lulled those footsloggers and the cavalry to wait until morning to come thundering across that field in a wave to overrun us. Not knowing our true numbers, I think, will dissuade them. In any case, that's the plan, cover your tracks."

Marcel wondered if it would work. What Nathan was attempting—to delay the Confeds into wandering about trying to find out where and in what direction his troops had headed—seemed logical. But as this long day had shown, logic seemed at times the last consideration in times of war.

Marcel walked to Nathan and motioned for him to follow, stepping deeper into the woods. He turned. "Using the words 'you are' as in 'you are going to slip out of here and head north,' just exactly, what in the hell does that mean, *mon capitaine?*"

Nathan rubbed his troubled arm. "It means just what you would suppose it to mean, that I am staying behind to kindle the fires, and when they come in the morning I'll do whatever I can to delay them. Maybe I'll wave that pretty blue shirt of yours and have a nice chat with Lieutenant Browning, whatever, it's not of import to you. Do as you're told, head north, then when clear, west toward Vicksburg, tend to the Fifth Michigan boys. I'll meet you on the trail . . . God willing."

Marcel stared at Nathan, the flickering of the fire casting a deathlike glow to the captain's face. Marcel started to turn, then reached out and grabbed Nathan's hand, shaking it vigorously. "*Bonne chance, mon ami, bonne chance.*"

Marcel went to Lem first to see if he was able to ride. After hearing an "I be fine, Mr. Farge," he quickly gathered the troops and had them mount, exhorting them to move quietly with Israel leading the way. They slipped quickly north, away from Nathan and the roaring campfires.

Taking pains to cover their tracks, the group was now thirty-odd riders moving single file across the open fields. The moon was up and shone brightly as horses and riders made a long shadowy parade across the plowed ground.

Marcel stopped his mount for a moment and cupped his ears with his hands, thinking he had heard a horse whinny in the far distance. The myriad of night sounds blended as if one to help deaden his mounted troop's slow retreat across the rich farmland. He stayed rooted for several minutes, listening for the jingle of the various buckles and straps of his mounted troops' harnesses to subside. Once again he cupped his hands and turned slowly in his saddle. There it was again, to the west, a horse or maybe many horses making their animal sounds—a snort; a whinny; a gelding calling to a mare, protesting his lost manhood; a young colt trouncing the ground, feeling the tension in the air. Marcel spurred his mount past his riders and got to the head of the group. Waving his hand high above his head he made a circling motion. As the mounted souls gathered, Marcel once again held his arm high for quiet. In a restrained but firm voice, still with arm extended, he began.

"Unfortunately our little ruse with the campfires may not have worked. We've got troops to the west, maybe a quarter of a mile."

Various murmurs of protest rustled among the horsemen. "How in hell . . . ?" "Riding out, the hell with it." "Sure as the sun rises this is a disaster."

Marcel let them go on for only a moment. "*Fermez la bouche.*" He spat. "Shut your mouths and listen."

There was complete silence, as if a leader had arisen. "We're in this together. Anyone who thinks he would have a better chance alone against probably thirty mounted soldiers and at least that many of a trained cavalry company ride on out. Our only hope is staying strong and together . . . what I think might be happening is either the mounted troops from the train or this new company of cavalry are trying to flank our former position at the campfire. They don't know *our* whereabouts as yet. We'll continue on."

Someone from the back made a protest and moved their mount through the throng up close to Marcel. In the weak light Marcel could see it was Wilma.

"What about Captain Parker, what's his chance?" Wilma whispered.

"Indeed, what of him, Mr. Frenchman?" A voice from the rear.

Marcel looked to the expectant faces. "Parker's words to me were, 'It's not of import to you. . . . Do as you're told.' " Once again, he looked around the group to reiterate, " 'Do as you're told.' His thoughts were with you, he knew too well what it would mean to stay behind and try to cause a diversion. His sacrifice, if it's to be, will be in vain if we as a group don't stay together . . . what will it be?" Marcel raised his arm as a sign. Slowly the rest of the thirty-plus horsemen started to raise their arms.

The Fifth Michigan men looked struck. Marcel didn't know many of their names but among those he did know, Fitz, Watson, Kendall, and Harris all expressed their distress at this plan. They didn't want to see their captain stay behind in such a dangerous position.

Marcel finally interrupted them with the logic he figured would work best with these soldiers. "I understand you men being upset but I must repeat—your captain wasn't asking your permission—he said, 'Do it.' "

Their arms came up. Reluctantly, but they came up. They were together. The group moved farther north, then, following Marcel's lead, dismounted. He once again called the troops into a tight circle. "Water and feed your horses, take on water, and some *repas* for yourselves."

"What's a '*repas*'?" someone called out, a light spattering of laughter seemed to relax the nervous men and women.

"After we're refreshed, we'll head west a half mile then back south, trying to get the horsemen into a flanking position where our rifle fire will rake across the axis of the enemy. In other words we've got a better chance of hitting someone if there are a dozen or so horsemen lined up in a row . . . comprenez-vous?"

They all nodded, but some of the Friendship gang looked puzzled.

"Once we've hit them hard we'll try to encircle them, pushing them off the open plowed ground into the trees where they'll find it hard to reorganize. When they're dispersed, we'll ride a giant circle heading east in a group, then bear north. Finally, back west and a full-out retreat. All we can hope for is a delay, and hopefully discouragement on their part. . . ." Marcel waited. "Questions?"

The group fell silent.

"All right, let's get to it." Marcel made his way over to the group of the Fifth Michigan ex-prisoners. He found Watson. "How do you feel?"

Watson nodded in the affirmative. "We're okay, I think a couple of the men feel kind of weak, but we're up for it. I wish we were better armed, we've only got three rifles among us. The others supplied us with their sidearms, so I guess the best we can hope for is to make a hell of a lot of noise."

Marcel looked over the thin worn soldiers. "I want all of this group to stay close to me, the Fifth Michigans and the hangers-on. Don't get yourselves shot, or Captain Parker, when we see him next, will have my hide."

The group enjoyed Marcel's humor.

"Mount up." As Marcel eased into his saddle, he checked his Colt, resolutely spinning the cylinder, then snapping the heavy metal drum back in place. The Spencer rested easily in its scabbard under his right leg. All appendages seemed in place. If only, he wished, he were as confident and ready as his weapons. It seemed extremely bad luck that they had barely begun and were obliged to deal with an enemy that was so unpredictable. The idea of having to attack a superior force with less than a healthy group seemed foolhardy, and yet knowing the vagaries of war, they might just succeed. Once more, he thought, a battle awaits. So let's not keep my stubborn Southern compatriots waiting.

The horsemen headed west, in the far distance to the south they could make out the flickering of Nathan's campfires. Marcel raised his arm. They were in a depression in the loose earthen field. Several hundred yards or so to their left they could see a long line of horsemen silhouetted against a night sky. Marcel pointed toward the band of riders and turned in his saddle to see his people as one, gazing at the distant troops.

Marcel reasoned they had surprise on their side. The Southern troops would be fully expecting fire from their front as they closed on the campsite. He rode on for fifty yards then once again raised his arm, making a sweeping gesture for the horsemen to form a line abreast. After having done so they wheeled into their positions, the extreme left side holding steady as the right swung about. Marcel thought it not too bad for a motley band of guerillas. Now, he knew, would be the most important moment. He needed to move closer and attack before the Southern mounted troops charged toward the woods being fortified by Nathan's gallant army of one. As his horsemen stood silently waiting, he rode quietly along their front, stopping to check on Lemuel who insisted that he was fit and ready as did the bank of ex-prisoners who smiled at him. It was a crushing responsibility, this leadership.

Marcel loosened his Spencer and checked its rounds. He had been fortunate to acquire such a fine firearm, they were indeed scarce. Then, simply taking a position at the front of the thirty-five riders, he motioned with his hand for them to follow. At a gallop they headed toward the fires and the unsuspecting cavalry. As they neared, Marcel stood in his stirrups and raised the Spencer, waiting, waiting until the last possible moment. He could see through the darkened haze that the cavalry men had dismounted and were leading their horses in what was probably an attempt to surprise what they thought were the renegades and ex-prisoners in the woods.

It was a break certainly for Marcel's raiders. He steadied his carbine and opened fire along the line of men and horses. Not being able to tell if he had hit anyone, he quickly reloaded and fired again as his whole line of would-be cavalry followed him with a withering cross fire. He could hear distant screams and a bugler attempting to signal an alarm—*tut-ta-taa-tut*—then he was cut off, as if suddenly grown tired. The men in gray attempted to organize a defense but with very little return fire. Marcel could see a number of horses running free, scattered by the withering rounds from his men. They charged among the routed footmen, dealing them heavy losses. A few of the men had regained their mounted positions and were attempting to fight back but there was no doubt, it was a rout.

In the midst of the brief skirmish, the moon suddenly moved out from behind a long dark cloud, exposing a chaotic scene of men running, horses either dead on the ground with their masters or sprinting for cover to the distant trees. The gunfire continued, a cry split the night air to Marcel's left—it was one of his people. Marcel wheeled his horse and, still firing rapidly, moved toward the screaming. It was one of the Friendship gang, on the ground beating the earth with his legs, clutching a darkened wet stomach with both hands. Before Marcel could alight, a voice from a horseman to his left called out to the fallen rider.

"How bad ya hit, Hiram?"

The supine form lay begging. "I'm a goner, Tom, do me quick, I can't abide it . . . do it, Tom, please."

Marcel rode off with Tom's pistol shot still ringing in his ears.

The fight seemed to have moved off to the east, his guerillas chasing a group of running cavalry men attempting to regroup. Marcel shouted to his people to encircle them. As the horseless troops stopped to fight, the band of horsemen indeed rode in circles around the stationary troops like wild Indians. Marcel could see that the eight to ten horseless cavalry men were attempting to surrender as the Friendship gang cut them down without remorse. Marcel shouted to his troops to break off and re-form, but they were so scattered it was near impossible. He finally managed to settle a large group of the ex-prisoners who were reveling in the demise of the decimated Southern cavalry.

"Form up on me!" he shouted. A number of bodies lying awkwardly on the soft earth proved the victory decisive. Sparse gunfire still came from the tree line and Marcel wondered how Nathan had fared, if in fact he had been a victim of rounds from his own troops or if he had managed to take shelter. He would check the woods after he organized his troops. Once again he bellowed, "Form up!"

It was hard to tell in the dim light exactly how much damage had been done but it had been extremely fast and deadly. Musket fire echoed somewhere off to the east. Marcel continued to call to his people to form up. Finally, it seemed the whole group was excitedly gathered. "You did good, men—"

Wilma quickly answered, "Thanks a treat, General."

The men thought this to be funny.

Marcel held up his arm for quiet. "Let's head out east as planned. Once what's left of these cavalrymen and the mounted troops from the train get back together there's going to be hell to pay. Where's Israel?"

"Here, Frenchy."

Marcel smiled in spite of himself. "Lead the troops out of here. I'll catch up with you. I need to check on Captain Parker."

Israel swept his arm on high and wheeled his horse toward the lightening eastern sky. As Marcel watched the horsemen, he caught a glimpse of Lem valiantly trying to sit upright in his saddle, but instead listing to port like a leaking ship. He marveled at the black man's courage.

The woods were empty, the coals from the banked fires glowing red in the dank woods. Marcel rode carefully through the tightly grouped trees. At the main campfire close to where Nathan had exhorted Marcel to "slip on out of here and move north," Marcel found his own blue shirt, used to signal Lieutenant Browning, stretched out on the ground with rocks holding it in an arrow shape. Tied to the bottom of the form was a small piece of Nathan's blue-and-yellow pennant from his dark hat. The arrow pointed west.

By the time Marcel caught up with his troops they were bivouacked in a group of sheltering oaks off a dirt road heading north.

"Thought we might wait for you here, Lafarge. Seems like we'd be heading up this road later."

Israel moved his mount closer to Marcel. "That fellow Willoughby got himself hit, I couldn't tell how bad." Willoughby sat astride a bay mare, his left arm pinned tight against his side. Marcel could tell from his quick short breaths that he was gut-shot. "How you doing, Dad?"

The older man nodded. "I've been better, that's for damn sure. . . . If I could get this mare on wheels it would be a might smoother, I'll tell you."

Marcel forced a chuckle. "You want me to take a look?"

Willoughby winced. "No, sir, I'll keep up, carry on, sir."

Marcel surveyed his people, most of them scattered about, resting in the warming first light. "Mount up, we've got to keep moving."

They answered with a considerable bit of complaining but the troops indeed saddled up. They headed north for an hour then turned west. Taking to the trees, they hoped to stay hidden. The awakening sun felt warm on their tired backs as they wound their way in a serpentine line through virgin woods of pine and oak.

Marcel continued to check on the condition of the ex-prisoners and Lemuel, who now rode with his chin on his chest rocking back and forth, more dead than alive.

They had stopped briefly for a cold breakfast of dried jerky and tea. Most of the horsemen collapsed on the moist grass of the densely clad forest only to be roused several minutes later with, "Saddle up, move out."

Marcel had noticed that Dad Willoughby hadn't gotten off his horse. "You couldn't step down, right?" Marcel asked.

There was perspiration on the older man's face, rivulets of sweat collected in his graying whiskers. He couldn't answer Marcel. His tightly clamped teeth gave his mouth and jaw the lie to "I'll keep up."

Marcel called out, "Hold up, troops." Willoughby sat like a stone on his mount, afraid to breathe. Marcel had several of the men ease him off his horse and onto the ground as Israel rode up. Marcel motioned toward the stricken Willoughby. "We need a moment."

Israel's concern was genuine. "I'll set up a perimeter."

Marcel rinsed his kerchief in water from his canteen and bathed Willoughby's face. "What's your first name, Dad?"

The man's eyes darted from side to side. "Phil, but my mother always called me Pie."

"My brother's name was Phil, or rather, Philippe, which I guess you could say was the same."

Phil slowly moved his head in agreement. "Are we making small talk . . . 'til it's over, sir."

Marcel clutched Phil's hand. "Well, soldier, as they say, 'There comes a time. . . .' Just try and shut your eyes and breathe easily, Philip." The dying man moved both hands to grasp the blood-sodden jacket gathered around his waist. He began fighting for air, and then very quickly he was gone. Marcel regretted they couldn't take the time to bury the man, but they wrapped him tightly in the remnants of a Sibley tent and hoisted him into the lower branches of a century-old oak. The body safe from the night animals, they rode off while Marcel recited the Lord's Prayer.

It was a quiet set of horsemen that moved out, death being the silent partner riding with them. Each man knowing that Phil Willoughby's death could have very well been their own. The random musket ball having had no design, simply choosing the eldest this time.

As they picked their way through a stand of sycamore, Marcel was reminded of an episode concerning his brother Philippe when he was a child. He remembered his father appearing at a friend's house in the middle of a lavish birthday party for a fellow thirteen-year-old schoolmate and, at the top of his voice, inquiring whether Marcel had, in fact, filled his brother Philippe's boots with porridge. Marcel recalled looking around the suddenly quiet party, asking his father if they could speak of the matter at a later time. Of course they could not, and if Marcel was embarrassed it was of his own doing, insisted his father. He remembered the elder Lafarge unbuttoning his frock coat and unhitching his belt while Marcel fought the tears that threatened his blushing cheeks. Hearing the giggles from other children while being paraded across the salon, he knew he had never moved his eyes from his father's angry face. Brandishing a toy sword, he recalled speaking to his friend Bertrand, saying he was being called away on an important secret mission. He assumed Bertrand could manage to provide their troops with the proper sustenance. He was sorry he would not be able to share in the festive *gâteau* and wished Bertrand, *"Joyeux anniversaire, au revoir."*

Marcel's father delivered the first blow before Marcel had completely crossed the room. He never flinched but began singing "La Marseillaise." Bertrand applauded, followed by the rest of the children. He urged Marcel, "Head high. Head high, comrade. We will carry on the good fight." Most of the other children of French lineage picked up the familiar refrain of the French national anthem. Tears streaming down his face, Marcel raised high his sword, head held aloft in defiance. His father, muttering to himself, astonished Marcel when he ceased the beating. *"Mon pére,* your arm seems to have lost its resolve. Are *you* ashamed?" Marcel remembered the rustle of clothing as his father put his belt back on. Through clenched teeth, he spit out that his son would be the death of him, his defiance and arrogance inexcusable . . . he was at his wit's end. They walked through a manicured garden, and a woman's voice called out to wait a moment. Who was that, he wondered? Strange, he couldn't remember. He could see the woman's face. He thought she would be upset if he didn't recall who she was.

As the group slowly began to trail, Marcel called out to Israel to take the point. A worrisome itch at the back of his neck made him turn, and each time he felt as if he were being watched. He stopped his mount and waited for several minutes. It was reminiscent of last night's battle. A sense of movement coming his way. He pulled his mare off the trail and headed down a ravine, then back up a steep hill. At the top, the view was clear back east and to the south. A shiny glint pulled his eyes back to where they had come through the woods some ten minutes earlier. He shielded his eyes from the sun with his hands and moved his head slowly across the eastern skyline. There it was again, a polished belt buckle possibly or maybe, he thought, simply the morning sun catching a reflection off a pool of water. A puff of smoke, a moment of silence, and then the unmistakable sound of a musket shot and the dreaded whistle of compressed air as the ball came whistling past his head. As he wheeled his mount off the hilltop and bounded down the side of the hill, Marcel's thoughts reverted to the close call on the stalled train as he and Nathan had made their way through the vestibule. Was it the same sharpshooter, he wondered, who had driven the wood splinter into his hair, down and to the right? In thinking of it, it seemed weeks ago since the encounter at the rail siding; was it just yesterday?

CHAPTER 30

April 1865

B y the time Marcel caught up with his troops they were a mile farther on through the trees. He approached cautiously as they were spread out in a line abreast with their guns at the ready. "Israel, it's Marcel, I'm coming in."

Israel rode out to meet him. "We heard what sounded like musket rounds. Didn't know what was up."

Marcel slid off his horse. "No, it was a single round, what you probably heard was the echo off these hills." Marcel led his horse toward the waiting troops. "Men, we're being followed."

Wilma coughed discreetly.

Marcel looked her way and nodded. "People." Then there was quiet laughter. "We haven't shaken them. Let's hightail it. If they're following in strength, we'll have to stop and fight." Marcel led them through the trees; he ordered the Fifth Michigan boys and the other prisoners from the train to stay close as they zigzagged at a controlled pace. After twenty minutes they came upon the opening to a large gentle valley and Marcel signaled for the horsemen to form a circle around him.

"I see no reason to go any farther without trying to resolve this." He looked at the tired group. "We don't know if the folks that took a shot at me were just a scouting party or the main body. Either way, I intend to find out; we're going to split up into two groups, one on each side of this valley. Get yourself high enough on the side of the hill so you're firing down and not across into the rise on the other side. I'll be down in the center of the ravine with—" Marcel looked around at the expectant faces. "Wilson, drag your reluctant ass alongside of me, my friend, we're going to be bait."

Wilson spurred his horse into the clearing alongside Marcel. An arrogant smirk frozen onto his face, Marcel could see an uncontrollable lip quiver as the man drew closer. "You weren't planning on living forever were you, Wilson?"

Wilma laughed. "I'll ride with ya, Frenchy."

"No need for the woman, Lafarge." Wilson said.

Marcel nodded. "Israel, stay with the Fifth, our friends from the train, Lem, and Toby." Toby? It suddenly occurred to Marcel that he hadn't seen the irascible freeman since leaving Nathan and the fires. Christ, Nathan was right about that useless bastard—he had found a way to save his own hide by running off when the attackers would be preoccupied with either the camp or Marcel's retreating company. He reined in his anger—he couldn't be distracted by it, that luxury wasn't his when he had responsibility for so many men's lives.

But the others must have come to the same realization as one of the Friendship bunch remarked, "Yeah, you can dress 'em up, but a shiftless nigger is a shiftless—"

"Enough!" Marcel would not brook being interrupted. "Spread out on that north bluff there. The rest of you take the south rise, remember what I said—be sure you're high enough that you're shooting down, not raking your friends on the opposite hill. . . . Mr. Wilson and I will be having a smoke here in this clearing. Don't fire until we start to move out, the Confeds will come through that opening back there"—he then turned and pointed toward the end of the clearing. "When we decide to run, and we reach that dead pine hanging over the ravine, open up."

There were no questions as the riders took their places up in the tree-lined bluffs and rises. Marcel urged his horse into the large bowl-shaped clearing. He quietly dug into his knapsack and retrieved a pouch of tobacco as Wilson nervously tried to steady his horse. While they waited, Marcel carefully rolled the fine tobacco grounds into flimsy corn silk. He looked at Wilson and ran his tongue slowly lengthwise along the homemade cigarette, never taking his eyes from the man. He twisted the ends and handed the finished treat to him.

Wilson shook his head. "Never touch 'em."

Marcel grinned at the would-be gambler. "It wasn't an offer, it was an order."

With shaking hands, Wilson took the cigarette as Marcel rolled another. "While we're killing time I'll tell you a little story, Clete. Back on the train at the siding, one of the Reb sharpshooters winged one at me, missed by about six inches, drove some splinters into my hair; it was close. Just now, up on the hill I believe that same man tried again . . . down and to the right. Sooner or later that fellow might get lucky. Now, as we sit here enjoying our ciggies, probably one of two things will happen, either the man is alone and he's settling his rifle in the fork of a tree for another try, or . . . he's with a patrol of ten to a dozen troopers who'll come hoopin' and hollerin' down into this gully and you and I will simply ride off into the brambles, trying like hell not to get shot, while our friends up in the hills do their best to cut them up." Marcel struck a match with his thumbnail and reached out to light Wilson's cigarette; then his own. Smiling, Marcel cupped his hands and sucked in; as the flame followed his inward breath of air he continued to stare at Wilson. Flicking the match away, he winked at the worried horseman. "Bait."

They didn't wait long, what sounded like a dozen horses could be heard, their heavy hoofbeats amplifying off the surrounding hills. Wilson stretched his head from side to side, his horse, sensing his tension, pranced, while Marcel sat calmly waiting for the gap between the trees to be filled by the Southern horsemen.

"What do you think, Wilson, will it be the cavalry or the mounted men from the train?"

Wilson remained mute.

"The cavalry took a beating last night when we attacked them from behind, whereas the soldiers from the train were embarrassed and shot to hell at the siding. Either way I look for them to have smoke pouring from their ears. . . ." Marcel nudged Wilson's horse with his toe. "Don't you?"

Wilson tried to spur his horse away but Marcel caught the reins and snugged the horse and rider up close. "Don't be anxious to leave, my friend. Wait until I say so, *comprenez-vous?*" Marcel could see dust forming above the trees to his front. It wouldn't be long; they were coming hard now, he could hear the pounding weight of the first riders. As they appeared, it was evident from their undisciplined array that they were the mounted soldiers from the train, not the cavalry.

Marcel fired two shots at the horsemen with his pistol and released Wilson's horse, spun his own mount in a half circle, and with a "Whoop" started at a dead run down the open valley. Pistol fire could be heard behind him along with the occasional rifle and musket report. Wilson's horse took the lead, the rider stretched almost horizontal on the mount's back. His arm flailing wildly, he beat his horse with the reins.

Marcel could see what he thought was the dead pine where he would be clear of his own troop's gunfire from the hill above him, but before reaching it, in front of him, Wilson's mount's legs unexpectedly folded under him and horse and rider went down hard—whether from a Confederate round or a rabbit hole, Marcel didn't know—but Wilson rolled into a dusty, hardened creekbed and came up running. Marcel shouted to him, and as the man turned, he caught him under the left armpit and swung him onto the back of his horse. Wilson grasped Marcel around the waist as withering gunfire erupted above them. His troops had resisted firing until the last possible moment. Marcel hazarded a quick glance back to see as many as six or seven riders down, the rest pulling up and retreating back into the woods where they had come from. Marcel looked over his shoulder at Wilson.

"Catch one of those stray mounts as I ride by." Marcel sprinted hard to catch one of the frightened Confederate horses and Wilson scrambled onto its back before he was properly seated and was unceremoniously bucked off. He lit hard, but held onto the reins of the frightened mare and remounted.

He called out to Marcel, "I owe you, Reb, whether it's a round in the back of the head or a shot of whiskey. I'll decide later."

The gunfire from Marcel's guerillas had subsided as he ordered them to cease fire. "Pick up any rifles and ammunition that you can," he shouted, "and quickly form up on me, do it now, double-time!" He looked hard into the hills, then once again yelled out, "Casualties?" He breathed a sigh of relief as there was only the sound of men and horses scrambling down into the valley floor.

They quickly gathered weapons from the fallen horsemen and silently moved away from the bloodied canyon floor. Marcel kept them at a gallop for a number of miles until they finally came upon a fast-moving stream.

"Water your horses, grab something to eat . . . boots and saddles in ten minutes . . . Israel, get someone to ride back a ways and keep watch." As Marcel checked on Lem he heard a shout from the Friendship group.

"Pat Thomas is missing, damn it all to hell." When Marcel

inquired of the missing Pat Thomas, he was told he had last been seen on the southern bluff with the rest of the Friendship gang.

Thomas's friends were working themselves into a lather. "We gotta go back for him."

"How in the devil are we going to do that?" Marcel stepped into the group. "If we go back we'll all be killed, damn it, use your heads. Wilson, see if you can find Thomas and be quick about it, we'll set up across this stream behind those boulders and trees. We'll wait an hour, no more, be back here, or you'll be on your own. . . . All right people, listen up, the rest of you cross the stream, take cover and get some rest, take the horses deeper into the woods, make sure they're well tethered . . . let's move."

With great reluctance Wilson rode out, back the way they came. As he passed Marcel he attempted a sneer that died in the making as his fear overcame him.

Marcel unsaddled his horse and rubbed her down with grass. He fed and watered the animal before resaddling and walking the mare back among the other tethered horses. They sat behind large boulders and trees, each man quietly contemplating his own destiny. They should have been making tracks westward. This to a man they knew, but to leave a fellow behind was difficult. Marcel lay facing the streambed, his Spencer resting easily, pointing east. He had sent Wilson on this mission of mercy not because he thought he was the best man for it, but because he disliked the man to distraction. He wondered if he had been fair to the missing victim, Pat Thomas.

An hour passed and then another and still they waited. During this time Marcel was able to put a name to the woman's voice from the birthday episode. It was his friend Bertrand's mother, Madame Bonet. Lovely in a delicate pink chiffon dress, she came hurrying up to Marcel and his father. What was it his father said . . . something about an excuse, the earlier "interruption" even before Madame Bonet could speak. She, in turn, berated his father for coming into her home in the midst of a celebration to reprimand his child. Marcel's father, he recalled, continued to defend his intentions but she corrected him; that his intent was not to punish but to embarrass his child and in so doing, he had brought embarrassment and contempt upon himself. She stated the father was never to set foot in her home again, and requested that he remove himself from her property immediately. Marcel's father tried to explain himself but the woman would have none of it. At one point, Marcel had turned to his friend's mother. *"Faire des excuses, madame."*

"N'est pas nécessaire." She reached across and touched Marcel's cheek, then followed them down the long gravel path until they vanished under the ornate steel gate.

Marcel stood, wanting to shake the long-ago memories of his brother and father. He asked Israel to bring in the outrider on watch so they could move out. He needed to shake his daydreaming. He had no more than finished his words when a horse could be heard, coming from the east riding hard; someone was shouting.

"Don't shoot, hold your fire. I'm Wilson," he called out. "Hold fire." The horse plowed quickly through the streambed. "They got Thomas and the outrider, my man Buckles. Ah, Christ, I saw 'em, they was trussed-up like mummies." Wilson kept babbling like an incoherent child. Marcel walked to him, slapped him hard, and the man finally stopped. Gasping for air, Wilson finally told his story. He had gone out half a mile or so when he heard voices. He could see through the trees a large group of mounted Confederates. Buckles, whom Israel had assigned to watch duty, and Pat Thomas were hog-tied and being kicked while thrashing around on the ground. Hearing this, the Friendship gang rose en masse to get their horses. Marcel stood behind a boulder, calmly looking across the stream.

"You'll only get halfway across that water before their riflemen will cut you down. But you fellows suit yourself. You usually do." The Friendship gang waited. Marcel could see glimpses of horses and men gathering just beyond the tree line. "If you want a fight you'll have it soon enough . . . here they come." They could hear the bugler's call and with that the mounted horsemen burst through the trees charging toward the streambed, hesitating for a moment before driving their mounts into the unknown depths of the rushing water. In doing so they remained open targets for Marcel's band of guerillas. Several men fell and the rest retreated back beyond the tree line. They had stopped the initial attack but to a man they knew that there would be more coming. Marcel told his men to use their ammunition sparingly. They settled in. Throughout the midmorning and into the afternoon the Confederate troops kept up a steady barrage of rifle and musket fire, the rounds singing off rocks and boulders. Marcel was at the front of what turned out to be a **V**-formation of heavy boulders. He could see practically every one of his troops, signaling them early on to spread out so that they would appear to be a superior force. Occasionally he would either call out or point to someone to fire, to let the Confederates know they were still there. He tried to form a pattern of fire, first the extreme right and then the left and so on.

Later it occurred to him that the opposing side might try to flank him so he sent scouts down the streambed on both sides to watch for troopers trying to gain their exposed flanks. The battle wore on into the late evening, several attempts by the mounted soldiers had been thwarted, and although Marcel's troops experienced only minor wounds, it felt to him as if it were a stalemate. Browning's troops had twice attempted crossing maneuvers through the waist-deep water to Marcel's left only to be turned back by withering fire from his ex-prisoners. Several bodies were sprawled across the edge of the stream on the opposite side, a wounded horse with its saddle hanging beneath its belly continued to cry out in pain. The animal stumbled up and down the width and breadth of the watery passage as if looking for its master.

Just before dark a shout came from the other side and what appeared to be a cavalry company guidon was being waved from the edge of the woods. Marcel called out to cease fire.

A voice from the far side, strong without a hint of fear, answered, "Captain Parker, it's Anthony Browning, let's talk."

Marcel wondered what the man was up to and shouted back, "What do y'all want?"

A tall figure emerged from the tree line. The yellow pennant from the guidon hung limply.

"Meet me in the middle of the stream, Parker."

Marcel said to Israel, "I'll go meet this toad again. Leave three strong men and their horses with me, one on each flank and one in the middle well hidden. Once I get into the middle of the stream, pull back the rest of the troops and head west. Do it quietly. I'll keep him talking as long as possible, don't stop, we'll catch up with you. . . ." Israel moved back to his position as Marcel once again reminded him to move quietly. Marcel waved his neckerchief in the air and waited for Browning to come to the edge of the water. Once there they eyed each other momentarily, then stepped into the icy stream. As they met in the center, the long lantern-jawed Lieutenant Browning pushed the guidon staff heavily into the rushing waters to gain a footing.

"You're not Parker, where in hell is he?"

Marcel eased closer to the tall soldier. "Captain Parker is busy with otherworldly duties right now, he sent me as his emissary. What can I do for you, Browning?"

There began to spread a gleeful look on the long-faced lieutenant. "He's dead, isn't he? Damn tootin', he's dead."

Marcel simply smiled. "No, he's not dead, monsieur, matter-of-fact he's very much alive, but considered that his temper would be better served if he sent me to speak to you. You see the good captain was royally incensed at your disregard of our flag of truce the last time we met. As you might remember your troops blatantly fired at us before we were able to quit that sacred field of honor. You in your cavalier way, after agreeing to let us go back to discuss our possible surrender, disregarded all that is holy in terms of gentlemen speaking civilly about the vagaries of war—"

The lieutenant stamped his guidon angrily into the cold stream-bed. "Stop this nonsensical bullshit, sir, before I have you summarily horsewhipped."

Marcel eased his derringer from his vest pocket. "Well, sir, there's bullshit and then there's . . ." He dropped his charming smile. "Don't move an inch, Browning. You were given ample opportunity back at the first surrender talks to do the right thing. You were told the war was over. I imagine when your cavalry troops arrived they verified what we said to you of Lee's surrender, yet here you are in this mad pursuit trying to reinforce your manhood by extracting some measure of revenge for your superior officer's death. Granted it was murder, but as explained by Parker earlier, the culprit has been summarily punished."

The officer looked doubtful.

"He was shot in the face, man, not once but four times, and this was explained to you on that so-called field of truce. . . . What more do you want, Lieutenant?"

The shivering lieutenant tried to regain the upper hand. "I have explicit orders to recapture the Union prisoners and return them to Andersonville."

"Now it's my turn to say stop this nonsensical bullshit. You have no orders now, nor did you at any time have orders directing your men to fire on unarmed prisoners of war." Marcel knew he was stretching a point, but also knew that he needed to keep the lieutenant occupied for another ten minutes.

The sun had disappeared behind the spindly pines, a darkening gray sky held the two figures in the middle of the stream in a near comic tableau.

An angry Lieutenant Browning held himself in check. "When

we previously met, I observed you possibly as a compatriot. Was I mistaken?"

Marcel wondered how much he should reveal to this man. "Compatriot," he mused. "Coming from the Latin, come together. A fellow countryman or colleague . . . indeed. . . ." Marcel eased off and smiled at the trembling soldier. "You could say we both are men of the South and as such share that particular breeding, therefore we could be considered for all intents, compatriots . . . but the word also implies a closeness of soul, perhaps a bonding if you will." Marcel worried if he could go on without the man stomping off in disgust. "Friendship, *mon ami*, or *gentillesse*, would imply simply that we are of like spirit—therefore, friends. Which as you can see, with this weapon in my hand, tiny as it may be, to call us compatriots may be evading a stark truth. . . ."

The lieutenant regripped the guidon with both hands. "I came here under a banner of truce, and scoundrel that you are, you have the audacity to flourish that relic at me?" He paused. "I sense that you're stalling, what's going on?"

Marcel attempted a stern countenance. "You asked for a meeting in the middle of a waist-deep streambed, now pray tell me who's stalling?"

The lieutenant gave Marcel a devilish grin and lifted the water-soaked guidon, waving the pennant high above his head. Fifty yards behind him at the edge of the tree line, a bloodied Pat Thomas and Billy Buckles came stumbling out, their arms bound behind them, their legs now free. Several horsemen herding them on either side kicked them to the ground.

"What say you now, Mr. Flowery Speech, with your cowardly *tiny* weapon?" The lieutenant lowered the long pole of the guidon, resolutely driving it into the rushing water.

Marcel felt trapped by his own devices. He looked to his left and to show strength he shouted, "Men of the second platoon, sound off!"

A moment of silence and then a strong voice sang out, "Second platoon's all present and extremely ready, Mr. Lafarge."

Marcel smiled and turned to his right. "First dragoons report." Silence again.

"First dragoons report, damn it."

A voice from downstream finally yelled out. "Dragons are here and ready, Mr. Farge!"

Almost on top of that report, Marcel could identify Corporal Watson's strong voice from behind him. "Fifth Michigan's here, *sir,* and I got a bead on Lieutenant Browning's right eyeball, if needed."

Marcel watched as Browning looked nervously back at the tree line where his troops waited. "Lieutenant, we've reached an impasse. I suggest you release my men over there and—" Before he could finish Browning drove the guidon's steel-pointed top toward Marcel's startled face. Missing, he then dove headlong into the icy waters. Shots from across the woods whistled past as Thomas and Buckles began running toward the stream. Marcel fired two rounds from his derringer, which at that distance was about as effective as a child's slingshot, and then scrambled for cover in the cold water. He held his breath and crawled across the rocky bottom of the waist-deep streambed until he was, he thought, twenty yards down from where he had started. Springing from his frozen bath he dodged the relentless fire from the Confederates and crawled onto the boulder-laden shore, quickly taking cover. He had lost his beloved derringer. Somewhere in that icy streambed lay the diminutive weapon, lying empty and lost. He had a fleeting thought to retrieve it but dismissed the moment as the insane stretching of a scared soldier's rattled mind.

He could hear screaming from the opposite bank; Pat Thomas had been shot in the back as he ran from his keepers. On his knees at the water's edge, he was cursing and trying to thrash his way out of his bindings. Marcel retrieved his carbine and started sliding back into the water to assist him when he heard another musket round crack heavily into the man's head. The top of his scalp and skull came away in a red blur as Pat Thomas's lifeless body fell stonelike into the frigid water. Farther downstream he could see, floating facedown, the dead body of Billy Buckles. Marcel pulled back behind his boulder and tried to catch his breath. He sat with his soaked jacket pressed into the cold stone, trying to will his reluctant body to action.

Finally a call from Corporal Watson revived him. "Mr. Lafarge, we're taking pretty heavy fire, don't you think we should . . . vamoose?"

Marcel took a moment to control his breathing and then thought, yes, to leave hastily might not be a bad idea. "You crawl over to whoever answered to second platoon, get them and rabbit back to the horses. I'll get the 'dragon' from yonder." Marcel fired his Spencer twice to cover Watson and then he retrieved his lonely dragoon from a neighboring boulder. The young man who Marcel had relieved of his duties crawled alongside of him as they tried to make their way back to the horses.

"Damnation, I was scared blind. When you called out, I didn't know for beans what was a dragon, hope I did right?"

Elbowing his way along the rocky ground, Marcel assured him that dragon or dragoon at this point, it really didn't matter.

At the horses they quickly mounted and sprang from the small clearing, musket and deadly rifle fire still whistling through the tree branches as the four horsemen hastily enacted their . . . vamoose.

After zigzagging for close to half an hour they finally found a trail and what looked in the darkening night like fresh hoofprints and road apples. Marcel was near frozen; the cool night air struck his waterlogged clothes like a winter storm. He dug his long cattleman's coat from his saddle pack and turned up the collar. It looked to be another long night.

In thinking back on their latest encounter Marcel was certain Browning would keep up the chase. The loutish son of a bitch had the bit in his horse face and seemed to be enjoying it. They found the rest of their band after the moon had gone down. He had checked on the Fifth Michigan boys, and had paid condolences to the Friendship gang over the loss of Buckles and Pat Thomas. Concerted grumbling came from Clete and the rest of his group. Marcel could tell they were fed up with the way the last two days had gone and were close to snapping.

Lem was worse. When Marcel first saw him he could barely stay in the saddle, his arms hanging limp at his sides, his head resting on the hard saddle horn.

Marcel felt caught in a dilemma. He knew they had a sizable lead on Lieutenant Browning's troops but any delay would certainly jeopardize that, so they continued on. Marcel tied Lemuel into his saddle, staying close by. Finally, Lem's near lifeless body sagged down the horse's side, his head bouncing near the mane. Marcel asked Israel to bivouac around the group of pines up ahead and to try and get some food and water into the men . . . ah, yes, and the woman. As the tavern owner shepherded the horsemen into the trees, Marcel ordered, "No fires, Iz, you understand?"

Israel nodded in the dim light.

Marcel cut Lemuel's ties and eased him off his mount onto a blanket away from the other men. "Your wound has opened up, Lem. Can you hear me? It's Marcel. Lem, what can I do to help you with the pain?"

Lem's parched lips moved but nothing was said. Marcel searched his pack for the metal whiskey flask. He poured a small amount of the warm liquid down Lem's throat. This time a raspy voice answered, "Captain?"

"No, Lem, it's Marcel." He squeezed Lem's hand.

"Cap'n, do I still got my freedom paper? Would ya kindly check, suh?"

Marcel rustled Lem's interior coat pocket.

"It's right here, Lem, sure as shootin'." Lem's weak grip on Marcel's hand started to fade. Marcel crouched lower and spoke in Lem's ear, reassuring him he was a freedman and would spend his days walking proudly. His kinfolk honoring him, all singing, "Kingdom coming, sisters and brothers, Lord let the kingdom come." Lem's breathing became more uneven. He coughed softly as a bubble of blood formed on his lips. Marcel wiped it away as Lem's body began to relax. One last deep rattle. Marcel closed Lem's eyes. Had his life like so many others been squandered? God only knew the answer, he thought.

They made a cairn of stone and said a few words over Lem, then drifted away, each man with his own thoughts.

They needed rest, but after his troops were fed and the horses watered they pushed on. Most of the ex-prisoners could barely hold up their heads. The horses followed more like sheep, nose to tail, as the band moved slowly along a little-used footpath in the deep Georgian woods. After several hours they crossed a picket fence and came upon a group of outbuildings and a dilapidated barn. The farmhouse close by had been burned to the ground; a stone chimney stood as a monument, in a mound of charred rubble. A lush grape arbor stretched seventy feet, connecting the barn and a large toolshed.

"Troops, listen up. We're all exhausted," said Marcel. "Take care of your animals and then bed down, clear out that toolshed. Iz, put as many of the horses in there as possible; the rest turn loose in that corral. We'll all get some rest, I'll take the first watch." The small farm was situated on a hill looking down into a forest cut into squares by open fields. Behind what used to be the former farmhouse, a dense wood continued to sweep up a long gentle rise heading west.

Marcel's time on watch dragged on endlessly. More asleep than awake, he guided his mare around the modest homestead. Finally being relieved of his duties, he exhorted Israel and his new pal Wilma of the need to stay awake. He took care of his mare and then collapsed among the thirty-odd exhausted bodies lying on the hay-strewn barn floor.

CHAPTER 31

April 1865
Dry Forks, Millers Ferry,
Old War, Fresh Blood

T he Confederates caught up with them the next day at first light when most everyone, including the man on watch, was still asleep. The first shots penetrated the barn's thin weatherworn slats, letting strong beams of sunlight streak across the dust-laden ceiling. Israel sat up in the far corner with Wilma next to him—both looking stunned. Marcel called out for the troops to man their arms, then rushed to the back door of the barn. Crawling quickly through the ash-strewn rubble of the farmhouse, he peered around the blackened fireplace.

Down below, stretched across a grassy meadow, stood nearly fifty mounted horsemen who hadn't bothered to take cover while firing indiscriminately at the outbuildings of the tiny farm. Marcel could see the horse-faced Browning galloping casually behind his troops, waving a saber high above his head. . . . Brandishing a toy sword like Bertrand, Marcel's birthday friend of yore.

The angle of the hill kept the Confederate soldiers from firing into the barn much lower than head height. Marcel's immediate reaction was to try and get his people to the horses in the back toolshed and run. But the more he surveyed the situation the more he liked what he saw. They owned the high ground.

After spreading his men in a semicircle around the deserted farm, he ordered them to conserve ammunition. He crawled to Israel, Wilma, and several others who had taken cover behind a stone wall in front of the burnt farmhouse.

"You've got a good spot here, Iz. . . . it looks like Browning thought we might just pack it in and surrender. He's fallen back into the tree line. At that distance he won't be very accurate. Watch for a flanking maneuver from the right coming up that road. When they come, and they will, that's where it will be."

Israel nodded, never taking his eyes off the distant trees.

After checking the horses, Marcel continued to hustle between the men scattered around the farm. He took two of the Friendship gang with picks and shovels from the toolshed and, skirting to the right of his entrenched troops, guided the men undercover, down to the road. There were several spots where the road dipped from erosion. Marcel picked one that he knew he could see from the farm. Hiding behind various bushes and trees the three men dug a trench across the width of the roadbed and covered it with twigs, branches, leaves, and dirt. Once again he knew that this would only be a discouragement, not a deterrent.

Back at the burnt homesite, Marcel waited and watched. For the past half an hour there had been very little gunfire coming from Browning's troops. To the northeast he heard what was once again the Confederate bugle, calling for assembly. From the same area, a line of horsemen appeared. Marcel counted eighteen, they kept milling about as if to confuse Marcel's troops of their number.

He stood behind a tree in the middle of what was once the front yard of the homestead and yelled, "Men, listen up. They'll not come from the northeast where you see them gathering. It's a ruse. The main body will come up the road off to your right. Let the troopers now in view come ahead, they'll have to stop at the lower fence line. Wait for the main group on the road. Hold your fire."

Marcel knew that when Browning realized Marcel hadn't fallen for the false attack, he would already be committed to the road. Marcel didn't know if his trench would stop the thirty to forty horsemen, but it would certainly slow them down. Browning had taken his main body a mile or so farther west before committing to the dirt road. Although expecting the attack, Marcel and his troops were still startled when the horsemen came pounding down the road, bugles blaring and several dozen grown men screaming.

Marcel chilled at the Comanche-like yell that he knew so well. His instructions to his troops had been for them to wait for his signal. It became chaotic when the first of Browning's horsemen came over the small rise in the road and stumbled into the ditch. Men and horses went down in painful heaps—the first of them having tripped in the trench, others following close behind falling over the downed horses and riders. Several expert horsemen finally got through only to find themselves alone on the road to the farmhouse.

Marcel screamed his own version of the Confederate battle cry and opened up with his Spencer on the trapped horsemen. They were quickly cut down; others attempted to cross the pile of stricken men and horses but were turned back. The excited Confederate bugler called the troops into full retreat. The guerilla groups continued to send rounds into the writhing men and animals until a pronounced stillness settled within the group of vanquished horsemen.

Marcel hadn't been able to bring himself to fire at the wounded men, his former compatriots and their horses, but he also hadn't called for a cease-fire. "Reload, people, and keep a sharp eye. They may try to come again." The original false charge had petered out, the would-be cavalrymen having lost heart at the sight of their fellow horsemen's slaughter on the road. Browning's arrogance had once again cost him dearly.

Marcel could just make out the cavalry's bivouac in the distant woods. Several fires were started and with the long glass he could see men milling about in the dense forest. The guerilla band were ordered back to rest in the barn. They were assured by Marcel that since Browning's troops had started fires, they could also. It was their first hot meal in days. Marcel was standing by the barn door when Clete Wilson approached him.

"Wanted to say what I couldn't say the other day, Lafarge." He dropped his head as if thinking. "I never liked you, always thought you to be a might cocky and kinda know-it-all, putting on airs and such." He laughed self-consciously and moved his hand nervously along his thigh and waited while Marcel continued to drink his acorn coffee.

"But having got that off my reluctant tongue, you done me a deed, pardner, pulling me up on that horse. A damn good one, I'll tell you, and I'm obliged . . . truly." Wilson started to walk away but turned. "I'll be standing watch tonight, to do my share. I've talked to the men and to a soul, they're with you."

"I'll relieve you after the second watch around 4:00 A.M.—"

Wilson continued his retreat.

"—and Clete . . . no sleeping on watch, apologies or not."

Marcel posted several men on the perimeter in the early evening and turned in for a well-deserved rest. It was difficult to sleep, he kept reliving the past thirty-six hours—what he could have done differently, what might have been. He finally drifted off only to awaken with a start after what seemed like mere minutes. He lay listening to his tired mind, scrambling for an explanation of where he was and why.

Just outside the barn a low fire held a charred coffeepot. The rank acorn coffee brought him to consciousness quickly. He looked at the time on his battered silver pocket watch; near enough to four to relieve Wilson. His hand brushed the empty vest pocket where his derringer had resided for so many years. It was mere metal and bone, he reminded himself, easily replaced. But there was, despite his best feelings to the contrary, a foreboding, a true sense of loss. . . . Back to Clete, he felt he couldn't let the man off the hook. Too much water passing down that particular creek to just forget and forgive. Marcel waited in the dark for Wilson or one of the other outposts to make a move, but there was nothing. He felt a chill in the warm night air. Something seemed wrong. Marcel stepped into the barn and quickly found Israel in his usual spot. He shook the man's arm off Wilma's shoulder. When he awoke, Marcel held a finger to his lips and signaled for Israel to follow him. Marcel waited a few steps from the door.

"What's going on?" asked Iz.

Marcel signaled for him to follow. "I can't find Clete or the other Friendship outposts. Check by the toolshed. I'll head down to the perimeter wall, meet me back here."

They were both gone only a few minutes when an angry Israel appeared back at the barn. "The horses are gone, goddamn it."

Marcel took a moment. "You're sure . . . all of them?"

"I could see a few grazing off in the woods"—Israel kicked at the corral fence—"but couldn't tell how many. We can probably catch them, rattle a feed bucket or such."

Marcel swung around into the barn, almost immediately coming back. "They're gone."

"Who?"

"The Friendship gang."

"Holyee Kerist Amighty, those bastards."

Bastards, indeed, they had taken almost all of the food. Marcel couldn't even guess how they had organized their thieflike departure. He stood in the center of the barn more stunned than surprised. Wilson's pitiful attempt at apology and camaraderie should have been looked at for what it was, sheer bald-faced bull crap. Still, a part of him was not disappointed. Wilson and Sangnoir had been his idea, they had been trouble from the beginning, and Nathan, he reminded himself, had gone to some lengths to point that out to him. He realized one of his failings to be his uncommon attraction to the darker side of life, the seedy characters and despots found along the Mississippi River. All souls to their own devices, he thought. He moved smoothly into an overwhelming urge to break Clete Wilson's bastardly neck.

"Fifth Michigan, on your feet . . . get up."

The tired ex-prisoners stirred, several having to be physically shaken to come back to life.

"Fifth Michigan, listen up."

One of the ex-prisoners from the train, a hanger-on, spoke up. "Does that mean the rest of us can go back to sleep?"

Marcel ignored the weak attempt at humor.

"The Friendship gang has departed for healthier climes, check your weapons." Languid movement ensued, with no one really fully awake nor for the most part truly understanding the exit of the eighteen-member rowdy gang. "Listen, damn it, have they taken any of the rifles or handguns?"

"I'm missing a rifle, Mr. Lafarge. Stacked it up with the rest of 'em near the barn door last night." It went on like that . . . in the end only the handguns and three rifles remained—Marcel's, Israel's, and one that a prisoner had wrapped his arms around as he slept.

It took them nearly an hour to round up the horses; there were fifteen. Marcel assigned the lightest men to pack double on the largest, strongest animals.

They trailed west behind the toolshed, having crept out of the barn under cover of the grape arbor. Israel led them through the trees, skirting broken dried branches and other noisemakers. Marcel stayed at the deserted farm for nearly half an hour, simply listening. It was the beginning of a lightening sky, the early morning birds starting their endless quest for food. Somewhere deep in the distant wood, an animal screamed. A wounded horse from the previous day's battle or maybe, Marcel thought, a man whose wounds transcended mere mortal's thoughts of what most humans understood to be a cry of pain.

I pray, Marcel thought, they don't follow us, let this be the end.

17 April 1865
Vicksburg and Camp Fisk, Mississippi

N athan arrived at a makeshift train station in Mississippi that was still in Confederate hands. It was the terminus for crossing the Black River into Yankeeland. He knew his soldiers from the train and Marcel should be nearby if all had gone reasonably well. Hopefully, with Nathan's holding action back at the campfire, and with the added protection of the Friendship crew, Marcel had a comparatively easy journey through Alabama. As soon as he made contact with the rest of his men at Camp Fisk, he would find Marcel and arrange to get them all together for the next step—a steamer north.

In deference to his friend's wisdom of life and Southern ways, Nathan simply walked through the mob of gray and butternut soldiers milling about to where the road narrowed over a bridge of land. Most of what the Rebs were guarding against here was an enemy coming the other way from Yankeeland; they were unsure what to do about people crossing from their end. Nathan was scrutinized, but not questioned. Really, what was there to ask? The war was more or less over except for the last gasps of General Forrest in Mississippi and others in Texas. But the Confederacy was officially . . . officially what?

That confusion was probably the result of the Confederacy having gone to such pains to recognize the sovereignty of each state. It made it difficult at times like these to know who was in charge, to say nothing of the worth of Southern money. Lee had surrendered. Months earlier he had been given overall command of Rebel forces, not just the Army of Northern Virginia. Was everybody now supposed to lay down their arms? Nathan thought his nation was about as unsettled as it could be. It was now clear to most that the nation would remain one—that the Union would prevail—but all other reality was cast in some strange hues.

As Nathan headed south, the pickets along both sides of the river appeared lackadaisical. He passed Federal soldiers, arms crossed, leaning over their rifle muzzles, watching their young blue-coated associates standing unarmed in a gully that served as a makeshift no-man's-land. They were talking to some equally young and unarmed Rebs. He caught enough of the loud banter to confirm his suspicion; lift from young men the burden of killing one another and they forget war and politics to talk about women.

He thought about that all the way to Camp Fisk. It was something that his men in the Fifth Michigan had gradually stopped doing at Andersonville. There came a point when even the thought of a beautiful woman couldn't distract from the misery. Even now, with his own health largely restored, he found his few intimate interludes to have been periods of desperate intensity followed by a dark emptiness—*le petit mort,* the French called it. Now he knew why.

But the world of romance seemed not quite as remote since seeing Darien. He dare not even think of missing her; she had been an unattainable dream and despite what she said, he doubted a serious relationship with her was ever to be. And then, the conversation stopper; he was a father. Really? That was a whole world of reflection that he would have to put off a while longer. If he didn't, it would overwhelm him. Nathan's world had changed during those few minutes in Annapolis speaking with Darien; he wasn't sure how, just that it had. His quest to free his men hadn't lessened, but in some way it no longer was the only thing that could possibly matter to him.

But enough—he had to get Darien and Sean out of his mind and pull himself together. As he made his way on the trail to the west gate of Camp Fisk, mulling how he could get an audience with the camp's commanding officer, something occurred that for him was rare—a pure stroke of luck. He came upon a colonel's retinue standing by as their officer let a sergeant apprise him of some vexing telegraph problems affecting Vicksburg headquarters. As Nathan made to pass around them, he heard someone hail him.

"Parker . . . Captain Parker, is that you? I haven't seen you in some time. Is all well?" It was Colonel Prescott, whose troops had found him when he first arrived in the Vicksburg area. Nathan felt his spirits rise.

"Well, sir, things are better all the time, now that the war seems on the brink of being over."

The colonel removed his glove and shook Nathan's hand. He was actually considerably warmer to him than Nathan would have expected, given the conditions under which he had left Vicksburg some months ago.

"How about your Fifth Michigan lads? Was that ever settled, Captain?"

"Former captain, sir, but I'm hoping to close the book on that issue in the next couple of days. I believe they have been sent to Camp Fisk."

"Ah, bless them then. This arrangement Henderson and Fisk put together here has been a lesson for all of us. Your soldiers are indeed lucky. And Parker, while here, you will remain a captain when addressed by fellow officers."

"Thank you, sir, but I wonder if you would be so kind as to help me meet the officers in charge of the camp. I've come a long way and would like to ensure they're well and the final steps have been taken."

The colonel glanced away and hesitated a second before replying in the affirmative. He would do Nathan this favor, but he obviously was not thrilled about it—he probably thought their meeting would be just ships passing in the late afternoon. Now it would seem rude not to accommodate the man to whom he had been so friendly. Prescott instructed his men to let Captain Parker fall in with them as they entered the environs of Camp Fisk.

The camp was protected more by agreement than by stockades or iron. The guards were mostly just for keeping general order—it seemed silly to guard against an attack that could only gain the Confederates a contingent of sick men they weren't able to care for in the first place.

Prescott led Nathan into a comfortable-looking home that served as camp headquarters for the Federals. They waited alone for a bit before they were addressed by a servant, a black man, who walked into the room with a tray of what looked liked real coffee and some confections. Nathan took the coffee and declined the rest. The Negro told him in a deep Southern accent that he conveyed apologies for the others, but they were discussing some problem with the Confederate officers. He actually used the word *conveyed* and seemed confident in his diction; he was clearly educated and native to the area. The South sometimes struck Nathan as a complicated place.

But the brief delay was welcome as far as Nathan was concerned; he needed the time to regroup. From the porch of the house he could see a distant tree line dip where it conformed to the Black. He was actually looking back into "Rebeldom," as everyone, including the

Rebs, called it. He wiped his brow. Mid-April and already there was a tinge of mugginess in the air. It wasn't so much hot as it was wet. With the river water up higher than most years, the mosquitoes were especially healthy and seemed unimpressed with truces and talks. The bastards were out for blood and seemed little dissuaded by the smudge pots on the porch.

Nathan had never seen Vicksburg from this vantage point. He was four miles south and east of the riverfront near Camp Fisk. The war-torn town pushed up from the surrounding green like a man's head emerging from a swamp. It occupied high bluffs but appeared stark, after being denuded of trees in endless bombardments. It would take more than a few years for those to grow back. The tree damage was more noticeable from this vantage point than from inside the town during Nathan's stay a few months ago. In the town itself, the starkest scars from the war, besides ravaged homes, had been trenches and caves dug into hillsides where people lived during the bombardment. While Prescott lingered on the porch, Nathan wandered into a well-appointed meeting room—it seemed this was where the business of the parole camp was conducted.

"Ah, Captain Parker." Nathan almost dropped his coffee. Another colonel coming in had banged open the door as he spoke. Nathan jumped to his feet and saluted before remembering he was no longer required to do so. The fellow just smiled at the faux pas and advanced with his hand out.

"I'm Colonel Fisk and I understand you're here to check on your men." He glanced behind him as the others came in and continued, "Here's Colonel Prescott. You two certainly don't need introductions. You'll meet the others momentarily."

Two other Federal officers walked into the room. They were lieutenants. One had a sheaf of paper and a pen. They weren't introduced and not seeing a uniform on Nathan, they just nodded and smiled. All seemed busy and distracted with their own affairs.

Then Nathan saw another officer enter the room wearing a gray uniform. All rose, including Fisk, as a courtesy to the man. He walked around and shook hands with all of them in much more than a perfunctory way. He introduced himself as Captain Henderson of the Army of Tennessee.

At Fisk's invitation, Prescott explained that Nathan would like a moment of their time at the end of the meeting to ask the whereabouts of the remainder of his company of Michigan mounted infantry. He believed they had recently been moved from Camp Sumter to Camp Fisk.

"Ah, Captain Nathan Parker, is it?" Henderson asked with his brow up, as if trying to recollect something. "Parker's Rangers."

"Yes, sir." It was Nathan's turn to be surprised.

"I believe you had the misfortune to serve some time in Camp Sumter yourself before being one of the few to escape."

"Yes, sir, I did." Nathan decided it was not in his interest to pursue that any further. It would be uncomfortable if Henderson should mention the unnecessary killing of a sergeant of guards during his escape. He glanced at Fisk, hoping he would continue.

"We'll pursue that later, gentlemen," Fisk said. "Now to business on the next exchange." After looking over a list in front of him, he looked up to Captain Henderson. "We're having the devil of a time getting confirmation of that request for medical supplies—it's that clause about equitable distribution to parolees from both sides." Glancing back toward Vicksburg, he said, "It seems the damn telegraph lines have been down for almost three days, since the night of the fourteenth."

The others shook their heads at the inconvenience and continued on to issues with which they could cope, with or without outside permission. The group seemed used to working together. They spoke without contentiousness and only an undertone of negotiation. There were still problems with the release of Rebel soldiers from some of the Northern prisons and conflicting guidance from

Washington. Nathan thought the group was trying to meet the spirit of their superiors' orders while expediting the exchange with all haste. Sometimes they simply agreed that they hadn't seen a particular piece of official correspondence if it would unduly slow things down.

Much of the discussion was of marginal interest to Nathan. He thought the work was important, but the details were too unfamiliar to keep his attention. He gazed through a window to the courtyard where a number of soldiers, blue and gray, probably Fisk's guards and Henderson's escort, were passing the time chatting. They were interrupted by a courier riding up at a fast pace. The man dismounted without exchanging greetings, handed his reins to one of the blue-suited cavalrymen, and walked out of sight toward the front door of the meetinghouse.

The soldiers milling in the courtyard watched him disappear and laughed at a remark made by one of the group, probably about self-important people who rode up and didn't say hello. Nathan turned his attention back to the negotiations while waiting patiently for the opportunity to find out specifics of his own men.

Henderson began wrapping up a point of discussion. "And so, gentlemen, I believe if we agree to keep the newest arrivals in Rebeldom until sufficient room becomes—"

"Sir!" All quieted down as one of the house lieutenants rushed through the door and blurted out the salutation before being acknowledged. It was unusual to have a full colonel interrupted so unceremoniously by a lieutenant for anything in either army. The man was literally white and shaken. What in hell had happened that it would so rattle a veteran officer? Nathan could see in the outside foyer the courier he had seen ride up in such haste. Fisk rose and accompanied the lieutenant outside the door. The others could hear the beginning of their conversation.

"Sir, pardon me, but I thought it urgent for you to know that—" The door closed.

A moment later, Fisk reentered. He had a stricken look that mimicked that of his lieutenant. He stood up straight, took a breath, and said in a formal voice, "Gentlemen, it is with deep regret that I must be the one to inform you that President Lincoln has been shot. . . . It is expected he will not live."

After some gasps, the room was silent except for the sound of breathing. Nathan was as speechless as the rest. Perhaps the world had finally spun out of control.

Fisk added, looking down as if in a trance, "Word just came by one of the riverboats."

"Good God!" came Henderson's reaction in a low voice.

Prescott looked up, pale, and in a quiet tone replicating the Confederate officer, he said, "Now we know why the telegraph lines have been down—it was purposeful—controlling the flow of information."

Nathan was dumbstruck. Lincoln? For some reason that seemed impossible, it made no sense. Why now?

As if listening to Nathan's inner voice, one of the lieutenants asked Colonel Fisk, "Well, sir, was it an act of war?"

Fisk quickly replied, "We don't know yet, other than it was a murderous act."

Henderson stood and said to the group with great solemnity, "Gentlemen, this was no act of war by the Confederacy, of that you can be sure. And as strongly as I believe in our cause, I would say that I'm certain there is not an officer in my command who would maintain his oath of service if such a dishonorable thing were ever done in our name."

Fisk said, "We know that, Captain. But I suspect the reaction to this news will be extreme for a while. So, if you don't mind, I would ask you to return to your lines. To ensure safe passage I will have you and your men accompanied by a detachment of Federal cavalry."

Seeing his chance, Nathan interjected, "Colonel Fisk, with your permission, I'd like to accompany Captain Henderson back to his lines."

Fisk looked to Henderson, who nodded in reply.

Minutes later Nathan found himself sitting on a flour barrel, holding the reins of a borrowed horse, waiting for a cavalry detachment to be assembled. Like some of the soldiers sitting nearby he was immersed in his own thoughts. He would soon head to the Black River in the company of Captain Henderson, his men, and the Yankee escort. Even from this distance he could hear the tolling of a bell in Vicksburg.

★

NATHAN REMAINED GLUED to his perch on the flour barrel, absently slapping his borrowed horse's reins across the palm of his hand. The mount, an old warrior himself, stood waiting patiently.

After a quest that had taken half a year, Nathan was almost back to his men. One would think he'd be feeling excited or fulfilled. But his hands shook with fatigue, his head swimming in a vain effort to sort out everything that had happened. If only he had time to clear his mind—he wasn't quite ready to see his men.

Being directly associated with Captain Henderson would help in his dealings with the Confederates. But this latest bit of news— Lincoln—it didn't seem possible. Nathan was slow to show any belief in the workings of God. It hardly seemed part of a grand design when the country was coming apart at the seams. But fate—that was a concept that gave him greater pause.

Nathan thought there was supposed to be reconciliation in the air, but now President Lincoln was dead, the carpetbaggers were clogging the shipping rosters on the Mississippi, and Sherman's sentinels, the chimneys of burnt homes, dominated the countryside in many places besides Georgia . . . at least many places in the South. Lord, there was nothing a goddamn bit "civil" about this war.

His men didn't need to see him like this. He needed time; time to clear his head, sleep, be their leader again. More than eight months in that hellhole. How had they done it? He felt he would have gone crazy if he had spent any more than his three months of incarceration. His men thought him a hero, but he had gladly accepted the risk of an escape attempt rather than spend more time at Andersonville.

Nathan didn't know what he would have done if someone else had been chosen by the men to escape. All he knew was that he now carried a great sense of guilt. He had sworn to one last commitment; he would bring his men home again.

How was Nathan going to emerge from this war? Perhaps he would finish his one remaining task and never think of it again. Was that possible? Was he going to bring back the smell of blood and death to Darien and Sean? Sean. The boy had looked him in the eye and froze him in place when he did. This was his son? What did it mean to be a father? The boy was his seed from time spent in illicit love in the arms of Darien, a creature whose lovemaking had raised him to otherworldly heights. But Nathan often wondered if she was real—it didn't seem possible that she could exist in the same world as this horrendous war. Which world was really his?

A corporal with a high-pitched voice advised him they would be departing shortly. Nathan jumped, startled from his deep reverie, and the corporal apologized. Nathan assured him that the fault was his own and thanked him for the warning. He could see the blue and gray mixture of uniforms assembling so that the blue surrounded the gray in a protective embrace. Some of the young soldiers joked. They recovered from distressing news much quicker than the senior soldiers on each side. Nathan pulled his weary body into the saddle. A brisk signal from the lieutenant and they were off to the outskirts of Camp Fisk.

As they headed to Camp Fisk, Captain Henderson confirmed

Nathan's hunch that his remaining Michigan lads were probably lined up with many others on the east side of the Black. That's where the Confederates held them until properly exchanged. Fisk was allowed to send Sibley tents and supplies out for the use of the prisoners and told his own men not to inquire who else might be eating the food as long as the prisoners were fed.

Nathan continued to marvel at the imagination and nerve these officers showed when disconnected by a thousand miles from their leadership. They treated orders with respect, but politely disobeyed them when necessary. Each was a loyal officer to their respective side, yet made room in their hearts for people caught in a brutal war.

They had not left the camp too soon. An unruly mob enraged by the assassination headed out from Vicksburg. Recently released Federal prisoners from Camp Fisk vented pent-up anger over this most recent outrage. It would likely blow over when people got their wits together, but the shock had thrown things into an up-roar. Nathan hoped his efforts to retrieve his own men would not be harmed by this incident.

A platoon of Federal cavalry led by a Lieutenant Hadley fell in with the small Confederate escort and moved them back toward the Black River. A loud crowd of men appeared off to the right side of the road as they approached the bridge; most seemed to be ex-prisoners. One of them threw a rock that almost hit Captain Henderson's horse. Hadley put his hand up, slowing his riders to a halt. He nudged his mount over toward the men clustered in a knot near the road.

"You! Soldier!" The men fell silent. He rode up to the rock-thrower and said, so that everybody nearby could hear, "This man is under a flag of truce and under my protection."

"Yeah, but, Lieutenant, them Rebs killed our president."

"I ain't going to say it but one more time. This man has gone to great lengths to help secure your release. He is under my protection.

If a stone is thrown, or even a further word is thrown at him, I will personally ride back here and blow your goddamn head off. That understood?"

"Well done," Nathan muttered to himself under his breath.

The group of ex-prisoners seemed to get hold of themselves and lapsed into silence, some trudging back to their tents. The mounted group continued at a businesslike pace and clomped over a bridge the Rebs had secured at the Black. A number of Rebel troops stood at a makeshift gate. "Lordy, sir. What's going on over there? They been yelling some stuff about murder and the like, can't figger it."

Captain Henderson looked down at the sergeant who had spoken and said, "Keep a reinforced watch tonight. President Lincoln's been assassinated and the rowdies are having their sway for a bit." He let his words sink in for a moment. The sudden quiet of the Reb soldiers showed the point had hit home. There was a time they might have cheered such bloody news but they were obviously far from that point now—murdering Lincoln boded well for nobody.

Before continuing on his way, Henderson stood up in his stirrups, turned, and waved a thank-you to Lieutenant Hadley. The latter nodded in response and led the Federal cavalry unit back to their own side of the river while Henderson pushed on to his command post with Nathan. Outside a large white tent, a corporal stepped up and took the reins from his captain as Henderson briskly dismounted.

As soon as the corporal led his horse away, Captain Henderson called out, "Lieutenant Brewster!" His tone was clipped. With the recent unsettling news, Henderson was making a point of keeping things in tight order. "See that our visitor here is given access to the prisoners. He's looking for his own unit from Camp Sumter, Fifth Michigan."

"And when I find them, sir—"

Henderson interrupted Nathan. "When you find them and sign a statement that you can and will take responsibility for them, I'd be more than happy to see them leave. One thing we're not running short on these days is Federal prisoners for exchange."

It struck Nathan how things across the river were so different in some ways and so much the same in others. Brewster was a ramrod-straight veteran officer that even looked a bit like Lieutenant Hadley. Nathan didn't relish facing disciplined Southern regulars in battle, but he was glad to see them here—he felt better that his men were under their care.

"Captain, the Michigan boys probably ain't far, but gettin' around out here at night, with all the new 'uns coming in . . . it might take a while—it's running on to full dark now."

"True," Henderson addressed both of them. "Maybe you could find them a lot easier in the morning, Parker. The groups out there change every day."

Nathan replied quickly, "Actually, that will do fine, Captain. I'm exhausted, sir, and would rather have my wits about me when we find my men . . . might I lie down somewhere?" The captain looked at the lieutenant, who nodded.

"I can set him up in my tent, sir. There's plenty of room now that Lieutenant Borden is off to Selma."

Nathan thanked the lieutenant and addressed Henderson with one more request.

"If I might prevail on you for one more thing, sir?"

Henderson nodded for him to continue.

"I see you have civilian supply wagons returning empty to the depot across the Black almost hourly. If you permit us to hire one in the morning to transport my men and me back there, I would pay the man handsomely."

"Fine, Parker. But if you pay the handler a moderate fee and send us back a wagon of supplies that we don't have to requisition, it would be even finer."

Nathan shook hands with Captain Henderson and let Brewster guide him to his quarters. He could hardly remember falling onto the blanket in a corner of the lieutenant's Sibley. It seemed it was midmorning light coming through the flap that wakened him, then he realized it was Lieutenant Brewster shaking his shoulder gently.

"You was sleepin' like a dead man. I reckon you'd want me to wake you."

Disoriented, Nathan rubbed the sleep out of his eyes, and thanked the lieutenant. He stepped out of the tent and was greeted with a virtual sea of shelters around him. For a second he thought he was back in Andersonville, then grasped that it was an uneven, wide line of tents and other shelters extending back at least a mile east along the road. Brewster walked up and handed him a cup of coffee.

"Thank you, Lieutenant. After I throw some water in my face I'd like to look for—"

"Yeah, well, while you was asleep, I checked around and they tell me that your men are probably down near that big elm just off the road. Ya see it?"

A few minutes later, Nathan, now fully awake, made his way through a jumble of soldiers and supplies toward the elm. He found he had a dread building along with his excitement over finding his men at last. Stopping for a minute, he took a deep breath and continued on his way.

As he got nearer to the big tree, he thought he recognized a fellow sitting on the side of the road leaning on his elbow. He was taking in the sun a little away from the others. Emaciated, yet tall, he looked as if he had aged five to ten years in the last six months. It was Weed.

Nathan began feeling through his vest pocket as he quietly walked around behind him. He pulled out the locket he had been given by the young man for safekeeping in October. He kneeled beside Weed, who was still unaware of Nathan' presence, his empty stare fixed someplace in the distance. Holding the locket by its thin chain, he extended his arm over Weed's head and lowered it slowly in front of the young man's face.

Weed's jaw dropped. He leaned forward and wrapped a shaking hand around the locket, then jerked his head backward to look at Nathan.

"Sweet God," was all he could say. He held the locket tight and let his captain wrap his arms around him. Nathan said nothing.

After several minutes, Nathan asked how he was doing. It was just to make conversation, as it was plain how he was doing. Weed clutched Nathan's arm, holding the locket bunched tightly in the same hand. Nathan tried to be strong for his men. That's who Nathan Parker was, the captain of his men if he wasn't another goddamn thing. But it was hard to keep his composure. Furtively, he wiped a tear from his cheek.

Several other Union soldiers turned and quietly watched the two of them. Out of the corner of his eye, Nathan saw Lieutenant Brewster approach. He stopped a few feet away and kneeled, but also kept silent.

Suddenly Weed seemed to come alive. He stood himself up with little help from Nathan and turned to the strange men around him. "This is Captain Parker, the leader of Fifth Michigan."

The others watched quietly. Weed pulled on Nathan's sleeve, saying, "Sir, we've had a few losses, it's been kinda hard, but you gotta come see the rest of the men."

Nathan glanced at Brewster, who nodded consent, and let Weed pull him along. The young man tried to tuck his shirt into his pants and Nathan noticed they had no unit markings on them. They weren't the correct size but they also weren't very old; probably issued to replace his prison rags by the Union medical people that Henderson was letting in.

"I know you don't brook no sloppiness, sir, but sometimes we have no heart left, now look here." Weed jutted his chin toward a group of men who were all apparently from Andersonville. You could tell them by the unbelievable emaciation, which had gotten so much worse since Nathan's escape. Those from Cahaba seemed thin and exhausted, but those from Andersonville were walking nightmares. Their skin drooped where it used to cover muscle. Some looked like human skeletons covered with paste-paper. But you could see the results of Fisk's and Henderson's recent efforts. The black layer of filth and soot was gone and the odor of gangrene was only noticeable as he walked by certain men because it didn't blanket the whole camp. Somewhere they had been washed.

"Jesus, for godsakes, men, look, it's the captain!" Peregoy uttered the words and a number of faces looked at Nathan with the same dumbfounded expression.

As he stood there, each of them got to his feet, some helped by others. It probably made a bizarre scene, these skeletons in uniform standing and saluting a well-fed fellow who wore no uniform.

"At ease," Nathan said. "Are you all being fed now?"

"Yessir, but we can't eat much, you know. We done shrunk our stomachs."

"Where's, I mean . . . there's five of you . . ."

"Sir," Peregoy interjected, "There's four as didn't make it. Ricketts, Murphy, Corby, and Borrows."

Jesus, Nathan thought, the damn camp sickness was always the worst killer. He looked around him at the crowd of silent watchers, then turned back to his men. "I want you all to clean your area and put everything in military order. Understood?"

There came a chorus of "Yessirs."

"Tuck your shirts in, and, and . . ." Nathan couldn't speak anymore. He walked over and hugged each man.

Nathan gathered his men around him. "An open wagon will be here soon. When it arrives I want you all to have your bedrolls wrapped and ready for transport."

CHAPTER 33

April 1865
Marcel

T hey traveled for almost two days without a sign of Browning's troops, heading always west. Their view expanded, the countryside opening to streams leading to dense woods and occasional pastures. The trails fed into farm roads and small villages. Provisioning at general stores, people gave them hard looks but little trouble. Near the town of Dry Forks, they rested.

Marcel, ever-vigilant, scanned the eastern horizon. If, he reasoned, Browning was following them, why hadn't he attacked? They were obviously a smaller group now, some of the riders packing double, a band of desultory horsemen extremely vulnerable. No, he reasoned, they were free of Browning. They had given up, he decided. There was just one thing that bothered him, he had seen it yesterday and now, once again with his long brass eyepiece, he panned the horizon. There it was, a small dust cloud, certainly not Browning, probably only one or two horsemen, maybe it was nothing. After all, he reminded himself, after the recent four years of unpleasantness, it was a free country. They pushed on. Dry Forks was only twelve miles or so from Millers Ferry, where they would cross the Alabama River. Marcel hoped to make the crossing by nightfall. Israel and Wilma rode alongside.

"We're gonna part company down the road apiece, Frenchman." Israel grinned.

Marcel turned in his saddle and surveyed the two. "Heading up Tuscaloosa way?"

Wilma nodded and eased her horse up next to Marcel, punching him hard on his upper arm. "You bastard, I owed you that and more." She then grabbed him by the sleeve and, pulling him close, threw her ample arms around his neck to kiss him on the cheek. "You saved our unworthy butts, Frenchy, I love ya, so does Iz."

They enjoyed a moment of shared adventures. The Fifth Michigan and the hangers-on joined in, not really knowing why but simply enjoying the camaraderie. As they neared Millers Ferry the light started to fade. The ferry had shut down for the night so they bedded down the best that they could. Marcel made himself a smoke and stood silhouetted by the fire. Something, he later remembered, caused him to turn and look into the yellowing eastern sky. One moment he was standing and then the next—it wasn't until he was halfway to the ground before he heard it, the musket round. Somewhere on the left side of his stomach, a white-hot poker probed his innards. Down and to the right. Well, he thought, the marksman finally corrected for windage and a dozen other variables and got it right.

He could see bright vivid colors and rushing water. A distant voice calling him was his mother, he was sure. *"Marcel, mon chéri, vas tu bien?"*

He nodded to his mother. *"Oui, je vais bien, Mama."* He didn't want to concern her. He thought of his brother Philippe and of his father, although less so of his papa, he was somewhat shamed to admit. Feeling something damp at his mouth, he tried to brush it away.

"Marcel," the female voice again. A pinch on his cheek and then another on the opposite side. He opened his eyes. It was Wilma.

"You've been hit bad, Marcel. Try this water." He let the cool liquid run through his mouth. Somewhere in his mind there remained sure knowledge that water wasn't good for a stomach wound. He ignored the thought and drank. Immediately, a new wave of pain enveloped his torso. It was so complete that it covered every inch of his chest and arms, wave upon wave surged through him, somewhere a faraway voice screamed to stop the pain, he wondered what manner of man would cry out so shrilly, and then, nothing but vivid images of fallen horses, men running, their mouths agape, arms hanging by mere threads of skin, and fire. A lake of fire and decimated bodies.

There were times he knew where he was, and what had happened to him. He was aware of vague faces looming, mouthing platitudes and hopeful encouragement. Then they would dissolve into a white-hot blinding agony. He couldn't get away from it. He willed his body to flee from the gripping torment, but each time he began to feel better a new excruciating wave of torture swept through him. He had dreams of fallen men and screaming animals. In what he thought was a moment of clarity he wondered about the health of the ex-prisoners. He saw them shaven and their hair properly cut, standing at attention in clean uniforms being addressed by Captain Nathan Parker. The captain extolled their virtues and congratulated a certain Frenchman for tending them well. In the distance under a sprawling oak, a figure lay covered in a white sheet. Who was that? Marcel wondered.

It was so for several days. When Marcel next awoke, they were in Selma, Alabama. Israel and Wilma along with the help of Corporal Watson had managed to put him on a wagon with several layers of blankets for the trip to Selma. He was able to sit up; the deep pervasive pain had subsided. Laudanum, he suspected.

"A doctor looked after you, Marcel." Wilma patted him on the hand. "You ate, had some soup, I gave you a powder, looks as if you're a might better."

Marcel looked around. "Where's Iz?"

Wilma scanned the eastern horizon, and then secretively said, "He went huntin'."

Marcel understood. Maybe it would be better to let it go, he thought, call it a tie. Not look for restitution from the lonely marksman. He drifted off. When next he woke, Israel and Wilma were making a bed for him in a boxcar on a train. The men of the Fifth were also there. Some of them sick, others simply tired and discouraged. He marveled at the transformation from his dream of their sparkling countenance. Their hair had once again become disheveled, beards long and matted, their clothing caked with grime. Missing was the figure in the white sheet. Wilma set a canteen of water next to him and a small paper sack close by.

"The doctor said you're okay to travel. It's less than two hundred miles to Bovina, which is outside of Vicksburg. Iz remembers Captain Parker saying if he made it out alive he'd go to Camp Fisk east of Vicksburg where the rest of the Fifth are. We figure it's the closest stop." Wilma watched him. "Will you be all right?"

Marcel raised up on one elbow. "As long as the laudanum holds out." He grasped the small sack and brought it to his lips.

Iz, who had slipped out of the car next to Wilma, thought that was amusing. "It has been quite a time, my friend. By the way, when next you're in Tuscaloosa stop by for a drink . . . better not bring Captain Parker, though, I don't care for his idea of a good time." The train lurched. Wilma and Israel walked a few steps next to the open boxcar door.

Marcel started to speak and then coughed heavily. Clearing his voice he called out to Israel, "Your hunting trip, how did it go?"

Israel simply drew his hand across his throat and smiled.

The trip west went quickly, Marcel drifting in and out of a

drugged sleep. When next he awoke he found himself once again in the back of a buckboard headed for Camp Fisk. He could feel both the front and back of his blouse soaked with blood. Now there seemed to be no need for the laudanum. He was only half awake, the rhythm of the buckboard alternately pressed his body against his wound and then relieved it, pressed and then released. Pressed . . . he dreamt once again, vivid, bright collections of reds and oranges. From nowhere he remembered a commander during the siege of Vicksburg screaming like a treed cat.

"You be a Celt, then yell like the furies." Celt or not, he remembered joining his men in their "WHO-who-ey" as they swept across an open field trying their Rebel best to assault the very souls of the Yankee troops.

He wondered if it was day or night. Once again a lake, and on the water men and women with raised arms as if to signal, to call out, yet he heard nothing. Was there a house behind them, on fire? No, it's the farm. The monumental fireplace. He thought of Lem and his stone cairn and, pushing against him, a familiar voice.

"You'd do anything to get out of work, wouldn't you?"

He opened his eyes. It was Nathan Parker.

CHAPTER 34

April 1865

Outskirts of Vicksburg

M arcel tried to raise himself but couldn't; he lifted a feeble hand.

Nathan lifted Marcel under his head and shoulders and moved him into a more comfortable position. Nathan was dumbfounded. It was the last thing he expected to see—his friend grievously wounded. He knew there had been fighting, he'd even heard it. But once they were truly free of the engagement where Nathan had played red herring at the campfires he hoped and believed they would make it on to Fisk with minimal problems. Watson had filled him in on the whole amazing story.

"There's fire, Captain . . . oh, the men, did you see them? Are they . . . I saw my blue shirt and your torn piece from your hat . . . charming . . . where have you been, these many days?"

"It's a long story, Buck-o, but not as wild as yours from what I hear."

Marcel seemed to relax, finding shelter in Nathan's strength.

He began once again to drift off, but suddenly roused and asked, "What happened? I didn't think you were going to make it."

"After causing those Rebs a bunch of confusion and bad times I thought I was finished, but I got away when your boys opened fire on the cavalry."

"That right? Good. Good."

"Later I was all but caught again but was saved by a lone gunman. He took down two of the patrol that snuck up on me and chased off the rest."

"Lone gun . . . who, what gunman?"

"It was Joe Toby, Marcel. He found me and was of a mind to kill me until he decided to take a stand against the crackers."

"Joe Toby . . . *vraiment* . . . really? Did he get . . . did he die?"

"No. Afterward he stood there pointing a .44 at me for a full minute. I finally said 'Thanks, Mr. Toby.' " Marcel listened wide-eyed with his mouth half open, so Nathan continued answering his unspoken question. "Then he shrugged his shoulders, turned, and rode off."

"No lie? Why . . . why'd he do that?"

Nathan, feeling deeply concerned for Marcel, didn't want him using his remaining strength, but knew he was stubborn about having his questions answered. "I don't rightly know, except maybe he'd somehow finished something in his own mind. . . . That's what it looked like to me anyway."

Marcel seemed to ponder that a moment, then changed the subject. "Nathan, I'm gonna die, ain't I."

"Yes, sooner than later, friend, so I want you to listen to me." Nathan felt himself well up; he could hardly speak but he needed to say some things.

"Marcel, my men told me how you led them to salvation."

"That's a bit thick, don't ya . . . don't ya—"

"Shut up and listen, Marcel." Marcel quieted.

"Look, there's nothing thick about it. I was wrong, I thought I'd not make it out of that camp that night and I did . . . because of Joe Toby—the man I couldn't abide and who you talked me into taking on this mission."

Nathan could tell Marcel comprehended him, but was starting to drift in and out. "I was wrong about you, too—I thought you'd get away without much grief once the firing stopped between your men and the cavalry."

"It was that damn Lieutenant Browning. Crazy son of a bitch, he never stopped coming."

"I know, I wonder why he was so damn wild-eyed—it didn't make any sense, the goddamn war was over. . . . What drove that man anyway?"

"Nathan, you don't get it, *mon ami*—you want to know what drove that Reb?—look in the mirror. Then look at me. See? I found out what it's like to fight Nathan Parker."

Nathan was momentarily quiet—he didn't expect such an answer and needed time to absorb it, but it would have to be some other time, not now.

But Marcel rambled on. "'Nother thing, you know your only weakness? I'll tell you . . . only weakness . . . always thinking. Yeah, always thinkin', fight too goddamn much with your head, alla time fightin' with your head, Nathan Parker, you gotta use your heart . . . you got a great heart."

"Well, forget all that, Marcel, and listen to me!" His voice was tight and tense.

Marcel mumbled something inane about Nathan being too excitable.

"Marcel, you have to know that I think what you did back there was about as fine a piece of military leadership as I've ever seen. Four of my men who went on to Camp Fisk are dead, Marcel, four, damn it! You had eleven in your care, Marcel and they're alive. You know what saving those men meant to me and it was you who brought them through."

Marcel seemed to become suddenly coherent. "We did it, Nathan. I used to wonder what was so important about those particular men—but now I see, their lives don't mean much to the world or to the war but they meant everything to them . . . and you . . . and now to me. We couldn't change anything about this damn war, except maybe one damn thing . . . and by God, we did it. We saved them, partner."

The effort to speak his piece seemed to drain Marcel. He stopped and gasped a few breaths, then a tight smile formed slowly on his face.

"Nathan, it ain't so bad now, except I'm feeling cold." A thick trickle of blood started to ooze from the crevice in the side of his mouth. "Thass funny, things taste strange, maybe like iron . . . something . . ."

"Copper maybe?"

"Yeah, like that. Say, tell me about your son, Nathan."

"My son? How did . . . ?"

"You have one, right?"

"Well, yes, I suppose . . ."

"Don' suppose . . . if you have one, nothing matters more, even your men . . . or me." Before Nathan could respond, Marcel added, "I think I had one too, but he died . . . he died in my wife. . . ."

"What? Marcel, I don't understand what—"

Suddenly Marcel waved his hand dismissively and decided an important point was yet to be made. "Nathan, there are people in the water, Captain. I've dreamt it, and now I see it clearly, animals and people and fire . . . too many, just way too many. . . ."

Nathan attempted to comfort him. "Fire and water don't mix so well, Buck-o."

There was no response from Marcel. He had taken a deep breath as if to submerge himself away from flames and his breathing became very rough. Suddenly he sat almost upright.

"Nathan."

"Yes?"

"Do you know 'The Marseillaise'?"

"The what—?" Then Nathan felt Marcel grow limp as the red Mississippi earth gathered yet one more soul.

★

NATHAN HAD ALL of his men gather in a semicircle. In front of them, a figure lay in a white sheet under a sprawling oak. Sixteen men of the reunited Fifth Michigan, most almost too weak to walk, had insisted anyway on standing for the ceremony, hats in hand.

Nathan stood silent a long moment, then said, "This man was a free spirit and a rogue. He accepted no rulings of authority or power. He was hurt inside, but a great warrior. He is the reason you are all alive . . . and he was my friend. May his memory live in all our hearts."

There was a general chorus of "Amens" and "Rest his souls." Nathan turned and walked away as the men of the Fifth Michigan and hangers-on, as Marcel had called them, lowered the shrouded body into a hastily dug grave.

★

"I WANT TO know everything about our men who've died so I can begin the letters."

"Yes, sir," came the chorus of replies. The soldiers hadn't been apart long but even after a couple of weeks separation, they were happy to be reunited. Nathan sat amid the sixteen men that remained of the twenty-three with whom he had been sent to prison. The men that weren't rescued on the train he hadn't seen for seven months. He had a pen and paper that a heavyset woman in a white smock had given him. She was a nurse from Vicksburg who, with a good number of others, had volunteered to help. That explained the scrubbed appearance of his men. At least they looked like reasonably clean corpses.

Nathan had found his men and they were damn near freed. The only thing stopping them from leaving immediately was the need for orderly dispatch. Federal officers were making arrangements for riverboat travel to Memphis, Cairo, St. Louis, and many other points up the Missouri and Mississippi from there.

Nathan's feelings were torn. He was gratified to see that so many had made it, no matter how hollow-cheeked they were. But the dead weighed on him terribly. Worse was his conviction that if he didn't move quickly, his men were not going to last much longer. Even with all the improvement to their circumstances, the former prisoners were dying at an alarming rate. No one was trying to kill these men now. The problem was yanking them back fast enough from the Grim Reaper of neglect that was already almost on top of them.

After Gator, Bender had died smothered in the tunnel; Rawlins had expired at Andersonville; Corby, Murphy, Ricketts, and Borrows had died either at Sumter or on the way here. They were so far gone, the timing was critical; it was like the abuse to their bodies and souls was exacting its toll in death knells even as conditions improved.

He addressed letters to families that tore him apart. Men dying by the hundreds in battle formation was hard enough to deal with. But these fellows were dying over months, their souls withering away in baby steps in pace with their bodies. For three solid hours, he sat with his men and wrote, "I am deeply sorry to inform you that your son . . ."

They did it together. Nathan asked for particulars about the personalities of the deceased, maybe a tender story, something personal to include in the missive. In a way it was terrible, in another it helped not only his men but him. They became animated and cried, but they also came out of themselves just a bit. Some of the heat seemed to be working its way back into the souls of the Fifth Michigan mounted infantry. Captain Parker was back.

Mustered out or not, Nathan demanded all the formalities of discipline and order, and the men responded. "Clean Barsky's blanket for him, roll him out, and freshen up his pillow and clean his sores—look at those damn bedsores—can't abide by that. And those tent flaps, keep them wrapped with three twists of a tie and close them at nightfall."

"Yessir."

"I'm going to town to see about a boat." Nathan quieted for a moment as Barsky let out a moan when the men turned him. When his breathing returned to normal, Nathan continued. "Barsky, Cotter." These were the sickest men.

"Sir?" came two weak responses.

"You are not going to die, because I damn well haven't given you leave to die. Is that understood?"

"Yes, sir."

It wasn't as crazy as it sounded. Nathan believed Barsky and Cotter would be more likely to make it if they felt compelled by his order.

Peregoy suddenly roused himself. When he spoke there was some gristle in his voice. "Damnation, look at these guys, Barsky and Cotter. Hey, you got all the food in the world now and you won't eat it." A few weak smiles started to play around the other men's lips.

Peregoy looked to Nathan. "No, Cap'n, you can't make 'em happy—they keep complaining about their shrunk stomachs and how they rattle when they walk." Nathan let the slowly recuperating banter continue.

Vrenka then said in a solemn tone to the wounded men, "Barsky, you can't have Cotter's watch if you die first."

Nathan heard a feeble "Rot the luck" from Barsky. He turned and walked abruptly away. There were no good-byes, he was simply an officer leaving his men for a while.

★

WHEN NATHAN ARRIVED in Vicksburg, he walked directly to the Wheeler. The fellow at the desk was in the process of telling him there were no rooms when Nathan recalled an observation once made by Marcel that most problems were born of inertia—although Marcel called it dead-ass habit. He was convinced that these venal concerns were best solved with guile and money.

"Believe I already have one," said Nathan. "Would you please check under Lafarge?"

"Ah, you speak of Monsieur Marcel Lafarge."

"That's him. I'll be waiting for him here." Nathan passed the man two silver dollars. He wasn't sure how much Marcel would have given him but it seemed to suffice. Nathan missed his friend and somehow this bit of skullduggery made him feel better, like a salute to Marcel's spirit.

"Yes, indeed, you have a room, here's your key, sir."

Nathan spent the night, and the next one, getting supplies and as much medicine as he could lay a hand on. It took a couple of days, but on the night of April 23, Nathan's men were formally released and taken by carriage at his expense to the Wheeler. They arrived at 5:00 P.M., just two hours after Barsky had died in transit.

Nathan counted the remaining greenbacks bequeathed to him by Marcel. He had enough to pay for the large suite they crammed into, their steamer fares, a coffin for Barsky, and some left over. On the morning of April 24, Nathan led his men to a bluff overlooking the river and sat them under one of Vicksburg's few remaining maple trees near the steamboat landing. They were finally all together and free and Nathan should have been elated. Indeed, part of him was bordering on the edge of tremendous relief. The other part was increasingly uneasy.

Although most prisons were just beginning their process of release, Nathan had already managed to have the Fifth Michigan cleared for the trip north. But he didn't expect the enormous crowding at the docks. It seemed the whole population of some camps had gathered and were vying for rides. Men seemed willing to clamber onto any ship heading north. The large steamboat being loaded as he watched had a huge swarm of wounded and emaciated men being helped along the gangplank. To Nathan it appeared like the danse macabre with long lines of skeletons clambering aboard. This ship, *Sultana,* was the one on which he had secured passage for his men.

He wandered onboard himself to see where he could comfortably berth his ailing soldiers, but a virtual flood of tattered blue uniforms wrapped around stick figures had already taken over almost all the available deck space. He didn't know much about seafaring but the ship seemed smothered in its human cargo—this couldn't be right, or safe, even for these extreme times.

He reflected that it must take incredible force to move a dead weight like this against the current. The whole idea of steam power was marvelous to him. That heat and expanding steam could move such a behemoth reminded him just how far industry had come in this industrial age. Now he especially missed Marcel. Besides having been a sailor, Marcel was a lover of powerful machinery and alluded to them even in his last words. Nathan didn't consider himself superstitious but he couldn't get Marcel's ravings out of his mind: "There are people in the water." "Alla time fightin' with your head, Nathan Parker, you gotta use your heart."

Suddenly, he felt the ship heave shoreward as hundreds of men piled to the starboard side. It looked like someone was setting up a camera to take a picture of the fantastically crowded vessel and the soldiers had moved en masse to get in the photo. Nathan walked about the vessel examining the decks and noted that even the boiler deck was crammed with soldiers. Two engineers poked at the firebox, talking to each other in muted voices, "It's okay, patched already, oughta hold."

Nathan returned to the heavy gangplank crowded with officers and overheard one say, "Jesus, hope the colonel got his palm crossed with silver for getting this mob on." Another man, a nautical-looking fellow with aquiline features bronzed from the sun, stood next to Nathan, puffing on a pipe. Shaking his head, he turned to Nathan and remarked, "Too many, just too goddamn many."

With that, Nathan made up his mind. As a final nod to Marcel, he would follow his heart and just do what felt right. Who knows what Marcel meant in his fevered rants about "fire in the water," and there being "too damn many." Nathan had just seen intelligent, logical thinking end up in the slaughter of more than a half million men. He was going to act on his instincts just like his French lunatic friend. He made his way hurriedly off the vessel and told his soldiers to stand by while he sought passage on the next ship—the *Olive Branch*. It seemed damn near empty, but for some reason they weren't letting people on her and were squabbling over letting them on a third steamer, the *Pauline Carroll*.

Christ, the war was barely over and already the clerks and greedy officers were taking bribes, so he did what Marcel would have done—he took ten silver dollars out of his pocket, much of his remaining fortune, and shoved it in the hands of a deck officer on the *Pauline Carroll*. While self-important, greed-driven arguments between brokers from steam lines and Federal officers carried forth on the gangplank, he ushered his men through a cargo loading hatch and comfortably ensconced them amid some cotton bales, under a roof and out of the wind. It would arrive later that evening and head north only hours later.

The lads from the Fifth hardly blinked an eye—the other soldiers being transported were on their own and had to think for themselves. But their captain had things in hand—they were heading north and would soon find their old lives; at this point that was about all they could ponder—if they were to admit it, they had finally begun to imagine a world in which their family wasn't the Fifth Michigan or a household run by Captain Parker. Not only did they get on a boat with no crowds but both it and the *Olive Branch* slipped away while the arguing was still hot and heavy about the *Sultana*. The *Pauline Carroll* only had about a dozen other soldiers on it and the *Olive Branch* was empty.

Nathan watched a couple of his men find the energy to wave and hoot at the huge mob on the *Sultana* as they pulled north—the men on the other ship made a few obscene gestures in a good-natured sort of way in return.

For his own part, Nathan was beginning to separate from his own obsession. He wandered back to the Wheeler and ordered a rye whiskey. Within a few moments he heard someone calling to him—it was Colonel Prescott.

"Hello, sir, I—"

"Parker, I've got something I need to tell you." The colonel seemed to have already had a few drinks; he fumbled with some papers as he withdrew them from his pocket. He unfolded them, sat down next to Nathan, and waved the waiter over for a bottle.

"I can't believe with all that's going on the man has time to be so vindictive, but listen here, I've a missive from General Grant that concerns you."

"Grant?" Nathan couldn't imagine what Grant would want with him.

"After a bunch of unrelated things he gets to 'the matter of Nathan Parker.'" Prescott glanced up at Nathan and informed him, "He asked in a previous cable if I had heard anything further about you as he had received word of problems you'd caused in collusion with a certain Rebel renegade by the name of Marcel Lafarge. I sent him a cable three days ago that explained that you were well and had retrieved your men and were shipping them home.

"So, here he goes on: 'Having engaged in a number of criminal actions contrary to the express orders of the commanding General of the United States Army, I am in process of remanding his Medal of Valor, his honorable discharge, his pension, and, hopefully, his freedom if I can find a civilian prosecutor to bring charges. I want him imprisoned and his men held in Vicksburg until further orders—he might not be under my purview at the moment but his men certainly are.' "

Nathan felt as if a rug had been pulled from under him. How could the general be so ornery and petty when he had just won a war? Prescott took a long gulp from a glass and said, "He adds one thing further," and continued to read from the paper.

"Prescott, I can't believe that son of a bitch did it. Tell him that there is one recourse he may have that would allow him to reacquire his honor and have his crimes overlooked. I want him to swear an oath that within three months of receipt of this document he will reenlist in the army and serve as my adjutant. With faith in our united nation, Ulysses S. Grant.' "

Nathan, his head in a daze, sat across from Colonel Prescott a full minute before even drawing a deep breath. Prescott filled both of their empty glasses and stared at Nathan while absently tapping his finger on the table.

"He said all that in a cable?"

"No, it came on the morning mail special from the *River Queen*. Parker, I hate to do it but I'll have to detain your men . . . I could always say I wasn't able to find you. . . ."

Nathan stopped a passing waiter and took an empty glass from his tray. Then he laid it on the table next to the two full glasses of whiskey. "Colonel Prescott, may I prevail on you to please fill this other glass?"

With a puzzled look, Prescott complied. Then, Nathan rose to his feet and asked the colonel to join him in a toast. Prescott stood, glass in hand.

Nathan said, "I reckon I have no choice but to comply with General Grant's offer. But first, I ask you to join me in a toast to my friend, Marcel Lafarge."

Prescott, looking vastly relieved that he wouldn't be forced to detain the men of the Fifth Michigan, raised his glass. Nathan slowly spilled Lafarge's drink on the Wheeler's floor as he solemnly recited, "To blackguards and bastards and full-breasted women."

Nothing was going to surprise Prescott this day anymore. At Nathan's urging, he blearily refilled all three glasses.

Nathan again spilled Lafarge's on the floor. "To that devil, General Grant." Prescott drank as Nathan finished his toast, "May he step on his own red dick."

★

NATHAN PARKER WALKED down Liberty Street in Cambridge. He was in dress blues with the newly applied insignia of a full colonel. His stride was slow and tentative. When Darien saw him, she stopped pruning a thick patch of roses in front of her home. They drank each other in deeply with their eyes for several moments.

"Welcome home, soldier."

"Well, I guess Cambridge *is* my new home . . . in a way."

Darien walked up to Nathan, whose breathing had pretty much stopped. She ran a finger down his cheek and said, "I didn't mean Cambridge."

"Darien, so much has happened, the war . . . Harmon's death . . . and what would people say? . . . And there's Sean, whose father . . ."

"Look, Nathan. These have not been easy times for anybody and there will be a lot of adjusting going on. As to Sean's father, I'm speaking to him. After what all of us have been through, I think we'll be able to work out life's complications, don't you?"

Both turned when a boy ran out to the street, a dog nipping playfully at his heels.

"Hello, Sean."

"Hello, Mr. Parker. Great to see you! Have you come to stay for a while?"

Nathan looked at Darien. She answered the question on his face with a smile. For the first time in what seemed like ages, Nathan Parker felt great emotion, but not the type that came with desperation, quiet or otherwise.

EPILOGUE

★

N athan Parker weathered a period in his country's history, which was, by any measure, a time of great desperation, little of it quiet. It was a blessing for his men that Nathan had faith in his friend's ravings when he opted to send them north on the steamboat *Pauline Carroll*. Marcel's last words kept Nathan's men from a maritime disaster of incredible proportions—one truly appropriate to follow a war and prison experience of such a similarly disastrous nature.

Seven miles north of Memphis, the side-wheel steamer *Sultana* blew its boilers in a terrific explosion. More men died than on any other shipwreck in American history—including the *Titanic*, forty-seven years later. Somewhere between 1,500 and 2,000 men, most just released from the Andersonville and Cahaba prisons, burned to death or drowned. But in such desperate times, their ordeal rated a single paragraph in the April 28, 1865, *New York Times*. Indeed, how many of us have even heard of the wreck of the *Sultana*?

The War Between the States was a time of unfathomable bloodshed. More Americans died in the Civil War than all other American wars and conflicts combined—and that at a time when the nation had one-tenth the population it does now. Yet a soldier's chance of survival for a given period was less at Andersonville Prison than it was on the battlefield.

Nathan never got to meet Henry David Thoreau—he died in 1862 after several years of poor health. His death meant little to the American people at the time, not solely because of the war, but because few but the highly educated read *The Atlantic* and his star had just begun to rise. Dr. Holmes' son, Oliver Wendell Holmes, Jr., survived his own wounds in the Civil War and went on to become perhaps the greatest of American Supreme Court justices.

Nathan eventually married Darien Crosby. Mrs. Parker blessed him with three more children in addition to his son Sean. Sean attended VMI and went on to become a major in the U.S Army during the Indian Wars. At the age of thirty, he left the military to never return. His new chosen profession was photography and astronomy—young men are nothing if not changeable.

Nathan's next oldest son with Darien eventually became a soldier of fortune who signed up with Teddy Roosevelt's Rough Riders. He was known for his daring raids, yet generous gestures toward men he had captured. And, too, he always had a ready smile for the ladies. His name was Marcel Parker.